UNCERTAIN PARADISE
1973

PART ONE

JOHN W. CASSELL

INKWATER
PRESS

On the run from vengeful mobsters and numbers-hunting federal agents, John Cassell and Connie Quintana arrive on the Isle of St. Margaret's shortly after John's twenty-fifth birthday in January of 1973. Whites familiar with the Caribbean island quip: 'it's THEE place to visit if you're a hurricane'. But John and Connie know there's no storm quite as deadly as that caused by an angry Mafia don. They need an out of the way place to come.

THIS IS A WORK OF FICTION

DEDICATION

In the event this is my last book, I want to dedicate it to those of you who have been my faithful readers… and even those who have read my stuff casually. It is often said that breaking into the 'big time' in published literature is tough. Proper marketing of a book takes a substantial amount of energy and creativity. Several of the authors with my publisher have done that and have seen their cherished works "go places".

That accomplishment eluded me, though my works were no less cherished. Though writing books was something I always wanted to eventually do [ask any reporter who waited out a jury with me in my twenty-five years as a trial lawyer], I got into it very late, after I had reached that time in life when that small voice whispers 'it's now or never, buddy', and when the energy required for such an undertaking as marketing or promotion was no longer there.

Fortunately, though, my dream was a comparatively modest one and so came true in the mere writing of Crossroads, Odyssey and Hell's Quest. I wanted to "tell my story" for anyone who cared to listen. I wanted it documented… a matter of record. Those three books, covering the years 1969-1971, told the story of my young adulthood, the times in which it occurred, or a combination of both.

Having accomplished my goal, I noticed that the 'novel' bug had bitten. It was fun taking certain activities in life, both ordinary and extraordinary, and putting them down on paper… weaving them together into something fun to write and, for me at least, fun to read. Thus was born DeVilliers County Blues and Uncertain Paradise. I pictured myself writing far into the future, but the nemesis that was to take my profession from me also managed to steal my beloved hobby as well.

Where there is life, there's hope, however, and should the opportunity again occur I will grab it for all I'm worth. But for now, thank you, my readers. God bless you.

John W. Cassell
Albuquerque, NM
April 14, 2007

TABLE OF CONTENTS

THE CHARACTERS OF UNCERTAIN PARADISE

John Cassell-Protagonist
Connie Quintana-his companion
Wilfred Gwynne, trade representative, Pan-Caribbean Council,
Miami, Florida

POLITICIANS AND OFFICIALS

David M. Phillips, outgoing Royal Governor
Major Peter Hill, 18th Berkshire Rifles, Commandant
of the garrison, Ft. Cornwallis
Edward Andrew Markham, outgoing Principal Secretary
Sir Bertram 'Bertie' Tibbets, incoming Governor-General
Desmond Colgate, Leader of Our Destiny Party (ODP),
holding 15 seats in 22 seat Parliament
Jocko Cummings, Speaker of Parliament
Norbert Perkins, Leader of Opposition National Liberation Party
(NLP), holding 7 seats in 22 seat Parliament
Nat Webster, NLP MP
Emory Jack, President of the House of Councilors
Chief Constable Maurice Jenkins, Commander,
Royal St. Margaret's Constabulary
Solon Grimes, Esq, Solicitor-General of St. Margaret's

PORT ALBERT YACHT CLUB

Perry Herbert, Australian expatriate naturalist
Lars Sandstrom, cannery Foreman (Danish expatriate)

Marvin David Hillary, president of Caymans Bank and Trust Ltd.
(Canadian expatriate)
Donald Autrey, Taro Planter (American expatriate)
Mark Clendenon, charter boat skipper (Canadian expatriate)
Peter Huggins, solicitor
Philip Doran, taro planter (South African expatriate)

ISLANDERS AND OTHERS

Serena Blackstone, Colgate's mistress
Derwood 'Woody' Crenshaw, guerilla commander
Damien Andrews, editor, *Port Albert Clarion*
Chung Lee Park, mercantile operator, Port Albert
Percival Dudleigh, solicitor
Sybil Jack, Cassell's Mistress
Kwan Lu, mercantile operator, Mantilla
Melissa Torreon, John and Connie's housekeeper
Colby Hanlon, John and Connie's groundskeeper
Emil 'Curly' Howard, Port Albert taxi driver and guide
Rev. Damian Wallace, vicar of St. Martin's Mission,
headmaster of Church of England Mission school
Dr. Margaret Detweiler, Belgian expatriate, founder and physician,
St. Margaret's Clinic
Graham Jack, John and Connie's driver
Rory Peebles, Guerilla commander
Capacious Cargo, Esq., Cassell's solicitor, Court-martial
Fortunus Jack, Patriarch of Jack Clan

INTERISLAND AIRBUS SEAPLANE

Ted Callison-Captain
Chuck Kirschner-First Officer
Chuck Donovan-Loadmaster

THE CABINET

Desmond Colgate, Prime Minister
Dollie Fishbine, Notary General and Deputy Prime Minister
Millard Cotter, Home Secretary
Morton Gentry, Minister of Defense

Albert Seachrist, Foreign Secretary
Granville Browne, Attorney General
Clinton Hatter, Minister of Economy
Daphne St.George, Minister of Welfare and Education
Thompson Ritter, Minister of Posts and Telegraphs
Duncan Kleiner, Royal Household Secretary

ARMED FORCES

ROYAL ST. MARGARET'S MILITIA

Colonel Paul Christian, Commandant
Lieutenant Colonel David Moreland, Commander,
Fedderson Company
Lieutenant Colonel Romulus Augustulus Jones, Commander,
Sedona Company
Captain Toussaint DeFreeze, Commander, New Britain Platoon

ROYAL ST. MARGARET'S AIR MILITIA

Group Captain Eugene P. Hayes, Commandant
Flight Lieutenant John Cassell, Deputy Commander-Operations
First Subaltern Felonious Burns,
Jr. Deputy Commander-Maintenance
Second Subaltern Victorious Preston,
Commander-New Britain Airstrip
Air Sergeant Major Rufus Killebrew
Flight Sergeant Tino Prentice
Flight Sergeant LeRoy Crewe
Flight Sergeant Aaron Sampson
Flight Sergeant Lucien Reeves
Flight Corporal Emil 'Curly' Howard
Aircraftsman Chungu Fumo
AircraftsMan Micah Dooley

THE HOUSE OF COUNCILORS

Emory Jack, Lord President
(Magenta gown with ermine stole)

GOVERNMENT MEMBERS

(Black gown, blue yoke)

Felonious Burns Sr, Leader

Vitrus Kaufman

Morris Dolan

Dred Scott Phipps

Olive Fishbine

Canny Fenton

Mitre Fisc

Oscar Melton

Anise Welton

Deal Winters

OPPOSITION MEMBERS

(Black gown, red yoke)

Kyle Szabo, Leader

Harlan Debke

Taro Windom

Martin DeWeese

Art Kraft

CHAMBER OF COMMERCE MEMBERS

(Black gown, white yoke)

Olaf Torgeson

John Cassell

Tran Van Choy

Perry Herbert

Apple Jack

THE DIPLOMATIC CORPS

David M. Phillips, British High Commissioner,
Honourary Consul for Commonwealth Nations
Colonel Heriberto Córdova,
Ambassador of the Peoples' Republic of Cuba
Donna Goldstien, Minister, United States Legation

Vladimir Kurtz, Minister, Soviet Legation,
Honourary Consul for Warsaw Pact Nations

Desmond Brathwaite, Jamaican High Commissioner,
Honourary Consul for Caribbean Basin Nations

General Antonio Imbert y Colona, Minister of Argentine Legation,
Honourary Consul for Organization of American States nations

Doris Freidburg, Minister of Israeli Legation

Pierre Loeb, Swiss Consul

Emile LeGrande DuBois, Consul for Republic of France

Hans Van Tyne, Consul for Kingdom of the Netherlands,
Honourary Consul for North Atlantic Treaty Organization Nations

ISLAND PATOIS

The People of St. Margaret's converse in a commonly understood language made up of simple English and a corrupted, or at least colloquially adapted, form of Swahili. Here are some of the more commonly used examples appearing in the book.

Mgeni	foreigner
Maggierock	Isle of St. Margaret's
rafiki	friend
jumbe	'boss' or 'leader'. As used on the island, however, particularly when addressing whites, it is often derogatory, implying a sort of mental linkage in the speaker's mind with a slavemaster
Mume	husband
mke	wife
watu	[our/a] people
nchic	ountry
hodari	brave, valiant
hatari	danger, peril
safari	journey
ndiyo	yes
mwenyeji	Master of the House
salamu	greeting
yetu	our
Move to de calypso beat	Taking it easy, sleeping, desert, generally not participating in white anxiety

Chapter One

BENEATH THE TEMPEST'S VEIL

Monday January 1, 1973: New Year's Day, 0030 hrs: aboard the Soviet Nuclear Powered Submarine *Novy Mir* somewhere in St. Margaret's territorial waters

The rhythmic beeping at a variety of sound frequencies from the navigational and defensive systems of the Soviet Navy's Murmansk Class nuclear powered submarine *Novy Mir* had been the only sounds audible on the conning tower for the past thirty seconds. Two officers, clad in powder blue open collar shirts with miniature shoulder boards and navy blue trousers, stood intently eying a console of dials and digital displays.

"A world-class feat of navigation, Captain." The lean officer on the right, Lieutenant Commander Yuri Dobrynin, the *Novi Mir*'s executive officer, spoke with admiration.

"Eighty meters... seventy-five...," intoned another similarly clad officer sitting at a console nearby, intently eyeing the dials in front of him.

The officer standing on the left drummed the calloused fingers of his massive right hand against the small table as he registered both the compliment and the status report. Soviet Navy Commander Vladimir Kamarov knew damned well it was a feat of world-class navigation. Not that the world would ever know of course. That was because his actions over the past three hours had committed a technical act of war by the Soviet Union against the United Kingdom of Great Britain

1

and Northern Ireland. The gamble was, of course, that they would complete their mission and get away before anyone would ever find out... at least until it was too late.

"Sixty meters... fifty-five..."

"Night vision lighting," Kamarov called. The command was repeated, plunging the conning tower into a dimly red-lit world of beeping machinery and taut, anxious faces.

"Forty meters... thirty-five..."

According to the instruments, the *Novy Mir* was approximately half a mile from the rocky coast of a God-forsaken British-held island some one hundred fifty nautical miles northeast of Barbados. If Kamarov's charts... and instruments for that matter... were accurate, he was little more than one hundred yards north of some deadly shoal waters that stretched for miles southward to the deep water harbor at Port Albert. It was these very shoals that had destroyed the American slaver *Annabelle Treen* in 1845 and led to the populating of the island by the cargo of slaves in its holds.

"We're at periscope depth, sir," called the helmsman in his white tunic displaying the chevrons of a leading seaman.

"Very well," Captain Kamarov replied. "Level off!"

The command was repeated.

"Idle both."

That was repeated as well.

"Air or surface contacts, Mister Kornilov?"

"Negative, Captain," the sonar officer responded. "Heavy weather up top."

"Very well." Kamarov glanced at the Zulu Time chronometer mounted on the near bulkhead. It was some thirty minutes into 1973 where he was at now. "Meteorology report?"

A thin officer with thick glasses looked up from his console. "Nor'easter up top, sir. Sustained winds of forty knots... two to four foot swells."

"Very well." Kamarov swallowed. "This is as close as I'm taking her to that can-opener of a coast."

"Like they told us at briefing in Havana, sir," the executive officer, standing next to Kamarov, again spoke up. "This place is a real hell-hole. Hurricanes from July to November, foul weather much of the rest of the year."

"Raise primary and secondary periscopes," Kamarov called. Both he and his executive officer extended the handlebars and squatted down as the periscopes slowly rose. They each activated the night vision scopes as they peered outward into the swirling muck beyond. Kamarov recalled some other facts from the briefing as well. Over ninety percent of this island's population lived in shanties built of cardboard and scrap metal. After each terrible storm, they would go out and pick up enough materials to rebuild them. From then until the next storm, they would frequently identify parts of what had once been their homes now on the homes of the other poverty-stricken neighbors.

"Go to two-seven-zero absolute, Yuri Nikolaiovitch," Kamarov called to his executive officer. Both men peered for all they were worth into the greenish blob that appeared through their scopes as the coast. The *Novy Mir* was aiming for an incredibly small hole in the solid wall of rock that seemed to run from north of Port Albert all the way to Point Loma Hermose. On the map it looked like a tiny sawtooth hacked out of the island just south of the halfway point between the two landmarks. It was called Blankenship Cove. It was here the *Novy Mir* was to land its human and materiél cargo.

The Havana briefing had covered the fact that Great Britain was pulling out of this slag heap of an island on April 15. For the past two years, Marxist guerillas trained and supplied by Fidel Castro had been operating from the teeming shanty towns of Port Albert to the virtually uninhabited Central Highlands. Ambushing a taro convoy here... blowing up a telephone relay station there... spreading havoc and terror everywhere. London had responded with Bravo Company, 2nd Battalion, 18th Berkshire Rifles, a reenforced company of Infantry. Over the past eight months, a well executed series of counterattacks had exacted a heavy toll among the terrorists, and when the parliamentary elections were held the past month, the Marxists won only seven of the twenty-two seats in what would become the post-independence House of Assembly.

As the British military worked to consolidate their gains, Desmond Colgate, the incoming prime minister, worked to deny the Communists popular support. Things began looking bleak for the rebels. They needed more men... and equipment. Cuba was more than willing, but the problem was how to land the assistance safely. Early attempts on the sandy beaches south of Port Albert met with costly defeats.

One of the local guerilla commanders, Derwood 'Woody' Crenshaw, had been an avid student of the engineering feats of General Giap and the Viet Minh at the battle of Dienbienphu during his training in Moscow and Cuba. Now back on St. Margaret's, he had adapted some of these tactics by patiently tunneling through the rock from a jungle outpost atop the rocky cliffs down into Blankenship Cove, then installing a series of primitive, human powered lifts.

His plan was masterful... at least in theory. Today, on the fourteenth anniversary of the *Fidelistas* entry into Havana, the plan would be put into practice. Its base assumption was simple: the pitifully small British forces on the island paid virtually no attention to the rocky northeastern stretch of coast, because conventional military wisdom held that it was impossible to use as any kind of staging area for men or supplies. Now, however, if his primitive equipment worked, a substantial amount of badly needed matériel would be landed right under the noses of the British, laboriously hauled upward, and distributed among the guerilla forces operating in the 'heartlands'.

"Got it, sir!" Lieutenant Commander Yuri Dobrynin excitedly called as he peered through the scope. "I make Blankenship Cove broad on the port beam... two-seven-zero absolute!"

"I see it," Kamarov replied, the relief in his voice obvious. "Messenger?"

"Sir!" A young sailor in white tunic with the chevrons of an able seaman stepped forward.

"My compliments to Colonel Córdova... ask him to join me here."

"Aye aye, sir." The young seaman headed down the ladder from the conning tower.

"Action stations!" bellowed Captain Kamarov. Almost immediately, the rhythmic throbbing of a gong sounded throughout the vessel as men hurriedly made their way to their posts.

In less than five minutes all hands were at their posts and the gong stopped. A trim youngish man with colonel's insignia on his collar, intense dark eyes, thick, curly black hair and a heavy moustache, uniformed in the dark green fatigues of the Cuban People's Militia, appeared on the conning tower with another similarly uniformed Cuban with the insignia of a lieutenant. The Cuban lieutenant translated Captain Kamarov's conversation with Córdova.

"Your men are ready, Colonel?"

"Yes, Captain. All is in readiness. I trust your loadmasters are ready to assist us loading the equipment into the rafts."

Kamarov briefly eyed the Cuban colonel with hostility. While Córdova himself was clean and up to standards, the people he was bringing to the island smelled like goats. On the second day out of Havana, running submerged the entire time to avoid both United States and Royal Navy detection efforts, the angry Soviet submarine commander had raised the issue with him.

"Obviously you have no experience fighting in the jungle, Señor Capitán," Córdova had replied. "Should the imperialists bring in a unit of Gurkhas, as has been rumored for some time, my men would be detected by the smell of their bath soap. They are forbidden to wash under my orders."

Kamarov stared at the Cuban officer. "Obviously *you* have no experience running for weeks under water in a small metal box." Since that time, the two had barely spoken, and then only when necessary.

"Lieutenant Gorchev!"

A short while later, Gorchev appeared and saluted his Captain. "Deploy your men Mikhail Mikhailovitch... we are ready."

"Aye aye, sir." Gorchev and the Cuban departed the conning tower.

"Stand by to surface!" bellowed Kamarov. "Prepare to occupy surface action stations!"

"Surface! Surface! Surface!" the Captain called as claxons sounded throughout the vessel.

"Ahead standard both," the officer of the deck intoned to the telegrapher and helmsman. "Fifteen degree rise on plane."

The commands were repeated as a sense of keen anticipation gripped the crew.

At exactly 0102hrs on New Year's Day, amid furious winds and high surf, the *Novy Mir*'s bow broke the surface at a sharp upward angle, then leveled off. On the Captain's order, after a final scan for air and surface contacts, the engines were idled and the forward and aft hatches opened. Immediately after Soviet gunners ran for the deck guns and lookouts climbed the ladders on either side of the bridge, fifteen Cubans dressed in black with no insignia appeared on the deck as Soviet loadmasters hauled the cargo topside.

As Captain Kamarov in heavy windbreaker anxiously scanned the coastline with night vision field glasses, his crew quickly set to work completing their act of war against the United Kingdom. For a good thirty minutes, they would be extremely vulnerable to attack.

After anxiously checking one last time with the sonar and radar officer and learning there were still no contacts, Lieutenant Commander Dobrynin joined the Captain on the bridge. For a while the two silently scanned the coast with their glasses, all the while mercilessly lashed by the wind-whipped high surf.

"One good thing, Captain," he yelled above the howl of the wind, "we are nicely hidden beneath the veil of the tempest."

"Ah yes, Yuri Nikolaiovitch," Captain Kamarov replied soberly, "but aren't veils always getting rent in twain in the Christian Bible?"

"To be sure, Comrade Captain. But we have rejected such medieval tomfoolery."

"Yes, my friend. But the British haven't."

Monday January 1, 1973: New Year's Day, 0109 hrs: the Coastal Defense Watch Room, Fort Cornwallis British Military Reservation, Port Albert, Isle of St. Margaret's

"Brian."

There was something in the way Brian Callaghan's friend Arthur Ramsey said his name. The two were just past the one-quarter mark of what promised to be an especially dull midwatch. Sitting in the dark with four other rating and one officer personnel watching a needle turn on a dimly lit green scope when the major storm system now buffeting the island had everything keeping to port was bad enough. Doing it while serving a one-year posting to the small Royal Navy

Signals and Navigation Service detachment at Fort Cornwallis, Isle of St. Margaret's, made it worse. The fact it was the New Year's Eve holiday and they knew they were missing all the action back in Portsmouth was the final insult.

"What is it, mate?" Able Signalman Callaghan turned listlessly in Able Signalman Ramsey's direction.

Ramsey's eyes were wide as they remained riveted on his scope. "Would ya take a look a' that fer God's sake!"

"Caw!" Callaghan's eyes were now also riveted on the large blip on his buddy's scope. Then he got hold of himself. "Must be blow-back from the storm."

"Think so, eh? Here." Ramsey held out his earphones. Putting one to his ear after quickly removing his own headset, Callaghan heard the telltale 'beep' as the needle passed over the strange and scary sight... an audible signal it was something of appreciable mass... not one of the legendary midwatch ghost-sightings or spinach kicked up by the raging sea.

Ramsey had his recognition manual open and was flipping through the pages. He let out a gasp as he came to the one that matched the profile of the mysterious blip. Callaghan's eyes whiplashed in his direction. The legend underneath the profile Ramsey had found and was staring at, wide-eyed, said: '**Murmansk Class Nuclear Submarine, Soviet Navy**.' Callaghan took the book from him and read on. According to the Royal Navy's top secret intelligence, the blip now on his buddy's screen carried enough nuclear armament in its five intermediate range missiles to bomb the Southeastern United States and the entire Caribbean Basin back to the Stone Age.

"My *GOD!*"

"'ere now Callaghan... put a sock in it!" It was the stern voice of Chief Petty Officer Weston, Master of the Watch. He occupied a console at the very rear of the main room full of consoles, so he could keep an eye on the ratings as they worked. "Put yer backs into it, lads!"

Callaghan turned to Ramsey and motioned toward the chief with his head. Ramsey nodded, then picked up his intercom. "Chief, I have an unidentified surface contact... grid coordinates Tango-Eight."

Weston glanced at his grid map, then let out a smirk. Any surface contact at Tango-Eight would practically be aground on the deserted, rocky coast, if it wasn't impaled on the treacherous shoals of the waters immediately to the south. Besides, he knew damned well all ships had been ordered to remain in port. When he and his watch-mates showed up at the radar-sonar room shortly before midnight, to allow their eyes to adjust to the dark before relieving the watch at 0000hrs, the entire area was clear of all ships. "Whenner you blokes gonna learn to read a map... re-check yer data, Ramsey."

"But I 'ave, Chief... three times!"

The Chief muttered something inaudible, and no doubt unkind, then hauled his bulk to his feet and ambled over to where the two stunned signalmen sat, watching Ramsey's board. He took a look standing over Ramsey's shoulder, his eyes widening. "Blymie, man! Clear your machine and re-zero."

As the Chief watched, Ramsey did as he was told. The needle began turning once more as all three men now watched with their full concentration. As it passed over Tango-Eight, the blip re-appeared. "Lemme in there!" Weston barked.

Ramsey hurriedly stood up as the Chief slid into his spot. He worked for a while with the knobs and dials. "Good *GOD!*" He stood up. "Resume yer post, Ramsey... keep yer eyes on that blip."

"Aye aye."

With that, Weston quickly returned to his station and picked up his intercom, punching in three numbers. "Lieutenant Derby, sir, we have a major bogey sighted... Surface contact... Grid coordinates Tango-Eight." ...

"Aye, sir... I *know* everything's been ordered to stay in port." ...

Chief Weston angrily shook his head. "Aye, sir... I *know* there were no surface contacts when we relieved the watch." ...

"Aye, sir... within eighty nautical miles." ...

"Aye, sir... It checks out as a Soviet nuclear powered submarine... Murmansk Class." ...

Weston rolled his eyes. "I *did* that, sir... *twice* now." ...

"Aye, sir. Did that too." ...

"Correct, sir... Murmansk Class... about 'alf a mile off the coast it is. Almost dead between Port Albert and Loma Hermose." . . .

"Aye, sir." Weston had barely hung up the phone when the door to the room opened and a man in undress officer's whites wearing the shoulder board insignia of a sub-lieutenant strode to where the Chief stood waiting.

The two supervisors returned to Ramsey's board. They cleared it. They turned it off, then on again. They calibrated it. The horrifying sight remained the same.

"Great God Almighty," Sub-Lieutenant Derby sputtered. Then he turned to the Chief. "Keep an eye on this Weston, I'm calling Major Hill."

"Aye aye, sir."

Monday January 1, 1973: New Year's Day, 0124 hrs: the Residence of Her Majesty's Governor of the Isle of St. Margaret's, Government Plaza, Port Albert, Isle of St. Margaret's

Throughout the British Empire and Commonwealth, it was time-honored custom for the Sovereign's representative to hold a formal gathering of the colony's notables New Year's Day. Among the events that transpired at this gathering was the announcement of local residents who had made the New Year's Honours List from Buckingham Palace. Poised as it was on the threshold of independence, St. Margaret's was widely believed likely to have a name or two on the List this time round.

Thus it came to pass that as the Year of Our Lord 1973 moved toward the midpoint of its second hour, the lights burned brightly in the Official Residence of Governor David M. Phillips, even as buckets of rain driven by howling gale force winds furiously lashed at the building's many louvered windows, often drowning out the polite conversation going on around the long banquet table in the state dining room.

The political, economic and military elite of the colony gathered around the table in their formal dress now fell silent as the Governor tapped at the side of his water glass with a spoon. They were a diverse and interesting lot, typical in many ways of those locales in the world people only go when they're either running from something, or off on a great adventure.

The economic elite present included the hard-eyed, sunburnt taro planter Donald Autrey and his wife, as well as his equally brutal-looking competitor in the taro business, Philip Doran and his wife. Both couples had made the difficult and potentially deadly trip across the spine of central highlands to be in attendance this night. Until the coming of the cannery, their two gigantic plantations on the island's forbidding west side were the only economy this island had. Frequently the targets of guerilla activity, neither went anywhere without some impressive armament and a small army of mercenary gunmen. Tonight, they were in black tie, doing the best job they could at looking civilized. A thoroughly bored-looking young American multimillionaire in his mid-twenties, Gene Hayes, who'd arrived on the island a year ago and promptly founded a cannery and several other businesses occupied the kind of place at the table only money could buy. Marvin David Hillary, the mysterious Canadian who headed the Caymans Bank and Trust, the island's only financial repository, was there as well, along with the two suitably inscrutable Overseas Chinese mercantile czars, Kwan Lu and Chung Lee Park. What those two were selling besides expired cheese and cheap saucepans was anyone's guess, though it was safer not to guess at all.

Together these men formed the powerful Chamber of Commerce, which under the incoming constitution was granted the sole power to name a full one-quarter of the Upper House of the new Parliament. None of these men were native islanders and the Marxist guerillas had vowed to murder them all. But they weren't dead yet, and in fact clung to life and their positions of privilege on the island with all the tenacity of desperadoes who had nowhere else in the world to which they could safely run.

The political group subdivided neatly into islanders and colonial administrators. Governor Phillips and Principal Secretary Edward Markham, each in their impressive white uniforms with military and Commonwealth Service decorations, constituted the latter. The former included Bertram Tibbets, the soon-to-be Governor-General, ablaze in his regimental sergeant major mess dress heavily weighted down with medals attesting to his thirty years in British uniform, Desmond Colgate, the incoming prime minister, and several members of the new parliament. Even Marxist opposition leader Norbert Perkins was present, though everyone knew he was little more than a front man for the Communists. The real leader of the revolutionaries, Nat Webster, was nowhere to be seen.

The military contingent similarly reflected the islander-colonial split. Major Peter Hill, Commander of British Forces on the island, was present in his white-coated mess dress, along with Lieutenant Commander Colin Willhoyt, commanding the signalmen, carrier-borne helicopter assault crews and PT boats of the Royal Navy's contingent. He acted as Hill's overall second in command. Because of the unstable military situation, and Whitehall's determination that Britain was leaving this island behind, on time and with a minimum of embarrassment, Hill took orders not from Phillips, but directly from the Ministry of Defence in London. It was the island's armed contingent that for the time being answered to the Governor. Colonel Paul Christian, Commander of the St. Margaret's Militia, and Chief Constable Maurice Jenkins of the Royal St. Margaret's Constabulary were present in their Class A uniforms representing those forces.

Rounding out the attendees were the Reverend Damian Wallace, vicar of the Church of England's St. Martin's Mission which provided the island's only high school, Dr. Margaret Detweiler, who ran the island's only medical clinic, Perry Herbert, the tough, leather-faced naturalist who lived and worked all alone at his nature observatory on the windswept heights of Point Loma Hermose, and Captain Mark Clendenon, who as the skipper of the only boat on the island capable of making a quick getaway to Barbados or Latin America, was valued highly by the mysterious cabal of expatriates who constituted the island's white elite.

"May I have your attention please, ladies and gentlemen," Governor Phillips intoned with a smile. The room quickly fell silent, more likely because each of the expatriates half expected to hear that police agents from their home countries had caught up with them at last and had surrounded the residence than any courtesy toward the

Governor. "I have the distinct privilege of announcing unofficially the 1973 recipients of New Year's Honours..."

The door to the state dining room opened at that moment, revealing Captain Wilfrid Mackenzie, in dripping mackintosh and officer's cap standing with a servant in white tie and tails.

Major Hill turned in his direction in time to see him give a frantic wave. For some reason he glanced at his watch. It was 0124 hours on the nose.

Governor Phillips looked over at the doorway, then to Hill. "Go ahead, Major. This looks serious."

A trickle of laughter washed over the room at what was intended to be humor. Hill gave a neck bow to the Governor as he stood up and moved toward his adjutant.

"Her Majesty is graciously pleased," Phillips now resumed, "to bestow upon Regimental Sergeant Major Bertram Tibbetts the exalted Order of Knight Companion of the Thistle."

Loud applause and 'hear! hear!'s broke out from around the table. St. Margaret's Governor General would be known as Sir Bertram Tibbetts when he entered into his new duties April 15. The islanders present were obviously very pleased.

"Her Majesty is also graciously pleased to bestow upon Mister Desmond Colgate and Colonel Paul Christian the exalted rank of Commander of the Military Division of the Most Excellent Order of the British Empire."

As more loud applause and hear! hear!'s broke out, Captain Mackenzie began whispering into Hill's ear. Seeing his face turn ashen, Lieutenant Commander Willhoyt excused himself from table and moved toward the two soldiers.

By the time he arrived, Hill had already beckoned the servant to bring his mack and cap. The request for Willhoyt's was shortly added.

Hill was already buttoning his mack as the Governor turned to him. "My apologies, Your Excellency," Hill quickly spoke, "but we've some business needs urgent attendance at Fort Cornwallis. May we be excused?"

The Governor barely had time to ritualistically grant the permission as the three military officers hurried away to a perfunctory chorus of 'happy new years'.

. . . .

The British Army Land Rover raced through the flooded, darkened streets of the capital. The howling of the wind, the fierce beating of the rain upon every inch of the vehicle's surface, the screaming of its siren and the loud slap of the wipers made the perfect backdrop to the briefing the astonished Hill and Willhoyt were getting that a Murmansk Class Soviet submarine, armed to the gills with missile-borne atomic bombs, had penetrated deep into the colony's coastal waters.

"We should notify London at once, Peter," Willhoyt suggested.

Hill thought a moment, clenching and unclenching his fists. "No," he said at last, reaching for the field phone. He quickly turned the crank, putting the receiver to his ear.

"Hill here... Scramble the Helicopter Attack Group... top off with petrol... arm with full compliment of air to ground missiles... then *stand by* for further word from me. Got that?"...

"Very well."

"You're not seriously planning to attack her are you?" the incredulous Willhoyt gasped.

Hill was absently looking out the window, slapping the receiver of the field phone in his hands.

"It's going to be very difficult even flying those Sea Kings in this weather."

Hill nodded absently. "We'll have to try." He turned the crank of the phone again, putting it to his ear.

"Hill here... scramble the PT Boat Squadron. They're to fully arm and move with all possible dispatch to *block that sub*!"...

"Peter it'll take at least an hour for the boats to make it over there." Willhoyt was looking at Hill like he'd lost his mind. "We've GOT to contact London, Peter! That's SOP for the love of God!"

"Understood?"...

"Very well." Hill replaced the phone in its cradle, then turned almost as an afterthought to Willhoyt. "I'll use the Sea Kings to hold her where she is until the boats can get there."

"But for Christ's *sake*, Major! What if the sub commander miscalculates your intentions... what if..."

Hill's face appeared taut and drawn with concern in the dim glow of the dashlights, even as the Land Rover flew through the Main Gate to Fort Cornwallis, its siren screaming, the sentries barely having time to snap to attention as it charged past them, splashing the puddles of water through which it passed high into the air. An awful half minute went by. "I doubt he'll miscalculate my intentions, Colin. I intend to capture him."

"But..."

Hill again grabbed for the field phone, working the crank.

"But... you'll be court-martialed and broken out of the service, Peter!... if any of us are alive after tomorrow that is..."

"Hill here... have Third Platoon and Special Weapons Platoon fall out now... full packs and field equipment. Round up every lorry you need... take both urban assault vehicles and get them the hell to the heights opposite that sub. Contact me when you're in position. Understood?" . . .

"Very well." Hill sharply exhaled as he hung up the phone, then faced back to his second in command. "He's obviously here to aid the Communist guerillas in some way, Colin. I don't propose to let those bloody bastards think for a moment the British military will stand for that."

Willhoyt felt pale and shaky as he leaned back into the seat cushions, his brain going a mile a minute. Of the two, he was the naval expert. It appeared quite obvious the British force that could be marshaled against this powerful invader would be wiped off the face of the earth, along with everyone on this island, were the Soviet submarine commander of a mind to resist. He well knew a British commander would. That was SOP also. There was too much top secret equipment on board a nuclear submarine to *ever* allow it to fall into enemy hands.

"Oh God, Peter," he managed to gasp. "This is *utter madness!*"

Monday January 1, 1973: New Year's Day, 0149 hrs: the hangar and helicopter pad, 4th Ark Royal Helicopter Attack Group [detached], Fort Cornwallis British Military Reservation, Port Albert, Isle of St. Margaret's

As of 0149, 4th Ark Royal Helicopter Attack Group's hangar area and heliopad at the southeastern corner of the Fort Cornwallis Military Reservation was a madhouse of activity. Ground crews were pushing the four Sea King attack helicopters out into the furious storm where petrol lorries were waiting to top them off. Long, low trailers pulled by ground equipment were driven to each, where hydraulic lifts were used to elevate two racks of four Bolander-250 Air to Ground missiles, then attach them to the ships, one rack on each side.

Inside the briefing room at the north end of the hangar, twelve young men in dark green flight suits, with dark green helmets with internal headsets and oxygen masks cradled in their arms, were seated opposite a large map of the island and a schematic labeled *Murmansk Class Nuclear Submarine*. An officer in undress whites with shoulder boards displaying the rank of Royal Navy lieutenant stood in front of them with a pointer, gesturing toward the map as he talked.

"Thus you will approach the objective using a compass heading of 000 until you arrive at grid coordinates Uniform-six. There you'll switch to 030."

He turned to look into the faces of the youthful flight crews. "Your objective is equipped with up to ten Litvinov Ground to Air tactical missiles, two two-inch deck guns, and two additional .50 caliber machine guns. That's in addition to the five intermediate range ballistic missiles, of course. Weapons System officers watch your scopes from the moment you overfly the cannery. You won't get a whole lot of warning. A Litvinov firing will appear on your screen as a dull flash. Engage your ECM's immediately. You shan't be getting another chance.

"Should she engage you whilst over target, fire off all eight Bolanders at once." He paused to take a deep breath. "It's *just possible* that a massive strike will destroy her before she can trigger Armageddon. Anyway, it's our only hope."

A heavy sigh issued from the assembled flight crews.

"Should she *not* engage you, *do not* fire unless ordered. Position yourselves into the wind, making sure you're not obstructing each other's sight picture. Major Hill will be speaking to both the submarine and you on the international emergency frequency." Again he paused. "Are there any questions?"

"Bit of a daunt hovering in this heavy weather I'd be bound," one of the young warrant officers spoke up.

The officer nodded. "Unfortunately, we were unable to choose the day the Reds resolved to strike."

The young man nodded in return.

"Two platoons of Infantry are making for the area as we speak. The PT boat squadron will be along as soon thereafter as possible. Our hope is that something short of violence can be arranged. Major Hill will be talking to the sub commander throughout. In any case, lads, Godspeed."

The flight crews grouped around the coffee and tea pots, talking quietly among themselves. Several stuffed wrapped sandwiches sitting on a tray inside their flight suit pockets. Outside the hangar, all four ships had been started up, their rotors spinning at full idle. Ground power units had been pulled back… everything was as ready as it could be.

At exactly 0158, the claxon loudly sounded, sending the twelve young men running toward their ships. Crew chiefs assisted them inside, then swung the hatchways shut. A couple of the pilots pulled open their side portholes and gave 'thumbs-up' salutes. The lieutenant who had conducted the briefing now walked out into the raging storm and faced the four Sea King attack helicopters.

Clicking on a torch in each hand, he made a rapid circular motion with each on both sides of his head. The rotors of the four craft were throttled forward. Warrant Officer David Andrews of Horsham adjusted the microphone attached to the side of his flight helmet. "Blackbird One to Rookery… all checklists complete… all systems check out Oscar Kilo… all set to fly."

The lieutenant now positioned the torches to his sides, sharply motioning up and down. Blackbird One lifted off the pad. The same drill was followed with each of the four ships, as their ground crews watched in a heavy silence.

Major Hill and his regimental sergeant major watched the four craft lift off from their vantagepoint in the small, low air traffic control tower. He continued watching as they headed due north over the harbor. He found himself wiping away a tear, swallowing hard. His sergeant major seemed to read his thoughts.

"Pardon the liberty, sir, but, odd as it may sound, it still sticks in my craw that it's always the very best of our youth that have to pay for the failures of the older generation."

"And it sticks in mine that every older generation manages to bugger it all up."

"God be with'em," the sergeant major said quietly.

"Amen," replied Hill. They watched in silence until the four craft were out of sight. Hill let out a long, troubled, regretful sigh. "Let's get down to the Command Post."

"After you, Major."

. . . .

The rhythmic thumping of the Sea King's main rotor filled the darkened cockpit as Blackbird One, flying at an altitude of four hundred feet, moved across Port Albert's deepwater harbor. Off to the left, the two most brilliantly lit areas of the island, the Interisland Airbus Seaplane Terminal and Government Plaza, appeared as little more than faint blurs this night as the wind-lashed rain continued falling in torrents. Warrant Officer Andrews glanced at the chronometer mounted front and center between himself and co-pilot Dickie Whitfield of Shrewsbury. In the dim green light he made out it was now 0207hrs.

"JESUS WEPT!" the suddenly terrified pilot exclaimed as Blackbird One without warning dropped nearly one hundred feet, heeling sharply over to the left. Desperately fighting the stick, he managed to regain control, but the pounding of his and the two hearts of his crew was now competing with the rotor as the loudest sound in the cockpit.

"Air pocket," Andrews managed to gasp.

"The Old Man must be daft, sendin' us out like this." The tone of fearful panic in Weapons Officer Mike Rutledge's voice behind the two pilots was obvious.

Andrews continued to fight the stick, trying to keep Blackbird One on course. Heavy gusts were now frequently causing the four gunships to yaw. Another air pocket suddenly jarred his ship about twenty feet upward.

"I mean, 'ow am I to attempt accurate fire in all this? Good God, we're all gonna be..."

"Aw *stow* it, Ruts!" Whitfield now spoke up. The mission wasn't fifteen minutes old and the frayed nerves of this crew were obvious.

"We're gonna ALL get blown to 'oly 'ell!" The weapons officer was practically sobbing. "E's got no bleedin' right to do this!"

"CHRIST!!!" Whitfield suddenly bellowed as, out the starboard forward porthole, the giant blade of Blackbird Three's rotor nearly plowed into them. It had obviously caught one of the deadly air pockets and had been catapulted forward, nearly slammed into their side.

The three crewmen of Blackbird One were wide-eyed with terror. Awful things were happening thick and fast, on a mission that in the most ideal weather would be one that would try the souls of the most courageous.

Andrews adjusted the mike of his headset. "Blackbird One to Blackbird Flight... spread out lads... spread out."

"Roger One... Blackbird Four here... my temp gauge is reading hot. I may have to return to base."

Andrews and Whitfield exchanged a worried glance. They knew damned well what was happening. They also knew the other two crews were listening intently to what would transpire next. Andrews depressed his mike button.

"You so much as make a move to drop outta this formation Blanchard and, as God is my witness, I'll blow you outta the sky," Andrews began, shaking uncontrollably. Images of the deadly white-hot vaporizing flash of exploding atomic bombs had been haunting him ever since he first heard what they were being ordered to do in the briefing room. It was obvious Whitfield and Rutledge were terrified as well. Now at least one crew had apparently been discussing mutiny.

"That's tough talk Andrews," Blanchard now replied, his voice quavering. "You'd best..."

"SILENCE! ALL OF YOU!" It was Major Hill, speaking on the gunships' tactical frequency. For awhile, there was a deathly silence in Blackbird One's cockpit. It even seemed to drown out the beating rotor and howling wind.

Andrews held his breath, gripping the stick with a sweaty fist.

"Now listen, lads," Hill suddenly resumed in a quiet voice. "In a minute you'll be over the cannery. From that point forward you'll be picked up on the submarine's radar as a hostile force on a course to intercept.

"I've no idea what the sub commander will do in response. The gamble here is that, like us, he will do everything possible to prevent World War III. The problem, however, is that he is obviously here to deliver some kind of major assistance to the guerillas. Assistance calculated to cause your deaths, and the deaths of other British young men.

"I have asked you to do what... I've asked you to do, because I know of no other way to signal to both the rebels and the countries who now stand willing to aid them that we will exact a heavy toll from *anyone* who thinks they can take our lives with impunity.

"This is *NOT* some abstract showdown over national pride. I am not some posturing macho hoodlum. I am a very unhappy career soldier responsible for bringing as many of you back home to England on April 15 as I can.

"Granted the burden of this fight now falls on your outnumbered and outgunned shoulders... but you know bloody well that yesterday and last week it fell on the Infantry as they patrolled the deadly streets of Port Albert in their jeeps, trying to locate the next band of armed terrorists before they were able to strike... Sitting targets unable to protect themselves until the latest killer showed himself.

"Next week, it may well be the same again. The sooner we signal to our enemies that we will attack without mercy those who are trying to snuff out our lives... no matter *who* they are, and no matter *how powerful* their weaponry.... the sooner we ensure that we will be reunited with our loved ones.

"You've been here long enough to know the character of our enemies. They're all watching at this very moment, rubbing their hands with glee as this Russian submarine sailed right up to our coast and now sits there, doing whatever deadly deed they're doing. How many more of the people of this island will be willing to join their ranks tomorrow if they see Great Britain cower in the face of this threat? How many hundreds more will our soldiers have to look for among the sea of faces that silently watch them as they undertake their deadly patrols through these shanty towns?"

"You know bloody well... don't you?" There was a full minute of silence. "Right. Well there it is, lads... why I've done what I've done. Why I'm asking of you what I have. Why I have *not* as some have advised me, followed normal procedure and turned our fate, and the solution to this crisis, over to the politicians. They don't have to patrol the troubled streets of this unhappy land... we do. I'm going onto the emergency international frequency now... to raise the sub as you fly over the cannery and are identified by them as a threat... I'm counting on you lads... just as you count on the soldiers at other times in this unfair, unhappy fight.

"God be with you. Hill out."

Andrews wiped beads of sweat off his face as the radio went silent. "Switch to the EIF Whitfield."

"Roger." The co-pilot turned the frequency knob of the radio to where they would be receiving their instructions from now on.

"Watch your scope, Rutledge... we're over the cannery."

"Roger, Dave."

As the four pilots of Blackbird Flight struggled with buffeting winds and deadly air pockets, the gunships were now at the point their leaders believed would cause the Soviets to consider them a force intending to do them harm. The radio was now silent. Twelve terrified young men had gotten past their first crisis of nerve. The mission continued on course... on time.

Monday January 1, 1973: New Year's Day, 0212 hrs: aboard the Soviet Nuclear Powered Submarine *Novy Mir*, one half-mile abeam of Blankenship Cove, St. Margaret's territorial waters

Lieutenant Gorchev had just begun climbing the port side ladder to the bridge when a large roller caught the *Novy Mir* broadside, causing her to heel sharply to port. He managed to cling to the ladder for dear life, while the Captain and Exec clung to the true bearing compass on the rainswept bridge and the deck gunners wrapped themselves around the gun mountings. The roller broke over the submarine, then it slowly began to right itself as the cargo officer, specially attached to the crew for this mission, completed his journey.

"Last of the rafts away, Captain. Cargo holds now secured," he gasped, out of breath from his exertions.

"Very well," Captain Kamarov sighed with relief. "Well done, Gorchev."

"Thank you, sir."

Before the latest of an unending series of rollers had struck his ship, the Captain had been watching the rafts through his night vision glasses as they made the perilous half-mile journey to Blankenship Cove. Two, he knew, had already capsized. The rest looked as if they were going to make it.

Kamarov now spoke into his headset. "Port engine ahead two-thirds... starboard engine astern two-thirds... right full rudder."

"Aye aye, sir," responded the OOD. Kamarov heard the commands repeated, then watched as the sub slowly began turning, bow into the heavy surf.

"Come right ninety degrees to zero-nine-zero absolute, then put your rudder amidships and idle both."

"Aye aye, sir."

"Captain...," the voice of his sonar-radar officer Kornilov said it was ominous.

Kamarov gripped the bulkhead of the bridge in anticipation.

"I have four bandits on scope... bearing one-eight-zero... on a course to intercept. Interception in approximately twenty minutes, sir."

The three officers clinging to the bridge in the raging storm reflexively turned their heads to the darkened, storm-tossed horizon to the south.

"Identify and report."

"Aye aye, sir... I make them to be four Sea King attack helicopters. Each capable of carrying eight Bolander-250 air to ground missiles."

"And lo... the veil of the temple was rent in twain," Kamarov softly spoke to himself.

"Beg pardon, sir?"

"Oh... nothing, Yuri Nikolaiovitch. Just a bit of medieval tomfoolery we've discarded."

The exec seemed puzzled, distracted as he was by the previous communication. Captain Kamarov's broad Slavic face was screwed into a pose of deep concentration beneath the dripping officer's cap. A moment later, he looked up. "Thoughts, Yuri Nikolaiovitch?"

Lieutenant Commander Dobrynin's face was ghastly pale as he faced the Captain. "We don't have a leg to stand on, sir. Caught red-handed in an act of war. I say we dive and get the hell out of here."

"We're at zero-nine-zero absolute, sir," the OOD now announced. "Rudder is amidships. Engines are at idle."

"Very well," Kamarov replied. He leaned over into the hatchway. "Messenger!"

Within seconds the head of a seaman in a dripping sou'wester appeared at the hatchway. "Aye sir?"

"My compliments to Mister Konstantinov, Messenger. Request he join me on the bridge at the double."

"Aye aye, sir." The messenger disappeared below.

"Lay below Mikhail Mikhailovitch."

"Aye aye, sir." The tension in Gorchev's face was obvious. He shortly disappeared.

The Captain now turned back to his anxious exec. "How can we do that Yuri Nikolaiovitch?" He made a sweeping gesture with his arm in the direction of the Cubans fighting their way toward shore through the turbulent surf. "My orders are to land that cargo safely. If we were to leave now, the Sea Kings would show up and slaughter that force before it could ever secrete itself on the beach. It is our duty to remain until they are on-shore."

Dobrynin gulped nervously as Lieutenant Konstantinov, the *Novy Mir*'s Gunnery Officer now reported through the hatchway.

For a nearly unbearable half minute, there was only the sound of the howling wind, pouring rain and the roar of the surf as successive rollers continued breaking over the low-profiled submarine. Dobrynin and Konstantinov found themselves increasingly staring toward the south, as if straining to spot the Sea Kings the moment they appeared on the horizon.

"Andrei Anatolovitch..." Kamarov's voice was low... deliberate. His eyes were riveted on some distant point on the eastern horizon.

"Sir?"

"Have all officers put on sidearms at once."

Both officers gasped. The Captain had already told them his shocking plan. All officers occupying positions of authority around nuclear weapons were required to be armed when those weapons were being armed or deployed. This was so any attempt to interfere with the orders, which were, of course, to come from the highest political authority, would be met with lethal force.

"Arm all five nuclear warheads."

"But *sir*!" Dobrynin exclaimed. "We can't do that without an order in the name of the Praesidium of the Supreme Soviet!"

"Then elevate launching platforms aimed at their targets." Kamarov continued as if Dobrynin wasn't there.

Lieutenant Konstantinov just stood there, mouth open, face a ghostly white.

Kamarov now slammed a massive fist into the ledge of the bulkhead. "Now listen... both of you. We are caught red-handed in an act of war. The British have the right to arrest us. That is obviously what they've set out to do." He gestured in the direction from which the Sea Kings were coming.

"I must keep them busy until our Cuban friends are on the beach and the cargo is out of sight. Then I have to see that we get safely away. If you have any idea whatsoever of how to better accomplish that, then speak now... otherwise GET TO IT!"

The two officers jumped with fright at the sudden deep angry bellowing. Konstantinov happened to look up at one point to see both lookouts watching them, their faces a bloodless white, their mouths hanging open with fearful surprise.

"Launch the Litvinovs... blow this British force out of the sky, then run like hell. The evidence will fall into the sea and our government will deny we were anywhere close."

"I believe the British Commander is daring us to do just that, Yuri Nikolaiovitch. It is obvious he is acting contrary to his procedure as well. If we did that, he wouldn't wait for their politicians to accuse and ours to deny. He is obviously a warrior. He would muster both his and the American navy and hunt us down before we could ever escape."

"But..."

Kamarov angrily held up his hand. "He is a warrior... well so am I. My plan is to deal with him on that basis, so that hopefully all of us will come through." He angrily turned to Konstantinov. "Execute my orders!"

The Gunnery Officer swallowed. "Aye aye, sir." He disappeared through the hatchway as Kamarov reached for the intercom cabinet. Removing the microphone, he depressed the 'all stations' button.

"Now hear this! Now hear this! All hands, this is the Captain. We have been targeted by a force of Royal Navy attack helicopters who are minutes away, armed with air to ground missiles. I propose to confront the British with the credible threat of an overwhelming nuclear attack and thereby win us an out into the open sea, after accomplishing our mission. The orders will seem strange to you... even terrifying. You must, however, carry them out. Our threat must be credible, for we are otherwise in a most difficult position... alone among the seapower of the United States and the remnants of Great Britain's imperial presence in this part of the world... caught red-handed in an act of war.

"Obey these orders swiftly and I am confident we will come through. You have long since proved to me you are a body of men able to accomplish the most difficult of missions. That is what I expect of you now. All right... we've but minutes. Let's get to it!"

The Captain released the 'all stations' button. The first sounds of five panels in the main deck of the *Novy Mir* sliding open were heard as the Captain replaced the microphone inside the cabinet.

As Lieutenant Commander Yuri Dobrynin, the four Soviet deck gun crews and two lookouts watched with expressions of stunned horror on their faces, five launching platforms, each with a large white rocket attached, slowly rose from the bowels of the ship upward to the stormy, windlashed sky. The battle lines were now drawn.

Monday January 1, 1973: New Year's Day, 0235 hrs: the Command Post, Fort Cornwallis British Military Reservation, Port Albert, Isle of St. Margaret's

The Command Post at Fort Cornwallis consisted mainly of one large room, with detailed maps of the island and its environs on the walls, then a series of tables and counters on which sat telephones, recording machines, radio, radar and other sensitive electronic equipment. Major Hill, now in undress khakis and trenchcoat had arrived nearly fifteen minutes ago with his Regimental Sergeant Major and was now seated at the commander's console.

On the wall opposite, Sergeant Major Wickersham had just completed moving two red pins on the large map to a point just north of Port Albert. "Captain Schallert reports they're some thirty minutes from the heights," he called over.

"Very well," Hill replied as he reached for his radio microphone button.

"Peter."

He looked up to see Lieutenant Commander Willhoyt, now in heavy windbreaker and officer's cap, field glasses draped around his neck. "Yes, Colin?"

"One last time, Peter. I beg you to call London. The 4th Ark Royals will be making visual contact with the submarine in five minutes. In the strongest possible terms, I urge you to call off what will be a slaughter of our men... and possibly World War III."

Hill lowered his head to the dials and digital displays in front of him as every eye in the room turned in his direction. Letting out a deep sigh, he looked into his second in command's eyes with a face worn with torment. "I'd rather run that risk, Colin, than condemn the men of this Command to a *certain* death at the hands of a greatly increased and better equipped rebel force than any we've seen here thus far. We have to stop them, Colin. They're all watching us."

Willhoyt nodded, then stiffened. "In that case, sir, I request permission to personally lead my PT Boat Squadron... we're ready to shove off."

"Granted, Colin. Godspeed."

Willhoyt saluted. "You too, sir." With that, he turned and quickly left the room.

"Is this being recorded?" Hill now called over to the staff corporal manning the recording apparatus.

"Yessir. On two machines, in case one malfunctions."

Hill nodded. "Mackenzie... get on earphones with me. I want you to closely monitor."

"Yessir." The adjutant put on a headset.

Hill took a deep breath, glancing at his watch. It was 0235hrs. He pressed the broadcast button. "This is Fort Cornwallis calling the Soviet ship of war now encroaching on our coastal waters. This is Fort Cornwallis calling the Soviet ship of war now encroaching on our coastal waters. Come in and identify yourself, putting your commanding officer in voice contact with me... over."

He released the button as all eyes in the room not on headsets turned to the speaker mounted on the wall. Heavy static was all that could be heard.

Hill tried again. "This is Fort Cornwallis calling the Soviet ship of war now encroaching on our coastal waters... you are not free to disregard this transmission. If you do not acknowledge and report within thirty seconds, this Command proposes to blow you out of the water... *over*!"

More scratchy static was now followed by what sounded like low volume talking in Russian as everyone in the Command Post tensed.

"I think they're trying to find an interpreter, sir." Mackenzie whispered.

"You know Russian?"

"Wish I did. This is too bloody important for any misunderstanding."

"Think I'm making a mistake handling it this way, Wilfrid?"

For a long five seconds, Mackenzie looked into his commanding officer's eyes. "Yessir... but I know why you want to try. Godspeed, sir."

Hill nodded.

"Fort Cornwallis," a heavily accented voice now replied. "This is the Soviet nuclear submarine *Novy Mir*... I am its Captain... Commander Vladimir Kamarov. Over."

"Captain... I am Major Peter Hill, Commandant of Her Majesty's Forces on this island. An armed ship of war transgressing on British territorial waters commits an act of war. Over."

For a tense ten seconds there was more static, with low volume Russian talking in the background. "I'm listening, Major," the voice then replied.

"Captain, very shortly a flight of Royal Navy Sea King attack helicopters will be making visual contact with you. They will be dropping flares, but will *not*, repeat *not*... attack you so long as you do not fire upon them... over."

"How do I know I can trust you? Over."

"I am a military officer, sir," Hill replied. "I am not a politician... Over."

It sounded as if there was some low volume laughter mixed with the static. "Then we understand one another, sir. I am a naval officer... not a politician... over."

Hill managed a smile. "Very well then, sir. Under the rules of international law, I am ordering you to unload your guns, strike your colors and turn your spotlight to the sky. You will be interned and your government contacted. You will be treated with all respect due your rank... over."

"Very well, Major Hill... you have done your duty as a military professional... now I will do mine... If any attempt is made to board this vessel, I will drop five fifty megaton atomic bombs... one each on Houston, Texas.... Atlanta, Georgia.... Miami, Florida.... New Orleans, Louisiana... and Kingston, Jamaica... over.

Gasps could be heard throughout the Command Post as all eyes turned to Hill. For a second or two he closed his eyes, fists clenched, then he reached for the transmit button.

The loud sounds of the furious gale and the throbbing of helicopter rotors now split the tense atmosphere of the room. "Blackbird One calling Command Post on IEF as directed... over."

"Go ahead Blackbird One," Hill replied.

"We're over objective, sir. Request permission to fire flares... over."

"Fire your flares," Hill replied, leaning expectantly forward along with everyone in the room.

Two loud banging sounds were heard above the throbbing of the rotors and the howling wind. Two seconds later followed the sounds of two hollow explosions as the flares began their descent, lighting up the sky and surrounding seas.

"Jesus Wept!" a young voice gasped above the noise.

"My GOD!" sounded another.

Hill grabbed for the microphone. "Observe radio discipline," he snapped. "Over."

"My GOD, sir!" a breathless young voice replied. "It's Armageddon, sir! Repeat! Armageddon." It appeared as if his wind was choked off, then he recovered. "There are five guided missiles pointing up into the sky from the submarine, sir," he gasped once more.

"Are you *certain* they are not Litvinov tactical missiles, Blackbird One?" Hill asked. "Over."

"It's the real thing, sir!" the young man swallowed audibly. "The very end of all creation."

Hill collapsed backward into his chair, drumming his fingers on the table. Mackenzie was sweating as he clamped the earphones tight against his head, as if listening for some small sound. Sergeant Major Wickersham had stopped what he was doing and was watching his commanding officer intently.

An almost unbearable ten seconds later, Hill depressed the button. "Very well, Blackbird Flight... fan out... headed into the wind. If the submarine tries to get underway, you are to fire every missile you have... right down her throat... is that understood? Over..."

"Aye aye, sir," the still astonished young voice replied. "You 'eard 'im, lads... fan out."

"And at the very first sign of smoke from any of those missiles, you are to do exactly the same thing... but make certain at least two of you concur that this is what you are actually seeing. Understood?"

"Aye aye, sir. You 'eard 'im, lads. Blackbird Flight out."

The loud wind and engine sounds stopped, leaving only the static and low volume sounds in the background over the speaker.

"I trust we understand one another, Major... over."

"We do indeed."

"Your conduct seems a bit extreme... risking millions of lives... the life of the entire planet... over a technical act of war, Major... over."

"I notice you haven't claimed a mistake in navigation, Captain... over."

"No Commandant. As I said before... I am a naval officer... not a politician... I am one warrior talking to another."

"Well said, sir. Then I must tell you I am acutely aware that your violation of our waters is far from technical... you are either here to land supplies to the people who are killing my men, or performing some other act of assistance for them... I cannot allow that... over."

"Then you must also understand that I cannot allow my ship to fall into enemy hands... over."

Hill's face was contorted in tense thought for several heart-stopping seconds. "Yes, Captain, but I must show the people of this island, who are watching what is going on, that Britain will not permit *anyone* to give aid and comfort to these men who strike when our backs are turned... who kill the unarmed and innocent. I *cannot* allow that... over."

Above the hammering hearts of everyone in the Command Post, it appeared Captain Kamarov let out a heavy sigh. Then there was only static... that, and inaudible conversation.

Amid the unbearable tension, Captain Mackenzie leaned over to whisper in Hill's ear. "Sir, I think I'm picking up some kind of Spanish conversation in the background."

Hill turned to him. "That makes no sense, Mackenzie... on a Russian submarine," he whispered.

"It does if the aid being delivered is from Cuba."

"Good *God*! You're right. Do we have anyone here who can speak Spanish?"

"Lieutenant Cisco, sir. He spent five years posted at British Honduras."

"Ah yes." Hill looked quickly around the room, his eyes lighting on a young sergeant sitting at his console. Hill snapped his fingers and motioned the man over.

"Sir?"

"Listen lad... I want you to take a headset and one of those tape machines with a tape of this exchange thus far."

"Yes sir?"

Hill now looked anxiously over to the Command Post entrance, beckoning one of the military police guards posted there to him.

"Sir?"

"Take this NCO over to the vehicle maintenance complex, with lights and siren if necessary, and locate Lieutenant William Cisco... *wherever* he is. Got that?"

"Yessir."

"All right, sergeant. Go with the MP now. Tell Cisco I am ordering him to listen *this instant* to that tape and translate what appears to be a Spanish conversation in the background. He is then to call me here... *on the red phone*...immediately. Understood?"

"Yessir."

"Right. Make haste, the both of you." He gave them a very sober look. "You both know what's at stake here."

"Yessir." The sergeant went and grabbed one of the two recorders, with the tape still mounted in it. Then both he and the military policeman ran out the door.

Captain Mackenzie again leaned close to Major Hill's ear. "You've got to somehow stall things here, sir."

"Bloody right." Hill again reached for the microphone.

"Major?" Sergeant Major Wickersham was calling from his position across the room beside the large wall map.

"Yes?"

"Bit of an odd development, sir. Third platoon is taking small arms fire from guerilla positions to the north."

"On the *cliffs*?"

"Yessir."

Hill shook his head. "What the devil would a rebel force be doing there? There's no bloody way a submarine could land supplies up there."

"Agreed, sir. But the bullets are real."

"Good Lord... Tell Schallert to wipe 'em out... and to try to learn their identity."

"Very well, sir." Wickersham turned back to the telephone as Hill pressed his transmit button.

"Captain... there may well be a way out of this for men of honor. Over."

"I'm sure there is, Commandant... the trick is to find it. Over."

"Yes... well it occurs to me that, unless you are willing to disclose what you have landed and where... that you could hand over two of your officers to be interned. Over."

Excited low volume talking began raging in the background of the static. Some raised voices were even discernable.

A young man behind Hill suddenly burst out laughing. Hill spun around to see a blond-haired young man, uniformed as a Royal Navy signalman, laughing as he sat listening through his headset at a radar console. Seeing the Major looking at him, the young man put his hand to his mouth.

"Beg pardon, sir. I'm sorry."

"What's so funny?"

"At least three officers, including the sub's exec, volunteered to be interned the moment you were heard on their speaker."

"You speak Russian?"

"Some."

"What's your name?"

"Petrovsky, sir... Signals and Navigation Service."

"Why did you laugh?"

"Well, sir, it just struck me the Ruskis think their C-O is as daft as..." Now the young man turned scarlet. "Oh... sorry, sir."

For several seconds there was total quiet in the Command Post as all eyes were on Hill and the young signalman. "Go ahead, son, man to man."

"Well, sir...," the young signalman was still red as a beet, and now his voice was quavering besides. "It's just that I'd gladly grab a rifle and join in these deadly patrols... all my mates would too... if you'd stop risking World War III, sir. I 'ave a wife at 'ome, sir. Wouldn't want 'er to die. If someone's got to die, sir, that's our job."

Other than the static from the speaker one could hear a pin drop as all eyes now fixed Major Hill. "Hopefully it won't come to that Petrovsky. Grab your headset and come sit up here on my left. I may need you."

"Yes, sir... pardon the liberty, sir."

"What was the excited talking about?"

"The sub's captain was 'aving none of it."

As Petrovsky came forward to join Hill and Mackenzie, the submarine commander again spoke. "That is out of the question, Commandant. Would you surrender your officers to be imprisoned in a foreign country?"

"Frankly, Captain, I never thought of that until just now. I'd have to think about it. Are you sure you want to reject it out of hand?"

Petrovsky leaned over and whispered in Hill's ear. "The exec is practically *begging* him to reconsider."

"Human beings were never meant to *endure* pressure like this," Hill snapped. "Everyone's thinking of wives... children... We should never have spent our best brains and so much treasure inventing ways to destroy us all. God help me." Hill let out a heavy sigh as he began shaking.

Able Signalman Petrovsky put a hand on his arm. "Buck up, sir. You can do it."

He started to thank the young man when the red phone in front of him buzzed. Casting a glance at Mackenzie, he picked it up. "Hill here."

"Yessir... this is Lieutenant Cisco, sir... over at maintenance."

"Yes, Cisco, what did you find?"

"Not much, sir... there was lots of background noise and they obviously weren't speaking into a microphone."

"Were they talking Spanish?"

"Oh yes... there were two of them, apparently a lieutenant and a colonel... they talk like Cubans or Puerto Ricans, sir."

"What makes you say that, Cisco?"

"Lightening fast, sir."

"Were you able to make out *anything*?"

"The colonel kept talking about nuestros hermanos en la playa... con sus equipajes... brothers on the beach, and their equipment, sir. Does that make any sense?"

"Yes it does... go on."

"They were talking about 'him'... whoever 'him' was... having to protect them. No cabe duda que... there was no doubt that 'he' had to protect them. Make any sense, sir?"

"Yes... yes, go on."

"Well, sir, that's about all I could pick up, other than the lieutenant saying 'he' disagreed, that it wasn't in his orders... it was very confusing, sir."

Hill was practically hyperventilating. "Listen Cisco... this is very important. Were they talking about something in the past... or something in the future?"

"Well... I don't *think* so, sir. If I had to wager the family jewels, I'd say they were talking about something that very minute... like they were already there... in some kind of danger. That's my best guess anyway, from their tone and the tenses used."

"Thank you, Lieutenant. I think you better get over here with the men I sent. I may need you."

"Very well, sir."

Hill hung up the phone. "Wickersham?"

"Sir?"

"Just a second." Hill put down his headset and trotted over to where the Sergeant Major stood with the huge wall map. "Show me the location of the sub on the map... exactly."

"Right... here, sir."

"Are there any beaches around there?"

Wickersham laughed. "Not hardly... well... other than Blankenship Cove, but that's..."

"Blankenship Cove?"

"Yessir... right opposite the sub as a matter of fact... but it's a very tiny area, sir, with no communication to the cliffs except straight up the rock."

"Yes, but we never look there, do we?" Hill's heart was pounding.

"No... you couldn't haul any supplies up."

"Maybe..." Another thought struck him. "Okay, now where is Schallert taking small arms fire... in relation to the this cove?"

"Well, sir... actually, practically directly above it."

Hill stared blankly at the map, trying to make sense of it. "Who's the main rebel commander in this area, Wickersham?"

The sergeant major made a wide circular motion over the northern half of the island with a large calloused hand. "The entire Fedderson Region, sir, is the territory of Crenshaw."

Hill appeared lost in thought. Then his face brightened. "He's the chap who thinks he's General Giap... isn't he?"

"That's 'im, sir."

"I'll be God DAMNED."

"What is it, sir?"

"Maybe the solution to this whole bloody mess, Wickersham!"

The sergeant major stared at his commanding officer, his face a mix of puzzled astonishment.

"Tell Schallert to *hold that ground* until I can get back to him."

"Yessir." Wickersham reached once more for the phone.

Hill nodded, then turned away, a look of prayerful concentration on his face.

"We cannot accept your offer, Commandant," the Captain's voice now came over the speaker. "Over."

Hill trotted back over to his console, picking up the headset. "Well then, Captain, I invite you to make a proposal. Excuse me one second, Captain. Blackbird One... over."

Again the room was filled with the howl of the wind and the loud thumping of the rotors of the four Sea Kings. "Blackbird One, sir."

"Switch to your tactical frequency."

"Aye aye, sir. Blackbird One out."

"Sorry, Captain... I need to discuss petrol with my helicopters."

"Yes Commandant... I imagine that's getting to be a problem along about now. Over."

"Be with you shortly."

"Don't take too long, Commandant... your men don't have that much petrol remaining. Over."

"Sir?" It was Sergeant Major Wickersham from across the room. One hand gripped the telephone.

"Yes?"

"Commander Willhoyt reports PT boats have reached their objective."

"Very well. Have him fan out and arm depth charges."

"Yessir." Wickersham turned back to the phone.

"Oh! And tell him not to get jumpy if things get a bit noisy in the next minute or so."

"Uh... yessir."

Returning to his console, Hill depressed the 'transmit' button. "Captain? Major Hill... over."

"Go ahead, Commandant."

"You're quite right, we're rather at our limit on petrol. I may be ordering a gunnery exercise for our chaps before pulling them out. They will be firing upon British territory and *not*... repeat *not*... at you... over."

For a while, no sound broke the heavy static emanating from the speaker as the submarine commander was obviously considering his options. Finally, there was a heavy sigh. "You are within your rights, Commandant... over."

As all eyes watched him with extreme puzzlement, Hill now sprinted to the rear of the blockhouse, picked up a radio mike, turning the knob to the tactical frequency of 4th Ark Royal Helicopter Attack Group.

Monday January 1, 1973: New Year's Day, 0307 hrs: aboard Blackbird One, 4th Ark Royal Helicopter Attack Group [detached] above Blankenship Cove, St. Margaret's territorial waters

"Caw blymie!" Andrews gasped as he struggled with the stick. "The wind's picking up."

"Petrol's getting on to critical as well," Whitfield spoke into his intercom.

Andrews nodded as he scanned from side to side. Blackbird Three was on his port beam, Blackbird Two and Four his starboard. All were managing to keep a respectful distance from the certain death awaiting them if their aft rotors were slammed into those cliffs by a gust of wind.

"Rookery to Blackbird One." It was Hill's voice.

"Aye aye, sir... One here," Andrews responded.

"What's your petrol situation?"

"We've no more than thirty minutes over objective left, sir... the heavy weather's costing us dearly."

"Very well, Blackbird One... now listen closely. You should be just east of a tiny strip of beach known as Blankenship Cove... I have reason to believe at this very moment that a landing party is there... unloading supplies to the rebels. I want you to fire upon them and destroy them all."

Andrews looked at Whitfield, who returned a worried glance. "Aren't our chaps above there, sir?"

"Yes, One... somewhere close by."

"It'll be the Devil's own time sir... with this bloody wind."

"Understood, One... but we've no choice... good luck... Hill out."

"Here now, Davey... we'll take it." It was the voice of Blanchard in Blackbird Four.

"Right lads... now listen up...," Andrews now spoke, beads of sweat on his forehead. "On my command, we'll move forward to a point just about even with the sub... turn 180 degrees... training our spotlights on the cove... After that, Derek, it's all yours... got that?"

As the other three acknowledged the transmission, Andrews found himself uttering a silent prayer. "Remember lads... our chaps are somewhere right above."

"Aye aye," Blanchard acknowledged. Warrant Officer Trevor Howard of Newcastle-on-Tyne, Blackbird Four's weapons officer, opened the guard on his arming switch.

"Very well then," Andrews spoke. "Maintaining your interval... execute."

The four Sea King helicopters fought their way forward, then turned, putting the furious wind astern of them. All four trained their spotlights on the tiny strip of sand at the base of the cliffs.

"Will ya 'ave a look a' that!" a young voice gasped as piles of crates and several individuals in black came into view. They began swarming furiously around like ants.

"Have a care, Howard...," Blanchard gasped as he fought the stick, watching his artificial horizon bobbing above and below dead on. "Steady... steady..."

A furious gust of wind lifted Blackbird Four's tail high in the air. "HOLY CHRIST!" Blanchard bellowed as his three fellow ship commanders watched with pounding hearts.

Howard, busily arming the first two Bolanders, was jolted into his console. "Damn, Derek... you'll 'ave to do better than that."

As the young men shared a nervous laugh, Blanchard fought the stick. Blackbird Four began to right itself. Slowly, the artificial horizon dipped slightly below dead on. "Steady... steady... GO!"

Howard pressed the red button. Shooting tongues of orange blasted backwards from both sides of Blackbird Four as two projectiles shot forward at blinding speed. Downward they flew, shortly exploding with a bright orange ball of fire.

Cheers broke out on all four ships, but they were shortly stifled as a secondary explosion sent a colossal ball of fire up into the sky. The concussion of the blast caused all four Sea Kings to hurl violently backward, their windscreens pelted by bits of rock from the front of the cliffs... over half a mile away.

"My *God!*" Andrews gasped, reaching for the mike button once he had regained control of the ship.

Monday January 1, 1973: New Year's Day, 0322 hrs: the Command Post, Fort Cornwallis British Military Reservation, Port Albert, Isle of St. Margaret's

A dreadful silence filled the command post as all hands tensely waited the results of Major Hill's orders. Several men jumped with fright when suddenly the loud thumping of the helicopter rotors and the howling of the wind came through the speaker.

"Blackbird One to Rookery... over."

Major Hill closed his eyes in silent prayer for a split second as he depressed the button. "Rookery... over."

"Mission accomplished, sir. Landing party and supplies detected on beach. Two missiles fired forward hit their mark. *Tremendous* secondary explosion lit up the sky and finished the job. Obviously they landed a ton of explosives.... over."

Loud cheering erupted from every corner of the command post. Able Signalman Petrovsky and Captain Mackenzie threw themselves into an ecstatic embrace as Major Hill, still at the back of the room, now gripped the microphone, pressing the button.

"Well done, Blackbird Flight... Return to base... over."

More loud cheering erupted... on *both* sides of that two way communication. "Aye aye, sir! Blackbird Flight out!"

Every one was up, slapping each other on the back, shaking hands, in some cases embracing as Hill now took his place once more at the command console. Mackenzie started to congratulate him but stopped dead as he saw the ashen pallor on the C-O's face.

"What *is* it, sir?"

Hill now reached once more for the transmit button as he briefly glanced at his adjutant. "One more river to cross, Wilfrid... the one that will decide it all."

No one in the command post besides Petrovsky and Mackenzie heard Hill's words. It was something in his aura... the look on his face. Every one fell deathly silent once more, wordlessly taking their seats, their full attention on their Commanding Officer.

"This is Fort Cornwallis calling the *Novy Mir*... over."

Heavy static was the only sound now accompanying the dread silence in the room. This was the payoff of the Dance of Death the two warriors had been engaged in since the new year began. All hands, it seemed, realized it at the same time. You could cut the tension with a knife.

"This is Fort Cornwallis calling the *Novy Mir*... over."

More static was this time accompanied by shouted, excited Spanish in the background, then mumbled Russian. "Go ahead, Commandant..." Captain Kamarov's voice was practically toneless... eerie...

"We needn't detain you any longer, sir," Hill struggled to keep his voice modulated. "Have a safe trip home."

The sounds of bellowed Russian suddenly caused the background noises in the submarine to go silent. "Well done, sir," Kamarov now spoke above the deafening quiet. "Perhaps we will meet someday... eh?"

"A pleasure, Captain... though hopefully not upon the waters."

"A pleasure indeed... *Novy Mir* out."

As all eyes watched the speaker, there was only silence once more. To a man, the command post rose, giving Major Hill a standing ovation as he collapsed against the back of his chair, shaking.

Monday January 1, 1973: New Year's Day, 0331 hrs: aboard the Soviet Nuclear Powered Submarine *Novy Mir*, one half-mile abeam of Blankenship Cove, St. Margaret's territorial waters

All hands broke into boisterous cheering as Captain Kamarov closed the microphone at the main communications console.

"Lower the antenna, Mister Kornilov... prepare for departure."

"Aye aye, sir... and well done!"

Kamarov nodded. "Andrei Anatolovitch?"

"Yessir?"

"Secure nuclear armament... disarm the warheads."

"Aye aye, sir." An audible gasp of relief swept through the conning tower.

As Lieutenant Konstantinov repeated his Captain's orders in a strong voice, Kamarov and Dobrynin once more climbed the ladder toward the bridge. They hadn't yet arrived when the sound of the missiles being lowered into their silos brought a spontaneous cheer from the lookouts and gunners topside.

Out into the howling wind-driven downpour once more, the Captain studied the scene on the beach through his binoculars. The flames had already consumed most of the supplies and were slowly dying down, aided by the drenching rain.

Kamarov shook his head with disgust just as Colonel Córdova came charging up the ladder, shrieking in Spanish. His embarrassed lieutenant following behind.

"You must annihilate the imperialist force... blow them out of the sky!" the lieutenant translated Córdova's words into Russian.

Kamarov fixed Córdova with a look of disgust. "My orders do not include armed intervention against a British force acting on British territory, Colonel."

"To *hell* with your goddam orders!" the enraged Cuban spat.

Dobrynin and the Cuban lieutenant both jumped with alarm as Kamarov now grabbed the astonished colonel by his dripping slicker.

"Listen you... you military *amateur!*" Kamarov seethed, still gripping the colonel with two giant Slavic paws. "If those idiots on the beach had more respect for *their* orders this would never have happened. Their black outfits made them invisible against rocks... those sand-colored tarps would have made the supplies all but the same...."

"But what did they do? While I risked every member of this command to give them all the time in the world to secrete themselves in the cove... these bumbling fools stood around gawking at the military standoff!" Kamarov now shook Córdova violently. "You and your kind are little more than hoodlums... *playing* at war. And before I ever risk the lives of my men on your behalf again, I will make goddam sure that I am given professionals to work with... not juvenile delinquents in uniform. Now *get out of my sight* before I put you in irons!"

As the still furious Cuban colonel hastily retreated, the gunners and lookouts again broke into wild and relieved cheers.

"Where are the warriors nowadays, Yuri Nikolaiovitch?" Kamarov sadly shook his head.

Dobrynin just stood there, a very relieved look on his face, as the last of the panels walling off the silos could be heard sliding back into place.

The Captain now leaned into the hatchway. "All ahead standard."

"Aye aye, sir... all ahead standard." The submarine's powerful engines churned the water white as the *Novy Mir* began heading for the open sea.

"Lookouts, keep an eye on those PT boats."

"Aye aye, sir," they both responded.

"You know, Yuri Nikolaiovitch, I'm wondering how the British knew to look over at the cove. Once those men were ashore, they were all but home free."

"I know," Dobrynin responded. "Maybe it was dumb luck."

Kamarov rubbed his chin thoughtfully, shaking his head. "No... no... I don't think so. I had their full attention."

Dobrynin smiled. "You did indeed, sir. You played it brilliantly. I'm sorry my courage failed me there for awhile."

"It wasn't your courage. It was your devotion to your orders... to your duty. I did what I did because we were in a desperate situation. But if you had not attempted to remind me of the legal requirements for deploying nuclear weapons, I would have been disappointed in you."

"Well thank you, sir... very much."

The submarine was pitching wildly in the heavy surf as the running lights of the five PT boats were now clearly visible, arrayed all across its bow. Kamarov had taken to studying them through his binoculars, even as he suddenly let out a gasp.

"I've *got it*, Yuri Nikolaiovitch!"

Lieutenant Commander Dobrynin was also studying the scene ahead through his field glasses. "What sir?"

"How the British knew! It was that idiot Córdova! Do you remember when I was first talking to the British Commander?"

"Yessir."

"Córdova was constantly talking in the background. I'd bet you anything you'd care to wager that clever Limey son of a bitch picked it up through his headphones."

"Hmmm." Dobrynin shook his head. "The bastard destroyed his own men with his flapping mouth."

"Helped destroy them. They still could've saved themselves had they followed their orders."

The two officer informal court of inquiry was suspended as the submarine now drew to within yards of the PT boats. The two nearest on both port and starboard bows shone their spotlights to illuminate the path of egress for the Soviet ship of war.

As they drew abreast of the pitching, rolling British vessels, watching them silently in the darkness, the Soviet gunners and lookouts stared at the vessels with as much curiosity as the British sailors were eying them. One of the Soviet lookouts waved. The young Englishmen waved back.

Watching from the bridge, Captain Kamarov's eyes came to rest on a British Lieutenant Commander. The two smiled, then exchanged salutes as the submarine continued past, headed for the open sea.

"Lookouts below!" Kamarov bellowed.

After a final wave to the young Englishmen, the two Soviet sailors dropped into the hatchway.

"Secure topside and clear the decks!" The Soviet gunners now did the same thing.

Captain Kamarov now took a final look fore and aft, then leaned toward the hatchway. "Stand by to dive!"

A buzzer sounded as the command was repeated. Lieutenant Commander Dobrynin now climbed into the hatchway.

"Dive! Dive! Dive!" Claxons sounded throughout the vessel as the bow of the submarine headed below the heavy surf.

Taking a last look fore and aft with decks awash, Captain Kamarov lowered himself into the hatchway, grabbing onto the line, pulling it closed behind him.

As the last of the Soviet submarine disappeared beneath the sea, Lieutenant Commander Willhoyt let out a monumental sigh of relief. "Let's head for the barn, lads."

A huge cheer went up from the crews as the boats turned for Port Albert.

Chapter Two

NOT MY BEST BIRTHDAY

Wednesday January 3, 1973: on the Atlantic City Boardwalk, Atlantic City, New Jersey

Three days after the murder of Jerry Fischer anyone relying on the media for their version of reality would think the country was paralyzed with grief and despair. Politicians, clerics, community leaders of all races and faiths babbled on and on in each daily edition, talking about his goodness, his generosity, his love for humanity. It was getting so I couldn't stand to read *The Atlantic City Press* without losing my temper. The annoying thing was, though, that all the accomplishments cited were true. Jerry Fischer did indeed help many people with the money he made clawing his way to the top.

Maybe that was what got me most of all. I knew how *evil* the man was. I had watched him revel in my terror as he calmly gave the necessary signal for one of my closest friends, a guy who was as decent as a man came, to be bludgeoned to death and decapitated before my eyes. Over and over again as I read the daily paper, I kept seeing the heartrending sight of Dexter bowing his head, his hands tied behind him, on his knees, as his gooned out killer approached with the machete. The awful reality that was suggesting itself to my troubled mind was that much of the goodness... and greatness... in our world was little more than some grotesque by-product given off by the efforts of evil men gouging their way to wealth and power. There were sure plenty of other examples. It was an unnerving epiphany to mark my twenty-fifth birthday.

Yet I *had* to read the morning paper... to learn the latest on the manhunt for Fischer's killer[s]. So far, no one quoted in the press had identified the guy who did it. All the speculation thus far was confined to the Salt and Pepper Gang and Don Clemente DiStefano. DiStefano was the Mob's Boss of Bosses on the Jersey side of the Hudson River... the Salt and Pepper Gang was *me*.

Heaving my by now characteristic heavy sigh, I folded the paper and dropped it on the table. Swallowing the last gulp of coffee, I hauled myself to my feet and, after dropping three quarters under my plate, headed for the register.

The cashier looked listlessly up from today's Jerry Fischer front page article, taking my ticket and money without a word.

"Thanks," I mumbled as she handed me my change. I then stepped out into the foggy street, pulling the collar up on my London Fog topcoat as I did so.

I had awakened at the Seashell Motel in Margate City determined to celebrate my twenty-fifth birthday in *some* way. I finally hit on the idea of coming to the Boardwalk and eating at Child's Plain and Fancy, just like I used to do on those insanely happy summer days as a kid when the folks would bring me here from Philadelphia for a vacation. The smell of the salt air, the sight of that glorious beach and ocean, the sound of the lifeguard whistles and the clatter of hundreds of feet along the Boardwalk were all part of the joyful prelude to a pancake breakfast at Child's, followed by a *deliriously* joyful day on the Kentucky Avenue Beach, followed by an equally joyful evening on the Boardwalk... eating ice cream cones, watching my pinwheel spin in the soft ocean breeze, watching the red paint on the Sherwin-Williams sign 'covering the earth', getting peanuts to feed the pigeons, looking for one of the many places that sold captain's hats and plastic lifeguard boats. Then finally going to sleep with the window of our hotel room open to all the hustle and bustle below, breathing in the salt air, looking forward to another idyllic day tomorrow.

Atlantic City was a kids' paradise in those days. The fun never set. I don't think I was ever so happy for so many hours of the day as I was on those vacations.

My birthday idea was a mistake. Child's was closed. The Boardwalk was deserted. Nothing but ghosts from a long-gone era to keep me company. Atlantic City was dead. Most of the hotels were closed now, many in bankruptcy. Most of the town was out of work. Everything seemed to be decaying... returning to the earth from which it came, to be turned into something else.

I made my way slowly up Kentucky Avenue from the place where I'd finally located a greasy spoon. Peeling posters advertised long-closed cheap strip shows. The few bars that were open were catering now to the hard core alkies, their loud honky-tonk music blasting into the narrow street at 9:30 in the morning grated on my nerves, and my psyche as I struggled those last few yards to the Boardwalk. Past the closed businesses, past the New Clarion Hotel where we always used to stay... now closed, past all the other melancholy recollections of a world gone away.

At least the clump of my boots on the ramp leading up to the Boardwalk made the same sounds as were made by all those happy people all those years ago, but I wasn't sure if it was more of a comfort or a taunt. I was already fighting hard not to see all these closed, dismal, defeated relics of my childhood as a metaphor for my own life's path. *It's my BIRTHDAY dammit all!*

Once on the Boardwalk, I clumped my way to the familiar aluminum railing fence at the far side overlooking the beach. Glancing both uptown and downbeach as I crossed the deserted, dripping wet span, I could hardly make out the skyline through the fog. Even that was symbolic. The old Atlantic City skyline, according to the City Fathers, was soon to be no more. Many of those fine old Edwardian and Victorian hotels were slated for outright demolition... others for extensive renovation. The big solution was believed to be legalized gambling. It would shortly convert the old hollow shell to a noisy, slick, aluminum-plated replica of the gambling centers of Nevada... once they had the votes, that is. The thought made me wretch.

Letting out yet another heavy sigh, I propped a boot on the dripping wet bottom railing, folded my arms along the dripping wet top railing, then just stared straight ahead. The beach was just as deserted as the rest of the town. The sand was a brownish gray, the ocean, what I could see of it, was a field gray mixed with the white foam of the breakers, the sky was a deceptively dazzling whitish gray. *Gray... gray... gray.*

At least I wouldn't be here much longer. Connie McElroy had asked me for a week to give her time to close up the house she had shared with her beloved husband Harry in Brooklyn, then she would join me here and we would head south. In the opening hours of 1973, a week didn't sound either unreasonable or dangerous. But now, after yet another dose of the media hinting that the manhunt was getting closer with each passing day to arresting the murderers of Jerry Fischer, I had my doubts.

Of course I had a few things going for me. The girl I was planning to marry after I finally divorced Terri had left me close to $800,000 in her will. We had earned most of that together, though her part in it was infinitely greater. Up until yesterday, I was only counting on half a million, but the new management of J.B. Fischer & Company had discovered that additional monies were owed toward Nancy's commission on the Johannes Borg account. They had notified her lawyer Abe Horowitz and he had notified me. True to his word, he had gotten it for me in one thousand dollar bills, all of which were sitting in a briefcase back at the Seashell.

In the lapel of my sport jacket was the orange-blue-orange ribbon of New Jersey's Law Enforcement Medal of Valor, which undoubtedly would amount to practically a free pass through any suspicions of state and local cops I had anything to do with the murder.

Then too, I had Connie. She was as grief stricken over the loss of her husband as I was over the loss of my fiancé, but there was an energy that surrounded us this past year that made for some interesting possibilities. She was a tough Puerto Rican chick who at age twenty-four had been chief of staff to the notorious North Jersey political boss and Democrat Majority Whip in the New Jersey Assembly Edward M. 'Big Ed' Foley. I was a pretty resourceful guy myself. Together, along with two other guys, we had broken out of Fischer's insane asylum where we were all held captive as part of an enterprise the self-made tycoon was running to warehouse us and drive us insane. After making good our escape, we had enlisted the help of some New York and New Jersey cops and had finally managed to shut him down.

Fischer had his revenge however, and in three bloody hot humid July days at a farmhouse in upper New York State managed to kill our two brothers, the Jersey City revolutionary Abdul Jamal and a quiet unassuming New York postman named Dexter White. That was also when Connie's husband Harry McElroy was killed, along with our resident philosopher Moses Worthington. Connie and I survived, but sufficiently shattered so that we each spent some serious time at a Saratoga County sanitarium. We were released in the fall, each determined to kill Jerry Fischer, even as he was brought to trial in the case we'd helped to make against him.

Those plans were unwittingly foiled, however, by the numbers-hunting FBI, who in exchange for the promise of some testimony against Clemente DiStefano, successfully prevented the State of New Jersey from bringing him to trial and me killing him at the courthouse. They also had all but guaranteed that he would never otherwise be brought to justice for what the press had called The New Chatsworth Massacre.

But as sometimes happens, the Law of Karma, or whatever, stepped in and foiled the feds' plan to reap both headlines and numbers in 1973. Jerry Fischer, along with his bodyguard Dan Mahoney, had been gunned down in the parking lot of his office building on New Year's Eve, and now the hoopla over Watergate was even preventing the frustrated FBI from getting headlines they would otherwise have expected searching for his killer[s].

That was the rub. This was a federal rap... and the feds had already photographed me, in my Atlantic County special sheriff's sergeant uniform, among the witnesses against Fischer at the Cumberland County Courthouse. My Medal of Valor counted for nothing among those bastards, and as the victim in a particularly brutal crime of Fischer's, I was an obvious suspect in his murder. Fortunately, Connie and I had made our escape from the murder scene apparently undetected, but the sooner we were out of this mess the better. Then too... there were those *other* people who would likely rather have me dead.

My maudlin thoughts were interrupted by motor sounds assaulting my ears from the direction of uptown. It wasn't the high-pitched, low volume whine of the modern rolling chairs, either. Surprised, I glanced in that direction.

It was a white over blue-gray Atlantic City Police cruiser. I watched as it slowly approached. Along with the decay of practically everything else around here, the Boardwalk was getting pretty shabby in spots. I found myself absently wondering, as the patrol car closed the last of the distance between us, if it would shortly fall through a rotten patch of Boardwalk. Of course I'd almost prefer rotten boards to what these same City Fathers had put down in some places. I didn't consider myself to be a neurotic purist, but *aluminum slabs* had no place on the Atlantic City Boardwalk! *Oh Christ! My birthday is turning out so depressing!* I had looked forward to turning twenty-five for a while now. I'd been hearing since I began driving at age eighteen that this was the year your premiums finally took a nosedive... that the insurance companies stopped considering you a hotrodder in disguise.

The police car pulled even with me and came to a stop. The lone cop inside cranked down the window. "Yo Cassell!"

"Yo Denny!" It was my old pal from the bus terminal two years ago... Denny Gardner. After we'd made our break from the asylum last February, he hid us in his apartment and was the first cop to believe our story and try to help us... him and his sergeant, Dom Pellegrini... another friend of mine.

"Hey man, thanks a million for dat Lincoln! I thought you was kiddin'!"

"You didn't act that way when I first came back from Morocco and told you I didn't have the money," I chided.

Denny reddened. "Yeah, I was seein' that car in my *dreams*."

I nodded, recalling his disappointment and mine when I'd been unable to come through.

Denny suddenly cleared his throat as if to change the subject. "Say, buddy, you ever heard of a guy named Sean Kelly?"

I tensed. I sure had. Knew him too. "One a' Fischer's bodyguards, Gardner... why?"

Denny's face grew serious. "Well then it's a damned good thing I ran into you."

"How so?"

"We got a tip outta New York City the guy was headed our way."

"No foolin'?" I was trying to act as 'normal' as possible. Denny knew only too well that I was a Fischer victim. I didn't want to make it any harder than necessary for him to 'look the other way'. "I wonder why."

"The tip says he's lookin' to kill the man got his boss." Denny was looking straight at me now.

Now it was my turn to redden.

"You armed?"

"Yeah." I patted in the general area of my waistband. Where my .38 snub nose rested in its holster.

"Okay, John... watch your back."

"I will... thanks, Denny."

"Sure buddy. That car is a dream come true, man... thanks again."

I gave him a grin and a wave as he resumed his forlorn patrol down the deserted Boardwalk. Denny had given me all kinds of fight training the year I worked at the terminal as a freight agent and he was just back from Vietnam, working as a security guard while waiting for a slot to open on the ACPD. I'd originally promised him a Lincoln *Continental* to help convince myself that Nancy and I really were about to become millionaires. Later, I was glad I'd done it because as one of the very few who even knew about all those diamonds old Mrs. Seabrook had left me, he helped keep me sane as I navigated that perilous summer and several kidnap attempts by gunmen working for Walther Van Der Groot. Finally though, all those fight tricks he'd taught me actually saved my life in Morocco a time or two, which made Denny even more worthy of an extra special present.

I watched as the police car disappeared into the fog in the direction of Downbeach. The tip left me with an eerie kind of feeling... as if all these deserted buildings behind me and stretching out on both sides weren't empty at all, but were places concealing a man who had obviously come to town to murder me. He was among them some-where... watching... waiting.

"Oh happy fuckin' birthday to you, buddy," I grumbled to myself as, now beset with a king-sized case of the creeps on top of everything else, I flung myself away from the railing, my reverie at an end.

Unfortunately though, my retreat to less scary realms immediately ran into trouble. I forgot where I'd left my car. Was it further uptown, on North Carolina Avenue? Or straight down Kentucky? I *couldn't remember.* As I struggled with the indecision, I heard that high-pitched, low volume whine characteristic of those new blue rolling chairs.

Why would anyone ride a rolling chair on a day like this? Seized with some undefined foreboding, my face whipsawed first in one direction, then the other, trying to place the sound. In the rapidly thickening fog, I was having no success. *Somebody might well hire a rolling chair if he wanted to quickly search the Boardwalk. Sean Kelly is, after all, no spring chicken. He's in his late fifties....*

The sound drew closer... or at least grew louder. *Fuck it... I'm gettin' outta here.* I quickly moved across the Boardwalk, then down the ramp onto Kentucky Avenue. I'd made it past the first three buildings when I turned back toward the Boardwalk to look. The rolling chair was there... just stopped. The heavy plastic cover was drawn across it, making it impossible to see who, if anyone, might be inside. The chair stood there for a while, then it turned and headed back uptown.

I realized I was probably psyching myself up, but it didn't matter. In the eeriness of the fog, obsessed as I was with the specter of various enemies closing in on me... then this tip... I was on the edge of panic. I turned once more toward Pacific Avenue and quickened my pace. I half expected the mysterious rolling chair to head down the ramp, but instead it disappeared... going back the way it came.

My footsteps now echoed back at me as I moved down the deserted street. My trip through the Atlantic City of my childhood was no longer an exercise in glum nostalgia, it was a journey into unholy terror. I quickened my pace even more, frantically looking both ways, occasionally spinning around behind me. The awful music blaring from the dilapidated bars was now almost a blessing, since it drowned out the sounds of those footsteps.

Reaching Pacific, I noticed a jitney heading in my direction. *Fuck this*, I thought to myself. *I'm ridin'... all the way to North Carolina.* I finally remembered that was where I parked my car. I often parked there because it was a wide street. I was far less likely to come back and find my car clipped by some drunken idiot trying to turn on the narrow streets in order to retrace his steps from the Boardwalk.

The jitney pulled to the corner and stopped. I hauled myself aboard, paid the driver, then collapsed nervously into my seat. There was no one else aboard. We made it just a few blocks to Tennessee Avenue, when a car on the opposite side of the street suddenly pulled out of a motel parking lot, misjudged the narrow turn necessary to avoid going into the other lane, and slammed into the fender of the car immediately ahead of us. The jitney driver barely managed to slam on his brakes in time.

All the while cursing in Yiddish... or maybe it was Russian... under his breath, he angrily pulled open his side window. "What the hell kinda' drivin' ya call that, fella!" he bellowed to the idiot who had misjudged his turning radius and caused the collision.

"Aw check yerself into a nursin' home, pop. Wit those coke bottle glasses a' yurs you prob'ly can't see nuthin'."

The driver of the car ahead of us jumped out and joined in the attack on the driver causing the accident. Soon all three of them were bellowing dark oaths and other insults at one another.

"Lemme out here," I finally gasped. He didn't hear me. Obviously his hearing aid was turned way down. I had to repeat myself several times.

It took a while to get the driver's attention. When I did he turned on me angrily. "What's your problem kid? You tink dis was MY fault?"

"No, I just..."

"It's you goddam kids cause all the accidents! They oughtta..."

"JUST LET ME OUT!" I bellowed. Once I was through the doors onto the sidewalk, we exchanged angry upward swatting motions with our right arms as I resumed my troubled, now practically obsessed, journey.

Leaving the angry, gesturing drivers behind, I continued up Pacific. Once past the accident, my footsteps again were echoing in my ears, only now it sounded as if there was another pair of footsteps walking at almost the same pace. I spun around... and saw nothing. I stopped, and the sound stopped too.

I was past South Carolina now. My goal loomed ahead. It seemed as if the only three vehicles driving the streets of the Southside had found each other and collided. Everything else looked so deserted in this fog.

Reaching my old church, I turned left toward the 'honor' parking lot. This was something of a joke because every hustler in town, it seemed, would take turns popping out of the shadows, introducing themselves as the attendant and demanding the money you were about to shove into the slot. *That's okay, after this I can take a joke.* I could see my yellow VW up ahead. *I'll just pick up something from Casel's Supermarket back in Margate and take it to my room.* With Sean Kelly somewhere on the loose, I needed to lay low. There could, after all, be only one person he would come to Atlantic City to hunt down.

I was in the alley now. The shortcut to the parking lot. It was *very* deserted. I'd almost made it to the point where it opened into the parking lot when powerful arms clamped on my neck from behind and yanked me backward. In a flash I reached back and ripped at one of my attacker's ears, but he must have seen it coming because he shoved me with considerable force over one of his legs, sending me crashing into several trash cans, knocking some over and me seeing stars.

Hearing his approach, I managed to roll to one side, then begin to haul myself up. Now I got a look at him. It was Kelly all right. He lunged, knocking me once more into the trash cans. We rolled around for a while on the suddenly litter-strewn asphalt, grunting and groaning, making attempts to gouge that were unsuccessful. I finally managed a poorly aimed chop to his windpipe that allowed me just enough time to stagger to my feet. He did the same, and I shortly heard the tell-tale click of a switchblade opening.

Kelly was no doubt back in Hell's Kitchen now as he maneuvered toward me, an evil look in his eyes. I thought of my .38, but realized wearing the bulky topcoat he'd probably be on top of me before I'd ever have it out. Instead, I grabbed at one of the upended trash cans and flung it at him with all my strength. It caught him on the arm holding the knife, knocking him backward. Taking advantage of a short window of opportunity as he struggled to regain his balance, I lunged for him, knocking us both to the ground with him on the bottom. Grabbing his wrist, I repeatedly slammed it against the asphalt until he let go of the knife.

During this time, though, he managed to land a heavy open-palmed roundhouse on my ear, knocking me over. Once again we were rolling around on the ground. Kelly managed to land a knee into my stomach, then push me away long enough to stagger to his feet. He next tried a kick, but I managed to roll away from the blow and get to my feet. Unfortunately, this maneuver had put me with my back to him and he now closed the distance, clamping an arm across my throat.

Again we struggled, locked in a stalemate, in the darkened silent alley. I tried to grab the back of his legs so I could slam into him and knock him down but his grip was too strong. I couldn't get low enough. Our struggles wound us up alongside another parked car, our grunts and groans and the scraping and squeaking of our boots on the cement were the only sounds.

In desperation, I reached back to his neck, then doubled over as fast as I could. If done right, this flips the opponent over on his back... but I didn't do it right. Sean Kelly now came slightly around past my shoulder, almost facing me. His powerful arms slid under mine as his hands clamped onto my forehead and began jamming my head back. I collapsed over the hood of the parked car, desperately fighting his efforts to get his fingers closer to my eyes. After struggling for what seemed like hours trying to defeat this hold, I suddenly got smart and jammed my leg upward.

It wasn't directly on target, but it was close enough. Kelly let out a gasp and let go long enough for me to land a hard swat downward onto his glasses, driving them hard against the bridge of his nose. He let out a groan and stumbled backward. Hoisting myself quickly up onto the hood, I saw his hand go inside his coat pocket. I kicked outward, planting both feet square against his chest as hard as I could.

Kelly's hand came flying out of his coat, a .45 automatic clattering onto the cement, even as he fell backwards out of control. He landed onto the cement with a crash and just lay there as I pounced, gasping, on the .45... picking it up.

Kelly's hands now covered his face, wiping away the blood starting out of his nose. "Kill me, Cassell," he gasped. "I ain't good fer nuttin' any more... go on and kill me."

I somehow wobbled to my feet holding the .45. My chest was heaving so hard I thought I was going to pass out. For a while we just looked at one another... for a time unable to catch our breath.

"I said kill me, you stupid mick," Kelly finally gasped again. "I can't do nuthin' no more."

"How come you didn't just blow me away, Sean?" I gasped a few moments later. "You had me dead to rights back there."

He managed a bitter smirk. "I was gonna hijack you... get you to confess what you did. No fool like an old fool... huh?"

"You did all right, buddy," I panted. "I hope I got half your wind and strength when I'm your age."

He eyed me with anguish. "I didn't have what I needed, kid. You killed my Boss... I shoulda' killed you."

"I didn't do it, Sean."

Kelly eyed me for a few moments, then managed a wheezy laugh. "Sure, kid. You're gonna tell me DiStefano did. That shows how much you know. Why..."

"Yeah," I interrupted. "They had the testimony all worked out. I heard."

Kelly seemed to eye me with something bordering on respect. "That's right. So if it weren't you... and weren't DiStefano..." He stopped, then shook his head. "Don't tell me you're gonna pin it on the little broad."

"No... she didn't do it either."

Kelly made a face, then made an effort to stand up. I reached out and hauled him to his feet. He nodded, then again searched my eyes with his. "Okay then... who?"

"I'm not gonna tell you I didn't want to Sean. I'm not gonna tell you I wasn't there. But it wasn't me... and it wasn't Connie."

Kelly now leaned against the other parked car, wiping occasion-ally at the small amount of blood still coming from his nose. Then he faced me once more. "Well then... who?"

I reached out his .45 to him, butt forward.

For a few moments he eyed me with astonishment. I suppose I was taking a gamble, but I didn't really think so. Kelly now eyed me with something approaching gratitude. "You're okay, Cassell," he said as he took it, stuffing it back inside his coat.

"Come on, man. I need a drink. Help me celebrate my birthday."

"Your year's off to a great start, kid. But I won't screw it up any fur-ther. C'mon, I'll take you to a place nearby. Serves great Irish." With that, after we'd done all we could to bat the filth off of our topcoats, he put an arm across my shoulders and we retraced our steps toward Pacific Avenue.

The place he had in mind was a dingy spot on Virginia Avenue named 'The Winner's Circle'. At high noon on this foggy midweek January day, the place had a few losers inside and nothing more. We found a table, ordered a round, then resumed eyeing one another.

"So you witnessed it?" He asked as the waitress set the drinks down and departed.

"Yup."

"What were you doin' there?"

"I was waiting to kill him."

"And you ain't gonna tell who pulled the trigger?"

"Nope."

"Was it anybody I know?"

I shot him a look that made him chuckle in spite of himself. "Okay, Cassell. I believe you. And I won't press you any further."

I nodded, then stuck my hand across the small table and we shook on it. "Where do you go from here?"

Kelly shook his head. "I dunno. Miss Colleen don't want me around no more. She's offered to let me stay on in the back cottage but..." Kelly stopped, then began shaking, obviously fighting back tears. "I dunno... nuthin's the same any more."

There wasn't much more to say, but we sat there not saying it through two more drinks. Finally he stood up, dropped two bucks on the table, then made an effort at putting on a brave face. "Happy birthday, kid. Many happy returns." He took my hand, weakly shook it, then turned to go. The man had been with Jerry Fischer since the Thirties, had remained loyal to the last... and now he had nothing and no one.

"Wanna come work for Connie and me?" The words were out of my mouth before I knew what I was saying.

Kelly whiplashed in my direction, studying my face hard. "I ain't lookin' fer no charity kid."

"This won't be. We're moving to some foreign country... a real hell hole... We gotta lay low. It's gonna be tough."

"Good idea kid. I guess you know word on the street is that you did it."

I didn't. The news didn't exactly surprise me, but it still gave me a hollow twinge in my gut to hear my worst fears confirmed. I swallowed, still awaiting his answer.

"I'd be a good hand fer you, kid."

"I know you would."

A smile stole across his face. He stuck out his hand again, pumping mine with considerably more vigor this time. "Deal, kid... uh... Boss."

"Okay... grab your passport, just a couple changes a' clothes, then meet me at this address." I reached out and handed him the card of the Seashell.

"Will do... see ya tomorrow, Boss."

"Bye Sean."

. . . .

My next birthday surprise awaited me as I arrived back at the Seashell Motel a few hours later. At first I couldn't see any signs of a driver, but the black sedan with small antenna on the roof and New York plates pretty much gave it away.

I walked over to the bulkhead and surveyed the deserted beach. He wasn't there... or at least anywhere close. I next went to my room and opened the door with my key. His tired black sport jacket hung on the chair, his service revolver rested in its clip-on holster on the table. He was stretched out on the bed, the knot on his tired old black knit tie pulled down a couple inches, his threadbare plaid shirt open at the collar.

He'd obviously been sound asleep, but before I was across the threshold had pulled himself to a sitting position. "Yo Cassell," he mumbled thickly, scratching his head full of oily black hair. "I was wonderin' when you were gonna get back."

"Hi Rick," I ventured cautiously. "To what do I owe *this* honor?"

Detective Sergeant Rick Gariglia of the Manhattan South Borough Command, New York City Police Department now hauled himself to his feet, yawning noisily. That done, he went for the sink and splashed some water in his face as I took off my topcoat and threw it across the bed. Then I just stood warily watching him.

"Do I need an excuse to drop in on an old buddy?" he retorted in a mock-insulted voice, all the while wiping his face with the hand towel that hung by the sink.

I nodded, a sarcastic look on my face, as I folded my arms across my front and leaned against the wall. "For a social call, of course not." I gestured with my head towards the front door. "But with New York City on the brink of bankruptcy, I doubt your boss authorized the use of that car out there for a social call."

Rick smiled, then knotted his tie in the mirror, buttoned his shirt, clipped the holster to his belt, then with one motion grabbed the sport jacket and turned to face me. "Know any place we can get some chow in this burg?" he grinned, obviously choosing to avoid answering yet.

"Sure." Eyeing him all the while, I again picked up my topcoat and we headed back outside to my car. Within minutes we were driving up Ventnor Avenue toward Arnie's Delicatessen on Lancaster. The Kramer Brothers had finally retired, selling their legendary eatery. 'Arnie', whoever he was, had done a pretty good job of continuing with their peerless cuisine.

"God Cassell, you smell like a distillery," Gariglia frowned as we began hunting a parking spot on Lancaster around the corner from our destination.

"I'm old enough," I grumbled.

He reached over and tapped a calloused finger in the area of my left lapel, obviously about to make reference to my Medal of Valor, the ribbon of which was clamped there. "You ain't settin' a very good example to the youth of New Jersey, buddy." He withdrew the hand and glanced at his watch. "Bein' soused at three in the afternoon."

"Maybe the event that led to my gettin' it has somethin' to do with it."

"What? The election of 1972?"

Rick knew me too well. Suddenly we were both convulsed with laughter.

"Seriously," I finally continued as we walked the short distance to the deli and went inside. "I'm celebratin' my birthday, Rick, if you must know."

"All alone?" He made a clucking noise with his tongue.

"With Sean Kelly."

His face whiplashed in my direction. "You serious? I was about to mention him... give you a tip we got..."

"Yeah, I know. Fortunately one a' Dom's guys already passed it on... about half an hour before he jumped me."

We chose one of the many empty booths. The cheerful, heavy-set lady who always seemed to be in black ambled over and handed us menus. As Rick perused the selections I told him the rest of the story, leaving out my travel plans, but including the job offer.

"You pulled a rabbit out of a hat there, Cassell."

"I guess the old guy was desperate."

"Yeah... say, what's this baked bean malt they got here?" His eyes were back to looking incredulously at the milkshake selections. The menu, for as long as I could remember, had featured both a baked bean and a lox malt, for the ungodly price of fifteen bucks.

I laughed.

"Nah! They gotta be kiddin'!"

The lady was coming back now with an order pad. "Go ahead... ask her." I already had... quite a while ago, so I knew the answer he'd get.

"You gentlemen ready to order?"

"Say, Miss," Rick's tone was unbelieving as he pointed at the spot on the menu. "Is this for real? Do you really carry somethin' like this?"

'Mrs. Arnie' laughed. "If you're willing to pay fifteen bucks, we're willing to make it for you."

The three of us laughed, then we placed our orders. Mrs. Arnie took our order slip to the back. "Anybody ever took 'em up on that?" Rick continued, still entranced.

"Not as I know of. But it's sure a conversation piece. Like if you're a kid here on a first date, and you're a little tongue tied.... it's an automatic conversation topic. It's a pretty cool idea."

"Yeah... no foolin'."

We made small talk until the food came, then I plunged right in. Rick eyed me for a while, taking bites here and there. I watched him until I could stand it no longer, but it wasn't just idle curiosity... Rick was suddenly *uncomfortable*.

"You wanna talk about the baked bean malt," I asked him, making the obvious reference.

"Heh heh." He looked down, then up at me, wiping his mouth with the linen napkin. "Happy birthday, Cassell... did you kill Jerry Fischer?"

I stumbled over the bite of Arnie's magnificent corned beef, cole slaw and Russian dressing on rye I'd been chewing at the moment. After a short coughing spell and a couple swallows of my black and white milkshake, I looked him in the eye. "Thanks... no."

Rick looked positively relieved. "Know who did?"

"Did what?... Have a happy birthday? Or kill Jerry Fischer?"

Rick grinned. "The latter."

"This official, Rick?"

"Yes."

"No."

"And unofficially?" Rick and I were very close. We'd been through a lot together last year. Much of our relationship had involved keeping life and death secrets, so in a minimum of words we were able to signal one another exactly what we meant. No elaboration was necessary.

"Yes."

"Care to tell me?"

"Don't you think it'll just complicate your life Rick? Knowing... but not knowing?"

"The fuckin' FBI is loaded for bear on this one, John. They wanna talk to you. I threw 'em off, sayin' you'd mentioned somethin' about goin' to New Mexico, but that won't keep you safe for long."

"Thanks man."

"Sure, buddy. Those two bastards Griggs and Boxwell... the ones that threatened me, remember?"

"Sure do."

He caught my involuntary grin, even as my face shot to the floor. Suddenly, he was looking at me *very* suspiciously, breaking into laughter at the same time. "They each have a broken arm." He reached over and yanked my face upward until I was forced to look at him. "Or did you know about that?"

"Officially?"

"Yes."

"No."

"And unofficially?"

I burst into laughter myself, with Rick joining in all the heartier. It was several minutes before he could compose himself. "Way to go, Buddy!" he finally wheezed, even as he wiped his eyes with the napkin. "You deserve another a' them medals just for that!"

"I couldn't possibly accept one," I wheezed in return. "That was a labor of love. Connie helped me out quite a' bit."

"Oh... you two are speakin' again?"

"Yeah... she finally got medicated for her depression. We're speakin'."

"Glad to hear it."

The rest of our dinner passed in tall tales and small talk. Rick never renewed probing into the subject of his visit. We had long since finished dinner and were back at the motel, standing in the dark by his car at 5:30 that evening before he finally brought it up again.

"Take care, man... Happy New Year," I'd just finished telling him as we shook hands.

"Yeah... uh... Happy Birthday," he'd responded.

Looking over his shoulder, back toward the motel, I caught a glimpse of a silhouette standing in near darkness at the corner of the building, looking my way. It was his movement around the corner that had caught my eye. Seeing another person there, he suddenly froze. I recognized him immediately. He was my third birthday surprise of the day... the killer of Jerry Fischer and Dan Mahoney. I tensed at the sight of him, and Gariglia caught it, spinning around to follow the path of my eyes. The shadow quickly ducked behind the building.

Rick turned back around. "What was that look all about, Cassell? I could a' sworn you saw somethin' just now."

I looked down. "Nuthin', Rick."

He eyed me curiously, then took a deep breath.

The shadow must have heard me speak Gariglia's name because he reappeared, seemingly trying to decide whether to make himself known.

"John... I think I gotta know..."

"Know what?"

"Who killed Fischer." He looked me square in the eye. "Unofficially, of course."

"Why Rick? Tell me that? Is this your case?"

He shrugged. "Yes and no."

"What's that mean?" Eyeing the shadow as inconspicuously as possible, I noticed him paying keen attention to the conversation.

"I mean Fischer was a federally protected witness, so that makes it a federal beef. On top a' that, Griggs and Boxwell got in a lotta hot water for bein' falling down drunk while their star witness got bumped off. Still, though, this happened on our turf and my boss gave it to me."

"And you wanna know because..."

"And I wanna know because I got pretty close to several a' that bastard's victims. And after the feds saw to it he skated completely free of answering for those horrible crimes... well... I figgered I'd take myself off it if I'm just gonna find out *officially* it was someone... well... I got close to."

"Like me."

"Yeah, Cassell... like you."

I nodded. The shadow was now silently moving in our direction, looking straight at me. He'd obviously heard what he was hoping to hear, and had made a decision of some sort. I always knew he was the type of guy would likely turn himself in... but I didn't want that to happen. I hated those feds too... *at least* as much as the two men now in my field of vision. I considered their conduct morally reprehensible to the nth degree. "Okay, Rick," I quickly whispered, causing Gariglia's eyes to widen. "I'm about to tell you... next thing I say... *unofficially.*"

Rick was looking at me very confused.

"Hi Joe," I called out.

Gariglia jumped with surprise, then quickly spun around as Fallon closed the last of the distance between us. "I'll be *God DAMNED!*" he quickly gasped under his breath.

"Evenin' gents," Fallon spoke, forcing a smile on a face otherwise contorted with pain and uncertainty. In a word, he looked a mess. His eyes were red, the flesh on his face seemed to sag with the effort of fighting the Law of Gravity, he looked hungry, broke and exhausted. Only his iron clad stubbornness was recognizable... he was trying hard not to show the disastrous turn his life had taken. Perhaps if Sean Kelly hadn't showed up ahead of him he'd have taken me in. Sean had, but in the course of our contact I had managed to find out. I guess I was ready for Fallon.

In many ways his problem was worse... much worse, than Kelly's. Fallon was a hunted man. And his crying jag at the murder scene convinced me his conscience hadn't been entirely reconciled to what he'd done. That kind of problem was bound to worsen with the passage of time.

"Hi, Joe." We shook hands. "What brings you down here?"

"Sean Kelly, mick... He's gunnin' for you. Headed down here early this morning. I came to warn you. He thinks you..." Fallon stopped, then made a 'you know' gesture with his head and hands.

"Cassell already took care a' that, Joe." Gariglia jumped in.

Joe looked worried. "Yeah? What happened?"

"He put him on the payroll! How's that for fancy footwork?"

I think Gariglia threw those lines out to see what Joe would say. If he did he was disappointed. Joe just looked at me, *utterly stricken*. In a flash I knew why. Though he would never ask in a million years, he was hoping I'd give him a job. In the initial confusion of hearing Gariglia's revelation, he was likely convinced that killed any chance of an opening. Joe's look *scared* me.

"Uh... yeah, Joe. I'm tryin' to hire some guys," I quickly spoke, accentuating the plural. "In fact, I wanna talk to you, and I'm just goin' with Rick here to celebrate my birthday. Why don't you join us?"

"Oh, I couldn't."

"Couldn't celebrate my birthday? It's a custom in my family that the birthday guy treat his friends to a big meal."

Joe looked at me puzzled. He'd never heard of a custom like that. Looking at me all the while, he shortly was obviously wondering if this was a ruse for charity. I gazed impassively back. "Naw, mick, I just wanted..."

"Damn you, Fallon, this has been a shitty enough birthday for me..."

"Why so?" Something in my tone registered as genuine, but comparing my life to his, Joe would have been hard put to figure out why I was having a bad day. He was perfectly right too.

"Look, buddy, we'll explain it all over a thick, juicy steak. Come on."

"Well look, Cassell," Gariglia now spoke. "Since you finally got some company, I really gotta be gettin' back to the City." Ever since I mentioned another meal, Gariglia was practically turning green. He'd eaten quite a bit at Arnie's. I didn't see how I was going to manage either, but Joe's demeanor shrieked 'suicide', so I'd have to try.

"Why?" I asked. "What's the panic?"

"Oh... I gotta get taken off this case I'm workin'... I got a conflict."

We exchanged furtive grins. "I see... well take care, Rick."

Fallon now looked at him astonished. "Don't you wanna talk to me, Sarge?"

Gariglia just grinned back at him, clamping a hand on his shoulder. "Don't think so, Joe. Other than to say *well fucking done*."

"Well done? But why would you say that?"

"Because... you shouldn't turn down Cassell when he needed someone to fulfill that old family custom with him. And when you came along it was a godsend to me because... Well, I'm having an attack of flu right now and couldn't eat a *bite*."

For a good half minute, the two men just stared into each other's eyes. Fallon with his look was saying he knew exactly what Gariglia was really saying and was overwhelmed. Gariglia with his look was saying that he knew Fallon knew, and he was telling him in no uncertain terms he was considering any thought of suicide by the old street-brawling Irishman a real waste.

All three of us were trying to hide misty eyes when Gariglia pumped first my hand, then Joe's, then got in his car and departed without another word.

Some ten minutes later, Joe and I were driving to Zaberer's on the Black Horse Pike. We were completely silent up to the toll booth on the Margate Bridge. Once past there though and zipping through the total darkness of the marshes, I could take it no longer.

"Look, Joe, I don't have Rick's finesse, so I'm gonna give it to you straight."

"That's the way I like it, mick."

"Okay... I know what you did New Year's Eve... and I'll just bet you know I know."

"You and the dame weren't very quiet at times."

"Yeah.... Now it just so happens I gotta take it on the lam. Connie and I both do. The feds wanna try to pin it on me, and for all I know Don Clemente hasn't forgiven me for giving him shit fits throughout last year by keeping those ledgers. Bottom line: I gotta split. Now I want you to come with me as my main bodyguard. I hired Sean for Connie."

"But Sean has sworn to kill the person who killed the boss, John."

"We don't have to tell him do we?"

Fallon just stared out the window into the blackness, lost in thought.

"I guess the only worry I have is that you're gonna be uncomfortable carrying that inside you with him so close by."

Fallon nodded.

"Because, you see, Joe, I've already told him I intended to kill Fischer, and was just prevented by someone else doing it first."

"You *did?*"

"Uh huh."

"What was his reaction?"

"Well, we'd already had a fight, so a certain amount of hostility had already been worked out."

Fallon turned toward me now, an amused expression on his face. "No kiddin'? How'd it turn out?"

"I kicked him in the balls."

Fallon laughed.

"Then I took his gun. After he had a chance to bleed a little, I helped him up and gave him the gun back. He then told me he wasn't gonna hassle me about it any more."

"You're learnin', mick."

"Yeah... well you've already beat me up so many times... Anyway, get what I'm sayin'? Maybe when the time is right you two should just settle it the Irish way. I'm a mick too, so I'm not gonna fire anybody for fightin'.

I guess that was what Joe Fallon needed to hear. He barely noticed I had my whole steak wrapped in a doggie bag as he demolished his, talking all the while about our new life somewhere in the Caribbean. I guess it wasn't my best birthday ever... maybe not by a long shot, but before it was over I'd managed to hire two very capable bodyguards that would make Connie's and my life in a strange new world a bit more bearable. It didn't hurt as well that it was salvation for the two of them.

Chapter Three

LEAP INTO DARKNESS

Monday January 15, 1973: the offices of the Pan-Caribbean Trade Council, Miami, Florida

"Mister Gwynne will be right with you," the gorgeous, miniskirted West Indian receptionist told me as she hung up the phone. I could have sworn she added a split second 'extra look' into my eyes as she said it, but Connie was standing right there, so maybe not.

This was our third visit to the offices of the Pan-Caribbean Trade Council. Located in a converted warehouse in a place where a West Indian section of Miami met a Cuban one, we originally had our doubts the place would be of much help in answering our somewhat unique needs, if indeed they were unique. But I had learned about them from a full page ad in *The New York Times* Sunday supplement, so I decided to go on in and give them a try. After all, you didn't take out full page ads in that paper unless you had some money to spread around, and if an outfit like that had money to spread around, I reasoned, they probably knew what they were talking about.

. . . .

Turned out I was right. The PCTC was really four organizations rolled into one. The first was a kind of library, a resource center where you could read the latest information on just about every island in the Caribbean Basin. This was where people like us usually started out, or so that same gorgeous receptionist had told me on our first visit. After looking at a leaflet with a general overview of the area, Connie and I figured that Anguilla and the Isle of St. Margaret's were the two most likely candidates for us to flee to. They both spoke English and were poor.

It was at that point we graduated to the second level or organization: a counseling center. Here you were assigned a 'trade representative' who took extensive personal information from you and related it to the places you were considering. It didn't hurt that your trade representative was usually from one of the choices you were considering *and* that he had diplomatic status... usually the rank of honorary consul... for one or more of your choices. It was here we were introduced to Wilfred Gwynne. He was from the Isle of St. Margaret's and was its honorary consul here. This meant he couldn't be hassled by the feds trying to learn what you may have told him to assist in finally making up your mind.

Gwynne was a stocky sort of guy, very dark, with a very British cast to his speech. On our last visit to PCTC he managed to convince us that, of the two, St. Margaret's was probably the better choice. This was because, unlike Anguilla, which had refused independence from Britain back in the late Sixties, St. Margaret's had actively fought for it, and in fact was becoming an independent nation in April. This, Gwynne had pointed out, what with the money we were bringing with us, would greatly enhance our ability to 'dig in' to the new country and enjoy all sorts of privileges and immunities otherwise undreamed of. He mentioned that among one of the very first bills the incoming prime minister was putting before the new parliament in April was a 'dual citizenship' measure that would shortly net us St. Margaret's passports and the right to participate in the civil life of the country.

"What's the benefit to that?" I had asked him.

He smiled as he lit a cigarette. "Well, Mister Cassell, of course I can't say for sure what will happen once you arrive, but I wouldn't be a bit surprised, what with the money you will be bringing with you, if the Chamber of Commerce might consider putting you in the Upper House."

"Of Parliament?" I gasped incredulously.

"Yes. Under the new constitution, they get to name five members and as of this moment only have about two or three selected."

This hit me totally out of left field, but Connie said we ought to seriously think about it as an advantage. "Surely," she had whispered to me, "a Member of Parliament would enjoy police protection from any mobsters that might accidently blunder into the place, and likely immunity from extradition in the event the feds located us and wanted to bring us back."

We left the PCTC offices that time with St. Margaret's the likely choice, and with another handout containing information about the place that we eagerly pored over that evening at our little rented house shared with Joe and Sean across the road from the ocean in a little suburb of Miami Beach.

ISLE OF ST. MARGARET'S FACTSHEET

Compiled by the Pan-Caribbean Council, Miami, Florida

LOCATION LAT 15N LONG 59W (north northeast of Barbados)

SIZE: 20 miles at widest point; 150 miles in length from Point Loma Hermose to Ormsby

TOPOGRAPHY: spine of uninhabited Central Highlands run north-south; rainforest-covered western slope; rainforest-covered eastern slope tapering into narrow sandy beaches from Mantilla to Ormsby . Highest point: Mt. Linley 2310 meters

Type of Government: Crown Colony until April 15, 1973; thereafter Member state of British Commonwealth. Post independence government: 22 seat Consultive Assembly to become 22 seat Lower House of Parliament, called House of Assembly. Executive formed from majority or parliamentary coalition in the Lower House. The breakdown as of Independence Day (elections held December 20, 1972) will be:

1) Our Destiny Party (ODP)- 15 seats (left wing socialistic)
2) National Liberation Party (NLP)- 7 seats (Marxist-Trotsky ite)

Twenty seat Upper House called House of Councilors acts as nation's ultimate court of appeal. It can veto a law passed by the

House of Assembly for one year. Ten members are appointed by the governing party or coalition, five by the Opposition and five by the Chamber of Commerce. Councilors serve ten year terms. Its presiding officer is called the President of the House of Councilors and is appointed along with the Governor-General. The President serves as a 'lieutenant governor-general' as necessary and ranks as Deputy Head of State.

Head of State is Governor-General appointed for life by British Crown from a list of between one to three persons provided by the Prime Minister serving at the time of a vacancy. Governor-General may rule by emergency decree for up to ninety days, with a ninety day extension authorized, after which there must be an election. May veto legislation but veto may be overridden by two-thirds majority of House of Assembly. A veto which is not overridden requires an election be held within sixty days. Governor-General may be impeached for high crimes and misdemeanors by two-thirds vote of House of Assembly. Trial is by the House of Councilors which may remove from office by two-thirds vote.

Courts: mayor and aldermen of municipalities handle misdemeanors sitting as magistrates in panels of three assigned by mayor. Misdemeanors committed in 'heartlands areas' [outside municipal boundaries] tried before nearest available 'heartland justice of the peace'. Court of Queen's Bench sitting at Port Albert tries felonies and de novo appeals from magistrate and JP courts. Trials conducted by presiding justice with two island-born 'assessors'. Unanimous verdict required for conviction. Appeal is to House of Councilors which usually hears and decides cases in panels of five as assigned by President. Plenary appeals are rare but are authorized in certain cases.

Infrastructure: deepwater port at Port Albert, Highway One (graded gravel road) runs from northern end of Port Albert to Ormsby; Highway Two (graded gravel road) from Government Plaza in Port Albert to Settlement of New Britain on west coast.

Population: 35,000 inhabitants (est 1970). Population heavily concentrated on southeastern coastal plane. Largest settlements:

1. Port Albert: 20,000
2. Ormsby: 9,000
3. New Britain: 3,800
4. Mantilla: 1900

Ethnicity: Black (94%-mostly descendants of cargo of slaves escaped from the American slaver Annabelle Treen when it foundered in dangerous shoal waters in 1845 north of what is now Port Albert. Vessel was being pursued by two Royal Navy corvettes, HMS Ormsby and HMS New Gatwick, when all were overtaken by an approaching hurricane), Caucasian (4%-not counting some two hundred soon to be departing British troops), Overseas Chinese (1.5%), Hispanocaribe* (0.5% -this group, unique to St. Margaret's, are widely believed to be the descendants of the crew of the obscure explorer Don Diego Alvarez y Coborubias, who never returned from a voyage begun at Cadiz in August of 1699. This conclusion is based on the surnames of known crewmembers Torreon and Mantilla found on the island and the explorer's noted inability to spell. It is believed he named the northeastern most tip of the island 'Puente Loma Hermose' when he probably meant Hermosa. Most reliable historical speculation is that his vessel foundered in a hurricane, with only a few of the crew making it to safety, where they mated with the remnants of a prehistoric Indian culture which has since become extinct).

Economy: fishing port facility for Atlantic-Caribbean fishing fleet, cannery, cocoanut farming (eastern slope from south Port Albert to Ormsby), taro plantations on west coast.

Currency: British pound with widespread acceptance of American dollar. Caymans Bank and Trust Ltd. (no affiliation with Cayman Islands) acts as central bank and depository.

Climate: tropical with hurricanes frequent July to November.

Transportation: access island by seaplane from Barbados.

Security: Royal St. Margaret's Constabulary (150 officers throughout island). Currently a company of British Infantry at Ft. Cornwallis. Organization and training of St. Margaret's militia currently under way. To replace British troops April 15, 1973.

Great Britain currently maintains a larger than usual military presence on the island due to guerilla activity encountered in the agitation for independence. The transition team has requested their presence until Independence Day to prevent disruption of services and infrastructure.

Health and Education: St. Margaret's Clinic located in Central Highlands on Highway Two about three miles outside Port Albert; Church of England Mission School, St. Martin's Mission. Offers high school level education to limited student body: est. 125 in 1970.

Communications: some two hundred telephones are currently in use. There is a five thousand watt radio station founded in 1971.

Health issues: malaria, dengue fever, occasional outbreaks of typhoid fever following pollution of drinking water after hurricanes.

Population change: largely stagnant, though ten to fifteen mission school graduates are given scholarships to British universities each year.

RELOCATION INDEX: Economic investment: 1.5 Quality of lifestyle: 1.5

The Relocation Index is compiled by the Pan-Caribbean Council as a public service to potential immigrants and investors: 10 is most desirable, 1 is least. CAUTION: all ratings subject to change and are necessarily subjective to a degree. Persons interested in traveling to the Isle of St. Margaret's for the purpose of considering either investment or relocation may obtain visas from Pan-Caribbean Council trade representatives, who are honourary consuls. PLEASE NOTE HOWEVER that persons desiring to invest or relocate for a period extending beyond April 15, 1973 should visit the Transfer of Power Office, Government Plaza, Port Albert and should NOT rely upon documents issued by the departing colonial administration.

"God what a dump!" I sputtered to Connie's giggle as we passed it back and forth in bed that night.

"Well, John, that's what we've said all along we need to find. I mean, after all, Don Clemente isn't gonna be building any gambling casinos in a place like that!"

I sighed, shaking my head, putting my arm around her as we snuggled together, letting the 'factsheet', as it was called, fall to the floor. "We sure got ourselves into one fine mess, didn't we?"

"It wasn't our fault. The main thing now is to stay alive until we're eliminated as suspects in Fischer's murder, and we find out whether DiStefano has forgiven you for holding out with the ledgers. It won't be forever, darling."

. . . .

Thus it came to pass that we were back once more, into the third, and for us final, layer or organization of PCTC... the travel agency. The fourth layer was a commercial trade organization for people setting up concrete business arrangements with the governments of the various Caribbean countries represented. Concreteness hardly described our situation. We brought Sean and Joe's passports inside with us while they stayed outside watching our rental car, a very good idea we were told on the very first day we arrived here. We'd made up our mind... St. Margaret's it would be.

Connie busied herself looking at some tastefully done travel magazine put out by Barbados' Ministry of Tourism as I lit up a Chesterfield and leaned back in my chair. At one point I happened to look over at the receptionist. She had apparently been looking at me because she gave me a dazzling, penetrating smile which shortly put my pulse through the roof. My estranged wife Terri Edwards used to say that women could sense whether a man was 'getting any' or not. Connie and I slept together and loved each other, but we weren't in love and we didn't have sex. She was still in mourning for Harry. I had been in exactly the same spot last year as we were getting to know one another as fellow captives in Fischer's human warehouse. I still missed Nancy, would probably always miss her, but I was starting to come out of my funk physically.

As a result, I was starting to get a lot more playful with Connie, but I knew all too well what she was going through and respected it. Respect, however, is no cure for restlessness. I wondered as I returned the receptionist's gaze, if that's what she was picking up on. Maybe she'd just read our application, however, and knew I had $800,000. Her intercom buzzed and she picked up the phone, carrying on an inaudible conversation. I noticed for the first time her nameplate: 'Sybil Jack,' it said. *Odd name for a gorgeous, caramel-colored beauty*, I thought.

Further thoughts were interrupted by Sybil. "Mister Gwynne apologizes... he is ready to see you now."

"Uh... thank you," I stammered, still in the grip of libido as we stood up. "We know the way."

She nodded, giving me that dazzling smile once more. Like Connie, she had fabulous white teeth that, like Connie, perfectly complimented her dark complexion.

. . . .

"Ah! Mister Cassell! Mrs. McElroy! Come in," Gwynne cheerfully called as we arrived outside his office. "As a matter of fact I was just in the teletype room in touch with your new home."

We nodded, smiling as we took our seats, handing him our four passports. He quickly checked them, then took out a rubber stamp and inkpad and stamped our visas into them. "Now remember, as soon as you arrive you need to visit the Transfer of Power Office... it's on Government Plaza." He took out a single sheet of paper from his desk drawer which turned out to be a map of Port Albert, drew a red circle around a small square, then passed it across to us. That's the place."

"Why do we need to go there?"

"To make sure the new, post independence government grants you a visa. You'd be surprised how many people forget things like that when they don't take care of it first thing."

"Oh... okay... Where will we be located?"

"There's a fairly decent little place right close to the Interisland Airbus Terminal and Yacht Club I can book for you... 'Lady Jane's Guest House'... that's the spot if you want convenience. Then, a short ways down the coast is a settlement called Mantilla. This is where you'll likely buy your house... all the elite reside there. It has beautiful beaches as well. Now if you're looking for a resort atmosphere, I can book you into the brand new Hotel Hayes. It's right on the Mantilla beach."

Connie and I looked at one another. "I could use a swim... let's take that," I suggested.

"Okay."

"Jolly good... consider it done. The Hotel Hayes it shall be." Gwynne reached for a very thin folded up newspaper from his credenza, wheeled his chair around and handed it to us. "This just came in today. Had a spot of bother over New Years, apparently."

THE PORT ALBERT CLARION

A HAYES PUBLISHING COMPANY LTD NEWSPAPER   3d   2 JANUARY 1973

BRITISH SECURITY FORCES FOIL MAJOR GUERILLA LANDING! FIFTEEN INVADERS FOUND DEAD ON BEACH!

Connie and I exchanged a look which again recognized what a hell hole the place was. Gwynne seemed to read our minds and faces, smiling as he took the paper back. "Ten to one they're Cubans I'll be bound."

"Really?"

"Yes... apparently our local guerillas have some tight alliance with Castro. They tried another landing south of Mantilla last year... also got slaughtered."

"Do you think the incoming government will be equal to this challenge?" I asked, taking the words out of Connie's mouth.

"Oh yes. Desi Colgate is quite a popular leader. The guerillas can't seem to make much headway."

"Against the British Army perhaps... but when they leave..."

"When they leave, we will have a fully trained militia," Gwynne interrupted. "You two might consider joining it. There's a Mantilla unit being formed now."

Connie and I exchanged looks. Since our escape from the asylum, she had tried many times to draw parallels between my experience in Morocco with Nancy and our experiences. After the horror of New

Chatsworth, however, she was no longer drawn to the lure of us serving under arms together. That suited me fine.

"Yes," I responded diplomatically as Connie looked away, "we might just do that. What is the policy on personal weapons... bringing guns into the country?"

"Strictly forbidden by law." He was looking hard at me, inviting another question.

"Uh... well... is there any way around that?" I had long since learned that Gwynne was more than happy to tell us how things *really* stood, not just what the rules were on paper.

"Talk to Chuck Donovan when you board the seaplane in Barbados."

"Chuck Donovan?"

"The loadmaster. Many things are possible with his friendship."

"Ah! I get it." I tapped my wallet.

"Yes... you do get it!"

"Any duty on incoming money?"

"You pay a premium on any amount above five thousand if caught by a British customs inspector." Gwynne was looking hard at me... smiling.

"Chuck Donovan?"

"Chuck Donovan. I have a feeling you two will get on quite well in your new home. You're just the kind of people we need."

Connie and I exchanged a weak smile. "We're looking forward to it." Gwynne either had no ear for sarcasm or simply believed that eight hundred grand was eight hundred grand. We were, after all, his pigeons whether we griped or gawked. He simply nodded pleasantly.

"Now I've booked you on Trans-Caribbean leaving Miami a week from today. You'll catch the Interisland Seaplane at 0730 Tuesday morning and be in your new land in time for an early lunch.. Or a very late breakfast." He handed us four ticket folders.

"Thank you, Mister Gwynne."

"You're most welcome... *oh*! I almost forget... I've two signals for you here." He pulled two teletype sheets out of our file folder. "Let's see... Hmmm! Looks like you have an appointment to meet with

Desi Colgate and Clint Hatter at Government Plaza the following Thursday."

"Who's Clint Hatter?"

"The incoming Minister of Economy. Well, you two, it appears St. Margaret's is really looking forward to your arrival!"

"Yes it does." *Or the arrival of our $800,000*, I thought to myself.

"Now this other one," his brow was furrowed. "It asks of you, Mister Cassell, did you enter Spain in 1969 in a VW bug?" He laughed, then looked at me, puzzled.

"Good God!" I gasped. "Who could possibly know that?"

"Did you?"

"Yes... I did. Hitchhiking in no-man's land. Our ride had gotten stopped by the French border guards, leaving us stranded. Fortunately, it turned out. But who could *possibly...!*"

Gwynne was smiling. "Well then you're really in luck. This is from the bloke who picked you up... Eugene Hayes."

"My *God!*" I gasped. "What a small world! Gene Hayes! He's actually in St. Margaret's?"

"He's not only there, he's on the way to owning the place. Our biggest investor!"

"No foolin'!"

"Yes... he says if you're *that* Cassell, you and your lady love are to be his guests for that meal I mentioned. Do you want me to cable him for you?"

"Oh yes... absolutely!"

Connie seemed relieved we at least had an influential friend on the island. Maybe things were falling into place after all.

Thursday January 18, 1973: a small house on the outskirts of Miami Beach, Florida

Opening my eyes the Thursday morning before our departure, I noticed through the cedarwood slats of our blinds that it was just turning gray outside. A look to my left showed Connie still fast asleep, dressed in her klunky cotton long nightgown. *Last year*, I recalled somewhat ruefully, *when our emotional circumstances were reversed, she would wear short, lacy negligees to bed. Oh well... give her time... I under-*

stand. I really did too. It's just that my frustration level was rising with the return of emotional health.

Letting out a sigh, I stumbled to the dresser and pulled on a pair of blue nylon running shorts, then, grabbing my Chesterfields and lighter, felt my way across the tile floor of our bedroom and living room to the kitchen. Putting some water in a pan and the pan on the burner, I opened the door leading to the back patio and went outside.

I guess the temperature was probably in the high sixties. Many of the locals wouldn't come outside without jogging suits or windbreakers, but to me, after the bitter cold of New Jersey and New York, it was so warm I didn't even need a shirt. Leaning against the wooden railing, I lit a Chesterfield and smoked as I gazed across the road, through the stand of palm trees, to the beach.

It was going to be a beautiful day. A long stripe of orange clung to the horizon out to sea as the sun made its final preparations before sticking its head up. The water was a deep bluish gray. There was even some surf this morning. I decided a walk on the beach would be just what the doctor ordered to kick this day off right. I had no plans. Everything was in readiness for our journey. Connie had mentioned last night that we might play some tennis, but other than that, I was free as a bird.

I went back inside, got a styrofoam cup from the cabinet instead of my usual mug, spooned in the coffee and creamer, then stirred in the boiling water. The first essential cup of the day all made, I returned to the bedroom long enough to grab deck shoes and a teeshirt, then grabbed the coffee and slipped outside.

Our postage stamp front yard was small white stones in place of a lawn. There was a sidewalk leading to the street, but for some reason there were always enough stones lying on the cement, no matter how often Sean or Joe swept, that it was wise to put on the deck shoes before stepping off the molded concrete slab that substituted for a front porch. Taking the first few blessed gulps of the coffee, I headed for the road, crossed over, then took a seat on the wooden bulkhead just beyond the row of palm trees, getting seriously to work on the remainder of the coffee.

I realized as I took in this glorious orange-gray world of surf, sand and palm trees, that I was a very lucky man. I had a woman who loved me, I had money... I even had two very capable bodyguards.

I also had to flee the country, and in moments of quiet reverie like this it wasn't long before that fact loomed larger and larger in my mind, blotting out the appreciation of all the many blessings and filling me with a frustrated *rage*. The coffee done, I crumpled the cup and dropped it into the wire trash basket at the far side of the bulkhead, then slipped off my shoes and began walking. I wondered what life on the Isle of St. Margaret's was really like. Despite the feel of the cool granular sand under my feet and the gentle ocean breeze in my face, I shortly was grumbling to myself about being the only guy in the world with hordes of money who couldn't even decide where he would get to live. Worse than that, I *had* to live in some kind of hell hole, because those were the only places it was unlikely I'd stumble into one of Don Clemente's mobsters.

What would life in St. Margaret's be like? I had to hand it to Gwynne. He definitely didn't try to hide the ball from us, make us think it was some replica of Waikiki Beach except with lower prices and wider boulevards. That was quite a gesture of candor that he did, in the middle of a conversation about the resort beaches of Mantilla, pulling out a newspaper talking of the interdiction of Cuban guerillas trying to land. *No... I knew what I was getting into... I think.* I wondered what it would feel like taking a morning walk like this on a beach that could at any moment be used for the next landing of hostile Communist soldiers aiming to conquer the island.

So far in my life, my experiences of war and peace had been rigidly compartmentalized. Living in America, I never knew what it was like to live in a place that could at any moment be turned into a fiery hell of mortar shells and falling bombs. Even my brief but intense experience with war had entirely taken place climbing our way up hostile mountain trails and dragging ourselves, half dead with starvation, across the fringe of the world's worst desert. I just had no idea what it would be like living in a place that might very well look like this, then finding myself in the next five minutes cowering in some ditch hoping to God I wasn't going to get blown to pieces or *burned*.

Getting burned... I think that was one of my biggest fears. When I took Nancy to that makeshift military hospital in Fez to try to get her some help, we saw all sorts of horribly disfigured young men, contorted with awful pain, lying on litters everywhere in the corridor. The worst of these were the burn cases. It was so dreadful, so tragic, we couldn't stay long enough to see the doctor. *What would it be like?*

I was so horrified, I had to stop and catch my breath. As I did so, the feel of the sand beneath my feet and the breeze in my face began to revive me. I wiped the beads of sweat off my forehead, then looked around. The lifeguard stand was just ahead. I made for it, then climbed up and sat on the uncomfortable wooden bench, pulling out my cigarettes. Lighting up, I leaned back and enjoyed the tobacco as I watched the waves crashing against the shore, turning into turbulent, boiling masses of white foam, then pulling back, becoming bluish gray water once more.

Dengue fever... malaria... *what was the other one? Oh yeah, typhoid fever. Good God! And that's even when no mortars were falling. No bombs... no Communist soldiers. What was there... one clinic? Up in the mountains? What about medicine? Obviously there was no corner Walgreen's. Did they even have medicine? How good was this Dr. Margaret Detweiler? Did she have any help? What did dengue fever feel like? Were there Communist guerillas in the mountains?*

Oh God, I'm turning into a world-class schizo case! I field stripped the now dead cigarette, tearing the paper with my thumb, letting the remainder of the tobacco float away in the breeze. Then I crumpled up the small remaining piece of cigarette paper between my thumb and index finger, putting the tiny dot in the pocket of my shorts. Vaulting down from the lifeguard stand, I resumed my walk, this time to the water's edge. The ocean was cold, but felt very welcome as the tail end of the incoming waves now engulfed my ankles as the water raced to shore, then turned and headed back again. I had always loved the ocean. It was the place I brought my worst problems. It could always calm me, given long enough.

The sun was above the horizon now, turning the water bluer and the sand much whiter, casting an orange-gold glow on the whitish poured stucco walls of the houses across the road. I paused for a moment to look at ours. Kind of a nice place. I was sorry we weren't staying longer... *sorry I had to leave at all...* Connie intruded on my thoughts. Her lovely petite body, long black hair, dark, dark eyes. She'd had short hair the very first day I met her, shackled to Louella in the yard of the disciplinary barracks. But Connie had learned in short order that I liked long hair, so that had been the last time she'd cut it short.

Connie was putting the make on me then... only I couldn't enjoy it because I was grieving... The only girl who put the make on me... and it had to be then... I was ready now. I was DYING for her... only now Connie was grieving. I couldn't give her the love she so desperately sought. And then Harry had come along and for nearly five months Connie enjoyed what a very hard life as a Puerto Rican chick living with seven others in a two room apartment in Newark of all places had denied her all along. And then Fischer had taken it all away.

Overcome once more with bitterness, I struggled to get a grip, but I was losing. My forced departure to a poverty-stricken land, my grief-stricken girl who *just couldn't* make love... all this money but no way to enjoy it... feds... mobsters... *AUGGGH!*

There was only one solution to this rapid downward spiral. *Oh but I couldn't! Oh but you must!* I was practically gasping for air as I faced the pounding surf, sticking lighter inside the cigarette pack, dropping cigarettes, shoes and lighter on the sand, taking off my teeshirt.... Dropping it to the ground. *It's so goddam COLD! But you MUST!* I had gotten to about the middle of the beach now, between bulkhead and water. My brain shrieking at me all the while to *cut it OUT...* I began trotting back toward the water. Then sprinting. The thought of that icy cold water engulfing every inch of me had me in hysterics. It would be *so COLD!* I was running now. My eyes bulged, my mouth let out a blood curdling rebel yell as I charged into the water and dived.

OH MY GOD! It was sooooo fucking COLD! I popped up... I dived again. Under a wave... out past the breakers... I flipped over on my back... floating over the swells like one of Atlantic City's lifeguard boats. I flipped over again... I dived... I caught a high wave heading for the shore and rode it in. I was a fairly good body-surfer... always had been. The wave took me until my chest made contact with the sand. My legs washed sideways and I rolled over before I was able to get my balance. Then up on my feet, full of wet sand.

Nice ride! I charged out into the water once more, diving under an onrushing wave. Coming up... paddling... then swimming... then flipping over on my back. Another nice wave was coming... I rode it in. This time I leap-frogged to my feet before getting into the too shallow water. I was clean, but one more time. Out again, then in.

I felt *fabulous* as I went over to where my teeshirt marked my supplies, got out a cigarette and lit up. *GOD THAT FELT GOOD!* My blood was coursing through my veins, warming me all over. The salt water dripped from my hair and moustache, and between that and my wet hands had soon destroyed the cigarette. *Fuck it! Home for some coffee. I'll have one when I'm dry.* I hadn't grown up an island kid for nothing. The ocean was always my friend in times like that. Full of thoughts of Connie and the way she looked in those negligees she no longer wore, I headed for the house very pleased with myself.

The rule here was the same as it was in every other seashore community I'd ever lived. Before you exposed the floors and the drains of indoor plumbing to the rigors of sand, you *washed yourself off... outside... using the outdoor shower or hose.* There was no way I was going to use the outdoor shower, but I obligingly made my way to the side of the house where the spigot was.

Just as I was crossing the sidewalk, our next door neighbor came out onto his porch, gripping his briefcase, all suited up. Seeing me showing the obvious sights of having been soaking in salt water he shook himself violently, as if freezing cold, then flashed me a big grin.

"Man, you crazy as a bedbug!" he shook his head, laughing.

"It's not half bad, Marty. You oughtta ditch that briefcase and tie and join me!"

He shook his head once more as he headed for his car. "You crazy as a bedbug, man!" Marty was a nice guy. He had played poker several times now with Joe, Sean and me. His wife Danielle had introduced Connie to the local fashion hot spots, such as they were. They were from the West Indies. I know he'd said from where once, but it hadn't stuck with me. It wasn't St. Margaret's.

Giving him a final wave, I headed for the hose and turned on the tap. That done, I reached for the trusty towel I left hanging on the hose rack for just such occasions, then wiped off the worst of the water with its sandy, clammy terrycloth, then headed inside by the back patio.

Connie was in the kitchen, bent over a skillet which smelled of sizzling bacon and eggs. Connie always cooked them together for some reason. The orange light was glowing on the coffee pot resting on the counter.

"Hi John," she called without looking up.

"Hiya, Klunk," I challenged back as I came up behind her, throwing my arms around her front and squeezing. "Thought you'd sleep all day."

Connie leaned briefly into me. "AHHH! You're wet!"

"Of course I'm wet." I snuggled against her neck, kissing her on the ear, the cheek, the ear again.

Connie visibly tensed. "Come on," she attempted, trying to shut me down without hurting my feelings.

"I *am* coming on, baby," I whispered, continuing the kissing, gripping her tighter. "Can't you tell?"

She tried to shake loose without appearing upset... tried to fake an appreciative giggle. "You're gonna make me burn this."

"Let it burn, baby!" I gripped her tighter still. Her warm, dry body felt wonderful. I resumed the kissing.

"Hey... come on... *cut it out!*" She was obviously uncomfortable.... resentful of my blatant violation of our 'truce'.

I let go, turning away. "Yeah... yeah... sorry, Klunk." I was being a piss ant and I knew it. Even that nickname, riding her over the loss of those negligees, was unfair. I don't know how many times I'd shut her down last year when she tried to be affectionate. It was nothing personal, it just came with the grief. Her first unconscious thoughts as she felt me closing in had no doubt been that it was Harry. I had always seen Nancy too. I knew what she was going through... I knew she was right. I was just so horny after my duel with the ocean... she felt so *good. Aw, fuck it!*

"Sorry," I sighed, taking a mug from the cabinet and pouring some coffee.

"You want some of this?" she chirped, using that phony bright voice she used when nervous and trying to change my mood... trying to keep it from sliding where she knew it was going... and *why*.

I *detested* that voice. But maybe it was because I always heard it in these moments of put-down... of frustration.

"Yeah... yeah... sure," I mumbled, making it sound as ungrateful as I felt. I collapsed heavily into the kitchen table with the mug of coffee in tow. Locating my cigarettes once more among the teeshirt, I stuck one in my mouth and lit up.

For a while, a heavy silence reigned in our little kitchen, filled with the aroma of cooking bacon and brewing coffee... and the smoke from my cigarette. Connie was scraping with the spatula much more than she needed to. I was staring at the patterns in the formica tabletop much more than I needed to.

"Where's Joe and Sean?" I broke a silence of several minutes as we sat eating.

"Up and gone. They asked if you needed them... I said no."

I looked at her.

"Well we *are* going to play tennis today, aren't we?"

"Oh! Yeah! Sure!" That suited me fine. Just watching Connie move around the court in her short, pleated tennis skirt made it all worthwhile. On top of that, she was damned good competition. Connie made up for her lack of formal training in the game by playing it with the same bitter, driving, unrelenting energy that she played the game of Life... the kind of energy that only someone who'd clawed their way out of a dingy Newark tenement could possibly understand. No matter who won, we always wound up in a kind of wrestling match, started by one pretext or another. It was the closest I could come nowadays to what I *really* wanted to do with her.

She smiled, obviously reading my mind. "Well then," she glanced up at the kitchen clock, "we'd best start to get ready... don't you think?"

We were smiling again. "Sure." I got up, kissed her, then went in to commence my preparations. Within two hours we were both in our tennis whites and making for the door.

The telephone rang. "Oh shit!" I grumbled, then slowly went over and picked it up.

"Mister Cassell?" It was Sybil Jack.

"Yes?" I kept my voice modulated, but after all the libido-driven misadventures of the day thus far, my heart was suddenly pounding.

There was a silence at the other end. *That babe is reading my mind.* "Yes?" I repeated.

"I'm so sorry but can you come down? Mister Gwynne says he needs to talk to you."

"Really? What about?"

"Well, I don't know, sir... but I think this has something to do with your wife... uh, Mrs. McElroy, being from Puerto Rico... he wants to talk to you...alone... about it."

Connie was eyeing me intently. I shrugged and made a face. "But we're just about to go play tennis... I'm not dressed for business."

"Oh that's no problem at all, sir. In fact, he'd like to see you over the lunch hour. So come as you are!"

"Oh...," I sighed, "all right... I'll be there."

Hanging up the phone, I fixed Connie with an unhappy look. "Mister Gwynne wants me at PCTC."

"What about?"

"Dunno." I walked over and kissed her. "I'll be back in plenty of time for an afternoon game."

Connie was as disappointed as I was, but we were only talking about a disruption of a couple hours. I called a cab and by 11:45 was let out at the old warehouse.

I walked inside just as several employees were filing out for lunch. Soon there was only Sybil and me in the reception area. She saw me, nodded, then picked up the intercom. After a full minute, she put it down. "Hmmm... he seems to have stepped out." She stood up, then walked by me to the front door and locked it for the lunch hour. She was dressed in her usual provocative manner... this time a red mini-dress and matching heels.

"Why don't you let me show you to the back conference room. I think that's where he wanted to talk." I followed her through the door, then down the darkened corridor to a closed door near the back. She opened it, then showed me inside, shutting the door.

I glumly hauled myself into a chair, looking at my watch. It angered me he hadn't raised any problem of Connie's status as a Puerto Rican before, and it also angered me he didn't want to talk to Connie about it... just me.

"I'm really sorry about this," Sybil whispered as she hauled herself to the table, her legs dangling about a foot away from me.

Seeing her do that, I looked up at her. She was smiling back. A very deep penetrating smile. She kicked her legs out in front of her, turning each one first one direction then the next. "So you're going to Maggierock, huh?"

"Where?"

"Oh that's what we call it. I'm from there you know."

"*Really?* Many chicks there look like you?"

"Are you kidding?" she playfully dug the point of her shoe into my chest.

I defensively grabbed at it... then found myself not letting go.

She didn't seem to mind. "Not many chicks *anywhere* look like me!"

"Well you're right there," I practically gasped as the other leg now joined the first in my lap.

"I've kind of wanted to know you better, Mister Cassell... being that we're soon to be fellow countrymen and all."

"Yeah." I was enjoying the feel of the nylon wrapping her fabulous firm legs. Sybil would flex her leg muscles now and then as I'd get to a certain spot... purring all the while about Maggierock and people needing to get to know one another better. It was definitely one of those conversations where the words didn't matter.

All pretense of whatever we were supposed to be pretending vanished less than a minute later as Sybil's divine body dropped into my lap and we began a furious, clawing make-out. Utterly out of my wits with ecstasy, I barely heard her whisper "would you see me home... I'm not feeling well."

But I heard enough. Our eyes met and we burst out laughing. "May as well get the other laugh out of the way," I gasped, "won't Mister Gwynne be upset I left before seeing him?"

Several minutes later, we finished howling at that one, and Sybil led me, both of us obscenely groping all the while, out the back to her little car and we began the drive to a high rise within sight, at least if you lived a few floors up, of Collins Avenue. Once inside her apartment, decorated with West Indian travel posters and artifacts, the usual activity under such circumstances ran its usual course.

I had no *idea* how much libido energy had built up within me, but it was almost *scary*. Two hours later we were lying in bed, tangled in one another, smoking Player's Navy Cut Cigarettes, a pack of which she kept on her nightstand. I was utterly spent... utterly satisfied. If Sybil wasn't, she did a damned good job of concealing it.

"You ever get home?" I asked, nuzzling her face with mine.

"I'll make it a point, John."

I let out a long, contented sigh.

"Are you going to live in Mantilla?"

"That seems to be what Mister Gwynne recommends."

"Well that's just fabulous, baby. You see I have a little beach house, on the outskirts between there and New Gatwick. That's where Serena Blackstone has hers. You've heard of her?"

"No."

"Well baby you will. She's the PM's mistress. Some say she runs the country... Or at least could if she wanted."

"You could sure damn well run the country if I were PM," I gasped after a short but pleasant make-out break.

Sybil giggled. "You're sweet, John. I want to see more of you once you get settled. Will you write to me here and let me know where you are... what you're up to?"

"Does a bear shit in the woods?"

She burst into laughter. "Good, baby. And if I haven't heard from you by then, I'll somehow find you the first chance I get back."

"Wonderful."

"Have you heard of Emory Jack?"

"No... he a relative?"

"A brother. We're a very large family... some fifteen or so brothers and sisters."

"You don't know for sure?"

She giggled again. "Actually it's easy to lose count. Half of us are actually cousins to the other half, but we were raised as brothers and sisters. You'll be running into us all over."

"Sounds good. So who's Emory?"

"President of the House of Councilors."

"Wow!"

"Yeah... we come in all shapes and sizes, all walks of life." With that, I reveled once more in Sybil's shape and size.

It was getting on toward late afternoon when we kissed goodbye at her door with the pledge we'd be doing a thing together in 'Maggierock'. I was walking on air. It was only as I made the walk down the long, dark hallway to the elevators that I started to feel the inevitable guilt. *Connie adored me... I adored her. I need to be patient... until she snaps out of this. If she ever found out I was having an affair it would break her heart.* I had just about reached the fire stairs a few feet from the bank of elevators when I decided that what happened between Sybil and me was only because of my building libido... libido that had found no outlet. *Okay,* I thought to myself, *the pressure's been released.* I took out the address Sybil had written for me on a little PCTC business card and began tearing it up as I walked the final distance to the elevators.

I'll make this up to Connie somehow, I vowed, feeling suddenly *rotten.*

The fire door suddenly opened. Into my path stepped about the biggest, meanest man I ever saw. Black as night, he must have weighed about 350 pounds or more. It was all solid muscle too. The demented gleam from his eyes was nicely augmented by a dark green do-rag wrapped completely around his head. He was about the scariest creature I think I'd ever seen... and he was blocking my path.

I tried to step around him, but with one quick move he clamped a giant paw around my neck and lifted me bodily a few feet off the ground, clamping my neck to the wall. He eyed me demonically. "You be fuckin' wit' my squeeze, jumbe."

My eyes widened with fright as he pulled me off the wall and gave a mighty push, sending me flying through the air, crashing into the floor and rolling head over heels back toward Sybil's apartment.

I was stunned by the impact... seeing stars. Through blurred vision at first, I saw him advancing toward me, a contemptuous look on his face. My vision began to clear. When he got close enough, I cut loose with a kick to his groin as I lay there on the floor.

He grabbed the offending foot, then jerked upward. To my horror I was once more completely off the ground. He then grabbed the other leg, hoisted me up... upside down... a full three feet from the floor then dropped me on my head, my legs once more flipping me over so that I wound up sprawled face down.

I had just managed to hoist myself up with my arms when he grabbed the back of my teeshirt. Again I was lifted off the ground, but the shirt shortly tore off my back and I wound up dropping to the floor once more.

Thoroughly desperate, I rolled over onto my back. He eyed me briefly with contempt, then reached down as if to pick me up. I hooked my tennis shoe around his ankle, then slammed my other leg into his kneecap as hard as I could.

At first, he just stood there, eyeing me with amusement. Then he grabbed for the ankle and twisted it, until I was face down once more. Then in a lighting fast move, he flipped me completely over, again on my back, but now my head nearest him.

"Hee hee hee... hah hah hah... HO HO HO HO!" The last part of that insane laugh nearly blew the walls apart. He reached down and pulled my arms up backwards.

Gasping with the pain, I stumbled backwards as much as I could to keep up with him. The hold was impossible. I had terrible pain no matter what I tried to do. Almost at the fire door again, he with one vicious yank stood me up, doubled over, facing away from him. He reached down, hooked a massive arm around my waist and lifted me up. Now completely upside down, my legs draped across his shoulder, he carried me through the door.

The hall had been carpeted. The landing he now stood on, with my head pointing directly at the ground was solid concrete. "I drop you on de head again... yeah, jumbe?"

"No... no please," I gasped.

"Hee hee hee... hah hah hah... HO HO HO HO!"

Damn that laugh was frightening.

"I tie you up and take you home, jumbe. You learn de manners." For a few awful moments he actually hung me over the landing, my terrified eyes seeing the five storey drop to the concrete below. "You behave now, huh jumbe?"

"Yes... yes... I won't struggle."

He laid me face down on the concrete, tying the remains of my teeshirt in my mouth, then taking cord from the pockets of his baggy trousers, tied my wrists and ankles. Then he picked me up like matchwood, flung me over his shoulder and started down the stairs. "Hee hee hee... hah hah hah... HO HO HO HO!"

Arriving at the building's underground garage, we went to a new big car parked nearby. He opened the trunk and laid me inside, then slammed it closed. As we began moving I briefly struggled against my bonds, but then realized if he opened the trunk and found me free, I'd probably get bounced off the sidewalk. I laid very still, my heart hammering.

I'd heard of those neighborhoods in big cities where the law no longer went. Where slum lords no longer tried to collect the rent. Where trash was no longer picked up. When the trunk was next opened, that's apparently where we were. As he hoisted me once more over his shoulder, my head down his back, some fifty or more screaming black children swarmed around us as he walked with me over two blocks.

The kids were sticking their hands in my pockets for loot. Finding none, one of them ripped the pocket almost completely off. "Hee hee hee... hah hah hah... HO HO HO HO!" My captor reacted as the kids were now pulling off my tennis shoes, then jerking at the socks, finally pulling them off despite the ropes. I felt my watch being ripped off from my wrist, again despite the ropes. Everyone smelled like a barnyard, trash was everywhere on the streets. A few walls I could see had 'NLP' spray-painted along with several other things

I couldn't make out. Some stoops I could see had teenagers lying on them, dazed on some kind of drug or other.

We turned at a stoop, the mob of kids now in a frenzy as they began pulling at my shorts. My captor mumbled something in a kind of patois and they stopped. We entered a door and were into a corridor that smelled of urine, garbage and cooking cabbage. He went up three flights of stairs and banged on a door. It was shortly opened. I was hauled to a bed over by a window and dropped onto my back.

For a few moments this evil giant stood over me. He was shortly joined by two other young men. Then the ropes were removed and the tennis shorts pulled off. Resting a gigantic knee inches from my head, the man opened the window and dropped the shorts out to the frenzied cheer of the swarm of street urchins. As the other two men now turned me on my face and re-tied the ropes, the giant led the street kids in some kind of chant. I only recognized part of it as English:

"NLP NLP NLP!
Blah blah blah
Blah blah blah
We be free!
NLP NLP NLP!
[and so on]

The giant was shaking his fist in time with the chant, the kids getting more frenzied with each chorus.

Finally he stopped, then waved, then closed the window to more loud cheering. "Hee hee hee... hah hah hah... HO HO HO HO!"

. . . .

It was long since dark when they turned me over on my back. The giant reached down and squeezed my cheek between thumb and forefinger so hard I thought he was going to rip it off. Then he eased himself down on the bed next to me, removing the gag.

"You be fuckin' wit' my squeeze, jumbe. Now I can hang you by de feet 'til de blood in de head make de eyes pop out, or you can pay de fine to de people. Whatchu want it to be?"

"I'll pay... I'll pay," I gasped through paralyzing terror.

"I'll pay! I'll pay!" he mimicked, causing the other two men to burst into laughter. "Poor little sissy jumbe!" He turned to the other two. "Oh look! De little sissy has de tears in his eyes."

"Please don't hurt me. Just let me go home. I'll pay you!"

He flashed an evil smile, repeated the pinching gesture until the skin turned purple, then tied the gag back in, got up and ambled over to a telephone. I looked around the room. It was lit with one kerosene lamp dangling from a cord in the middle of the ceiling. Empty, dirty cans were everywhere. The walls were spray-painted with that same 'NLP', with what looked like an attempt to do a black fist next to it. On one wall was a poster. It was a blown up photograph of a black man, the sleeves of his white shirt rolled up, open at the collar. Hate poured from his angry eyes and a powerful arm well laced with bulging veins was held upward in a clenched fist gesture. From an open door came the dreadful stench of a backed-up toilet. With the gag in my mouth I was doing all I could to calm my system, keep from vomiting.

He dialed some numbers then waited. Now and then my eyes would drift to the other two men. They stood there, arms folded across their chests, eyeing me with pure hate. I looked away.

"Lemme speak to Miss Connie, bwana." . . .

My eyes whiplashed to him. *He knew my phone number*!

"Miss Connie... we got your shack job... the blond jumbe. Don't speak, Miss Connie, just listen. You want to see you blond jumbe again, you bring one hundred thousand dollars to de bus terminal... south side." . . .

"Hee hee hee... hah hah hah... HO HO HO HO! Well you buy youself a compass, bitch." . . .

"Oh, you don't believe me, Miss Connie? Just wait... I put de jumbe on." With that, he walked over to me, picked me up by the arms and legs and laid me on the table. Then he did something with a finger to my thigh that felt as if all the tendons were twisted, causing me to shriek into the gag as he held the phone to my mouth.

He put the phone to his ear again. "You convinced, Miss Connie, or do you want another demonstration?" . . .

"Hee hee hee... hah hah hah... HO HO HO HO!" His expression hardened into a look of pure hate. "Just get the money, bitch. Two hours. We don't get de money... de squeeze hang from his head 'til de blood pop out de eyes. Hee hee hee... hah hah hah... HO HO HO HO!"

He hung up the phone, looking down at me with utter loathing as I lay helplessly stretched across the table. Then he muttered something in that same patois. The two young men joined him looking down at me. Then I was beaten until I lost consciousness.

Sunday February 4, 1973: on the outskirts of Miami Beach, Florida

Dawn broke gray and rainy this Sunday morning, but it still found me on the beach, sitting in the lifeguard stand, smoking a succession of Chesterfields, then field-stripping them. The ocean was gray and turbulent, and made for a scenic show. I was gray and turbulent, but I doubt anyone would have wanted to stare at my glum face for very long.

. . . .

I first regained consciousness from my farewell beating when I felt myself landing on sharp stones after the evil hulk stepped out of the car and threw me in my front yard. I had been wrapped entirely in a sheet, then the sheet had been tied in at least six places along its length. I was still gagged and totally immobile. Fortunately, Joe Fallon had been watching out the window in the darkened living room and immediately brought me inside.

Though amazingly unscarred on the outside by my experience, I was pretty banged up. All our departure plans had to be scrubbed while I recuperated. Money, however, conquers all, and Mister Gwynne, after assuring us he had *not* asked me to come see him that day, remade all our reservations, cabled both the prime minister and Gene Hayes, re-booked our rooms and otherwise made the delay of little consequence. A couple things resulting from the experience *were* of consequence, however.

To me, the most important of these was my sense of personal humiliation. I had turned as cowardly as they came before the experience was over... blubbering and begging for my life. Those people scared me to the depths of my soul, and the fear continued to persist. Besides that, I felt so guilty around Connie. She was understandably enraged at what had been done to me and not a little frightened herself hearing me shriek with pain as that evil man was threatening her. But because of the shameful way I got into the whole mess, I had to constantly tone her down from prying too much into what happened. I couldn't even allow my glasses to be searched for because I knew damned well that I'd lost them in the first contact with my kidnapper in the corridor outside Sybil's apartment. At the same time, fearing for my life for as long as I had during the incident, I was so grateful to see Connie again, to put my arms around her, to have her comfort me, that it just magnified my guilt over the whole thing. The very day it happened I had felt like such a man. In the aftermath I just felt like a scared little boy. It was *awful*.

The next issue was considered far more important by Joe and Sean, who were secretly told the whole story, and Connie in her ignorance. That was the *why* of it. The 'messin' wit' my woman' angle didn't wash. Besides the mere mention of it, there was nothing in the experience that suggested a jealous lover. This was *political*. That place I was held was obviously a hideout of some sort for radicals of some kind. Why would someone with a new car live in such a dump? In fact, the place really didn't look all that lived in. They had earned a quick hundred grand for their cause that day... but why that amount? Why not all $800,000? Joe and Sean both figured that if they knew to ask for that amount, they probably knew I was flush... so again the question became why didn't they take it all?

That question dovetailed nicely with the other subset of this issue... *who* were they? I didn't recognize the angry guy in the poster, so that was no help. No one mentioned St. Margaret's or Maggierock the whole time I was there. Yet there were constant references to the NLP, which we'd encountered in our factsheet. Joe and Sean both wound up concluding they didn't take it all because they *wanted* me to go on to St. Margaret's. They *wanted* me to become influential in the life of the country. That was the scariest thing of all... the *why* of that.

Having concluded they knew I had $800,000... and knowing for sure they knew my phone number... were carrying it around in their heads... the next question was *how?* The easiest answer was, of course, the PCTC. They had both pieces of information readily available. Okay then... *who* in the PCTC? Sybil was an obvious first suspect, but for that very reason had to be viewed with caution. She was almost too obvious. Her neck was hanging out in the whole affair about ten feet and she had damned little to fight back with. She lived alone, drove to and from work alone. She was easily retaliated against, and if these people knew anything about us, and even more the suspicions about us, they knew we didn't go crying to the cops, we retaliated. Sybil had to remain high on the list, but it really didn't *smell* like her.

Mister Gwynne? Did he show us that paper to try to get a feel for our reaction to the guerillas? His motive wasn't at all clear. Joe and Sean both figured it was more likely some unseen eyes that had watched us once they knew we had money and were going to their island. Sean even wondered about the entire PCTC, pointing out that there never was hardly anyone there, and how odd it was that its two most visible employees were both from St. Margaret's, just about the smallest and poorest country of the lot.

The mind boggled, but the apparency that they *wanted* us to go on to the island was the most ominous thing of all.

. . . .

We really were taking a flying leap into darkness here, I tensely concluded as I vaulted down off the lifeguard stand and resumed my troubled walk. There would be no libido-enhancing duels with the ocean this day. That was because I was in my windbreaker. I was in my windbreaker to conceal my .38 snubnose in the waistband of my shorts. Both Joe and Sean had chewed me out like a little kid, the dumb little kid I probably was, for going out to a strange rendezvous without them *and* unarmed. With a flair for Irish humor that I didn't appreciate, both of them promised they'd be the next ones to tie me up and throw my clothes to the howling mob if I did it again.

I walked for a while, then headed for the house. Connie's and my adventure was starting out with me at a very low ebb.

Chapter Four

GOD AND DONOVAN WILLING...

Tuesday February 6, 1973: Interisland Airbus Seaplane Terminal, Bridgetown Harbor, Barbados

Connie and I sat hand in hand inside the Interisland Airbus Seaplane Terminal, looking out on the giant British-built Granville-Wharton S-7 seaplane with twin Rolls Royce engines as it bobbed up and down in the harbor. We'd been traveling all night from Miami. We were *fried* but happy to be at the final leg of our journey.

She leaned over and kissed me on the mouth, a very worried expression on her face. "John, darling, a penny for your thoughts. You look so *beaten*."

By way of response I managed a weak smile and a squeeze of her hand.

"Is it something I've done?"

I turned to her, shaking my head, looking down. I was fighting back tears of shame. "Oh *no*, darling. It's just that..."

"*What*, John? What is it?"

I let out a long heavy sigh, shaking my head once more. "Oh Connie, I'm just so *angry* with myself! I turned so *chicken* with those guys... crying like a baby. I wasn't that scared in the barn."

"Well of *course* you weren't, darling. You're comparing apples and oranges. You fought them all you could. It was only when you'd done all you could do and were so helpless that your feelings ran away with

95

you. That didn't happen in the barn. We were fighting there to the very last."

Connie had a way sometimes of saying what I needed to hear. She was right too! I pulled the hand I was holding to me and kissed it. "Thanks, girl. You're mighty powerful medicine for me at times."

Her look grew very somber as tears now formed in her eyes. "I thank God for you too, John. You saved my life that day... at the farm... and I'll never forget it."

"You're sweet." We leaned in and experienced a much more joyful kiss.

"We really have been through so much together... haven't we?"

"I'll say."

Connie's reference only recalled to mind the riddle that continued to plague me. *They want us to go on to St. Margaret's... Why? What possible use do they see in me that was worth more than $700,000?* "Yeah... I'll say." I turned to her once more. "I love you, Connie."

"Now how about we go look at that sunrise?"

"I've gotta find that guy Donovan, Connie... before we board."

"I think he's a little busy at the moment, John." She leaned her head in the direction of the picture window looking out on the seaplane. A barge had been brought up next to it, and a conveyor belt passed across and anchored to the plane's hatchway. Using hydraulic lifts, several longshoremen were hefting large crates onto the belt and sending them into the cargo hold. Supervising it all was a man in an olive drab Army Air Corps officer's cap, otherwise dressed in khaki, holding a clipboard.

"Looks like you're right. Let's go see the sun." We stood and made our way to the door, then walked around on the wharf until we were facing east. The sun was just starting to rise over the capital of Barbados, turning the sky a flaming red in places not shrouded by the leaden clouds.

Connie gripped my arm with both hands and leaned her head on my shoulder. "Kind of symbolic, I think. This really is the first day of the rest of our lives... isn't it?"

I turned and looked into her smiling face. Our arms went around one another as we silently watched the sunrise. Connie's explanation had really helped me regain my self-respect. I cursed myself that I let my sense of shame over the whole thing prevent me from leveling with her before now... not that I *had* leveled... not really. But the cowardice issue had really been eating away at me, much more than the infidelity. I was feeling a whole lot better, even as I was registering how infernally *hot and humid* it was in the tropics. When we passed through the hatchway of the airliner that brought us from Miami, I felt as if I'd been thrown into a steam room. It was obvious this was going to take a bit of getting used to. But at least I had a peerless companion to do it with.

Our flight was scheduled to leave at 0730. By 0645, a good thirty minutes after Connie and I had resumed our seats inside, the conveyor belt had been taken up, the hatchway closed and the barge pulled back by its tugboat.

"I better go check now." I gave her a kiss on the cheek and stood up, heading for the counter.

Besides Joe and Sean, there were only two other people making the journey to St. Margaret's. Both had been on the plane from Miami with us. They were both up there at the counter, arguing with the agent in the island patois that sounded entirely like Greek to me. I waited for about fifteen more minutes... then they broke it off and stalked off into the coffee shop.

"Yes, sir?"

I moved up as close to him as I could get. "I'd like to see Mister Donovan please."

The agent shook his head, smiling. "That would be a bit difficult to arrange, sir. They're in the final checklists before boarding."

I took a twenty dollar bill from my wallet, pressing it into the agent's hand. "Would you try your best?"

"That's all we can do... our best. Isn't it, sir?" He was smiling, even as he nodded, then picked up the phone and dialed three numbers.

I stood away from the counter, pulling a cigarette out of my pocket and lighting it. I had nearly smoked the whole thing when one of those giant longshoremen came in, spoke a few words to the clerk, and was pointed to me. He came over, a harassed look on his coal black face, shiny with sweat. "You want to see de man? De man is very busy."

"I know." I pressed a ten dollar bill in his hand.

"We try... huh?"

"Great!" He led me out the back, through a corridor slimy with mildew. Doubling back onto the wharf, we went over to a slip at which was moored a small tender. Climbing down the ladder and getting aboard, the longshoreman revved the outboard motor, cast off the line, and we headed toward the seaplane.

It hadn't looked that way from our cozy seats in the terminal, but there was quite a chop to the water this morning. I enjoyed the ride immensely because of it. Within five minutes we came alongside the seaplane's cargo hold. "Boat alongside!" the longshoreman bellowed.

For a while, his challenge was met with just the sound of the water sloshing up against the giant seaplane. In the next minute, however, the hatchway was swung open and that same lanky, khaki-clad white man, now wearing sunglasses against the rising sun, came within view. He looked *busy*... and as if his word was law. I was feeling *very intimidated*.

"What is it?" he snapped, revealing a down-home country accent.

"I'm on this flight sir," I stammered. "I have a special cargo problem I'd like to bring to your attention." This was the line Gwynne told me to speak. The effect on Donovan was instantaneous, but not what I'd hoped it would be.

He rolled his eyes.

"It won't take long, sir," I gasped almost with desperation, visions of large excess currency premiums and impounded weapons dancing in my head.

"Aw hell," Donovan snapped as he reached out a wiry arm and practically yanked me through the hatchway. "Over here." He indicated a spot out of sight of the longshoreman. "Now who the hell keeps tellin' you people to bug me? Why cain't y'all obey the flamin' law fer Christ sake."

"Personal safety, sir." This time I held out the thousand dollar bill so that its denomination was very obvious. "It's worth a lot to us, sir."

Donovan's demeanor changed the moment he caught sight of the bill. "Reckon it is," he muttered. "Okay, sonny... whaddaya need?"

"We have a bag of weapons and briefcase of currency we'd like... uh... well... insulated from inspection, sir."

Donovan reached out and took the bill, stuffing it in his pocket. "Just the two bags?"

"Yessir."

He nodded. "Come forward once we're airborne... into the cockpit. Knock twice... then three times... then twice. Understood?"

"Yessir. Thank..."

"And bring the bags with you. I'll give y'all further instructions then."

I felt a rush of relief. "Thank you, sir! Very much!"

"Okay, y'all best git away from the side a' my ship. We gotta get ready to take on passengers."

It was a happy guy that made the return trip to the wharf. Pressing another ten dollar bill into the longshoreman's hand, I happily climbed out of the tender, mounted the ladder, then retraced my route back into the terminal.

. . . .

"Hey y'all!"

Connie and I had been dozing off and on throughout much of our flight. Chuck's voice roused us.

"We're coming up on the land a' the flea and the home a' the knave..."

Connie giggled as she looked up at Chuck with shining eyes. Something totally unexpected had happened on this trip. From the very moment Chuck saw Connie, there was an unmistakable electricity that seemed to sizzle between them. Chuck was built very much like me, but he was about Harry's age, maybe a little older. He had an interesting sort of job and was obviously very good at what he did. After Harry, I figured, Connie had developed an appetite for older, accomplished men. She just hadn't had the chance since Harry's death to display it.

"Thought y'all might like to see it from the cockpit."

"Oh *Chuck!*" Connie gushed. "That's really *wonderful!*"

We unhooked our seatbelts and fell in behind the lanky, accomplished loadmaster. *"Oh Chuck!"* I mimicked sourly under my breath, *"that's really woooonderful!"*

"John cut it out!" Connie hissed. "You're acting like a *child*!"

I sullenly shut up as ordered. Entering the cockpit, I gasped with awe in spite of myself. Connie did the same. The view through the wide, wrap-around windows was really impressive. There, stretched out below us, was this magnificent-looking island, its spine of mountains shrouded on both sides with forests, surrounded by a blue-gray ocean.

Chuck hastily arranged two collapsible seats and beckoned us to sit down, *demonstrating* for Connie, using her seatbelt, how to buckle herself in. I was right behind the pilot, she was right behind the co-pilot. Both men wore their headsets over those same World War II era officers' caps. Like Chuck, both looked old enough, though, also like him, obviously in fine shape. As we took our seats, the pilot was talking into his headset.

"Uh... roger Bridgetown Tower...," he spoke above the nearly deafening roar of the throbbing engines, "I'm approaching Loma Hermose now on a compass heading of 010, altitude 5,000 feet... requesting descent to 1,000...right turn to compass heading 090... over."

Looking out, we could see the northernmost tip of the island we'd read about all those times at the PCTC and our home outside Miami Beach. At the top of it, we could see a complex of small buildings huddled together on the windswept peak. Connie was *enraptured*. I was pretty impressed as well.

"Roger Bridgetown Tower... coming right to heading 090... descending to one thousand feet..." In short order, to Connie's delighted squeal, the island and the sea crawled up the right hand side of our field of vision, while above, below and all around was the empty sky. Then the island disappeared and the sea slid back below us as we straightened out.

"Stand by for pre-landing checklist, Chuck." At this point both pilot and co-pilot pulled a clipboard out from a pocket to the side of their seats.

I turned around to where Chuck was standing behind us. "I think he just said something to you, Chuck."

"He's talkin' to the co-pilot, buddy," Chuck replied to Connie's derisive giggle. I flushed hot and embarrassed.

The two pilots commenced an inaudible back and forth dialogue. As they talked, the co-pilot reached up and turned several knobs, dials and switches.

"Roger, Bridgetown Tower, acknowledge harbormaster clearance to land... commencing gradual turn right to compass heading 270 and final approach to Port Albert Harbor."

Once more the Atlantic Ocean slid over to our right and climbed up the side of our field of vision. "Oh this is *fantastic* Chuck!" Connie gushed. The rotten thing about it was... it was fantastic.

"John." Chuck was tapping me on the shoulder. I turned around.

"Okay with you if I ask Connie to dinner and dancing at a little place I know here? We're here overnight, then we take off tomorrow." He looked at me a little uncomfortably. "I won't even ask her if it bothers you."

It bothered the *SHIT* out of me. But I was at least decent enough to realize I had no right to deprive Connie of either a good time or stimulating company... for a change. Maybe I also realized that if Connie ever got wind of my dog-in-the-manger attitude, she'd never forgive me. Then too... there was my own infidelity... if that's what it really was. Morally and logically I was trapped.

"She does her own thing, Chuck. It's up to her."

He patted me gratefully on the shoulder, then leaned over and began whispering in Connie's ear. Once more my face was flushed and my eyes drilled into the floor as I registered the joy that stole over her face.

"You really don't mind, John?" It was Connie talking, looking at me hopefully, which bummed me out even more.

"No, dear. Have a ball."

Both she and Chuck exchanged broad, happy smiles as Connie gave me a grateful kiss on my cheek, then turned over her shoulder and began an excited conversation with Chuck. They kept their voices low. Connie's eyes blazed with excitement as I fumed and looked at the floor.

A cycling noise, followed by a shudder and a slamming sound reverberated from both sides of us. "Flaps down port and starboard... checking out oscar-kilo," the co-pilot replied to an inaudible command of the captain's.

The co-pilot now turned a knob on his seat handlegrip, then spoke into his headset. "Passengers take your seats and buckle up. We're on our final approach into Port Albert Harbor."

Connie was in seventh heaven as we began steadily losing altitude. Looming ahead was the island with a heavy concentration of low buildings stretching out before us in the foreground, the mountains off in the distance.

Our aircraft skimmed along in the water, barreling hell for leather toward the concentration of buildings, settling deeper and deeper into it until at last we were floating on our pontoons as the aircraft made its way to a point in the center of the harbor, facing what looked like the most modern building in sight. "Bridgetown Tower we have touchdown... all systems oscar-kilo... many thanks... out." Both pilot and co-pilot removed their headsets as we traveled the last of the distance to where some flags were attached to buoys.

Medium-sized fishing vessels were grouped to our right around a large mother ship. A freighter was on our left. A spit of land jutting out to our left had a pad on which sat two helicopters.

Chuck leaned in between us, his fingertips ever so slightly brushing Connie's shoulder as his hand rested on her seatback. "Off to the right there is the cannery, Connie. Those are the fishing vessels delivering their cargos. To the left there is a complex of freight warehouses, where most all of the island's supplies besides what we deliver come in on that freighter there."

"Ohhh... how *fascinating*, Chuck!"

"And at the extreme left there... see those helicopters?"

"Oh yes! How magnificent!"

"That's the helipad for a small attack group the Royal Navy has based here. They were in some hair-raisin' scrape on New Year's, but the Limeys are bein' real closed-mouthed about it."

"This is an amazing place, Chuck. So many things... all at once... right before your eyes."

"Oh barf."

"Did you say something, John?"

"No... just clearing my throat." To my boundless embarrassment, Chuck put a hand on my shoulder. The victor was being magnanimous toward the vanquished. And that's sure as shit what I was.

"Passengers, remain seated until we tell you," the co-pilot now was talking through his headset which he had replaced on his head after removing his cap. "A tender will be coming alongside to take you ashore, where you'll be processed through Her Majesty's Customs and Immigration. Please have your travel documents ready. You will be asked to fill out declaration forms by the British officials. Welcome to Port Albert, Isle of St. Margaret's. The local time is fourteen minutes after twelve o'clock. Thanks for traveling with Interisland Airbus... hope to see you again some time." The co-pilot again removed the headset.

We had all but come to a stop now. "Shut down one," the captain spoke.

The co-pilot turned some more controls. "One shutting down."

"And shut down two."

"Roger. Two down." Again he fiddled with more controls.

"All right, let's start the post flight checklist."

"Captain?" Chuck's voice sounded behind us.

The pilot turned around, a huge smile on his face when he caught sight of Connie.

"Like you to meet some new friends a' mine. This here's John Cassell and this gorgeous... uh well... this young lady is Connie McElroy. She'll be joinin' us at the Locker tonight. Guys... this is Captain Ted Callison and First Officer Chuck Kirschner."

The two managed a nod in my direction, then fulsomely welcomed Connie aboard. I just wanted to get *out* of there. It reminded me of some of my more humiliating moments hitchhiking with Roberta Larsen.

"We'll be lookin' forward to seein' you this evening, Ms. McElroy," Captain Callison added, grabbing the visor of his cap.

"Me too, Captain," Connie gushed. Connie was gushing a lot during this trip.

"The officers have got to shut this baby down and I got some work to do," Chuck Donovan now spoke as he leaned down between us. "Suppose I meet you at the terminal warehouse, folks." Those were the arrangements he'd explained when I first came forward, so I nodded in recognition. He again gave me a pat on the shoulder as I cringed.

We unbuckled our seatbelts and stood up, moving toward the stern of the ship where the tender was waiting to take us to the terminal. As we were once more smacked in the face with the hot, heavy air, I took in the vista of Port Albert spread out before us, the blue-gray ocean sloshing all around the seaplane and tender. We had arrived.

Tuesday February 6, 1973: the Hotel Hayes, Settlement of Mantilla, Isle of St. Margaret's

Connie sat at the small vanity table by the window of our fifth floor, beachfront room at the Hotel Hayes, pulling on her stockings and clipping them to the garters. Laid out next to me on the bed, where I lay trying to conceal my *jealous rage* by smoking a succession of Chesterfields, was a black miniskirt and a silky, root-beer colored blouse with spaghetti straps. I suppose the jealousy would have been there anyway. The rage was caused by the realization that she had never worn that outfit for me. In fact, other than her tennis skirt, I had only seen her in a dress once, and that was a knee-length black job she wore that day to Fischer's trial. I also recalled that had been the day she had avoided speaking to me.

All the while, Connie kept up an obviously nervous stream of banal small talk in that phony bright voice I despised. I began tuning her out. Our arrival at Port Albert had gone pretty smoothly. Gene Hayes met the plane as promised and shortly after we cleared 'H.M. Customs and Immigration' had taken us to the Port Albert Yacht Club for lunch. The Port Albert Yacht Club was an unpretentious place. Built of wood, the paint was peeling, the floors were uneven and squeaked, and the fare was less than fabulous. I had ordered a hamburger which, had I gotten it in the States, I'd have sent it back. It tasted *old*.

One thing the Yacht Club did have was a beautiful view of the harbor. Located at the very back-side of the 'C'-shaped coast, we had a fabulous look not only at the various watercraft moored there, but also the activity at the British military base and the cannery opposite. Upon hearing of Connie's plans for the evening, Gene invited me to accompany him on 'an important mission of state'. He was very mysterious about it. Our conversation mainly stayed on the topics of our time together in Spain and Andorra, wondering what had happened to Jim Crayford and Don Bremmer, our companions in part of those adventures, and my life since the time of our parting. Our conversation recalled to mind just what a clown Hayes could be at times, so I began to have fewer and fewer expectations for this 'mission of state'.

Chuck Donovan had also come through as promised. Once through the Customs House, he led us to a small yard at the side of the Inter-island Airbus Seaplane Terminal, where, from a crate stamped

'Cuban Mission: Diplomatic'
MISIÓN DIPLOMÁTICO de CUBA

he shortly retrieved our weapons and currency. I thanked him, Connie exchanged electricity with him, then we headed back to where Gene was waiting to take us to the hotel.

At this point in our adventure, I had already formed a few impressions about our new circumstances. The first was that it was bloody hot and close. The women tended to wear loose cotton dresses, the men khaki pants and white shirts worn outside the waistband. Gene had stressed that from here on out, we should be almost exclusively in cotton. The next impression was that, aside from the terminal and a building or two off in the distance which Gene said was Government Plaza, the place was something of a dump. Of course I'd only seen the waterfront area. But all the buildings seemed to be of rusty corroded, corrugated metal or decaying wood. I knew from growing up by the sea that the salt air was very corrosive and demanded a lot of maintenance for any structure, but here in addition was the added strain of the hot, damp atmosphere.

Finally, and in view of recent experience, to me most important, I noticed that everyone who had anything seemed very paranoid. A constable, dressed in an impressive black and powder blue uniform, stood inside the terminal building. Two British soldiers in navy blue berets and khaki uniforms with rifles slung over their shoulders stood inside the Customs House. I suppose neither of those sights would have necessarily registered paranoia if it hadn't been for what I saw as Gene escorted us to his Land Rover.

The first thing was that Gene, Connie and I had to scrunch in the back because the front was taken up by a driver and a shotgun... who literally was just that, and who carried one across his lap to prove it. The second thing was that we were followed all the way by another Land Rover with four more armed men. Gene acted like it was second nature, so I reserved pressing the matter until this evening, but I couldn't help notice that the security crew of our vehicle were definitely tense as we made our way down the coast to Mantilla along the gravel road somewhat grandiosely labeled a highway. Of course in this procession there was yet a third vehicle, the taxi that Joe and Sean were riding in.

The Hotel Hayes was okay... nothing more. It was obviously modern, but appeared to be little more than cinderblock and louvered windows... five stories of it, with thinly plastered walls on the inside. Over the louvered windows, which ran from floor to ceiling to catch any breeze God in His mercy might care to send, was placed screening and, on the bottom floor, something Gene called ratwire. On the ceilings both of the lobby and what proved to be our room were 'Casablanca' fans turning slowly. He said we'd do okay with an oceanfront room, what with the breeze and all. He explained that he'd considered putting in air conditioning, but then the windows would have to be sealed to prevent him going into bankruptcy, because utility costs were murder here. He added that if the windows were sealed his guests would probably die of heat suffocation, because the electricity was always going out, often for hours at a time. About the only good news of what was waiting for us in what Mister Gwynne had termed this 'resort atmosphere' was American 'AC' current. Apparently the British overlords had been unsuccessful in contracting the wiring of the island to a British firm, so an American company had done the job.

When we arrived, I observed an odd scene. Given Gene's penchant for clowning, I figured it might not be representative of 'employer-employee' relations here generally, but of course I didn't know. Pulling up in the gravel driveway in front of the building under an overhang, the security men got our luggage as Gene led the way inside. The lobby was totally empty. No one was at the counter. Gene got a monumental scowl on his florid face, stalked up to the counter and pounded on it.

"Hey!" he bellowed, pounding all the while. "One a' you hamburgers wanna come out here and work! We got guests!"

For almost a minute, there was nothing but silence. Then slowly there followed a rustling noise, then the opening of the door leading from the counter to the office. A scowling fat woman slowly hauled herself to where the register was located. "Keep de shirt on de back, jumbe!" she scolded.

I tensed at the speaking of that word.

"I move my feet to de calypso beat!" With that, she signed us in as bored as possible, handing us our keys. "Eric!" she bellowed like a fish wife, pounding her own fist on the counter.

A short while later, a teenager came shuffling out, studying us through listless eyes. "Take de jumbe to de room!" the fish wife bellowed.

"Ummm," the 'bellboy' groaned back, then stumbled to the elevator without picking up the bags. As Gene fumed the security men and Sean and Joe grabbed them and we headed up.

Our room was okay. The beautiful ocean view went a long way to silencing any predilection for grumbling on my part. But I was not destined to keep my cool for long, much to the amusement of Connie and the bellboy. "Hey!" I suddenly spoke up, "there's lizards in here!"

The bellboy eyed me with curiosity... like I was from outer space as Connie giggled. I turned helplessly to Gene. "Hey man, don't you got exterminators around here? We can't have *lizards* crawling up and down our walls! I'm no squeaky clean, ultra-privileged suburbanite... but I mean come *on!*"

Connie rescued me through her laughter. "Those are geckoes, John. They eat bugs. You won't be here much longer before you're really glad they're here."

I looked at all four walls, each of which had at least one of these great-great-great grandchildren of the dinosaurs on it, wondering how I was *ever* going to develop the mindset Connie acted as if would come second nature with a little time here. Apparently, the geckoes were provided free of charge by the management, and that was just the way it was going to be.

It was a kneejerk reaction, I guess, giving the bellboy who had done nothing but take up space in the elevator a dollar tip, but I did. He mumbled one more "ummm" then left without even opening the louvers on the windows.

Gene demonstrated how they worked, fuming all the while. Then promising to pick me up at six, he departed, still fuming.

. . . .

"*John!*"

I looked up. Connie was standing a few feet from me, all dressed now. She looked very nervous... she also looked utterly gorgeous, her long black hair tumbling to her shoulders, her provocative outfit perfectly complementing her divine complexion and body. "Were you asleep with your eyes open?"

"No... sorry... just thinking."

Connie swallowed. "Uh... how do I look?"

I cut loose with a bitter smile. "Come here." I crooked my finger.

She sat nervously by the side of the bed. I took her hands in mine. "Am I ever gonna see you in outfits like that?"

"Why do you think I packed it?"

"You look *stunning!*"

She recovered something of that dazzling, spontaneous smile. Continuing to look in my eyes, her expression grew serious. "John please... if you really object, please say so... I'll call and cancel if that's what you want."

The same thoughts that plagued me in the seaplane when Chuck first asked me for permission to ask her out came back into my head. Another one shortly intruded. I *never* went in for bars and nightclubs, especially in unknown neighborhoods escorting an attractive woman. To me, it was an open invitation to some s.o.b. to put the moves on her, then a fight. I'd certainly read and heard of such things, and had a somewhat similar experience on my first date with Serena Peralta in San Francisco when our car was impounded and we had to walk through some challenging neighborhoods to reclaim it. Bottom line: if Connie was ever going to enjoy such activity any time soon, now was her opportunity. *It was just unfair for me to stop her.*

"You go ahead, dear. Have a good time."

She had just leaned in to kiss me when the phone rang. Letting go of her hands, I picked it up. "Yeah?"

"De jumbe is here for de lady."

"Okay." I hung up the phone. "He's downstairs, baby."

She kissed me quickly, obviously worried I was going to grab on for a deep one and spoil her makeup job. Then rose and headed for the door. Pausing at the threshold, she faced me one last time. "Thanks, John. I'll see you later."

"Take care, Connie." I fought off a terrible foreboding as she closed the door and was gone.

She hadn't been gone two minutes when there was a knock at the door. It was Sean Kelly. He looked puzzled and worried. "I just saw Miss Connie get in the elevator, Boss." His eyes were wide. "Where's she goin' without me?"

"That Donovan guy from the seaplane offered to show her the town."

"And you *let* her?"

I shrugged. "You remember what I did a couple weeks back, Sean."

"And for that reason you're gonna *let* her?" His look was extremely disapproving.

I looked away, toward the window again, fishing in my pocket for a cigarette. "Well, you know Hayes and I are doin' somethin' tonight."

"Gimme the woid, Boss. I'll go get her." Kelly looked downright *anxious.*

I thought a moment, in the grip of my own paranoia. Finally I sighed. "Naw, Sean... leave her be."

He shook his head. "What's wit' you kids nowadays, Boss? Ya don't build happy marriages that way."

"You ever been married, Sean?"

He looked down. "Yeah... God rest her soul."

"Oh... sorry."

One more disapproving look and he was through the door.

. . . .

The sun was very low on the western horizon, already well behind the mountains, when Gene and I commenced our drive from the hotel in his Land Rover. The same vehicle with four gunmen followed along behind. There was no taxi this time, though. I gave Joe and Sean the night off.

"Why all the weapons?" I asked as we headed out onto the gravel road once more, back in the direction of Port Albert.

"Fuckin' Communist guerillas, man. They can be *anywhere*. You were smart to bring your two men, though when you get a house, you'll be takin' on some a' these hamburgers as well." He'd kept his voice low as he gestured toward the front seat.

"How come?"

Hayes smirked. "Call it... an island tradition. Like many primitive places in the world, John, this place is labor-*extensive*... not labor-*intensive* like in America. That's how the men feed their families. The women work as housekeepers and the like. When you get your house, a whole slew of 'em will come with it. You better not get rid a' 'em either... they'll burn you down... literally."

"Damn."

"Welcome to fuckin' paradise, buddy."

For a while we rode on in silence. I noticed as we passed through Mantilla that there were several very nice-looking estates heading up toward the mountains. Each one featured a large house with several little cottages grouped around it. Gene saw me looking in that direction.

"Your house is up there," he said.

"*My* house?"

"Well... assuming you don't wanna build one... and with these hamburger construction workers you better not less you wanna still be waitin' on your one hundredth birthday... you kinda move in when someone of your social class leaves."

"Oh."

"The Limeys are checkin' out April 15. The Principal Secretary, Edward Markham is lookin' to unload his... so you need to visit him at Government House one fine morning and talk about it."

"I see."

We were out of Mantilla now. Mountains rose up on one side, deserted beaches on the other. As before, both the armed men and Gene seemed to tense up, scanning the palm trees and hills nervously. "Seems like I'm gonna spend my whole life fightin' goddam commies, John." His tone was bitter. I had met him when he was just back from Vietnam. He was in Europe as a present to himself for surviving. From his conversation then it was obvious Gene wanted nothing more to do with war.

"How did you wind up here, Gene?"

"Same reason you did, buddy." He looked at me oddly. I had never told him the 'why' of it.

"You're on the run."

I reddened, then chuckled.

"Right?"

"Right."

"Fuckin' figures, man. Well I dunno who's chasin' you, but with me... it's my old man."

"Your *father*?"

"Yup."

"How'd *that* happen?"

Keeping his eyes straight ahead, he continued in a low monotone, his jaw tense with anger mixed with shame. "We're rich, John. My dad made a fortune in chemicals." He let out a long, frustrated sigh, then plunged ahead. "When I got back from 'Nam, I went to work for him, just like I was raised to do all my life. I guess I mighta' known it, but for some reason it took me a while to find out he was involved on the R&D end of napalm, agent orange, stuff like that."

Tears came to his eyes. "I was *in* Nam, John. I *saw* that kinda' shit up close. We started having arguments. Dad was one a' those

Republican contributors that was demanding we take over in Southeast Asia. Our arguments got more and more ugly." His fists clenched, he turned to me with something approaching an apologetic grin on his face. "Long story short, he offered me ten million dollars if I left the country and never returned while he was alive. If not, he said, I was going to be disinherited."

"Damn."

"Yeah... so anyway... I thought a' becomin' a hippie..."

"Freak."

He laughed. "You still get pissed about that?"

"Yeah, Gene. A hippie is a goddam wannabee."

"Okay... okay... but anyway, bottom line was, I didn't want to starve to death. I liked my comforts. So I took the money and ran."

"From what they told me in Florida, you're doin' pretty good."

He shrugged. "Little by little, man. The point was, I needed a place where my dough really stretched, and where I could do things my way. This place has no ties with America, believe it or not."

I happened to look out the window. The scenery was totally different now. Gone were the houses, gone were the beaches. In their place was mile after mile of the most depressing shanties I'd ever seen. Built of scraps of metal, wood, and lots and lots of cardboard, they hardly looked big enough for one person standing up. It therefore didn't surprise me that hundreds of people were loitering on both sides of the road, just hanging around.

Gene seemed to read my mind. "Lotta desperate poverty here, John. You see all those guys linin' this road?"

"Uh huh."

"If they hadn't caught sight of my small army here, they'd attack our vehicle, pull us out, and take everything we had, including all our clothes."

I suddenly remembered with a chill my experience that day in Miami. "Damn... this all the time?"

"Not all. You should see what happens when a British Army jeep comes along. You'd never know anyone even lived here, they can hide so good. There's also certain taxis that for some reason can come and go with impunity. I don't know how *all* of these people know who's cool and who isn't... but they do."

"What makes a taxi cool?"

"Well, I don't know for certain, but I think they're involved with the Communists. Donate their taxis for certain hours a week hauling explosives, stuff like that. Then Peebles gives the word and *everyone* leaves 'em alone."

"Peebles? Who's that?"

"Rory Peebles... the rebel commander in this region. Him and Webster, the overall leader."

I was suddenly feeling very frightened. "Is the new government gonna be able to hack it, Gene?"

He shook his head. "I dunno. Colgate seems pretty capable. And if we get the militia up and running we might just stay the course." His voice trailed off.

I looked at him. "Otherwise?"

He gave me a weak, worried, smile, then drew an imaginary line across his throat with his index finger.

Finally reaching the entrance to Fort Cornwallis, we broke out into the warehouse district we'd first seen upon our arrival. Then we were opposite the seaplane terminal. Turning left, we began heading toward the mountains. Our road took us through what looked like sleazy waterfront bars, through Government Plaza, through what Gene told me was the 'diplomatic quarter'. You could see the shanties beyond, but this area was clear of them.

"Say, where are we headed, man? What's this big mission?"

"We're gonna do some flyin'."

"Suits me." We were past all buildings now, following the gravel roadway as it climbed steeply toward the mountains.

"Say, didn't you tell me you were a DJ once?"

"Don't remember. But I was."

Gene got a hopeful look in his eye. "Wanna manage my radio station?"

"Where's that?"

"Up ahead here. I'd show it to you now but the turnoff to Hayes Airstrip is just up ahead."

"Sure are a lotta things named Hayes around here," I chuckled.

Gene's response stopped me cold. "It helps with the loneliness." He looked at me again, squeezing my forearm. "Glad you're here, John. I won't ask you to make any decisions tonight, but I'd like you to think about throwin' in with me in some way."

I was shaken by the sights of those shanties, and what Gene told me about those hordes of people, with no hope and nowhere to go, just standing by the side of the road... waiting. "I'm damned glad you're here too, buddy. Boy, I always thought islands with palm trees lapped by warm seas were paradise."

"If they are," Gene responded glumly, "it's a mighty uncertain paradise."

"Amen to that."

A turnoff to the right loomed ahead. "This is us," Gene noted. "You'd be surprised how many people lookin' for this place turn off at the prison."

"Where's that?"

"Next right ahead. About half a mile. Practically across from the radio station."

"Oh swell. I don't think the radio station sounds good."

Gene laughed. "Actually, what with the distance the two are from the road, you got about four miles between you."

I had been giving his radio station offer some thought. This bit of news was unwelcome. I had barely begun to digest it when our Land Rover made the right hand turn and began navigating a pothole-strewn path running about a mile toward what looked like a guard shack. On either side of the guard shack were heavy poles, with barbed wire running in both directions. The only problem was, it stopped about twelve feet from the shack running east, and about twenty feet running west.

"Great security," I joked.

"Hamburgers!" Gene spat. "This is the only airstrip on the island, John. Any chance we have to exploit the advantages of an airplane are totally destroyed by crap like this. They just don't seem to understand the urgency." Gene's already florid face was beet red with anger and frustration. "Any time the rebels care to, they can render that strip useless."

"They can cut fences too, Gene. What kinda' security you got here?"

"Hamburgers!" he spat. "The various platoons of our Militia take turns occupying this strip and protecting it." He let out with a sarcastic snicker.

The vista out the right hand side was awe-inspiring. Looking out the way we had come, the road appeared to drop steeply off to the sea. It hadn't seemed that steep when we were climbing, but maybe I was too entranced by the scenery to notice. Lush vegetation and palm trees on both sides of our road gave way to the buildings and urban sprawl of Port Albert, its first lights twinkling in the gathering twilight.... then the harbor and open sea beyond before my entranced eyes. "Damn this is a beautiful spot."

Gene looked at me through harassed and frustrated eyes. "Yeah... about like a coral snake is beautiful."

I started to pursue that thought further but our Land Rover had suddenly stopped. I looked up to see an empty guard shack with a big sign posted next to it, on the eastern expanse of barbed wire.

ROYAL ST. MARGARET'S AIR MILITIA

HALT!

THIS IS A MILITARY INSTALLATION. NO ADMITTANCE UNTIL CLEARED BY SENTRY.
TRESPASSERS WILL BE SHOT ON SIGHT.

AUTHORITY: GROUP CAPTAIN EUGENE P. HAYES
AIR MILITIA COMMANDANT

"Damn, Gene," I shook my head in wonder. "You sure wear a lotta hats around here."

Gene's hand was on his door handle, about ready to push it open. He looked in a towering rage. Hearing me he stopped, then turned in my direction, glanced at the sign, then collapsed back into his seat, exhaling sharply. Then he looked up at me, almost with sadness. "I'm the only guy around here willing to spend the money to turn this into an airstrip. I'm the only guy, so far, who owns a plane." He shrugged. "Yeah so they made me a group captain... that's just so I could hold my own with Colonel Christian when we're talkin' with Colgate about what we need to do. There's only me and eight ground crewmen in this so-called 'air militia'. One plane, a small tool shed, a hangar, fuel truck and tow rig.... some scaffolds."

"Who's Colonel Christian?" The last name fascinated me. I wondered if he was kin to Laura. She had told me her ancestors were from Kenya, and were first brought over as slaves.

"Head of the Militia."

I started to say something else, but Gene looked once more at the empty guard shack, turned a beet red, and pushed his way angrily through the door. "Lean on your horn, Oscar," he seethed as he walked to the edge of the guard shack. Our driver let out a long blast on the horn per instructions.

Gene stood there, looking murderously toward the hangar. "Will one a' you goddam hamburgers *come out and pull fuckin'* GUARD DUTY!" His face was so red as he bellowed it made the short blond curly hair on his head look almost electric lime.

I got out the other door, but stayed by the Land Rover. I wanted to concentrate more on the amazing vista stretching out to the horizon back the way we came, but Gene's rage and the whole odd circumstance of the 'air militia', sitting up here an obvious target for guerillas, was too engrossing. It looked like my old buddy Gene, already deeply saddened by the alienation from his family, and having sunk his entire nest egg into an island which teetered on the brink of conquest by Communists, was worrying himself to death, trying to keep it from happening.

At the hotel, his rage had seemed almost comical. It wasn't here. Obviously he had spent all kinds of time and money trying to turn this former narrow plateau covered with jungle foliage into an air base. Now he was seeing it, lying unprotected in the setting sun, despite the presence... I couldn't see anybody as I looked toward the hangar, but that's what he said... of a whole platoon of militiamen. He was feeling more than let down... he was feeling *betrayed*. I felt very sorry for him.

He bellowed once more, again having the driver lean on the horn. After another minute, I thought I detected movement over by the hangar. I watched the black and khaki blur as it got closer. It turned out to be a militiaman with a rifle slung over his shoulder, web belt, ammunition bandolier, flashlight, canteen and other indicia of guard duty in a combat zone. He was taking his time. A full four minutes after appearing, he came up to Gene and popped off a loose salute, keeping the rifle on his shoulder.

"You relax de nerve, jumbe Group Captain," the man said as he slouched his way into the guard shack, frowned, then came out.

"I've told you hamburgers you gotta post sentries all along the perimeter of this place. Where's Lieutenant Willett, for God's sake!"

"De Lieutenant be movin' his feet to de calypso beat, jumbe Group Captain."

Gene exhaled with frustration, shaking his head. When he next spoke his voice had an almost beaten quality to it. "Where's your goddam helmet, soldier?"

"I knew you not be de enemy, jumbe Group Captain." The militiaman had an expression on his face that seemed to wonder why Air Militia Group Captain Hayes had asked this dumb question.

As I watched this spectacle unfolding, I was more and more getting the impression that Hayes' title wasn't an exercise in ego as I first thought... it was a terrible burden... one that he, as an ex-grunt in Vietnam, would have been the last to want for himself. He had taken it, though, just as he had taken on all his other commercial burdens, because he was stuck here... and it was survive or perish.

Gene's head was down, still shaking. "And why wasn't this post covered?"

"We knew you not comin' 'til late, jumbe Group Captain."

"Uh huh. Get in there." He pointed to the guard shack, but it seemed all the starch had gone out of him.

The militiaman ambled inside, setting his rifle down. Gene once more entered our vehicle and sat silently, steaming, as the driver gunned the engine and we headed for the hangar. "Wait here," he told me as he got out and quickly went inside, slamming the hangar door with a force that made the three of us start with alarm.

I got out, gazing at the view back in the direction from which we'd come as the second Land Rover pulled in beside ours. Two jeeps and a troop carrier were grouped together nearby. For a good fifteen minutes there was shouting, then the sounds of movement of many booted men. The large hangar doors suddenly were slid open, as some fifty khaki-clad soldiers wearing British-style helmets and clutching rifles came sauntering outside and took up various positions in slit trenches, at a .50 caliber machine gun emplacement, and further down along side the runway.

Behind them came the guy who, judging from the two diamond-shaped 'pips' on each epaulet, just had to be Willett. Yawning, scratching his fulsome belly as he stumbled along, he paused to look briefly in our direction, then let out a fearsome belch, continuing listlessly on his way.

They were shortly followed by two men in blue coveralls, who entered one of the jeeps and quickly drove off down the runway. After them came two more men in a tow vehicle, pulling a twin engine Convair 880 out of the hangar. Once it was in position and chocked, and the tow vehicle disconnected from the nose gear and driven off, a fuel truck appeared as the original two men, now augmented by two others, began topping off the tanks of the aircraft.

Last of all came Gene. Now dressed in blue coveralls with epaulets, each having four stripes, he wore a revolver strapped around his waist, a flight helmet-intercom in his right hand and an RAF-style officer's cap on his head. The British insignia was replaced by a circle of black followed by a ring of green, with wings coming out from it and a crown on top. The Convair had that same target insignia on its wings and fuselage, with a square of half black and half green on its tail, the usual serial number and 'RSMAM' lettered under the wing nearest to me.

Standing at the hangar entrance, he beckoned me to join him inside. I headed in that direction. "Come this way, buddy," he called out as I got close. I followed him inside to a small room among a complex of rooms at the end of the hangar. He held up a pair of blue coveralls for me to see. Each of the epaulets had two stripes and the name tag under a pair of wings said:

ROYAL ST. MARGARET'S AIR MILITIA
FLIGHT LIEUTENANT
JOHN W. CASSELL

"Oh my God, Gene, you can't be *serious!*"

"I'm deadly serious. Climb in 'em." He tossed them to me.

"But I dunno anything about…"

"You're gonna learn. Get in 'em." He wasn't kidding. And looked as if he'd shoot me for desertion if I refused any further. I climbed out of my clothes and put on the flight suit. He handed me a holster which I buckled on, placing my own .38 and holster, which I now wore under my shirt everywhere, in the locker with my clothes. Then I climbed into the combat boots, which were just slightly small and picked up the flight helmet, facing him.

"How can you make me an officer?"

"Never mind. You are one. We're fightin' for our lives, Cassell, and you're gonna goddam well do your part. Now follow me."

I did. We went out to the airplane and climbed in. Gene ran through the preflight with me, forcing me to learn the different controls and steps, yelling at me as I'd stumble. Then we did what he called a 'walk-around', then I was ordered back inside. "And it's *sir* or *group captain* when you address me while on duty."

I wanted to make a sarcastic, almost bitter comment, but I no longer could. I was in the Air Militia now, like it or not. *Gene can fuckin' forget about me throwin' in with him, or however he put it*, I grumbled mentally to myself. I began thinking of how I could just *go*… somewhere else. This was all such a mistake. I was *very* depressed.

God and Donovan willing, we had gotten into this floating insane asylum with our weapons and money. I recalled him saying… Donovan, that is, not God… that he was taking off tomorrow. As I seethed with anger and frustration, I resolved to finish this 'mission of state', then grab Connie and all our things and make it back to the seaplane for a quick getaway. God and Donovan willing, we'd be back in Barbados by tomorrow evening.

Chapter Five

ONE FOULED-UP MISSION OF STATE

Tuesday February 6, 1973: Hayes Airstrip, base of the Royal St. Margaret's Air Militia, Isle of St. Margaret's

"Checklist complete," Gene sighed in a tone that was meant to be conciliatory as we sat in the cockpit of the Convair 880.

I was having none of it, staring angrily forward. *Hijacked into this comic book Air Militia... my girl off swooning over some goddam seaplane crewman, dressed in that outfit...*

A yellow scaffold on wheels was rolled up to the port side window. Gene slid the glass panel back as a young man in those blue coveralls, this one with three chevrons on the sleeves climbed up. "Starboard engine has been running hot in today's periodic maintenance, sir."

At the sound of him I looked over. He wasn't like the candy soldiers I'd met so far at the airstrip. He spoke English better than I did, his manner was crisp, professional, and military.

Gene checked the maintenance log the sergeant handed into him. "Whaddaya think, Burns?"

"Needs an overhaul, sir... but you'll make it tonight."

Gene made a notation on the clipboard, then passed it back outside the window. "Very well, Burns. Thank you."

The man nodded, smiled, then saluted. Hayes returned it. The sergeant than retreated back down the steps and the scaffold was rolled back.

The engines turned over and were revved as Gene pointed out several gauges it was important to check at times like this. I continued throwing my juvenile fit, but kept it to myself. The engines warm, we taxied along the tarmac, past several sandbag emplacements of the 'hamburgers', all watching with a kind of bored curiosity, their helmets off... their rifles in many cases lying in the dirt.

We reached the end of the airstrip and Gene turned our craft. We were nearing the last eight minutes of twilight now, the sky an amazing study of clouds and stars, set against a deep indigo background. It really was beautiful here. Palm trees and other vegetation were everywhere, the mountains, the urban sprawl and the sea all spread out before us, each in its place.

"Put on your headset, Cassell." Hayes' tone wasn't nasty, but my stonewalling of his earlier attempts to reconcile had clearly had their intended effect.

"Yes, *sir*!" I spat with mock crispness as I took the headset off the hook and placed it on my head.

"Militia One to Cornwallis Tower, over."

"Militia One," a British accented voice responded.

"Any of your chaps in the sky?" Gene asked.

"Negative Militia One... it's all yours. Nothing on scope throughout our airspace."

"Roger Cornwallis Tower... heading for the heavens." With that, Gene throttled our engines faster until the whole plane vibrated, then released the brakes, causing us to lurch forward, rapidly picking up speed as we began racing back toward the hangar from whence we had come.

"There's no air traffic control here, John," Hayes spoke as the Militia emplacements along the perimeter of the airstrip now zipped by us one by one, the Militiamen now anything but bored as they eyed us. "Still, I make it a point to check with the fort in case the helicopter attack group is up and running."

I nodded listlessly, trying to conceal the fact that this was all suddenly pretty interesting.

Gene now pulled back on the column and we lifted off the runway, motors loudly throbbing, heading for the sky. Passing by on the starboard side, right out my window, was obviously the radio station. Its large tower jutted up into the sky, its red lights twinkling in the twilight. The station consisted of a larger building of brick and two smaller ones, surrounded by a cyclone fence. A couple vehicles were parked there. Sandbags were stacked in the front of the buildings. Just inside the perimeter was a large awning with tables, chairs and even a cot visible underneath, given our altitude at that moment. Lounging under the awning at the side nearest the perimeter were some seven black men, dressed in regular clothing, which here meant loose white shirts and baggy khaki pants, clutching rifles.

"Your job," Gene suddenly spoke, obviously aware of my idle gazing, "is to scan the sky in as much of a 360-degree arc as possible... back and forth, up and down... over and over."

"Like a lookout on a ship?" I asked in a tone of interest I hadn't meant to reveal to him. I comforted myself in the knowledge that at least I hadn't mentioned any reference to 'sir' or 'group captain'.

"Exactly. Also it's a good idea to keep your headset on, even though it's highly unlikely you'll be hearing from anyone. Always remember, John, the most deadly factor in flying here is the monotony, the seeming ease of it all. It's hard to stay alert watching mile upon mile of empty sky, but that's what you've got to do. There is no telling what might pop up some day."

"What do you mean?"

"Many things, of course, from the helicopters at the fort to some shipment of ground to air missiles to the guerillas, maybe even an old MIG-15, or something. That's been rumored in the waterfront bars for several weeks now."

"You mean an actual air strike from Cuba?"

Gene shrugged. "There or somewhere closer."

I nodded. Gene now steeply banked our aircraft to the left. The lights of two settlements had been coming into view up ahead. Gene explained they were New Gatwick and Ormsby, the southernmost settlement. Our aircraft now headed out to sea, then continued its slow turn, eventually winding up hugging our coast line, heading north. I did my best as an amateur to keep watching the sky, but I was inevitably drawn to the view stretching out below. At the spot that had to be between the settlements of Mantilla and New Gatwick, my eyes scanned the strip of beach. I saw several very smart looking beach houses in a row, following the usual pattern of a larger house with several simple cottages grouped around it. I figured that Serena Blackstone was down there right now. *The Prime Minister's mistress.* I was *very* curious to meet *that* babe. *Some say she runs the country... or at least could if she wanted to... at least that'll be true after April 15.*

My mind was wandering. I'd never lived in a place on the cusp of two political identities. Obviously, the British were giving ground slowly. I figured they must be if they allowed what had to be the post-independence insignia to be displayed on this aircraft. I wondered about the other stuff, like Colgate's dual citizenship bill. Then my thoughts briefly drifted to Sybil... *Her house was down there too. Of course she was still in Miami.*

Gene was following a course of north by northwest. It was totally black now, and we had obviously left the coast behind and were angling northward over the spine of central highlands. "You'll hear many things about this area, John," he suddenly spoke up. "Locals call it 'the heartlands'."

I remembered a reference to that in the factsheet. The one we read at our rented house in Miami Beach. Connie was again intruding on my thoughts, my ego smarting at the thought of her out with Chuck Donovan at that nightclub. I struggled to get a grip and pay attention.

"There's no white presence here at all, other than Perry Herbert, getting his brains scrambled by the wind up on Loma Hermose. You'll hear stories of Stone Age villages deep in the jungle... white people vanishing without a trace... voodoo cults... more modern incestuous villages where everyone is a first cousin at least. And of course rebels... guerillas. This is their turf, John."

A shudder passed through me as I looked down into the blackness, wondering what our fate would be if we were to crash here yet somehow survive. I nervously looked out on the wing. The prop was turning reassuringly, the green beacon at the wingtip was blinking, just as it should.

"These mountains are incredible. I know you're gonna hear a lot about Highway Two. It's the road we took outta town to the airstrip, but it continues on, all the way to New Britain, a steamy malarial settlement on our west coast. Its reason to exist is as a terminus for the taro from both major plantations. One is directly above it, one below. Once the Limeys leave, you're gonna see a lot more taro convoys bein' ambushed. It's my guess the commies are gonna try to cut the road entirely."

"Is taro worth anything?"

"Around here it is. And with the island's entire crop securely in their hands, if the rebels can manage to cut the road, they could easily set up a Communist state on the west side. Then the Cubans move in with bases, troops and equipment, totally unopposed. Then they come over the mountains and slaughter the rest of us. That's my guess as to how they'll try to do it. In pieces. They keep flinging themselves at our east coast settlements, and getting rebuffed. I think it's all just to lull us into neglecting Highway Two."

"Have you told anyone about this theory of yours?" I was wide-eyed, with fear. It sounded really clever, and totally possible.

Gene nodded. "Colonel Christian discounts it." His face was taut in the dull, amber lights of the console. "I guarantee you, buddy, you're gonna spend a few weeks out that way totin' a rifle... we all are."

"In the factsheet I read it said the island was thirty miles wide. How long does it take to get from Port Albert to New Britain?"

"A day and a half... sometimes more. There's about two hundred miles of roadway... switchback... lots of it."

Damn! I remembered that same phenomena in Morocco. We were climbing for days to make just a few kilometers as the crow flies.

I glanced at the amber-lit chronometer mounted on the center of the console. It was now a little after eight, or 2007 hours, as Gene preferred. Either way suited me. Time was time... And it was relentlessly passing. April 15 was coming... those Militiamen didn't yet see the necessity for putting out perimeter security, unless their own officers were showing up. The British would be leaving... I was beginning to get a feel for Gene's sense of urgency, including his frustration at me for being so uncooperative. Looking down, all was blackness. Looking around, a few stars were visible among the clouds.

Again Connie intruding on my thoughts. What a fool I'd been. Now she was out with that... that HILLBILLY!

"Flight Lieutenant Cassell."

Gene's 'group captain' voice snapped me out of my jealous fit.... or worse, merely dragged me away from it. *Here we fucking go again*, I seethed to myself.

"Yes *sir!*" The phony crispness again fell out of my petulant mouth. *This place was like living in a schizo ward... Connie hot and cold... Gene an old pal, then Air Vice Marshal Dowding... I'm surrounded by LUNATICS!*

"Time to earn your keep." He pointed to a spot below my console. "See those stirrups there?"

"Yessir?"

"Get your boots into them."

Sullenly, I complied.

"That's the rudder... they work like the helm of a ship. All right... now grab onto the little half wheel on the column in front of you... but don't do anything... yet."

My heart was starting to pound. *The bastard's gonna make me fly the plane!* I was scared to death. My earlier thoughts of grabbing Connie and skipping out of here on that seaplane tomorrow morning were once again beguiling me.

"Okay... now look at this dial here." He pointed to one in the center of our two consoles. "That's your artificial horizon. That solid line there is straight and level flight... the one moving slightly above and below, tipping now and then is us. Watch it closely."

I swallowed. "Yessir." I was too scared to be sarcastic. But I was *angry.*

"All right... now pull back ever so slightly on the stick... that's it." The amber lights lit up an evil grin on his face. "You've now got the airplane."

Immediately, the line lifted above the 'artificial horizon'. "Get your nose down, Lieutenant," Gene barked.

I pushed the column forward. The line plunged below.

"Good *God*, Cassell! Get the goddam nose up! You're overcompensating!"

My hands were sweaty as I gripped the wheel. I didn't see how I was supposed to look where I was going if I had to watch that damned thing every minute. It turned out my troubles were just beginning.

"All right, Lieutenant... that's better." Gene eyed the artificial horizon with something approaching satisfaction. "Now... there are two instruments we use here to see at night. There's others, but let's learn these two."

"Yeah... let's," I sneered.

"This one is your three-sixty radar. The dot from which the needle turns is us."

I watched the amber scope. Up ahead... dead on our course... was this blip.

"Now this other one... look here."

My eyes darted to the scope he now pointed to. It looked like the angle of the left side of a triangle... with a line pulsating outward, then back. "Now that's your directional... shows where we're headed."

That blip was there too. "What's the blip?"

"Good *God*, Cassell! Get the fuckin' nose up!" While watching that other stuff, the line that was us dropped way below the artificial horizon. "Now I told you to watch that, Lieutenant."

"But I was *also* told to watch those other two," I snarled, injustice lacing every note.

"You just tell that to yourself as you're burning to death because you drove yourself into the ground. I'm sure it'll be a comfort."

Gene's sarcasm was enraging me. I hated being in these situations where I was the dummy, and could do nothing but take constant correction and criticism. My sweaty hands gripped the wheel with white knuckles as I fumed while trying to pull us out of the dive without going into a power climb... Gene now told me about those, reveling in my terror. While I spent too long watching the radar, he predicted, I'd climb so steeply the plane would stall and literally fall backwards out of the sky.

Son of a bitch! I'm scared to death of heights and that fucker knows it. That blip was getting closer on both those other scopes. "Will you *please* tell me what the blip is...*sir or group captain*!" I was trotting out the full sarcasm now.

If we were on the ground, Hayes and I would likely have started fighting at that moment. But he was enjoying his total sense of supremacy at the moment too much to worry about insubordination. The bastard had me by the balls, and was loving it.

"Mount Linley."

"Huh?"

"Mount Linley... highest point on the island." Gene leaned back in his seat. "You're headed straight for it, Lieutenant."

At this point I was thinking 'lieutenant' was about the lowest, most vile name a person could be called.

"That is if you don't crash us first into the trackless jungle below." The bastard could barely conceal a grin.

My eyes darted in terror over to the artificial horizon. Sure enough... we were headed down.

"And you might also notice your altimeter."

"My *what?*"

"This thingey here. I don't know if you've noticed, Cassell. But in all this piss ant flying you've been doing, we've dropped almost eight hundred feet." He let out a tired sigh. "You might wanna get us back up to 3,000."

Enraged and frightened out of my wits, I pulled back on the stick.

"Without goin' into that power climb I told ya about," he mumbled, barely suppressing a grin.

I eased back on the stick. The son of a bitch knew I couldn't punch him out.... cause then I'd be all alone way up in the sky with these conflicting gauges and meters and scopes. The altimeter showed us climbing... slowly. That blip was approaching... slowly.

"We gonna plow inta' the mountain, Cassell?" Gene asked in a bored tone of voice.

"*Well for God sakes,*" I screamed, "make up your mind! Do ya want to go to 3,000 or plow into the goddam mountain?" I realized how moronic what I'd just said was even before he burst into laughter. I was sooooo frustrated, tangled up and *scared*!

"Looks like you're gonna do both, Lieutenant," Gene observed in that 'bored' voice. "Who says lieutenants can't walk and chew gum at the same time." He chuckled some more.

"You realize you're gonna go down in flames too, don't you?" I pleaded, my desperation rising as once more the line on the artificial horizon said we were diving and that goddam blip just kept getting *closer*.

"I know how to parachute." Gene said nonchalantly, really sending me into terrified hysterics. "And get your nose down, Lieutenant," he threw in, correctly, once more for effect.

The sweat was now breaking out all over my face and body. Gene suddenly yawned, then unbuckled his seatbelt and started to get up. The blip was moving closer and closer to the angle on the directional scope. "Think I'll go aft and catch a smoke, Lieutenant... and put on my parachute." He draped his headset over the hook from whence he'd first retrieved it. "Lemme know if you wanna do anything about Mount Linley."

"God DAMN it!" I shrieked tearfully, all out of control.

"You're diving, Cassell," Gene muttered nonchalantly.

I think at this moment I was ready to begin punching his lights out, enjoying one last gesture of self-expression before burning to a crisp. But unholy fear continued to rear its ugly head. "Please! Air Vice Marshal! Group Captain! Sir or Your fucking Majesty! TELL ME what the FUCK to do!"

Gene glanced at the directional, then suddenly slid back in his seat. I think that scared me worse than anything else. "Turn, Cassell... to the right."

The blip was practically at the angle now as I struggled to recall... *like the helm of a ship...how DOES that work...*

"You got about ten seconds, Lieutenant." His face was tense... he meant it.

A loud series of beeps sounded from the directional. Panicked beyond reason, I jammed my left foot into the metal and swung the wheel to the right.

"*OH JESUS CHRIST!!!*" My erstwhile instructor gasped as the right wing dipped as the plane went into a yaw to port. Grabbing the column, Gene began a swift series of rudder, wing and altitude movements as the beeps got louder and both our eyes bulged with fright. I covered my head with my hands, praying every prayer I knew.

The beeping stopped. I removed my wet hands from my wet face. The radar and directional both showed a blissful absence of blips in our path. I collapsed backward into my seat.

"I think that's all for this trip," Gene gasped.

I was now too convulsed with shaking to cuss him out like every bone in my body wanted. "Yes, sir," I simply gasped back at him.

· · · · · · · · · · · · · · · · ·

The amber lights of the chronometer displayed 2122 hours. All had been blackness for some time now, though glances at that artificial horizon I was taking a certain pride in being able to read showed Gene had made a steep turn a while back. From my sailing experiences, I knew how to read a compass. We were headed back to the airstrip. Or at least in that direction. As the minutes passed I was starting to feel proud of what I'd learned. I was watching those instruments Gene taught me feeling like I'd been doing it for years. I had behaved like a 1950's comedic interpretation of a dumb girlfriend being taught how to drive, and I knew Gene was going to blackmail me with that for months to come... but I had *learned* something tonight.

I had just started to wonder if Chuck Donovan knew any of this kind of shit when Gene's anxious voice split the air. "Oh God, Cassell! Take a look... one o'clock low."

My eyes turned to look out and down. Flickering flashes of orange were raging in a loose, elongated oval pattern. I'd seen flickering flashes of orange before... in that Ministry of Interior helicopter over in Africa... *People were shooting!*

Before I could ask where we were looking, Gene hauled back on the stick and throttled forward. Our plane loudly vibrated as we climbed and turned back toward the north. "That's our base, buddy!" he gasped. "It's under attack... we're gonna turn back and go in low for a look. Hang on."

Before I could answer, the wing again dipped and we swung back around. Gene increased our airspeed as we began diving, preparing to make a quick pass over the battle area. My eyes were riveted in shifts on the altimeter and the bursts of orange now way off in the distance but getting relentlessly closer. Gene clamped his headset back on his head. Then he reached into the side pocket of his seat and tossed me a small looseleaf notebook.

"Gimme the radio frequency of the Fort Cornwallis Command Post, Lieutenant!"

"Yessir!" I quickly flipped through the book, then moved my finger down three-quarters of a page of frequently listings. The orange flashes were getting closer. They looked much more impressive at this much lower altitude.

"Hurry UP, God damn it!"

"Yessir! Sorry!" There was no more time for juvenile petulance. "It's 240.03, sir."

"Get it on the radio!"

"Yessir." I turned the knob... then depressed the mike button, talking into my headset. "Militia One calling Fort Cornwallis Command Post."

A British voice answered. "Roger, Militia One... Command Post here. Petrovsky speaking."

Gene took over from there. "Charlie-Papa, get me the Oscar-Delta.... Charlie-Papa, get me the Oscar-Delta... emergency! Over!

"Roger, Militia One... stand by...."

"Captain Schallert speaking... come in and identify."

"Captain... this is Group Captain Hayes in Militia One... the airstrip is under attack at this moment. I'm going in for a closer look... stand by, please."

"Roger, Militia One. Command Post standing by."

Gene now turned to me. "Lieutenant... go aft. There's a specially constructed hatchway... a small one in the fuselage. Pull it open, then load the flare gun from the box marked flares and watch the light above the main hatchway. When it turns green, fire one of the flares... when it turns green again, fire another... and so on... just as quick as you can reload... got it?"

"Yessir."

"Move out!"

I unbuckled, hung up the headset and flew out of the seat. My legs were practically numb from all the tension and sitting. I staggered back into the empty cargo-passenger area. I quickly noted the red light above the main hatchway. Pulling the small one open, I went to the box marked 'flares' and loaded one into the flair gun.

The light turned green. I stuck my hand out and fired. Quickly reloading, I fired when it turned green again. The engines were straining now. It turned green again and I fired as the hollow, banging explosions from the earlier ones sounded in the sky. The aircraft suddenly lurched upward, nearly knocking me on my ass.

"Return to cockpit, Lieutenant," Gene's voice now sounded on the intercom. For some reason 'lieutenant' wasn't sounding like a curse word the last several minutes.

Having just loaded a flare, I took the gun with me as I struggled against the intense upward angle. Collapsing into my seat, I buckled up once more, putting on the headset. The sky was all lit up, but I couldn't see anything because Gene had climbed steeply, turning back around for another pass.

I felt the turns with my stomach, but now we were straight and level again, heading hell for leather into the battle. The intense white light lit up the ground below as Gene and I struggled to make sense of what we were seeing. I guess in the end it wasn't that hard. Men clad in black were swarming over the runway and hangar area. Some bodies of men in khaki could be seen scattered about the flight line, and some seemed to be firing from that sentry gate.

Gene's eyes filled with tears. He was seeing lots more than I was able to. It was obvious our guys were getting slaughtered, but the extent of the defeat eluded me in my ignorance.

"Militia One to Command Post... guerillas have overrun airstrip... have detonated explosions on runway to disable it and now appear to be concentrating..."

Gene was interrupted as several explosions hit the wing and the engine out my window. I saw flashes coming from the engine, then, by the quickly fading light of the flares, dense clouds of black smoke. My heart jumped to my throat. "Engine on fire, sir!" I gasped.

"Command Post..." Gene now spoke with a quaver in his voice. "Request rescue attempt of surviving Militiamen... they're falling back toward Highway Two... over!"

"Any idea of the numbers involved?"

"It was a whole platoon... I see scattered gunfire from their positions... Maybe a squad or more visible... but I have an in-flight emergency, Captain... am switching to tower frequency... out!"

Gene was gaining altitude as the clouds of smoke got worse. He switched to the tower frequency as he turned the ship toward the coast. "Cassell, hit that toggle switch there..." He pointed. "Did the red light go off?"

"Yessir," I gasped.

"Okay, now hit that toggle switch next to it... turn the knob next to that to angle the prop blades to zero..." Gene quickly faced front, his right thumb depressing his headset mike button. "Cornwallis Tower...MAYDAY...MAYDAY...MAYDAY! This is Militia One... some twelve miles west of Mantilla heading east. I have an engine on fire and no place to land... over!"

"Roger Militia One... picking you up on scope... contacting air rescue... stand by."

My eyes must have been huge, but it was so scary there was nothing to do but work. "Blade angle all the way over, sir."

Gene reached up and pulled back on a lever above my console. The needle on three gauges in my field of vision dropped to zero. He had obviously just shut down the starboard engine. The prop whirled uselessly as flame and smoke shot from behind it.

"Okay, Cassell, now hit the third toggle switch and push the button below it!"

I did.

Gene didn't have to ask me the results. It was obvious the fire was still going.

Our stricken aircraft had reached the coast. Gene now turned us to the north and continued onward, losing altitude all the while. The lights of Port Albert loomed ahead, dwarfing the much more modest displays of Mantilla and New Gatwick below and behind us.

"Okay, buddy, here's the plan..."

"Cornwallis Tower to Militia One... over!" the British-accented voice interrupted him.

"Go ahead, Tower."

"Roger... Militia One... Major Hill has ordered a stretch of Highway One cleared for you to land. Military units from the base are organizing now to accomplish that. At the same time, he's scrambled the PT boat squadron. Continue to hug the coast line... if possible keeping yourself as close to the PT boats as possible. If the fire spreads to the wing, ditch in the water and the crews will pick you up. Understood?"

"Roger Tower... many thanks."

As we passed over the well lit-up British Military reservation, we could see activity in the area of the boats, though none had put to sea yet. Toward the front gate, a line of what the British called lorries, an urban assault vehicle and several jeeps were queuing up. Several of the lorries were field ambulances, as identified by the large red crosses painted on their roofs. Passing over the harbor, I saw the seaplane, moored where we had left her this morning. A thought of Connie again intruded on my terror. This time it wasn't jealousy at all, just the prayerful hope I would survive this and get to see her again. All the while my eyes frequently darted to the wing. The flames continued unabated despite several tries at the sprinkler. The prop had now stopped spinning.

Once over the cannery, Gene turned inland, then angled back toward the coast, headed south once more. As we passed the area of warehouses and sleazy waterfront bars, we could see what looked like crowds of people pouring out and staring up into the sky. That sight was nothing compared to what we saw as we headed south of the base once more and were overflying the southern expanse of shanties we'd passed through by car today. *Hundreds upon hundreds* of people were pouring out of them swarming around the highway.

Gene was also watching the spectacle, his face taut. "That's gonna be a tough scene to survive, buddy. I'm almost tempted to just ditch." He shook his head. "No... I've *got* to try to save this ship. It's all we have."

I uneasily watched the crowds swelling below us. "What do you mean 'tough to survive'?"

"They're gonna have us land toward the south. We'll come to a stop probably right where all those people are. Most all of them will flee when the Army shows up. But you can just bet there's a load of sappers in that crowd. They're gonna do all they can to have the crowd rush us.... strip the airplane and us... then... well, you know."

I looked reflexively down at the revolver resting in my holster. *Six lousy shots.* I knew I had no potential of talking him into doing anything with the plane his own mind hadn't told him was necessary, but I thought a gentle hint might be a good idea. I did NOT want to take on that mob. "Assuming we don't break up on landing, or that the ship isn't consumed by fire shortly thereafter... how is the plane gonna be salvaged, Gene?"

We were down to Mantilla again. Gene banked steeply to the left, then headed back toward the coast. A glance at the altimeter showed us flying at four hundred feet once he leveled off. "What do you mean?"

"Oh... how's it gonna get back up to the hangar area? Do you think there's anything left of your crew or the supplies?"

Gene's jaw tightened even more. "I guess we'll soon find out..."

A glance at the fuel gauges showed the needles indicating very low. On this pass, however, it was obvious several British Army jeeps and an urban assault vehicle were out on the highway now, moving down toward Mantilla. The few vehicles on the road were being forced over. The horrible mob scene had disappeared from our view as we again passed over the warehouse district. Jeeps were now blocking ingress to Highway One where it met Highway Two, while up at the cannery turnoff, jeeps were parked completely across the road. The highway was apparently all but sealed off now.

"Militia One this is Cornwallis Tower... over."

"Go ahead..."

"Captain Barclay reports we're almost in readiness for your attempt to land. Fire fighting units from the base are encountering difficulty with large crowds and intermittent sniper fire at the south edge of town. They will be held back until your landing. Unless you are prepared to ditch, you are directed to fly to a point not less than five miles beyond the cannery, then turn one hundred eighty degrees and begin final approach along Highway One... over."

Gene and I exchanged an extremely tense glance. "Roger Tower... over cannery now... commencing turn."

Gene now banked the aircraft to the right heading out over the water, then to the left, beginning a gradual turn back toward the highway. The flames were continuing to shoot out of the blackened engine. "Okay, Cassell... when we touch down, we'll play everything by ear. The main thing is to get out of the craft through the fuselage hatchway as quickly as possible before the flames overtake us..." He swallowed. "Ready, buddy?"

Heart pounding in my ears, I nodded.

"Here we go. Tower we're into our final approach over Highway One some six miles north of the cannery."

"Roger, Militia One... Godspeed."

We were steadily losing altitude now as we streaked along above the gravel road. Past the cannery... into the warehouse district. "Flaps down... wheels down and locked."

Looking outside, I could now see the large crowd that had poured out of the bars and warehouses clearly. In addition to small knots of British troops, there were several constables in their black and powder blue uniforms helping with the crowd control.

At the junction of Highway Two, there was a fairly large concentration of vehicles. We were now flying very low. Some fifty feet above the base we noticed the firefighting units on the road below us. They were already tearing in the direction we were headed.

Now practically at touch down, we flew just above a long line of lorries loaded with British troops in battle dress, field ambulances, and an urban assault vehicle. Ahead loomed a solid mass of black faces and white shirts.

We hit the gravel and bounced upward. The crowd was starting to scatter. We came down once more, the tires squealing with the impact. Gravel started swirling around in our field of vision, pummeling our windscreen and the remaining engine, which Gene had thrown into reverse to try to slow our forward speed. We both struggled with the brakes as we flew along the roadway... past large groups of people and several cars forced over to the side.

Repeated popping noises began to be heard. The glass just to the right of my head shattered with the impact of a bullet. Loud *thunk!'s* could be heard as more struck our fuselage. Gene and I both kept our heads down. The airplane squealed to a stop, as a sea of black faces and white shirts came charging toward us. A volley of gunfire from behind us made several of them suddenly turn away, but many continued coming.

Quickly unhooking our seatbelts, we made our way into the cargo-passenger area. I was clutching the flare gun in my hand. Gene got there first and turned the handle to the main hatchway. Gunfire, approaching sirens and a low but deafening roar were all we could hear as the hatchway was swung open.

I fired the flare gun point blank at the mob approaching us. There were several shrieks, then a very loud, agonized one as the flare dug into the chest of a man at the head of the mob, then exploded into a blaze of intense white light. People were screaming everywhere. The exploding flare stopped the people from closing on that side, but we could already feel the airplane being rocked back and forth by people on the other trying to turn it over. Up in the cockpit we heard the sound of breaking glass.

"My *God*, Cassell! We're *trapped*!" In desperation, Gene squeezed off several shots of his revolver as I did the same. He then reached up and pulled the hatchway shut, dogging it once more.

"Go check the engine!" he gasped.

I ran toward the cockpit, the rocking getting much worse. The sound of military gunfire was getting more pronounced... the screams and panic getting more incessant... the sirens getting louder. Reaching the cockpit, I now saw some twenty people at the port side windscreen, at least two with their heads sticking inside, trying to pull themselves in. In panic, I fired another round. Fortunately, it made them jump down and run away. Casting my eyes to the right, the fire seemed to still be confined to the engine and had not spread to the wing.

I hurriedly ejected the six spent casings of my revolver and pulled six replacements out of the bandolier on the gunbelt. As I tried to fit them into the chambers of the cylinder with shaking hands, I began stumbling back toward Gene. Off in the distance, a screaming sound was getting closer and closer. As I now passed through to where Gene was standing against the hatchway, revolver in one hand, the scream seemed right on top of us.

"HIT THE DECK!" Gene yelled. We dived to the floor. The aircraft suddenly stopped rocking as several loud explosions now sounded as if they were falling in our vicinity, followed by loud hissing.

"It's teargas," I gasped.

"Thank God! What's the situation with the engine?"

We could barely hear one another, the sounds of the panicking mob were so loud. But it was sounding like many more were fleeing. The rocking had stopped.

"Another miracle, Gene... fire remains confined there."

We gripped one another tightly, revolvers in our hands, until the sound of British voices were heard outside the hatchway. Opening it, very cautiously at first, we beheld some twenty British soldiers clutching rifles, their backs to us, facing toward the endless shanties. The smoke of tear gas was everywhere, though no longer concentrated enough to be more than a nuisance. The nearest white shirt and khaki pants was at least a hundred yards away, and seemed more curious than anything.

"You two all right?" A stocky NCO in the insignia of a staff corporal asked as he came toward us.

Gene nodded, then returned the man's salute once he'd gotten close enough.

The starboard wing was black but the fire was out. A couple of the base rescue people were standing at the front of the plane, large extinguishers on wheels with them. Further down the road toward Mantilla, another knot of British soldiers stood over four men lying face down on the gravel, their hands laced behind the backs of their necks. Two were in the white shirt outfits, but the others were in black.

I tapped Gene on the arm and pointed.

"Must be," he replied. We were both still in shock, acting like we were normal, unable to do anything else.

"Group Captain?"

Hayes and I both turned around to see an Army captain. "Barclay here... We're going to the rescue of the airstrip now. Care to come?"

"Yes," Gene spoke up immediately. The captain beckoned us to follow him and began moving toward the queue of vehicles behind the plane.

Gene turned to me, a sad, bitter look on his face. "I guess this is where you get off, Cassell... I don't know how we're ever gonna fix that plane."

"But..."

"You can keep those coveralls... just return the stripes, name tag and weapon to me sometime, okay?"

He turned away, not waiting for an answer, headed toward the trucks which were starting up. A thousand conflicting emotions hit me all at the same time. I had gotten a heavy dose of Maggierock reality this night. I had gotten a heavy reminder of my self-interest and personal concerns earlier in the evening. I hadn't slept in over twenty-four hours. Maybe I wasn't thinking too clearly. "Group Captain!"

He turned around.

"You can't *fire* an officer in time of war."

He looked at me oddly, then broke into a big smile. The two of us walked quickly to one of the lead jeeps and climbed in.

We would later learn that the British could realistically have either marshaled sufficient force to pluck us out of the airplane, and possibly save it from the mob, or counterattack in force at the airstrip. They opted to try to salvage Maggierock's pathetic Air Militia, then reclaim its base. Captain Barclay explained to us, as we now zipped along the gravel Highway Two toward the mountains, that the odd behavior of the mob indicated sappers. And if there were sappers in sufficient force to whip hundreds into a looting frenzy, the main attack at the airstrip was over. The base assumption was that the rebels were always short-handed as well, and simply couldn't do both at once.

"I just don't know how I'm gonna salvage that plane." Gene had a distracted, tormented look on his face as we flew past Government Plaza into the Diplomatic Quarter.

"Maybe the British will let you repair it at the base. Where we came to a stop isn't that far from it."

I barely had the words out of my mouth when Captain Barclay, who had been listening to some transmissions over a portable field radio on earphones, now turned and tapped Air Militia Group Captain Hayes on the knee as he sat with me in the back seat of the command jeep.

"The Major wants to know whether we should tow your plane to our base or blow it up. We can't keep a guard around it much longer."

"Tow it," Gene replied, looking at me as if that was the first break he'd gotten from Fate in many years. Barclay replaced the headset on his head, facing front once more. There was still the separate question of whether it could be fixed, but first things first.

As we passed the last of Port Albert and sped upward into the mountains, a thin plume of black smoke appeared above us and slightly to the right. Gene and I found ourselves riveted by the spectacle, each lost in our own thoughts about what may have happened, why...and maybe most important... what the next steps would be. His face betrayed the memory of his anguish at the state of security the Militia had maintained at his precious airstrip. I know he was haunted by the wide range of possibilities we might find awaiting us when we arrived.

His biggest fear was that the soldiers would be proved to have thrown their rifles away and run... back to shantytown, to mingle undetected among their erstwhile neighbors. Gene had invested a lot in this island. Being ignorant of military procedure and tactics was one thing... being lazy and a goldbrick when the heat was off was quite another. But turning tail under fire was something yet again. No one really yet knew how the St. Margaret's Militia was going to do against the rebels. The British Army was doing all the hard hitting thus far.

There was only one legend that Gene was aware of, but he wasn't sure if it were true. Militia drill sergeants were using it at the three week recruit school... to scare the recruits and whip up hatred for the guerillas. According to this legend, some time last year, a twenty man Militia unit was assigned to escort some of taro planter Philip Doran's trucks, loaded with provisions and supplies for his plantation on the return trip back over the mountains to New Britain. When the trucks were three days overdue, a search was organized. The burnt out trucks were found, their drivers stripped and slain, but not a single Militiaman was located. The drill sergeants told the recruits they were forcibly conscripted to fight with the rebels. Gene said that every time he tried to get confirmation from 'the Limeys' he'd draw a smile, but every time the tale was told, at least three recruits would 'move to de calypso beat,' as the local expression went. 'Deserted' was the more familiar expression. This would be the first confirmed test of their mettle, and the 'jumbe' who had as much of a stake here as its natives was very anxious, his anxiety only deepening the closer we came.

The plume disappeared as we got closer, because the thick foliage on each side of the jungle-forested mountain made seeing things at the same altitude off in the distance almost impossible. Nobody was doing much talking. My thoughts were of Connie, concern for my old pal, an occasional sensation that I was an utter idiot to have, in a moment of adrenalin-fueled emotion, thrown away the escape that had haunted my dreams on the airplane, and not a little insecurity over the issue that plagued Gene. All we could do was wait to find out. Whatever the answer, the soldiers who had so capably rescued us, and who were now riding behind us, no doubt lost in their own thoughts of England, were leaving in just a little over two months.

. . . .

A squad of British Infantry leading the way, Captain Barclay, Group Captain Hayes and Flight Lieutenant Cassell, revolvers drawn, cautiously closed the last few yards to the turnoff. The stench of death and gunpowder was unmistakable. We weren't kept in suspense long. Right there at the turnoff, seven Militiamen sat. Some had minor wounds, a couple were sobbing, but they were there, with their weapons. To Gene's boundless delight, the young sergeant that had so impressed me, along with two other men in those blue coveralls were with them.

Lieutenant Willett we were told, was dead. Some thirty Militiamen in his command were dead. At least two more of Gene's Air Militia were confirmed dead. The rest, some three Air Militiamen and about twelve of the other kind were unaccounted for. The British combat team now deployed to reclaim the airstrip. After firing several flares to illuminate the area they moved in as we watched.

There was no resistance. The rebels had fled. Their casualties were unknown, because they had all been removed. Nine Militiamen and another of Gene's mechanics were found hiding, terrified, in the burnt out remains of the hangar. I was able to salvage my .38 from the locker, but my clothes were destroyed. British interrogators set to work learning what had happened. The accounts were fragmentary and conflicting. The central truth that emerged was that the Militia was taken completely by surprise and blown out of its positions in the opening minutes. A hopeful corollary, however, was that many had kept on fighting, even as they fell back toward Highway Two or took refuge inside the hangar. The young sergeant was frequently mentioned by survivors as a source of leadership, as were two other Militiamen NCO's.

FREEDUM! NLP! COLGATE JUMBE LOVR DC

was found spray-painted on parts of the still standing hangar walls. One of the British NCO's told me the spray-painted leavings of the guerillas told the intelligence people a lot about the identity and characteristics of the rebel group responsible. He said these leavings told him the attackers were a unit of Woody Crenshaw's recruited from the very shanty town that had nearly dispatched us.

"Woody *Crenshaw?*" I'd asked. "Who's he?"

"Commander of the guerillas in the northern region," he'd replied. "Webster is the overall leader."

I'd certainly heard that before.

With Gene and the surviving half of his air force, I spent the next several hours rooting through rubble, picking up airplane parts, salvaging furniture, tools and the like. The young men were told I was Gene's executive officer, and would be a regular sight here from now on. The young sergeant was introduced to me by the unlikely name of Felonious Burns, Jr. I was also told there was another Felonious Burns walking around, and he was the Government Leader in the House of Councilors. Gene told me I would be seeing many 'colorful' names while I was here, especially within the Jack Clan. Gene knew nothing of my ties with Sybil. He mentioned them because he said at least one of them came with 'my house'.

Dawn was breaking with a magnificence I had seldom seen as I sat, exhausted, up against the front of the hangar smoking a Chesterfield. A gorgeous flaming red sunrise was displaying itself out at sea, long slivers of crimson like sunbursts lighting up the sky over Port Albert and the foothills stretched out below me. The Army medics had been hard at work on the wounded, aided toward the dawn by a gray-haired lady with glasses worn around her neck on a chain. She was all business, wore a white coat and a stethoscope around her neck, and was looked upon by the young sergeant and several other islanders practically with reverence.

"That's Dr. Detweiler," he had said shortly after she'd first appeared. "She has been helping us here for many years." It was obvious even the less articulate types among the survivors didn't consider her a 'jumbe'. I never heard the word mentioned once when she was being discussed.

It was only as the sun began to poke its head above the horizon that both my exhaustion and the stress of the night just past began to register on me. I was shaking so hard I could barely light the cigarette. That mob scene got more terrifying the more I thought about it. *We'd have been torn apart!* Easy to say, impossible to plumb the depths of emotion involved in the experience. My body was doing that for me.

"You doing all right, Flight Lieutenant?"

I looked up. It was the young sergeant. "Yes... I'm okay."

"Group Captain Hayes wants to see you, sir," he went on. He gestured. "Over by the tool shed."

"Okay." I hauled myself to my feet just as he saluted. I was so surprised I nearly knocked my brand new glasses off my face returning it, causing him to work hard stifling laughter, but he did.

"How ya doin' Cassell?" Gene asked as I joined him. They'd managed to salvage some of the commissary and were providing coffee to the British soldiers and our survivors, and of course Dr. Detweiler, when she could be persuaded to stop working on the seriously hurt long enough.

I shrugged. "Close call, wasn't it." I was still shaking so hard I could barely hold the coffee cup.

Gene smiled. "You'll get used to it..." his voice trailed off, an odd look coming over his face. "In a disturbing kind a' way."

I registered the look, but Gene had signaled he didn't want the thought pursued. Instead he now fixed me with a smile. "Thanks for joinin' this outfit, buddy. I appreciate it."

"I was drafted, *sir or group captain.*" I meant it as humor and Gene took it that way.

"No... I meant down at the plane... afterwards."

I looked down. "Oh... well... I guess there were too many good men in on the fight for me to just walk away."

He patted me on the shoulder and for several minutes we stood side by side watching the incredible sunrise in absolute silence. There really was no other way to watch a sunrise like that. It was *awesome.*

"These people deserve a chance," he spoke at last in as sober a tone as I ever heard him speak.

My face whiplashed in his direction. He kept his eyes riveted on the horizon. "I thought they were all 'hamburgers'."

Gene faced me, grinning weakly. "Some a' 'em." He paused for a while, obviously not finished. "There was a fair amount a' bravery here last night, Cassell." He shrugged. "Maybe it's this sunrise... maybe it's all we've been through last night ourselves... I dunno...anyway, the trick now is to take the emotion of these survivors, the men who acquitted themselves so well amid no leadership and a surprise attack... and somehow galvanize the rest of the Militia with it."

For another long while he just stared off to the east, then faced me once more. "Anyway, in the morning of our discontent and humiliation, I suddenly have *hope.*" He shook his head. "It didn't hurt that some lousy, worthless hippie...."

"Freak," I interrupted.

He smiled. "Yeah... well anyway, that you decided your place was with us." He patted me once more on the shoulder. "Well done, Cassell." His finger tapped at the stripes on my right epaulet. "You were a credit to those. See ya later, buddy... that's all... you're dismissed."

I turned in his direction and saluted. He returned it, then walked away.

Wednesday February 7, 1973: the Hotel Hayes, Settlement of Mantilla, Isle of St. Margaret's

It was nearly ten in the sweltering hot, sunny, terribly humid morning before the British Army Land Rover dropped me at the overhang in front of my hotel.

"Thanks," I called as I got out.

The NCO in the left front seat saluted. "'ave a good 'un, sir."

I returned the salute, this time sparing my glasses. The vehicle drove off in a cloud of dust.

Entering the lobby, I found it once more deserted. I realized my hotel key was back in my destroyed clothing up at the airstrip, compelling me to approach the deserted counter and pound on it, local style, with my fist.

"Keep de shirt on de back jumbe," the same fat black woman scolded as she ambled through the door some five minutes later. Taking in my sweat-soaked dusty uniform coveralls, the revolver in its holster around my waist, the revolver in its holster in my hand, the stripes, name tag and various other changes, most of them likely in my face since last she'd seen me, her face screwed into a monumental frown.

"Don't shoot de *lizards*, jumbe...," she scolded once more, doing a good job of mimicking my voice yesterday when I'd said the word. Obviously the bellboy had made the incident into something of a hotel-wide joke. "Dey come wit de room."

I leaned tiredly against the counter. It was really catching up with me now. I just wanted to put my arms around Connie, celebrate her existence, then shower and try to sleep in the raging heat. "I need a key."

"De key not grow on a tree... where's yours?"

"In de clothes, which burned in de fire at de airstrip," I answered sarcastically.

She smirked. "Two and six for de replacement."

"Deal," I sighed tiredly. "Put it on the bill."

"Deal," she mimicked, handing me another.

I dragged myself to the elevator, then up to the fifth floor.

There are times that with no clues whatsoever, you know you are entering a stricken house or room. There is something in the utter silence... a heaviness in the otherwise normal atmosphere. I had no sooner stepped in that I let out a gasp. Something was very wrong. I shortly found out what.

All of Connie's clothes and her luggage were gone. My heart pounding in my ears, my eyes filling with tears, I barely saw the note on the bed. It was a while before I could stop shaking long enough to read it.

The Hotel Hayes

QUALITY LODGING IN PARADISE

MANTILLA, ISLE OF ST. MARGARET'S

TELEX: PORT ALBERT 78-9943

Hi Darling!

Chuck is going to show me Puerto Rico! I have a chance to visit my grandparents for the first time since I was two years old! He's familiar with the island, and is even taking leave to help me.

I'll be back on the plane in two weeks. We came by this morning to talk about it with you, but you were gone.

Wish me bon voyage! See you in two weeks!

Love, Connie

I didn't bother to shower, to change, to even unbuckle the gunbelt. I collapsed on the bed, burying my head in my pillow, waiting for the exhaustion to rescue me. This had been one fouled-up mission of state, all right. Seeing it to its conclusion, I lost the one chance I'd been given to stop Connie from running off with that guy. I would have stopped her too. Throughout all the pain and trauma as the events of the mission had unfolded through the night, I severely regretted my response to Chuck's question... and later hers. Connie had given me every chance to stop it. In my woeful ignorance I had blown them all. I wasn't fooled by the promise of a return. What really plagued me, as Sean Kelly's words of reproach sounded over and over in my ears, is that she maybe thought by letting her go out like that... I just didn't care.

Chapter Six

THE MORNING OF OUR HUMILIATION

Wednesday February 21, 1973: the Transfer of Power Office, Government Plaza, Port Albert, Isle of St. Margaret's

In contrast to most of the inhabited portions of the island, Government Plaza was *beautiful*. Its four main buildings, well-maintained white-painted wooden structures with large windows and shady, columned verandas, were grouped in a square around a beautiful lawn with brightly colored, fragrant flower gardens. Dead center was a tall white flagpole, where the Union Jack snapped smartly in the ocean breeze.

At the north side, running alongside and parallel to Highway Two was the Consultative Assembly Building, soon to be called the Houses of Parliament. To the east, running parallel to Highway One but quite a ways west of it, was the newest building, rapidly being finished to house the Ministries of the Government. To the south, right next to the south wing of the Diplomatic Quarter, was the building housing the Transfer of Power Office, while to the west, just east of the Governor's Residence, was Government House, the Headquarters of the Colonial Administration, where I had come a couple weeks before to make arrangements with Edward Markham to purchase his house. That had gone smoothly, and as he had happily moved into the Bachelor Officers' Quarters at Fort Cornwallis, in eager anticipation of his return to England in less than two months now, I had since

146

moved in, with Sean and Joe, to his beautiful house on the 'Heights' in Mantilla.

Today, Sean and Joe had brought me, in our new Land Rover, accompanied by the 'shotgun' Graham Jack, who per 'island tradition' came with the house, to the second building I was to visit on the Plaza, the Transfer of Power Office. The occasion was my long awaited and twice-postponed meeting with Desmond Colgate, the incoming Prime Minister. They had picked me up at Sybil's beach house shortly after sunrise and brought me home to prepare for my visit. I had also been reminded to bring our passports, so that our visas could be issued by the post-independence government. We arrived in plenty of time for the appointment, allowing me another opportunity to enjoy the gardens and gawk at the machine gun emplacements and sentry posts an increasingly nervous colonial administration had deployed to prevent terrorist attacks.

I entered Colgate's outer office and somewhat nervously took my seat, some fifteen minutes early. He had indicated he wanted to meet with me before we ever arrived, apparently, according to Mister Gwynne, to convince me (and especially my money) to participate in the life of the new nation. I had been here now just a bit over two weeks, and on my own had done just that, including holding an officer's commission in its Air Militia and taking as a mistress the daughter of one of its most prominent clans. It was therefore just possible the Prime Minister now had other ideas about what our meeting should be about. The range of possibilities, many of which I'm sure I couldn't begin to guess, were the cause of my attack of nerves.

I had already seen him a time or two. At military formations of the Militia right after the blood bath at the airstrip, and more often and more recently at Serena Blackstone's beach house, when he would come to visit his mistress. Serena was Sybil's neighbor, so that made the Prime Minister and I neighbors by proxy. 'Off duty' he always seemed friendly enough. He certainly appeared to be a capable man. Nerves or not, I was looking forward to the chance to talk face to face.

. . . .

Gene Hayes had called the morning of February 7 the 'morning of our discontent and humiliation'. He was certainly right there. News of the slaughter reverberated through the island like a shock wave. Thanks to some fancy footwork by Colgate and his Ministers, however, it didn't have the impact the guerillas had no doubt intended.

On paper, it certainly should have. Thirty men dead out of a fifty man platoon. Half the trained airplane mechanics on the island dead. The island's only airplane temporarily out of action. The figures were shocking, and in the hands of a less capable administration could well have caused an end to Militia recruitment and many desertions in the units that remained. Such, however, was not to be the case.

That very morning, Gene was to later tell me, as I was lying distraught on my hotel bed, still in my filthy Air Militia uniform, Colgate summoned Colonel Paul Christian and Group Captain Hayes, as well as Morton Gentry, his Minister of Defence, Thompson Ritter, who in the innocuous guise of Minister of Posts and Telegraphs was really his propaganda chief, Home Secretary Millard Cotter, the 'top cop', Chief Constable Maurice Jenkins and Damien Andrews, editor of the island's only newspaper, owned, of course, by Gene.

The meeting was held in the conference room of the Transfer of Power Office, with Militiamen posted within the ring of steel created by the normal cordon of British troops. The orders issued to the Militiamen were to keep *everyone* out of earshot. Before it even began, Colgate issued orders to embalm the bodies of the slain soldiers and airmen and make certain there was a post-independence flag available for each of the caskets. Display of the flag was technically a crime, though Colgate had no problem getting consent from the Royal Governor, who was as panicked by what had occurred as the rest of us.

Colgate had been briefed on the disaster by Colonel Christian before sunrise, shortly after the British Army had reclaimed the smoldering remains of the airstrip. He immediately recognized the potential for a major guerilla victory in the battle 'for the hearts and minds' of the people. He brought in Ritter at once.

Ritter proved to be Maggierock's answer to Josef Göebbels. Educated at a British 'redbrick' university in journalism, he worked for a time on *The Daily Mail*. Colgate's offer of a portfolio, with the understanding he would be the 'architect of public education' in the post-independence government brought him home.

Briefed on the slaughter by his anxious chief, Ritter became *excited*. He readily recognized two kernels of truth that, if properly nurtured, would completely turn the tables on the guerillas. The first was the shattered remains of the platoon were found at the airstrip. The second was that they still had their weapons. Over the next two hours, as Gene, Felonious Burns and I rooted through rubble looking for parts and tools we could salvage, an exciting tale was spun before the suddenly fascinated Prime Minister.

Essentially, the story became 'Willett's Last Stand', where a heroic Militia Commander (Maggierock's platoons had commanders rather than leaders because they were designed as independent units), outnumbered ten to one, had fought the rebels to a standstill. Despite mounting casualties, and until his own death, he continually rallied his men to 'give not an inch to those who would enslave us!' Thus inspired, the embattled Militia platoon fought a bloody conflict of attrition, until the less motivated but numerically superior rebels finally fled in terror.

Ritter drafted a communiqué containing this official account. It was read on the radio, preempting JoJo Child's popular morning show *Funky Maggierock*. Soundtrucks with grim faced Militia escorts were sent into the north and south shanty towns, then down the coast to read it. He drafted 'consultative legislation' creating the St. Margaret's Military Cross, then awarding it to [almost] the entire platoon. Sir Bertram Tibbets personally decorated the survivors at a big ceremony in the Mahali, the walled-in field across from the cannery, then personally lay the posthumous medals on the coffins of the fallen, already draped with the green-black-green flag of the post-independence nation.

The ten or so survivors who'd taken charge amid the chaos were immediately given spot commissions, and sent forthwith to the British base for leadership training as well as motivational classes letting them know how brave and courageous they really were. This was an innovative and very constructive move. Those men *had* been brave.

Under normal circumstances, however, they would be condemned to live lives of disgrace, forever haunted by the bloody memories of that night. Under Ritter's plan, they learned pride in themselves, and their mere presence gave pride to the men around them.

It turned out Maggierock had a sort of 'artist' who once had gotten money from Lyndon Johnson's Great Society for painting one of those ghetto murals in a Miami slum. A contest was sponsored in the elementary schools inviting children to make a drawing showing Willet's Last Stand as they pictured it. One very precocious youngster drew a picture showing Willett, down on one knee, the look of a Man of Destiny on his countenance, his revolver pointed, the platoon guidon snapping smartly behind him, his men grouped around him, some with bandages tied around their heads, clutching their rifles. The ghetto artist was commissioned to turn this into a massive mural on one of the walls surrounding the Mahali, adding his own artistic interpretation.

Of course there were the four deserters to be accounted for somehow. A secret but massive manhunt was ordered by Ritter through Colgate to Chief Constable Jenkins. Privates Duke Grubbs, Meano Fittings, Jumbo Supplee and Marvel Hanlon were dragged, kicking and screaming, from various girlfriend's shanties and whisked away to the disciplinary barracks of the Militia headquarters at Fort Cornwallis. There, over the next several days, to their astonishment, they learned that at various crucial moments, the heroic Lieutenant Willett, knowing the end was in sight, dispatched each of these, the first three in a desperate effort to get reenforcements, the final one with a special brief to 'make sure our People know and never forget our heroic last stand.' Even Ritter gagged at the thought of decorating these men, but seizing on the pretext that their devoted attention to their orders had prevented them from falling victim to the final carnage, and participation in the heroism, they were awarded letters of commendation.

The mass Secular Communion of an entire People with its Heroes, both fallen and survived, went on for over a week. It was probably one of the most brilliantly conceived and executed exercises in 'historical judo', as Ritter privately termed it, ever pulled off.

For me, of course, the 'morning of our humiliation' had an additional and very personal significance. Devastated by the loss of Connie, I stumbled through each day, led around by the nose, first by Joe and Sean to the Caymans Bank and Trust to get most of my money in the vault, then to Markham's to get the house, then to Hayes Automotive to get our Land Rover. Group Captain Hayes, while reporting that my khaki uniform still hadn't arrived for the first few days of ceremonies, nonetheless saw I was present at the public celebrations in my Air Militia coveralls. When it did finally come, my Medal of Valor and Sheriff's Commendation ribbons were affixed and I was led around to the rest.

As the twentieth approached, I began frequenting the Interisland Airbus Seaplane terminal to get a peek at the passenger manifest out of Bridgetown. As I had feared, Connie's name was not on it, but another name was, and it coincided nicely with a conversation I had with Colonel Christian shortly after the funeral of the Fallen Heroes. Several of us had gone to the Yacht Club for drinks. After we had each had [quite] a few, the Militia Commandant took me aside.

"Let's go out on the deck, Flight Lieutenant... I'd like to discuss something with you."

I was pleasantly surprised by the attention being shown me by the Militia Commandant, so readily agreed. Before vacating my barstool, however, I paused for a final look at myself in the cracked, smeared mirror. My blue RAF-style officer's cap, with green-around-black target capshield flanked by wings and topped by the British crown had been the reason my uniform had been so long in coming, but the wait was worth it. The blouse was khaki, with short sleeves, just like the Militia's except ours was a lighter tan. My two stripes were mounted on each of the epaulets, gray with thin blue borders. Open at the collar like a shirt, it was as climate-compatible as such things could be. The sheriff's ribbons gave me the look of someone who'd actually earned the 'flight lieutenant' rank, the equivalent of a Militia captain. The Sam Browne belt with holster was the perfect top-off. Gene wore his with a British revolver that had a white cord running through a metal loop at the base of the butt. The cord then went up through both his epaulets and around his neck. I'd seen that look in many movies, but I didn't like my pistol tied around my neck, so I turned in the one he'd given me that first night, using instead my four inch .38.

Thoroughly self-satisfied, I passed from the steamy room out into the steamy afternoon, taking a seat across from the Colonel at one of the empty picnic-style tables placed on the deck stretching out over the water, shaded by an overhang. Aside from the aforementioned heat, it was a beautiful day and the harbor bustled with activity. My eyes inevitably drifted to the series of flagged buoys in its center where the seaplane would tie up when it arrived next Tuesday.

"How do you like our country so far, Lieutenant?"

"Very interesting," I answered with suitable ambiguity that drew an instant smile.

"We're glad you're here, and particularly so since you've chosen to participate in our society and help make a difference."

"Well thank you, sir. Occasionally I've felt a bit resented for doing so."

He brushed the remark off with a wave of his hand. "You'll find suspicion of outsiders everywhere you go. The people who count here know what's coming and appreciate the help, believe me."

"Do *you* think we're gonna have what it takes when the real shooting starts?" I was *very* anxious to hear his response to that one. Gene had told me he disagreed with his 'conquest in pieces' theory. As he obviously had all sorts of inside knowledge about the presence or absence of the resources that really counted, I was very curious as to how he saw the coming struggle.

He paused a moment, obviously thinking. "Right now...," he finally began slowly, "morale is at an all-time high. But *you* know, Lieutenant, better than most, having *been there* that morning, that it's all the result of some very clever smoke and mirrors." He let out a sigh as he gazed off toward the cannery. "I think the answer to your question really depends on what happens next." He shrugged, giving me a disarming grin. "My people every now and then have a disturbing tendency to relax a bit too much when they feel they're holding the cards."

"Most people do," I put in.

"Yes, but we *really aren't* holding the cards. It was all faked. I'm pushing my men just as hard as I dare, but the long term results are as

yet far from clear." He appeared beset with possibilities, many negative, as he finished the sentence. "If I could just locate a rebel force, I'd
love to follow all this hoopla up with a solid military victory... but the
fact remains they are a very capable bunch, and seem to vanish into
thin air when they want to."

"I think we should develop our air capabilities," I volunteered, "so
we could do some scouting." Gene had told me the Convair people
were sending mechanics and parts on the next seaplane, which would
arrive on the twentieth.

Colonel Christian just shrugged. "Well it certainly wouldn't hurt.
The problem with that is our country does not lend itself to a highly
mobile response... and that's what we would really need to capitalize
on such scouting."

There was no doubt about that.

"Are you familiar with your General Gavin and his theories?"

"Oh yes... and of course they've been honed in Vietnam... but you
have no helicopters."

"Yes." He eyed me closely. "Maybe some day, eh?"

I wondered if he were perhaps fishing for a contribution, like Gene
had done, buying the Convair out of his own pocket after building
the airstrip out of his own pocket. Of course Gene had ten million
to play with... I had close to half a million left after buying a house
and vehicle, and setting up a one hundred thousand dollar trust fund
for my daughter with Mister Hillary at the bank. "Maybe," I finally
replied, shifting restlessly in my seat.

He caught it and smiled. "There is a way that you can participate
further in our country, and have perhaps a boost for your morale."

That sounded too good to pass up. "Oh? How?"

"It's actually why I wanted to talk to you. Those of us who've been
watching you think you ought to take a mistress."

My eyes whiplashed to his. "Really?"

"Yes... a local girl of course."

"Of course were Connie to return..."

"In our society, Lieutenant," he interrupted, "it makes no difference."

"No?"

"No. It is customary... a social duty, in our society for the wealthy to take a mistress in addition to a wife."

Maggierock's stock was rising as I digested his words. "Yes?"

He nodded. "You see Lieutenant, as in your medieval culture, all our social acts revolve around the obligation of our people to feed one another. Thus, the wealthy are expected to claim a girl on the side. The interdependent obligations of such a relationship are rigidly fixed. She provides for your emotional and physical needs... on demand."

I had to admit he had me salivating along about now. I had been desolate since Connie left.

"You take care of her.... feed and clothe her... provide her with a home."

"Sounds very practical," I managed.

Colonel Christian burst into laughter. "The look on your face," he smiled. "I think you were meant to come here!"

"I always say everyone should do their part." We were both laughing now, the Colonel appearing quite pleased.

"Anyway, Lieutenant, we think the time has come for you to take this step. Are you willing?"

"Of course."

"Any of our young ladies who have attracted your interest?"

"Yes, sir. Sybil Jack."

He searched his memory. "Ah yes! One of Fortunus' girls... very attractive... smart too."

"Fortunus?"

"Yes... there were two brothers... Amadeus and Fortunus. They had many children. Amadeus died and Fortunus raised his brother's children as his own. Sybil is about the youngest, I recall." His face then darkened. "But she lives off-island. The idea here is to provide for our people at home."

"But she's returning on the seaplane... the twentieth. Of course it's probably just for a visit."

He brightened. "Well you can fix that."

"Really?"

Colonel Christian then went on to explain how the system worked. The wealthy man delivered gifts to the girl's family if she lived at home, to her house if she lived alone. Then he physically 'lay hold of her', as he put it, and took her to where the gifts were.

"Couldn't he just wait until she got home?" I asked, a little worried about carrying some girl off in public.

Christian burst out laughing. "Oh Lieutenant!" he gasped, coughing, "I think you're missing the point of it."

I certainly was, and my blank look must have convinced him.

"The idea here is for the wealthy man to demonstrate strength and absolute authority to the young lady. She gives up several things if she agrees. Culturally, we have found it more comforting all round if the man demonstrates his strength and iron will. With us, such strength is equated with strength of character."

My iron will had rusted from being out in the Rain of Life too long. I had to admit such an assertive come-on might do wonders for it.

I was very impressed when he told me that, under island custom, she had the final say on whether she wanted to accept the gifts, and that there was to be no yammering, weak-kneed pleading by the man if he were refused. On the other hand, if she did accept the gifts, also in the manner dictated by custom, she was yours from that time forward. Yours to support, feed and clothe, as well as support the children of the relationship.

"But of course Sybil has a career in Florida, and a beach house here. She probably wouldn't be interested."

The Colonel appeared to think a moment. "Don't be so sure. I think you should try. If she accepted your gifts, that would end the career. You would of course take her passport, and buy her beach house. That is the way it works. She is a Jack after all. I think she would go along."

My pulse was decidedly elevated by all this. Colonel Christian was adamant I should make the offer. Alone and lonely, it appealed to me. Without further delay, the Colonel took me to his Land Rover, then over to Kwan Lu's store in Mantilla, where I purchased the obligatory three cases each of tinned beef, taro, and salt fish, plus one cocoanut and a machete. Escorted by him, the security at the complex of beach houses readily passed me through and opened the door of her house,

where the gifts were stacked inside her door, the cocoanut and machete on top. After it was all stacked, we closed the door and headed
back to the Yacht Club and Gene who was going to take me home
after the post-funeral festivities.

"What's the cocoanut and machete for?" I asked the Colonel on
the ride back.

"If she accepts the gifts, she opens the cocoanut and kneels before
you, offering you a drink of its milk. If she rejects them, she hands it
back to you and you remove your gifts. Remember, now, the decision
is strictly hers, but if she accepts, you must immediately become her
master. She must not be allowed to return to Florida, unless you decide to take her there some time on a trip. To not assert your mastery
is a grievous insult to the girl and her family, no matter *what* she says...
once she's accepted your gifts, that is.

"And don't forget to wear your uniform. She is entitled to know
that you are playing a part in our country's welfare as she makes her
decision."

Literally *vibrating* with libido, I saluted the Colonel at the Yacht
Club entrance, then watched as he departed to go on about his busy
day. I had no idea what Sybil would say, but in my present mood I was
willing to give it a shot.

. . . .

"That ain't a bad custom, Boss," Joe spoke up as I waited with him
and Sean, consumed with nerves, on the other side of the Customs
House shortly after noon on Tuesday February 20. "I think I might
do some a' that myself."

"Got someone in mind, Joe?" I asked, somewhat amused, as I struggled to *stop shaking* like a leaf.

"Maybe I do," he replied, actually *reddening* for the first time since
I knew him.

Sean chuckled. "It's that housekeeper fer dat black fella two houses
down from us."

"Norbert Perkins?"

"Yeah."

I searched my memory. "*Tucan?*"

Joe's beet red face told me I was right.

"My God, Joe, she's young enough to be your granddaughter!"

"She's old enough, Boss," Joe snapped. "And besides, the object a' dis quaint little custom is to provide for her." He shot me a disapproving look. "Keep yer eye on the ball, Boss."

Sean dug an elbow into my side, grinning. "Yeah, Boss. Keep yer eye on the ball."

People were starting to come out of the Customs House now. My heart was hammering so hard at times I thought I'd faint. Some five minutes later, I caught sight of her. Sunglasses, yellow miniskirt and matching heels with white sleeveless top looking gorgeous with that deep mocha skin of hers. She was carrying a small suitcase.

"I don't think I can do this," I gasped, turning away.

Sean blocked my path. "Grow up, kid... uh, Boss. You been climbin' walls the last two weeks. Now you're gonna get laid or I'm gonna beat yer brains in... uh... Boss."

Laughing, shaking my head, I turned back around. Sybil caught sight of me and stopped dead. I couldn't see her eyes, but from the rest of her expression it seemed to me as if she were first surprised, then even frightened.

A red flag went up in my brain. But a big smile on her face chased it away as she came toward me. "Hi, Baby! Say! Is that uniform for real?"

"Yes it is, Sybil. I've had quite an interesting two weeks here."

She laughed. "Well, great. You'll have to come over some time and..."

She let out a gasp as I swept her up into my arms. "John! What the hell!"

"Quiet!" I gasped as Sean grabbed her suitcase and I started carrying her to the car. "I'm laying hold of you."

"You're *what*!"

"Laying hold of you. That's what they call it, isn't it?"

"Call *what*? Put me *down*!"

"Not a chance. You're takin' a ride, babe."

"John *stop*! I dunno what you're up to, but...."

"You be quiet or I'll put you over my shoulder."

Protesting all the way, but keeping her voice low, I carried her to the Land Rover where Graham Jack was waiting. Sybil caught sight of him. "Graham! Help me, will you!"

"Get the door, Sean."

"Right, Boss."

"Hi Sis." I wondered what Graham's reaction would be when he saw me 'laying hold' of his sister. I'd told him of course. But he was nearly three hundred pounds of solid gristle and not the quickest of thinkers so I couldn't be sure. So far, it seemed he was taking it like an islander should, at least according to Colonel Christian. According to him, the only people that would interfere would be a rival claimant.

As we closed the last of the distance, with Sybil kicking and protesting all the way, I nervously scanned for rivals. None had appeared yet.

"Graham, dammit! Will you *please*...!"

To my delight, my hulking security man came over and removed both her shoes. "I work for de jumbe Flight Lieutenant, Sis. You not move de feet to de calypso beat or you get de ladder in de nylons."

Sybil was positively livid as I put her in the back seat, then climbed in next to her. Sean got in on the other side. Then with Graham at the wheel and Joe gripping the shotgun, we headed down the road to Mantilla.

"How've you been, Sybil?" I gasped, becoming more and more concerned I was going to get the cocoanut shoved up my ass. But it felt good wrestling with her, and at least so far everything Colonel Christian said about the custom was proving true. Graham was certainly the acid test for that.

We drove on in silence. Sybil in an obvious rage. At one point we encountered a constable directing traffic at the turnoff for Fort Cornwallis.

"Officer!" Sybil called out as we were waved to a stop to allow a jeep full of British soldiers clutching rifles to turn onto the main road.

The constable leaned in.

"This man is kidnapping me!"

I must have been crimson. I know I was feeling really scared. The constable looked at the rank on my uniform and saluted. I returned it. "I'm just laying hold of her," I gasped.

He laughed, then waved us onward. "Ohhhhh!"

On we drove, past the throngs of people hanging out by the side of the road in shantytown. Past the point where the town disappeared and Graham and my other security men tensed. Even Sybil was quiet here. Finally we were passing through Mantilla.

"I got a house up there, Syb." I pointed out the window toward the heights.

She folded her arms across her front and stared straight ahead. I don't know how many times I thought of throwing in the towel, but I kept remembering the Colonel's warning that appearing weak was a grievous insult to both girl and family. I did *not* want to insult a clan with twenty million members like the Jacks. I'd also heard just enough to know that the girl's reaction was sometimes nothing more than a test of that resolve. I was thoroughly confused and way out of my depths, trying to adapt the mindset of another culture to my own fumbling ways, but I kept thinking of Connie... recalling with humiliation how my concepts of fairness had signaled something quite different... and cost me her love and companionship. I'd gone this far... there was no point in stopping now. Everyone so far had reacted exactly the way the Colonel told me they would. This was another world, and if I were going to prosper in it, I was going to have to emulate its ways. *Besides*, I reminded myself, *the custom vested in Sybil the final decision, so there really wasn't much more involved than a momentary delay in her plans.*

"You a pilot?"

Sybil's voice jarred me from my glum thoughts. "Huh?"

"You a pilot?" She tapped my wings with her finger.

"No...just an aircrew member."

"But you're an officer?"

"Yup."

"How'd you manage that?"

"Money."

She burst out laughing. Her attitude seemed to change. It was almost as if she were physically in the process of recalling my application at PCTC... and the $800,000 it mentioned. Maybe she was just realizing she was almost there and could soon hand me the cocoanut and end the whole disagreeable business. I was feeling pretty low by now. Only the thought of twenty million angry Jacks kept me going.

The beach house complex was a left hand turn off the road. Traveling a short way down a packed sand and pebbles trail, a security gate was encountered at which lounged some ten armed men. From here I could see the beach and Sybil's and Serena's houses. Two constables were stationed outside Serena's. They'd been there ever since 'Willett's Last Stand'.

One of the security men leaned in, then waved us through. We drove up to Sybil's and parked. "Can I have my shoes, please?"

"Nope."

"But I don't want to walk on..."

Further talk was interrupted as I again scooped her up and carried her toward the door. Joe went ahead and opened it with the key.

"How did you get the key to my house?" she asked with fury creeping back into her voice.

"Money."

This time there was no laughter. "Wait for me here, men," I called out as I mounted the concrete step above the tile patio and took her inside. Two yellow high heeled shoes came flying in after us, skidding across the floor.

"Welcome to de Maggierock, Sis," I heard Graham call. Then someone pulled the door shut.

I lowered her to her feet and stood there. She looked around, immediately catching sight of the traditional gifts. She searched my eyes. "You mean this?"

"Yes... I mean it."

"Hmmm... well, I have to return to Florida in a week, then maybe I...."

"No Syb," I interrupted. "That's not how it's going to be. Say 'no' if you want, but if you say yes, I'm walkin' outta here with your purse and passport. I'll leave you a five pound note to buy us some dinner, then I'll be back over this evening to eat it... maybe we'll have a swim first."

"I've spent too much time away from Maggierock to allow..."

"The *cocoanut*, Syb... Just say it with the cocoanut... One way or the other." I sat down on the sofa, waiting for her to brain me with it.

For several very disagreeable minutes she stood there. Sometimes she was looking at me, sometimes looking down. Once she walked around, obviously thinking. I pulled a Chesterfield from my pocket and lit up.

"I'm buying this house, you know."

"I'm buying it if you take me up on this. I will be taking care of you." It seemed as if she were testing my knowledge of the parameters of this what I was starting to think was an insane custom, with its bizarre little dance where the people aren't saying what they mean. Of course it wasn't long before I had to admit that the mutual responsibilities dictated by this custom certainly compared it favorably to the American practice of latching on to a girl, taking what you could get away with, then fading into the night.

My mind was starting to wander now. Thinking about what makes people different, and how customs evolve in the face of poverty that highlight obligation and responsibility. I was no longer sure *how* American society thought about sex. It seemed to be up to each individual pair, often, as I well knew, with the two members having very different views. Views that often were only revealed after the couple had gone a ways down the road. Here, at least, it was viewed with responsibility. I wished I'd had something like this to consider back in May of 1970 when I was being such a fool with Terri. Here, at least, people didn't play with the loaded gun until they had reached some kind of understanding about it.

Whack! The sound jarred me from my thoughts. Sybil swung the blade again with the precision of an expert, hacking a chunk out of the cocoanut. She was on her knees. Eyeing me all the while, she handed it up to me. I took a drink. She took a drink. Then we melted together for a rapturous kiss.

. . . .

"The Prime Minster is ready. Go on in."

I must have had a big grin on my face as I rose, acknowledged the secretary, and headed for the door. I had been recalling my first evening and night with Sybil. The candlelight dinner, the midnight swim. I hadn't felt so good in quite a while.

The Prime Minister rose from his desk as I came inside. Dressed very heat-compatibly in gray slacks and white short sleeved shirt open at the collar, he looked as capable as everything I'd heard about him indicated he was. His eyes had an intense, yet confident look. There was barely a gray hair to be seen in his short afro. He was lean, fit and possessed of a ready smile.

"Flight Lieutenant Cassell! I've been looking forward to this meeting. Please have a seat." I took one of the chairs opposite his desk, my eyes suddenly fixed upon a smaller version of the huge mural of Willett's Last Stand that now took up a whole wall where all the ceremonies had been. The one he had was done in oils and now hung behind where he sat.

Seeing my look, he turned and noticed what I was looking at. Flashing a grin, he turned back to me. "Well? What do you think of it?"

I shook my head. " I must say the battle did wonders for Lieutenant Willett's military appearance and bearing. That wasn't exactly how I remembered him that night."

The Prime Minster laughed. "I expect not."

"I thought you handled it brilliantly, sir."

He settled himself back into his chair, registering the compliment with a nod of his head. "These are times that try men's souls, Flight Lieutenant."

"It's encouraging to know our leaders can think on their feet. These rebels seem almost superhuman at times."

"They do indeed," he sighed, gesturing over to a credenza which sat under a window looking out on the gardens and a British Army sandbagged machine gun emplacement covered with an awning. A coffee pot, creamer and sugar sat on the credenza, along with ceramic cups and saucers and real silver spoons. "Can I offer you something?"

"No thank you, sir."

He studied me for a few moments. "I wanted to visit with you before you ever arrived."

"Yes, sir. I remember."

"At the time, my thought was to encourage you to participate in the life of our new nation."

I remembered that the first meeting was to be attended by the Minister of Economy. Today it was just the two of us. I nodded.

"But it is obvious you are ingratiating yourself quite well without any encouragement from me."

"Yes, sir. I've met some very fine people here. It's been easy."

He smiled. "Such as Miss Jack?"

"I knew her in Florida, sir."

"Oh yes." He grew silent again, for a while even looking down at his blotter on which sat a file folder. Then he looked up. "I understand you knew Mister Hayes before your arrival."

"I didn't know he was here. I met him in Europe a few years back, then lost touch."

The Prime Minister made a face I didn't quite know how to read, but it wasn't entirely positive. "I hope..." he began slowly, "you are not letting his... shall we say... somewhat negative attitudes toward my people cloud your judgment."

"I make up my own mind. But I think you should know, sir, Gene had some very inspiring things to say about your people the morning after..." I gestured to the painting.

He looked surprised. "Really?"

"Yessir. It opened with... these people deserve a chance. He said it in a moment of rather intense emotion."

"And it ended with?"

"It ended with... in the morning of our humiliation and discontent, I suddenly have *hope*... his exact words, sir."

The Prime Minister made a *well how about THAT* kind of face. "That's good to know, Flight Lieutenant. You see in the coming struggle our nation is going to have to... well... let's say *expect* certain sacrifices of our people. Sacrifices in attitude... speech... as well as the more obvious." He smiled, as if to throw me off the track of where those cryptic comments obviously led. "Let's just say I suddenly have *hope*," he mimicked my phrasing almost exactly, "for Mister Hayes."

I suppose I could have said something, but this conversation was suddenly off in some thicket where white outsiders were clearly subject to some enhanced scrutiny. He was obviously talking about some sort of restriction on civil liberties, possibly even reaching out to include people's thoughtless off-hand comments. No doubt Gene's constant reference to the denizens of this rock as 'hamburgers' had gotten back to him, and he was not amused. I gazed impassively back at him.

"Anyway, Flight Lieutenant, Colonel Christian is very impressed with you. And you made a mighty shrewd move in your choice of mistresses."

"She's a sweet girl."

"She's a viper."

I was *stunned* by that comment. Obviously Sybil had been under some kind of surveillance while in Florida. I didn't understand what led him to say such a thing, but I gathered it had something to do with her political attitudes, which I had never explored with her, and didn't intend to.

"You didn't know this?" He was eyeing me intently.

"No, sir." I could feel myself turning red.

He eyed me for a few uncomfortable moments, apparently convincing himself I was telling the truth. He smiled once more, releasing the tension in the room. "As I say, young man, a mighty shrewd choice. You are now in an ephemeral yet very concrete way tied in to one of the most powerful clans on the island."

I couldn't begin to decode that last remark, but I got the central point. I shifted in my seat.

"Anyway, Flight Lieutenant, I want you to know that I expect every citizen to do his duty in the coming struggle... each according to his ability."

"Citizen, sir?"

"Yes. As far as I'm concerned, you are one now. But when I push my bill through on April 16, it will become true to everyone and for every purpose. You have heard of my dual citizenship bill?"

"Yessir."

"Rest assured it will be in the Queen's Speech."

I nodded.

"I mentioned ability, young man. I understand you are a decorated lawman."

This meeting was really going in all sorts of unanticipated directions. Apparently I had been the subject of some snooping. I began to suspect this country had a genuinely secret Secret Police, and they were very active. "A special deputy isn't exactly a top of the line lawman, sir. But yes I was... am... one, and yes, I was decorated."

"You were a sergeant."

"Yessir."

"You are, as of this minute, a lawman here too."

I quickly stifled a gasp. Whatever he had in mind, and his come-on was making Gene's drafting of me into the Air Militia look like he was begging me, I was getting *scared*. This man didn't take 'no' for an answer. There would be no juvenile petulance here.

He held up a small white card. "This will be in your dossier at the Special Investigations Bureau. Naturally you cannot carry it or have it anywhere in your possession. But you are as of right now a lieutenant-inspector in that ultra secret agency."

I swallowed. "Whatever you say, sir, but you should know I've had absolutely no training in such things."

He didn't bat an eye. "Yet you brought down one of the most vicious criminals on your Eastern Seaboard with a very resourceful undercover investigation. And when your federal government moved to immunize him, you shot him dead."

Now I did gasp, eyes bulging.

"You will report directly to Home Secretary Cotter. You will be assigned tasks as I need them accomplished. Is that understood?"

My head bobbed up and down like some idiot. I was speechless.

"You will know when you have been assigned because the operative will include the code words 'Roberta Larsen' in your orders... understood?"

Once again I could only nod. I felt as if a ring of steel was around my neck, and this man turned the screw.

The Prime Minister then shrugged, flashing an almost boyish grin, again signaling a release of the tension. "It's just that there are some jobs that need a white man... and as of April 15 we will be locked in a bitter war for survival. See?"

"Yes sir."

"Now..." he reached inside the file folder drawing out a sheaf of papers. "I'm afraid I'm going to have to stage some rather elaborate cover for this meeting. It may interest you to know I've ordered construction of an airstrip running across Highway Two just east of New Britain. The Hayes Construction Company has the job. In a week's time, some twenty Air Militia recruits will be graduating from basic training. You will lead them as a military escort for the construction workers and equipment, across Highway Two to the construction site. You and your troops will remain as security for the construction until it's completed or until ordered home. Do you understand?"

Resisting the urge to pass out, I nodded. "Yes, sir," I barely managed to gasp.

He smiled. "Kind of an elaborate cover... eh?"

That was sure an understatement. "Yes, sir."

He reached over and handed me the papers across the desk. "On Wednesday March 7 you will assume command of your detail at Fort Cornwallis. The rest is up to you. You'll draw your supplies at Militia headquarters, check out your vehicles. Your NCOIC will be a Militia sergeant, not an Air Militia NCO. Understood?"

"Yessir."

"Needless to say, Cassell, it's in everyone's best interest to complete this project as soon as possible. Even if your assignment to it is only elaborate cover for the real purpose of our meeting. Understood?"

"Yessir."

He leaned back in his chair, letting out a heavy sigh. "Very well, then that's all."

I stood up, bringing my arm up in salute. He returned it. I then stumbled, gasping, out of his office.

Tuesday March 6, 1973: at the beach house, Settlement of New Gatwick, Isle of St. Margaret's

Dawn was just breaking when I opened my eyes, finding myself in our bed at the beach house. I glanced over to see Sybil, soundly sleeping naked beside me. Above our bed the Casablanca fan slowly turned.

Outside the louvered, floor to ceiling windows covered with ratwire, turquoise waves turned white with the foam as they pounded the narrow, white sandy beach littered with pebbles and seaweed. Overhead and behind us, brightly colored birds were chattering loudly in the banyan and cocoanut trees that engulfed our house and its satellite cottages.

Since leaving the Prime Minister's office, my life here had become almost unbearable, though physically nothing had changed. I think that even made it more ominous... there was nothing that I could fight or rearrange. *My mind* was doing this to me, based upon some seeds very cleverly planted by a Caribbean politician who, up until I met him, was the focus of considerable admiration on my part.

Now... I just didn't *know*.... That's what made it so awful. He left me with the feeling that my darkest secrets.... my entire life, was known to him. He went out of his way to demonstrate it to me in an off-handed way that only increased my sense of terror. Using Roberta's name as the recognition code... repeating the street rumor that I had killed Jerry Fischer as a fact... talking of my so-called undercover investigation and its target... my rank at the Sheriff's Office... even being aware of the frustrating of the trial by the FBI.... He was somehow aware of *all* of it. *And if he knew all that, what about my fear of Don Clemente and the reason for it?* Skillfully combining recited facts with things left unsaid, he had me in holy terror.

Then there was the fear of future unknowns he had so skillfully planted inside me. What were these 'assignments' going to be? He'd talked about them in the context of the coming death struggle with the Communists, and after a cryptic discourse hinting at the clamping of a dictatorial regime on this island that threatened all sorts of consequences for even the most unintentional behavior. He talked about them in the context of demanding we all make sacrifices... It was obvious these assignments were not going to be innocuous. They were going to *hurt people*, maybe worse.... and I was going to be the pawn that did the job.

On top of that, he had subtly yet with consummate skill managed to drive a wedge between me and the two people here I was closest to. Gene Hayes and Sybil Jack. I wanted desperately to tell them each what he'd told me, but he'd left me so terrified of his Special Investigations Bureau that I was afraid *they* might make some careless comment about what he'd told me that would get back to him, to the life or liberty-threatening detriment of them and me.

I had been so depressed when I left his office that the flower gardens outside actually appeared with the colors washed out. That same depression dogged my steps each day thereafter that I woke up. I was feeling it now. Dragging myself out of bed, I put on some cutoffs, got the electric coffee pot started and went outside.

The sun was coming up in a blaze of bright orange and pale blue. I barely noticed the sharp stones stabbing my feet as I stumbled to the waterline. My eyes went to the left... up the coast to Mantilla. To the right... taking in Serena's beach house with the two constables as sentries. The one standing on the beach side saw me and saluted. I returned it. *The soldiers that come today as an escort will come tomorrow as a firing squad....* The line from *Doctor Zhivago* that had always impressed me now came back as I turned away from the constable and cast my eyes back toward the mountains. My view of them was entirely blocked by our beach house and its setting of shady banyans and fluttering palms. Two new cocoanuts were on the ground, the sure sign that the ground crew hadn't started working yet. Cocoanuts disappeared quickly around here.

Turning back around, I headed for the ocean and charged in, diving under an onrushing turquoise wave. The water was warm. I swam around underneath for a while, then surfaced, flipping over on my back. The Equatorial sun was warming my skin. I closed my eyes letting it warm my face. I had scheduled a meeting with my NCOIC this morning at 1000 at the fort. I'd yet to meet him. I only knew he held the rank of colour sergeant and had served in the British Army, seeing action in the Malay Peninsula. His name was Lionel Thaddeus Matthias Ferdinand. We were to be joined by Winston Dekker, the Hayes Construction Company foreman, and Olaf Torgeson, the project engineer. They were, of course, making the trip too.

My mind wandered to yet another subject of terror... this mission. With all the heavy machinery we were hauling on huge trucks, the journey was estimated to take five days... Five days in the heart of guerilla country. Carrying valuable materials and equipment for a project that Colgate was seeing received daily headline publicity. "The showcase of our nation's coming development," he was quoted as saying. That's what our pitifully slow, lumbering convoy would be carrying across enemy territory... protected by raw recruits commanded by an untested, untrained rookie officer. *The publicity was making the rebels salivate to destroy this convoy and recoup some unjustly lost face on the eve of independence... the garrison being sent along to protect it made that result about as likely as anything could be with the risk of battle attached... WHY? WHY in God's name is Colgate DOING this?* It was almost as if he was *orchestrating* disaster... and for my dough you could drop the 'almost'.

Then, there was that *other* thing....

. . . .

Tuesday February 27, 1973: the Port Albert Yacht Club, Port Albert, Isle of St. Margaret's

Sybil was performing her duties as my mistress outstandingly. If we had started with a clean slate, if I had arrived here totally unattached, I'd have been in seventh heaven. But I *loved* Connie and remained devastated at her loss. I knew it was ridiculous, but something compelled me to go to the Interisland Airbus Seaplane terminal just before noon on the seaplane's next arrival day after the one she said she'd be on... and wasn't.

Her name wasn't on the passenger manifest. Sadly, I dragged myself over to the Yacht Club to drown my sorrows. I was sitting at the bar close to two in the afternoon when a familiar down-home drawl assaulted my ears.

"Hey... uh... aw shit... what's yer name...uh... CASSELL! Yeah! CASSELL!"

I looked up to see the lanky khaki clad figure in the bar's mirror, the olive drab cap on his head, accompanied by Captain Callison and First Officer Kirschner.

I wheeled around to face him. "Thought you were on leave." My look was as evil as I could make it.

"Just until I showed Connie to her grandparents, then I left her there and went on to visit my kids in Georgia."

"*What!?*"

He came over, taking the seat next to me.

"What'll it be?" The white-coated steward asked as I boiled with confusion.

"Make it a sour mash with water on the side." The steward nodded, then went over to the collection of bottles and poured the drink.

Chuck turned back to me. "How is Connie? Say I really appreci-ated..."

"She's not with you?"

The shock in my voice stunned him. He looked at me like I had seven heads. "With *me*? You kiddin'?"

I swallowed, breaking into a sweat. "But *Chuck*! She never came back."

His eyes bulged. "Man... that was all she talked about. What a wonderful understandin' guy you were..."

"But..."

He shook his head. "Man, that gets me *worried*. I dropped her at her grandparents. She told me she was heading back to Barbados after spending the five days with 'em until our next flight."

"Chuck," I gasped. "She never made it."

We went from there to the Royal St. Margaret's Constabulary Building, one of several that formed a ring around The Mahali, as the place where all the Fallen Hero ceremonies had taken place was called.

We sat in cane chairs eyeing the cracked linoleum, as three Casa-blanca fans turned on the ceiling, trying to breathe some life into the dismal [lack of] breeze coming in through the louvered windows looking out on the cinderblock wall sporting the mural of Willet's Last Stand. Fat mothers carrying crying babies seemed to be the main item today. Telling their problems to the large coal-black constable behind the counter. All of them, and both of us, were told to take seats. Meanwhile two other constables pecked away at typewriters sitting at desks behind the counter. A portrait of the Queen was mounted on the far wall.

Chuck and I did little talking. We'd already gone over it several times. Twice at the Yacht Club then on the way over here. He was convinced it was a police problem, I was paralyzed with guilt and fear.

A short while later a cocoa-colored man with short hair in a white flowing shirt open at the collar appeared at the counter through one of the offices beyond and waved us inside. "I'm Inspector Pereya," he intoned, shaking our hands.

We followed him down a stifling corridor, the heat only occasionally mitigated with the blast from an electric fan turning in an office we passed. His office was small, but its louvered windows opened out on the harbor. And he had an oscillating electric fan sitting atop a wooden file cabinet as well, so we were about as comfortable as possible.

The bottom line was, Connie was last seen by Chuck in Puerto Rico, but he remembered she had tickets on Trans-Caribbean for Bridgetown leaving the nineteenth. Inspector Pereya said he'd contact opposite numbers at the airports in San Juan and Bridgetown and go from there. When I mentioned I was commanding the convoy for the big showcase airstrip construction project and was leaving the first week in March, he promised he'd do all he could as quickly as possible, pull in some favors if necessary.

Chuck and I left, Chuck promising to check passenger manifests at every stop of the seaplane and let me know if he heard anything. I believed him. He seemed almost as distraught as I was.

. . . .

A wave smacked me in the face as I turned around to stand up. I wiped at my face, then began splashing my way toward shore. That had been exactly one week ago. Inspector Pereya reported Connie had left Puerto Rico, had arrived in Bridgetown on the nineteenth as scheduled. When the maids opened her room for cleaning on the twentieth, however, the morning of the seaplane's departure, her things were there but she wasn't. She had never checked out either. That was where things stood, only fueling my anxiety and terror, on the eve of this mission that looked for all the world like a scripted military and propaganda disaster in the making.

The ocean wasn't helping. I began walking toward the house, going over in my mind the things I wanted to discuss with Sergeant Ferdinand and the two civilians. All three had expressed concerns that we were sending a lot of valuable equipment accompanied by some highly trained men the island desperately needed on a dangerous mission protected by the military equivalent of cub scouts. They didn't have to tell me. Today, one of my sadder duties was to report the results of my efforts to enrich the mix a little... efforts that had ended in failure.

I had first gone to Gene. The Convair had been fixed by those company mechanics, and they had spent several days teaching the recruits some of their secrets. The idea I had brought up to him was for him to do some scouting for us in the Convair. That way we would at least have some advance warning if there were guerilla bands closing on us. He didn't even answer my proposal, chewing me out instead for taking *his* recruits on what was clearly the other Militia's job. It didn't seem to matter I agreed with him, or that my orders came from the Prime Minister. All the pressure of the last couple weeks had turned him into a raving maniac. He'd held himself together with the thought that at least he was about to get twenty better trained mechanics than he'd ever had before, when *I* had stolen them away from him, likely to get slaughtered in a job that riflemen were best suited for in the first place. He threw me out of his office.

I next went to Colonel Christian. He smiled and shook his head. "The PM tasked you with that job, Flight Lieutenant."

"I know, sir, but I was thinking... suppose you were to schedule... say... jungle maneuvers, which just happened to be in the same spot as where my lumbering convoy is traveling. That way, we'd have a greatly enhanced force to deal with any attack."

"What? All the way to New Britain?"

"Well... yes, sir... that's where we're headed."

He let out a patronizing sigh. "Sounds suspiciously like the Hayes 'conquest in pieces' theory."

"It's no theory, sir, it's where..."

"I have a whole highly populated area to defend here, Flight Lieutenant. I can't have my best troops off in the deserted heartlands with independence looming so close."

"But..."

"And besides, for your plan to really work, we'd have to keep having these... maneuvers... as you call them, until the airstrip is built." He shook his head. "No.. I cannot spare the men."

I was close to the house now, reeling with the failure to get help for my convoy, when I began to hear the sounds of thuds and grunts up ahead. I ran around the house. Not fifty feet away, practically in our front yard, three men were beating up one. All were black, none were wearing uniforms. Hurriedly, I retreated back toward the house, picked up the bush knife we kept in our shed at the side, and ran back, yelling at the top of my lungs.

Seeing me waving the bush knife charging toward them, the three men took off, leaving their victim collapsed in the sand. I went over to him. He was lean and muscular, wearing a white shirt with the sleeves rolled up and black dress slacks. He was bleeding profusely from a cut on the forehead.

I looked up toward the highway where the security people were always lounging around gripping rifles.... no one in sight. I looked toward Serena's house. Neither constable was in view.

"Hey buddy, we better stop that bleeding." I helped him to his feet, then threw his arm across my shoulder and walked him back toward our house.

Taking him into the kitchen, I got a clean cloth and began cleaning the wound in the sink.

"Ohhh... thanks, *mgeni rafiki*... thought I was a goner there."

I took some ice from the refrigerator and had him hold it over the cut while I went to our bathroom and got the first aid kit. Coming back out, I tore open the gauze pack in my teeth, then pressed it against the cut.

"Here... You hold on to that." He did.

I then got the adhesive tape and put some over the gauze. "You better lie down on the couch for a few minutes... till you're sure you're all right."

He nodded weakly, then stumbled over to the sofa and lay down, closing his eyes. "You took a mistress?"

"Yes... how did you know?"

He reached over with a muscular forearm lined with veins and pointed in the general direction of the gifts, still stacked by the door. I laughed.

"Adopting our customs, eh?"

"I plan to be here a while... figure I should."

He nodded, his other hand still clamped against the bandage, his eyes still closed.

"Want some coffee?"

At that point Sybil came in dressed in a teeshirt. She looked over at the man on the couch, then at me. "Being a good Samaritan, eh *mume*?"

"Get outta here dressed like that," I scolded. "That's for me only."

She giggled, grabbing at the corners of the teeshirt and putting on a mock-curtsey. "*Ndiyo mwenyeji!*"

I swung at her, aiming for her rear, but she lurched forward and ran out of the room still giggling.

The man on the couch smiled, even as he kept the bandage clamped to his forehead, blocking a view of his face. "That's the ticket, *mgeni rafiki*, keep her in her place."

It was a good forty-five minutes before the man felt well enough to sit up. When he did, opening his eyes, it was all I could do to keep from gasping. I managed though. "Well, *mgeni rafiki*, I am in your debt."

"Nuthin' to it, brother."

He came over, shaking my hand. "I must go now. Take care."

"Thanks... you too."

When he closed the door, I collapsed onto the couch, practically in a faint. *It was the man in the poster... hanging on the wall where those people kidnaped me and held me for the ransom. The one with the eyes burning with hate.*

Tomorrow would begin what in Island patois was termed *yetu safari a hatari*... our perilous journey. As I made preparations to leave for my meeting at the fort, it still hadn't occurred to me to link what had happened to Connie with the bizarre things happening to me. I was too preoccupied with the coming mission, and was an emotional basket case besides. Time would no doubt help me get a grip on things once more... but time was growing so desperately short.

Chapter Seven

YETU SAFARI A HATARI

Wednesday March 7, 1973: outside the Main Gate along Highway One, the British Military Reservation, Fort Cornwallis, Port Albert, Isle of St. Margaret's

"Tennnnch HUT!" Colour Sergeant Ferdinand bellowed as my twenty recruits, arrayed in four ranks of five, snapped to attention as I strode to the front of the formation. Ferdinand popped off a dazzling parade ground salute. "Detail all present SIR!"

"Very well." I returned the salute, then faced the men. They looked *scared*. I *was* scared, but seeing them so distressed gave me the courage to hide mine.

With the exception of Ferdinand, who wore the khaki Militia combat uniform, we were all in our blue Air Militia coveralls, garrison caps on our heads, blue British style helmets hanging from the side of our packs. I wore my sidearm, field glasses draped around my neck, they had rifles slung over their shoulders.

"You've successfully completed your basic training... had an additional week of anti-guerilla training given by the only Army in the world that ever beat a Communist guerilla foe. Your Sergeant served in that very war."

Out of my peripheral vision I could see Ferdinand swell with pride, also obviously impressed that I knew such stuff.

"I'd say that gives us a tremendous advantage." I took a breath. "You men all joined up in the wake of Willett's Last Stand... As some of you know, I was in the force that reached them immediately after they had driven off the vastly superior Communist force. I saw the fierce pride... the fire in their eyes. I *know* what the men of St. Margaret's can do upon the field of battle. You too, are the men of St. Margaret's. Now let's get on about this mission and get that airstrip built. The Prime Minister estimates the air link over Highway Two will save countless lives and prevent millions of pounds crop loss. Our task is an important one... and some of the best fighters in the world... men of Maggierock... *you*... have been chosen to do it. Let's get about it!"

I did a crisp left face toward Ferdinand. "Turn out the detail, Sergeant, prepare to move out."

"Yes SIR!" Another parade ground salute followed. I then strode crisply off toward the Command Land Rover, sitting second in line, hoping I wasn't going to piss in my pants, as Ferdinand bellowed the necessary orders behind me.

All had been made ready, beginning at 0500. Our convoy stretched out for nearly a mile. Most of that was taken up by the huge trucks hauling all sorts of heavy construction equipment. I knew nothing about tactics, of course, and so had chosen my vehicles emulating as much as possible what I remembered of Major Ben Khedda's tactics in the insurrection of 1971. Instead of one troop carrier, I chose five additional Land Rovers, to be occupied by four armed men in each, and scattered throughout the convoy. Walkie-talkies were in each, along with illuminating and signal flares. Win Dekker and Ollie Torgeson rode in a Hayes Construction pickup third in line. Their skilled workers, about twenty all tolled, rode in six other Hayes company vehicles, including the large transports. They were intending to hire the grunts of the project from among the heavily unemployed population of New Britain.

Pausing at the Hayes supervisory truck, I confirmed all their equipment was loaded and queued, then continued on. My assigned driver, a corporal, was already at the wheel. Sybil sat fuming in short shorts and an equally skimpy top in back. I climbed in next to her.

"*Must* I go, *mume?*" she pleaded. I announced it last night for the first time. She was livid, but I was unmoved.

"Yes, you must. Now no more about it, Syb." There were many reasons, I guess, most of them visceral. The one nearest my consciousness was the memory of... that man... practically in our front yard. *What was he doing there? Who was he coming to see? Why were all ten security men suddenly absent, so that he was able to come in unnoticed?* I had absolutely no answers for any of this at the moment, I simply reacted. Sybil was coming with me.

"*Ndiyo mwenyeji.*" She faced front, her arms crossed, her head down.

"Bloody good speech, Flight Lieutenant." Ferdinand's eyes said he really meant it. He hauled his stocky bulk into the front seat.

"Get us under way, Colour Sergeant."

"Very good, sir." He picked up the walkie-talkie and gave the orders. Some twenty engines of all sizes could be heard starting up.

I glanced at my watch... it was 0730. The skies were the color of lead and a stiff breeze was blowing in from the harbor. Throughout my time here, I wondered where all the foul weather I'd read and heard so much about was. All the days had been sunny and hot. This looked like the payback.

Thompson Ritter had organized a heavy turnout of 'the citizens of St. Margaret's' to see the convoy off. Actually, these were bureaucrats who owed their jobs to the Our Destiny Party. Their ranks were augmented by the family members they were ordered to bring along. Of course with all the unemployment, there were plenty of others drawn by the crowd and their own curiosity. They broke into wild cheers as we began moving down Highway One. Many threw ginger blossoms and palm fronds at the vehicles as they lumbered by. It was, I was told, the traditional 'blessing' for those embarking on a long, perilous journey, which also according to island tradition, was just about *any* journey.

Constables at intervals stood facing the crowd, positioning themselves between them and our vehicles. They were obviously looking for sappers. Frankly, I didn't expect any... not here... not today. In my increasingly suspicious, paranoid mind, I believed the whole point of this, no matter how little it made sense, was for the white *jumbe* to bungle the whole project somewhere in the trackless jungle. A successful attack now would reflect on other people. Once we passed the foothills where the radio station and airstrip were, the responsibility would fall on me. I knew it didn't make any sense, but that's what I believed.

Children ran along side of the vehicles as we were continually flanked by cheering bureaucrats throwing ginger blossoms. As we turned onto Highway Two I glanced toward the harbor, just in time to watch the seaplane take off. Once more my thoughts of Connie and the very suspicious fate that had befallen her paraded across my mind. The thought she might be lonely and frightened somewhere preyed on my psyche. I vowed to visit Inspector Pereya the very day I got back.

I tapped the sergeant on the shoulder. "Sir?"

"Tell those lookouts to scan the crowd goddam it." I was referring to the men in the lead Land Rover. They all appeared to be talking and laughing. In my orders to the detail, I stressed that *every* military member of the convoy was to scan the road and horizon beyond the entire time we were moving.

"Yessir!" Ferdinand got on the walkie-talkie and barked the order. The men were still young enough and rookie enough that they immediately turned their attention to the road.

"I don't see what good I'm doing here," Sybil grumbled.

I put a hand on her delicious bare mocha thigh nearest me. "The *jumbe* Flight Lieutenant always takes his woman with him." It was just a hunch, but from somewhere in my brain came the idea that the men would be impressed seeing their commander enjoying the prerequisites of power. I didn't know what I was doing militarily... frankly didn't know what I was doing period, but I was trying all the smoke and mirrors my feeble brain was suggesting.

"*Ndiyo mwenyeji!*" She crossed her legs, squeezing the lucky hand now with both.

At the same time, I had the strongest feeling that the presence of a Jack would retard rather than encourage Communist aggression. Of course I knew they were well aware of her presence. As I looked into the faces of the ginger-throwing bureaucrats, who were now beginning to thin out as the head of our convoy reached Government

Plaza, I figured that at least twenty percent of them would be flooding Crenshaw and Peebles with the news, if they weren't there watching themselves.

Our Command Land Rover was passing the airstrip. An order had recently been circulated by the Defence Minister Gentry that military formations passing the site of Willett's Last Stand were required to do an 'eyes right' with the formation leader saluting. I tapped Ferdinand on the shoulder, indicating the turnoff with my head. He got on the walkie-talkie.

"Detail! In yer seats! Tennnnch HUT! Eyeeeees RIGHT!" He and I dutifully saluted, a grin stealing over my face.

I well realized that this historical sleight of hand was for the good of the country. I also knew, or at least suspected, that irreverence toward this historical resource was likely one of the 'attitudes' that Colgate had hinted would have to be sacrificed. I figured those who had been there, such as myself, would be watched closest of all... and of course I had already made a wry comment in the Prime Minister's presence. In any case, I wasn't looking to add to my problems and so struggled against displaying the grin.

"Annnnnd FRONT! As you were." He put down the walkie talkie. I dropped the salute.

It was a story I'd heard from Colonel Christian that did it. Apparently, shortly after the unveiling of the Wall of Heroes (the mural) at The Mahali, Mrs. Willet and her two young children approached, to the snapping of photos and a reverent silence. Fortunately the child's voice didn't carry, and only Colonel Christian heard it besides the widow, but their eight year old daughter was said to have scanned the mural, all up and down the wall, going past the heroic figure on one knee with the pistol pointed and said... "where's daddy?"

Supposedly Mrs. Willett pointed to the heroic figure. "Right there."

The child is said to have replied "that's not daddy... that's a soldier." The Colonel only shared the story with people who had been there. It was a big hit.

The heavens opened. From behind us to the east, torrential rains swept across the convoy in waves, driven by a fierce wind. Visibility, even with the wipers going was very poor, but fortunately we were on a tame stretch of the highway.

Highway Two owed its existence to the taro industry. Built by the British first in 1962, it was exclusively designed for heavy, overloaded taro trucks. As a result, the primary goal became gradual road grade before any kind of speed or efficiency. As a result, the road was over two hundred miles long, its turns often so narrow and challenging that they could only be taken in the lowest gear. Even in a fast automobile, the trip took almost two days. We were looking at five, if lucky... and if this storm persisted, closer to eight or ten.

Part of the challenge was due to the fact that, unlike in Morocco, the mountains we were navigating weren't a single solid structure going almost unerringly in one direction. They more resembled the rows of spikes on the back of a stegosaurus. Deep gorges separated the rows of peaks. Thus we would climb up for several hours, then down for several hours, then back up again. I figured we did *not* want to stop for the night in one of these valleys, exposing ourselves to deadly fire from the heights, but then that's where the water was, so what was a body to do?

There were two exceptions along our route, the first one potentially attainable this first day. Lake George, it was called. Located on a high plateau of the first major row of mountains to the east, it was the headwaters for some incredible waterfalls that seemed to fall from heaven itself. I, of course, had never seen this, but that's what I was told. Militarily sound and compatible with human needs, this was the goal I set for us. Up until that time, we changed drivers and had 'latrine' breaks every three hours, but otherwise kept on going. Were the weather to prevent us from making the required distance, however, we would have to stop somewhere it was reasonably safe to chock the heavy vehicles. You didn't drive overloaded trucks at night on Highway Two.

As it turned out, we didn't make Lake George, but at 1702 came upon a gradual upward slope with a meadow stretching in both directions for a hundred yards or so. "I think this is gonna be our best bet today," I told Ferdinand.

He studied the terrain out the windscreen. Lake George was still way off in the distance and we had a little more than an hour of daylight left. He nodded, then gave the order to halt and fall out. We all put on ponchos against the ferocious downpour. The Hayes people chocked their trucks while we posted sentries and began work on our tents. Ferdinand, Sybil, Dekker, Torgeson and I ate together in my tent, our meal lit by a camp lantern hanging from its crossbar. The menu was American Army C-rations someone had sold the Militia's Quartermaster-General a while back.

One line of sentries ran along the highway side of the vehicles, the second at the perimeter of the meadow. The length of our convoy was a major disadvantage here. Half our outfit was required for sentry duty at a time. After our little executive group congratulated itself on having survived the first day, everyone scattered to their tents while Ferdinand and I divided up the 'OD' duties fifty-fifty. It was muddy and rainy. I found clomping around in two inches of mire in total darkness and a pouring wind-driven rain at 0300 less than fun, but at least we knew that it rained on the Communists as well, and the fury of the storm was making it hard for the sentries to fall asleep.

We passed Lake George at 1000 the second day and headed down. The rain had stopped, but its swollen headwaters now made for some spectacular waterfalls. Several hours later we were down in a valley when a red flair exploded beyond our vehicle, to the accompaniment of popping noises. Due to the length of the convoy, we hit on the signal flare idea, so that the rear could let the front know they were under attack.

Getting Sybil down on the floor of the vehicle, Ferdinand, the corporal and I jumped out. We could see muzzle flashes from behind and way above us. "They're too far away to do real harm, Flight Lieutenant," Ferdinand observed. "They've got no heavy stuff either."

Perhaps to the puzzlement of the men, we simply kept on going.

Such was not to be our good fortune later in the afternoon. Climbing an impossible length of switchback, mortar shells began falling from the heights ahead of us. I halted the convoy and we jumped out and took cover. Thus far, they hadn't found their range. The shells were exploding ahead and to the left. The problem was, other than know-ing they were ahead and above us, we had no idea where.

I scanned the switchback towering above us. "They've gotta be up there somewhere," I gasped. "Where?"

Ferdinand clamped the field glasses to his face. He thought he saw a wisp of smoke at one point. He marked it for me on our map.

"Can we reach that with our grenade launchers?" I'd asked.

An explosion to our rear was followed by a bloodcurdling shriek. Our heads whiplashed in that direction. "MEDIC!" One of our guys was yelling.

It looked like one of the Hayes pickups was on fire. "No," Ferdinand replied. "I'd say we'd need to be up about..." he marked the location on our map. It amounted to about five more miles of switchback.

For a couple frustrating, eternal minutes, the two of us studied the heights with our field glasses. "I hate to keep us here... we're sitting ducks while they hone their aim."

"Until we know what's up there, sir, that's all we *can* do," Ferdinand counseled.

"You mean..."

"Yes... that may be exactly what they want us to do... go charging forward in desperation... straight into an ambush."

I was feeling claustrophobic... helpless as I once more clamped the glasses to my face. There was no sign of anything else up there, but then that would be exactly the way a clever ambush would *have* to look.

"Okay," I gasped at last. "There's only one thing we can do. I'll take two men in the lead Land Rover and haul ass up there with launchers. We'll try to knock out that emplacement, and learn if there's anything else besides."

"You stay here, Flight Lieutenant," Ferdinand shouted above the din of another explosion. "I'll take it."

I thought a moment. The answer, the solution to this was all too clear. Heart pounding I turned to him. "We need you a lot more than we need me."

His deep cocoa face screwed itself into a frown.

"Besides," I went on, "these guys are goin' for our construction stuff. They won't waste valuable shells on one lousy military vehicle." I managed a grin. "That job is likely safer."

Ferdinand laughed. "Good luck, sir."

"Some kinda diversion would help... give us a chance to make that exposed dash. We got anything that would reach?"

Ferdinand thought a moment. "We have two Brownings and a thirty caliber... maybe if we spread 'em out and get 'em going all at once it might keep 'em busy."

"Set it up."

"Right, sir." Head down, Ferdinand bolted from behind our vehicle toward the rear. Two more shells landed, exploding toward the rear of the convoy, but off to the right.

After what seemed a very long time, the colour sergeant returned. "All right, sir," he puffed. "I've got the three men spread out... waiting for word on the walkie-talkie. You make your move and we'll open up."

I nodded, quickly holstering my revolver. "Watch Sybil, huh?"

He clamped a hand on my shoulder.

Running, head down, the short distance to the point vehicle, I arrived just as another blast hit the highway behind me, sending up showers of gravel and making a big crater. "They're gettin' closer," one of the men gasped.

"Anyone here an expert with the grenade launcher?"

A one-striper raised his hand. "Okay," I pointed to one of the others. "You drive. You other two, fall back to the Command vehicle."

I didn't have to repeat *that* order. Pulling out the launcher and a metal box of grenades, the rest of us climbed into the lead Land Rover. I looked back toward Ferdinand and signaled we were ready. Within seconds, loud bursts of gunfire sounded behind us.

"Okay driver... Move out!"

The Land Rover shot forward as the three of us held our breath. Up to the first turn... hauling ass along the straightaway to the second. All the while the sounds of our 'diversion' filled the air.

Our driver continued moving like a bat out of hell up the switchback. I was sitting in the front seat next to him. His eyes were wide, no doubt like mine. More rounds flew overhead, exploding ever farther below as we flew up the side of the mountain. "Dey not be seein' us, jumbe Flight Lieutenant," the driver gasped.

I had my glasses clamped to my face as we flew around the next corner. I could see wisps of smoke now. I vividly remembered at the date grove, the time those four men were headed for our jeep gunners with grenades. I was the only one of the three of us behind the jeep who could see them. "Yeah," I gasped, lowering the glasses as our journey around the switchback no longer permitted visibility in the right direction. "That adrenalin gets you mighty focused. The rain didn't hurt either. We're not kicking up dust."

He nodded, wide-eyed as he gripped the wheel, his foot jammed to the floor. We continued on another round of switchback. "Okay," I gasped. "We should be okay right about there." I pointed to a spot along the next straightaway with terrain level enough to park the Land Rover and get into position with the launchers. The underbrush was thick and tall. It was about the best break we were going to get.

"Yessir, jumbe Flight Lieutenant." The driver jammed on the brakes, bringing us to a stop a ways off the road in a stand of what looked like wild banana. Grabbing grenades and launcher, our driver taking his rifle, the three of us poured out of the Land Rover.

"This way!" I kept my voice low as I flung myself into the underbrush, my men right behind.

"What's your name?" I puffed, chest heaving, to the one-striper as I unholstered the revolver and we dived behind some rocks some fifteen yards further up the hill.

"Prentice, sir."

"Got a shot Prentice?" He squinted up and ahead. I handed him the glasses.

"No." He looked around. "Maybe over there." He pointed to a spot twenty yards or so further on. It was further up the hill and closer to the position, but more to the side.

"Suits me. Let's go!" The three of us scrambled up the rocks to the place Prentice had indicated, then flung ourselves into the mud, catching our breath.

"I got it, jumbe Flight Lieutenant!" Prentice gasped. For a while we listened as Prentice loaded a grenade into the launcher. We could hear explosions now as more rounds were fired. It appeared from the sounds that they had two mortars.

I clamped a hand on his shoulder. "Okay... take 'em when ready."

Leading Aircraftsman Prentice, squeezed off the launcher's trigger. We buried our heads in the mud once more as a tremendous white flash exploded above us. We could hear our men cheering below.

For a while we looked and listened, hearts pounding. Nothing. "Put another one in there for good measure, Prentice." He did. This time we heard a shriek accompanying the white flash.

I swallowed. I *hated* that sound. Its agony was so vivid. "Okay," I gasped, "let's move out." We scrambled to our feet, running and sometimes rolling down the hill back toward our Land Rover. Our driver gunned the engine, backed up, and flew back down the switchback toward the main body of the convoy.

"You're one hell of a driver," I gasped at one point.

"I drive de taxi in Port Albert," he gasped, wide-eyed. "I join de Air Militia because I a good mechanic. And dey have me put de face in de mud."

"Yeah, man. All of us." I patted him on the back.

The convoy sent up a cheer as we returned, full of mud, to our positions. It turned out one of the Hayes trucks, a pick-up, was blown up. Two of their people and one of ours were hurt. The remains of the truck was pushed off the mountain, the three men were transferred to the lead ambulance, and we set off once more.

We camped that night almost at a peak. There was no rain, the air seeming almost cool as the many jungle birds chattered at the rapidly setting sun.

"This is the best we're gonna do, Sir." Ferdinand had counseled when we reached the spot.

I looked at my watch. At the time we had almost an hour of solid daylight left. The jungle took over only seventy feet or so from the road, allowing excellent cover for a would-be ambush party, so I had my doubts. I pointed this out, but he was adamant. I nodded and he gave the necessary orders on the walkie-talkie.

We were in high spirits as we made our camp. Flight Corporal Preston, my driver, told me that our victory over the mortar emplacement 'won me great face' with the men. He went on to say that I was the first Air Militia officer to actually win a victory in the field. I, of course, knew that my own contribution to the victory had been negligible. But I also knew all about 'vibes' and reputations and quickly understood that both these elusive phenomena were working for me among the troops as a result of this afternoon's skirmish. It was a *very* fortunate break and I was grateful.

I stood at the hood of our Land Rover by the last light of day, scratching out citations for Leading Aircraftsman Tino Prentice and Aircraftsman Emil 'Curly' Howard. Sybil stood next to me, looking gorgeous and smoking a cigarette. All around the jungle fringe were frangipani, hibiscus, bird of paradise and philodendron. Ferdinand ambled by, noticing what I was doing.

"I admire that, sir," he began. "You know it won't get 'em squat though."

I looked sadly into his face. "There's damned little else we can try to do for 'em, Colour Sergeant."

Ferdinand nodded, then we watched the sun sink behind the row of mountains beyond. "Our goal for tomorrow," I sighed wistfully.

"Begging the Flight Lieutenant's pardon, sir..."

I turned to look at him. Up until this moment his look had always been one I would describe as 'distant' or 'military'. Now, his face wore a secretive look, as if he were on the verge of sharing some deep confidence. It instinctively made me uneasy.

"What do they have against you, sir?"

The question hit me like a bucket of cold water. I looked down, but not before he'd caught enough of my expression to crack a grim smile.

"Go in the tent, Syb. I'll join you shortly." I already knew Sybil was being watched by this mysterious and frightening SIB of Colgate's. He had already told me quite clearly he considered her a potential traitor. I didn't want her to hear any of this shit. This was *my* burden... she had enough of her own.

Her reaction was a surprise. It was as if she immediately sensed danger. I still hadn't told her about Colgate's remarks, but then I hadn't let her out of my sight since that day. When I was called away to Port Albert or the fort, I'd leave her with Sean. "*Ndiyo mwenyeji.*" With a brief nod at Ferdinand, she departed.

"I don't want you talking this stuff in front of her, Colour Sergeant." I wasn't about to tell him why. But in the atmosphere of suspicion and paranoia which had enveloped me since that awful day with Colgate, I wasn't going to take any chances.

"Sorry, sir."

I nodded. "You were saying?"

He reached in the pocket of his blouse for a pack of Player's. He offered me one, then lit up. "You know we're both being sacrificed, don't you?"

I looked away, taking a drag on the cigarette.

"I know why I was tapped for this assignment..." He took a long drag and exhaled. "But I can't figure you."

I faced back at him. "I think it's just that I don't know what I'm doing." I regretted the remark the instant it was out of my mouth, but there was no taking it back. *Why should I trust Ferdinand? Didn't Colgate tell me himself that a Militia NCO would be my second in command? He is very likely an SIB agent.* "I think they're saving their best officers for the death struggle on the east coast." It wasn't a *great* comeback, but it did render my last remark ambiguous. That just *might* help if they gave me a chance to explain.

"Maybe... but then this project is supposedly so important, I just wonder..."

Whatever Ferdinand was up to, I needed to end it before he tricked me into saying something I'd regret. "The PM is playing a difficult and deadly game, Colour Sergeant... Factors within factors within factors." I shrugged. "He's a very capable man."

Ferdinand snapped to attention and saluted. "Pardon the liberty, sir."

I returned the salute. "It's okay, Colour Sergeant. I'm very grateful you're here."

Whatever candor he'd been anticipating was clearly gone now. "Will that be all, sir? I'd best turn out the night guards."

I managed a smile. "Yes... that's all." He nodded, then walked away.

I finished the citations with a flashlight held under my chin, then walked, consumed with worry, the short distance to my tent. Sybil was waiting. She put her arms on my shoulders and kissed me. "Oh *mume*, is there anything I can do to help?"

I took her by the arm and we went outside, then walked along the row of vehicles toward the rear. "*Salamu, jumbe* Flight Lieutenant." I turned to see a small knot of my men smoking up against one of the Hayes tractor trailers. They stiffened as I looked in their direction. All were smiling, the one who had hailed me saluting besides.

I returned the salute, and the smiles. "The men respect you, *mume*," Sybil whispered as we continued along our way.

"I'll bet," I replied, squeezing her hand. "They probably wonder how I rated such a lovely woman."

Sybil seemed to smile to the depths of her soul. "It's because of today.... with the mortars."

"Oh... well, Prentice and Howard made that happen." We reached the ambulance, its interior lit up by a camp lantern. I helped Sybil up, then crawled in. One of our medics was changing a dressing.

"How are they doing, medic?"

He shrugged. "It could have been worse, jumbe Flight Lieutenant. They will all recover."

I nodded, then talked a while with each, especially the man in my command. I didn't have to tell Sybil the way she could help me. She stayed behind, holding their hands and talking with them for over an hour.

"*Salamu, jumbe* Flight Lieutenant." One of my sentries addressed me as I made the solitary journey back to the tent. I smiled in his direction, returning the greeting. I was finding myself getting attached to these guys. *They were all depending on me...* It made the riddle of this mission all the more difficult to bear.

I took the first OD watch, later crawling into the sleeping bag next to Sybil to the calling of several night birds and thousands of crickets.

. . . .

As we mustered for breakfast, I learned one of our sentries had been garroted to death. His post was along the fringe of jungle, the furthest to the west. The news hit all of us hard. The nearest sentries to him hadn't heard a thing past Colour Sergeant Ferdinand's periodic walk-by. Rumors were starting to circulate about superhuman enemies. That was nothing, however, to what occurred shortly before we shoved off.

I was looking at Ferdinand's submitted 'morning report' as the men were in the final stages of striking the tents when a terrifying amplified voice split the air.

"Soldiers of the *mgeni jumbe* Cassell...!"

At the hearing of the loud strange voice in the middle of nowhere, everyone dived to the ground. A second or two later, we were looking at one another, wide-eyed. Out of the corner of my eye I saw Ferdinand crawling toward me.

"You have made it to the third day! Most of you, that is! A demonic laugh split the air. "Poor Aircraftsman Locke! Took up arms against *Watu yetu* one time too many! He will now be on sentry duty in Hell for eternity!" [another demonic laugh].

We were all really spooked. I wanted to do something but so far was paralyzed. The voice had named our man who'd been strangled to death. Many of the men were looking at me, terrified. The two Hayes supervisors were also crawling in my direction, terrified. Ferdinand was almost there.

"Leading Aircraftsman Prentice! Aircraftsman Howard! You are next! But not in the way you are thinking as you cower in fear of *Watu yetu*! We know where you live! We know the loved ones who live with you! The Vengeance Squad will be paying a visit to them before you ever get to see the brothels of New Britain!" [more demonic laughter].

I shot an anxious glance at the point vehicle. Both men looked as if they'd been harpooned.

"Aircraftsman Crewe! Newleigh! Drayton! You will be next! You collaborated with the *mgeni jumbe* Cassell and the others!"

Ferdinand reached me, looking as pale as a dark-skinned man was capable. "Bad luck this, Flight Lieutenant."

"Those last three... what did they do?"

"The diversion you ordered."

"Ohhh." I swallowed hard.

"You think we don't know? You think the eyes of *Watu yetu* do not peer into your evil camp? Your evil mission?" [more demonic laughter]

"What kind of equipment is this, Colour Sergeant?" I fought to control the panic in my voice. The men were watching. I never made more of an effort to look unafraid, yet I was *terrified*.

"No idea, sir."

"I mean.... how far way is the person talking... the speakers?"

"No idea."

I looked at him angrily. The entire time I knew him, Ferdinand always seemed to know everything. When he didn't he managed to act like he did. I figured that was the standard issue senior NCO persona around young, green officers. Now, however, when even a little confidence would have gone a very long way, he was apparently helpless. I was too busy to think, but my instinctive reaction told me something was very wrong with this picture. "All right, God damn it, get me the radio frequency-finder... now!" This was a piece of primitive survival equipment common for military formations here. It indicated on a true bearing compass the direction from which a transmission from an open mike was beamed. People lost in the trackless jungle could follow it to rescue.

"Right sir!" He stood up, but ran down the line of vehicles doubled over.

"You gotta stop this, Flight Lieutenant!" It was the anxious voice of Win Dekker. He and Torgeson had now reached me from their pickup.

"Got any ideas?" I looked back at him with frustration as I hauled myself above the Land Rover's hood and clamped the field glasses to my face, scanning off in the jungle beginning only seventy feet beyond our line of vehicles.

"Don't try to look for us *mgeni jumbe* Cassell!"

I lowered the glasses, heart hammering.

"You and your kind have been declared redundant by history! Your men know of the all-seeing eyes of *Watu yetu*! You don't! Your culture has long since lost its soul! As of April 15 you and your kind will be gone from our island forever!"

Ferdinand came back, handing me the device. I switched it on... nothing. I turned to him. "What does this mean?"

His eyes widened.

"Oh come on, Colour Sergeant!" I snapped in a frustrated frightened rage. "Don't *you* give me this supernatural shit. When does this thing fail to get a reading?"

Ferdinand just shook his head. Fortunately, Dekker was there. His outfit used that equipment too. "It means there's no radio transmission, Flight Lieutenant"

"So they're close by? It's some kind of PA system?"

He nodded.

"Well *fuck* this shit!" I stood up before Sybil could stop me and bolted to the point vehicle. "Get that launcher and a grenade, Prentice. Lob one into that thicket."

He just stared back at me, frightened beyond belief.

I opened the door of the Land Rover and got it myself, along with the box of grenades. I fumbled around trying to figure how to load it while the amplified voice now began a chant that made my blood run cold. I'd heard it that one other time, when I had been as terrified as Prentice. At the time though, I had no ear for island patois. But a lot had changed.

NLP! NLP! NLP!

Hodari Watu yetu!

Hodari nchi yetu!

We be free!

The grenade finally went in with a click. I pointed the launcher up over the first row of trees, then pulled the trigger. The grenade flew upward as the chant continued. It seemed to have an eerie effect on the men, as if maggots were crawling up their skin. The grenade exploded... the chant continued.

I reached for another, swung the launcher to the left and pulled the trigger. "Good bye doomed soldiers of the *mgeni jumbe*! Until next time... if you are alive to hear!" More demonic laughter filled the air as the second grenade exploded... then silence.

For a while we held our positions, waiting for a possible attack. None came. After a minute or so, I hauled myself to my feet, headed back toward the Command Land Rover, wiping beads of sweat from my face with my sleeve. "All right, Colour Sergeant! Move 'em out!"

Ferdinand and the rest of them stood up. "Right! You heard the Flight Lieutenant! Stow the last of the gear and mount up!"

No one moved. Ferdinand bellowed some more... no result. He turned and fixed me with a look of helplessness that didn't fit an NCO in *any* army, much less the British.

I moved further down the line of vehicles, nothing in particular in mind. All I knew was that the warmth and magic of last night was completely gone from my soldiers' eyes. They looked hostile... fearful.

"You better do somethin' about this," Dekker whispered from behind.

I spun around. "No fuckin' shit. Just what do *you* suggest?" I was angry now... that very special kind of anger Fate sometimes sends to rescue someone from paralyzing fear.

By way of answer, Dekker drew his handgun.

"Put that goddam thing away!" I snapped.

"These jablonies ain't gonna give you much more time to reassert control here Flight Lieutenant," he sneered back.

I pointed angrily toward his holster and he put the weapon back, crossing his arms and staring at me with contempt. I could hear Sybil's light tread coming up behind me. Again I turned. "Get back to our vehicle, *mke*... I'll be along shortly."

It seemed her smile would split her face when she heard the island patois name for 'wife' spoken. She'd been calling me 'husband' since our second day. I didn't like it, thought it was adding a layer of dishonesty, perhaps even hopes that would only be frustrated were Connie to be found, and otherwise ruin what was a very candid custom. But these were unusual circumstances. I *needed* her warmth, that closeness she seemed so anxious to share. I realized I owed her for this... we'd have to do some reshuffling of our relationship... if either of us survived that is. According to Colonel Christian, once you beheld one another as 'mume' and 'mke', you were all but engaged. It had been okay as long as I hadn't fallen in with it too. In my desperation and terror, though, I had.

"My place is with you *mume*," she whispered, moving up beside me, staring defiantly back at the soldiers who were staring defiantly back at me.

I gave her hand a squeeze. "Well just let me do the talking, *mke*... 'less you want a hellacious spanking.... if we come out of this, that is."

I heard her softly giggling as I now faced the bulk of my men. The Hayes skilled labor were grouped around them too. I took a deep breath, shaking like a leaf. "All right, men... now listen. You are not soldiers of the *mgeni jumbe* Cassell. You are soldiers of the Prime Minister... the nation.... the *Watu* or 'people' that Communist who was talking over a loudspeaker kept trying to claim for himself."

I turned and gestured back to the Command vehicle, noticing that Prentice, Howard and the other two from the point vehicle had gathered 'round as well. "Back there, I have the Prime Minister's written orders... I'll be glad to show you if you want."

The men's faces remained blank… hostile. I took a large gulp of air. "On April fifteen, the British are leaving. This is something you've fought for now since Ghana's independence in 1959... Do you know Ghana has been ruling itself that long now? They didn't have to *sell out* their freedom to Communists! To exchange one kind of slavery for another. And neither do you.

"Don't you *realize* that fighting people like that voice trying to scare you was what Willett's Last Stand was all about?

"Don't you understand that..."

"How did that voice *know* which of us did what yesterday, jumbe Flight Lieutenant?" One of the special weapons crew interrupted.

A dead silence descended over all of us. That was the $64,000 Question all right. *I needed to think that one through and this was sure no atmosphere to do it in… Yet I had no choice. Actually it was a riddle in*

two parts. The first was relatively easy, but I had to get them both or we'd
likely all be dead by sundown... me at the hands of the men... them as they
fled, a disorganized mob, back toward Port Albert, to be picked off by sniper
fire like ducks in a shooting gallery. "What's your name, Airman?"

"Crewe, sir."

"Oh yes. Well, there's only one way that could have happened. It's
why Aircraftsman Locke was killed...."

I clearly had their attention now.

"Someone in this camp went out... through that jungle... and contacted the rebels. Someone who, masquerading as a brother, knew all
of it. Hell, anybody here knew all of it."

"But... everyone is here, *jumbe* Flight Lieutenant."

"I know. He's back with us."

"But how could that be, sir?" another airman spoke up. "How would
the traitor know to find the rebels in the dead of night?"

It was a damned good question... and it focused me. Suddenly I
knew the answer, and it nearly made me vomit. All the rest of it could
have been anyone in the camp... just as I said. But there were two little
pieces of information, the most important having just been pointed
out to me by this airman, that made the traitor stand out like a sore
thumb. I stumbled backward with the nausea of the revelation. All
eyes were riveted on me now.

I turned around, my knees threatening to collapse beneath me at
any moment. "Colour Sergeant?"

"Sir!"

The blood rushed to my eyes, turning the world red as I drew my
revolver and fired three shots at pointblank range. As it was, the first
one still went wild. The other two embedded in his chest. He toppled
backward on to the ground.

For a few moments a ghastly silence descended over our little
group. I first remember turning my gaze upward from Ferdinand's
lifeless body, looking into the terrified eyes of Torgeson, Sybil and
Dekker. Then beyond to Prentice and Howard.

Fighting the urge to faint, I turned back around. My men were
wide-eyed as they studied me. I holstered the revolver, then looked

down, then back at them again. Even the ever present jungle birds were silent. Swallowing hard, I took a deep breath.

"It's like this, men...," I began haltingly as the medic knelt over Ferdinand's body taking readings. "Last evening, Colour Sergeant Ferdinand insisted we stop here. As you may remember, we had plenty of daylight left to find a spot not so hemmed in by the jungle.

"He was just too experienced to make such a move," I looked them in the eye. "But I was too inexperienced to see it. But of course this had been arranged in advance. He *had* to stop here. The heavy underbrush so close to our bivouac gave him a chance to make quick contact with the Communists... to give them the information that made it look as if a supernatural force were peering with evil eyes into our very midst. Quick contact... say... in the course of a walk-by."

The other men who were sentries with Locke were nodding.

"I think that's why Aircraftsman Locke didn't sing out when he was attacked. He thought it was his superior noncommissioned officer... and it was. But it was also a Communist in our midst."

The ghastly silence continued, but the men were looking at one another, exchanging nods.

"Flight Corporal Preston!" I bellowed.

"Sir!" My driver came up behind me, standing at my side.

"Flight Corporal Preston, you are now the ranking military member here. I am surrendering my sidearm to you." I unsnapped the holster and removed the revolver once more, handing it to the astonished and not a little nervous junior NCO.

I turned back to the men. "All right, men, here's what I want you to do. I want you to assemble together and take a vote. Whether to remove me from command. I realize I face a court-martial for what I just did, but I happen to believe that this was orchestrated so that we would never come out of this alive.... any of us. Therefore I had to act immediately. Now... if you vote to remove me, Flight Corporal Preston will assume command and I will travel as your prisoner. If you vote to keep me on, however, I will re-assume command and there will be no more said about this until I contact my superiors when we arrive at New Britain. I now ask you to retire and make your decision."

"Sir?" Another of the young airmen spoke up.

"Yes."

"What do you think is going to happen, now that Colour Sergeant Ferdinand is dead... to us I mean... on this trip?" Several of the Hayes civilians and my soldiers were nodding at his question.

"I'll tell you. I think the Communists are very short-handed at the moment. What have we faced so far? Some desultory rifle fire from the heights that barely reached us and a deadly assault, but by only two mortars. I think they're massing for some independence show-down somewhere else. I think that's why they needed a plant among us. So that their meager resources would have maximum effect. This little thing today was supposed to make you desert... and would have ended the mission. It was all very cleverly done."

There were several nods. The birds were starting to sing again.

"From here on out, whatever limited resources they have will have to stalk us from the jungle. If they try to shadow us from the road we will see them. They are going to have a very difficult time mounting a serious military challenge to us from here on out.

"Of course, whoever will be in command, myself or Flight Corporal Preston, will make sure we stay alert."

There were smiles here and there from the men, all closely listening.

"For as you know, a bullet fired from a small, weak force kills you just as dead. But I think the death of the traitor will throw our pursuers into darkness. They will wait for inside information that will never come."

Several nods were seen among the men.

"Any more questions?"

The soldiers looked back and forth at one another, several shaking their heads 'no' at me. "Very well then, retire and make your decision."

The men in blue now formed a large circle and began talking. I stumbled, shaking, back toward the Command vehicle. Dekker and Torgeson were staring at me as I went by. "This is one goddam stupid move you're making, sonny," Dekker snarled.

Sybil was gripping my arm tightly. I don't think any of us knew how to take what had happened. I now wished... desperately wished... I hadn't been so hasty. I believed I was right, but twenty-five years of living, much of the last of it on the Road, was more than enough to convince me that 'rightness' was but a make-weight in the mix. I had shot a black man... on the eve of independence... with Colgate already constantly being called a 'jumbe-lover' for attempting to marshal as much help for his poverty-stricken country as possible, no matter what color the people offering it were.

"Maybe," I replied, voice quavering. "But you better bloody well believe the men hold the fate of all of us in their hands at this moment." I gestured toward his holster. "You'd a' maybe gotten two before they canceled your ticket. At least this way I'm getting them to assume responsibility for what they have the power to do anyway."

"Yeah but..."

"And who knows... I might survive."

He couldn't help but sympathize. Maybe at some level he also figured I was right. He nodded, and Sybil and I continued on our way.

Colgate... I gotta get back to him...rethink this whole business...when my head clears. Who assigned Ferdinand? Colgate had told me it would be a regular Militia NCO at the beginning. Was it him? I think at that point I was quite resigned to death by firing squad, provided I lived through this crisis, of course.

Sybil and I sat in the grass on the shady side of the truck. At one point I looked at her, consumed with... *something!* "Sorry I brought you along on this, *mke.*"

By way of reply, she wrapped her hands around my arm, leaning against me.

A while later, I glanced at my watch. It was 0820. Much time was being consumed, but it wasn't wasted. The Communists had us by the throat that morning. At least it was possible with this delay the mission would continue. I think that's why I wasn't catching any flak from Dekker.

"*Jumbe* Flight Lieutenant."

I looked up, some fifteen minutes later, into the blinding sun. Flight Corporal Preston was silhouetted above me, his arm out, handing me my revolver, butt first. He seemed very nervous.

"The men want you to stay on, *jumbe* Flight Lieutenant. They say you have... uh...well...that you have..."

"Have what, Preston?"

"Well... uh... *balls*, sir."

As Sybil, Preston and myself burst into relieved laughter, I hauled myself to my feet, holstering the revolver. "Get us under way, Preston."

"Yessir!" He saluted, I returned it, then he went off, bellowing the orders.

"Howard!" I called to the erstwhile Port Albert taxi driver as he made his way with Prentice and the others back to the point vehicle.

"Sir?"

"You're my new driver."

"Yessir, *jumbe* Flight Lieutenant!"

Within twenty minutes, we were under way once more. Back on the mission that was never supposed to make it. Preston lacked Ferdinand's crispness and polish, but he was non-Communist and wanted us to survive. With the pitifully few resources I'd been given for this job, that counted for plenty.

Friday March 30, 1973: the Hayes Construction Company site, just east of the Settlement of New Britain, Isle of St. Margaret's

Win Dekker studied the newly completed airstrip with satisfaction as he stood beside me, now dressed in my khakis, just outside the company trailer. Standing with us was the Mayor of New Britain, Peter Cressey, Flight Corporal Preston and taro planters Philip Doran and Donald Autrey. A short ways down, the eighteen surviving members of my detail stood, in three ranks of six, also in khakis, their rifles slung over their shoulders. The additional death was caused by sniper fire during the building of the airstrip. The Communist harassment here had been as weak as on Highway Two, though I shortly figured out why. The Communists *wanted* the airstrip built. If they were able to seize the western half of the country, it was the ticket in for supplies and troops from their Cuban ally.

I glanced at my watch. It was 1030. The Convair, flown by Group Captain Hayes and carrying Prime Minister Colgate and several of his Ministers, was due any minute. This was the Big Day, the opening of the airstrip.

. . . .

We had first sighted the unfinished, rotting wood buildings of New Britain's low, shabby skyline the evening of March 13. The men, quite understandably, rejoiced. For me, the occasion was a mixed blessing. My Amended Morning Report for the fateful day of March 9 read as follows:

MORNING REPORT SUPPLEMENT

Manpower status [here indicate present, absent but accounted for, awol, etc.]

Absent from duty: hospital---- one A/C Harrett
------------death: two C/S Ferdinand; A/C Locke
Present: commanding officer, NCOIC-rplacement, 18 EM

[here indicate unusual circumstances of complement]

C/S Ferdinand summarily executed for high treason by
Commanding Officer. A/C Locke strangled while
on sentry duty. F/Cpl Preston new NCOIC----
A/C Howard new CO aide.

Submitted by: *John W. Cassell, F/Lt, RSMAM 9 Mar 73*
Approved by: *John W. Cassell, F/Lt, RSMAM 9 Mar 73*

Ministry of Defence Form MR 1-SUPP use only when amendment required

We were met upon our arrival by Captain Toussaint DeFreeze, Commander of New Britain's Militia platoon. As we were of equal rank, there was a minimum of ceremony. As Flight Corporal Preston busied the men with construction of their tent city in a field of weeds standing between the New Britain Settlement limits and the construction site, Sybil and I were shown to a house standing on stilts in the same field. Made of the same unfinished, rotting wood that seemed to characterize all of New Britain's structures except for the rusted corrugated metal of the warehouses belonging to the two planters and the hundreds of shanties, it promised to be a challenging battle with termites and other vermin.

While Sybil set to work hiring servants, I scratched out my transmittal memo to accompany our morning reports, calling Group Captain Hayes' attention specifically to the one showing the killing of Colour Sergeant Ferdinand. I added a brief explanation of my reasons, then was escorted by the captain to the Ministry of Posts and Telegraphs office, where I was assured it would be put on the next taro convoy, said to be leaving in a week.

That unhappy chore out of the way, I returned 'home' to attend a briefing for the men on the various sentry posts we would use and procedures we would follow in guarding the construction project. After that, I indicated I would buy several pigs for a big celebratory barbeque if the men would be willing to set up the traditional underground island ovens necessary to cook them. Then they were given passes to hit the bars and brothels of this steamy, miserable settlement.

Flight Corporal Preston spent the next several days attending Aldermens' Court on behalf of the several members of our outfit arrested that first night for fighting. Once past that headache, the construction began and Sybil and I set seriously to work on the barbeque. It was a huge success, and very much appreciated by the men, many of whom now had 'steady dates' from the brothels to bring along.

Construction was completed in the three calendar weeks remaining in March, despite day long downpours one out of every three days we were here. Other than the blessed boost for my morale provided by Sybil, the days passed with me commanding and climbing walls, climbing walls and commanding. Our routine was varied several times by having all our men move inside with us when the tent city was buried in a sea of mud, once when I was summoned to meet with the two planters, who had heard of me and wanted to meet me in person and finally meeting with the Mayor, the Militia captain and the Hayes people to go over plans for today's ceremonial opening.

Throughout this time, I remained plagued with thoughts of Connie, concerned over when the guerillas would drop the other shoe and worried over my impending court-martial. Nobody had mentioned word one about it to me, and the one mail pouch that arrived with an Autrey return trip from Port Albert contained no military mail at all except for our orders to be ready for today's formal opening ceremony. On the positive side were the close relationship I'd formed with the men and Sybil's devoted attention.

. . . .

"There it is!" Preston exclaimed, pointing up in the sky.

We all watched as the Convair made a low pass over the airstrip, then straightened out and came in for a landing. Often with laughter, Preston and the men had worked with me for many hours toward those final evenings, teaching me the formal moves for the ceremony. Now was to be the payoff. I think I was more nervous about this than at any time on the mission.

The Convair taxied to stop opposite our formation, its giant props turning. Then the red beacons topside and below cut out as Gene shut the engines down. My eyes met Gene's once as he sat in the cockpit those final moments. His expression was impassive. The hatchway swung open and a gangway of sorts lowered.

"PreSENNNT HARMS!" I bellowed as the Prime Minister appeared at the hatchway to the cheers of the bureaucrats and the hundreds of unemployed turned out for this ceremony.

Colgate came down the steps, shaking hands with the Mayor, the planters, the Militia captain, Win Dekker and Olaf Torgeson. When he turned in my direction, he had a very odd look on his face. The nearest I could interpret it was puzzlement... that I was still around. But maybe I was projecting.

He was followed in short order by Defence Minister Gentry and Minister of Posts and Telegraphs Ritter. Then came Gene followed by the newly created, in the wake of Willett's Last Stand, First Subaltern Felonious Burns, looking very good in his khakis with one and a half stripes on each epaulet. At the last came three aides of the Prime Minister.

The handshaking over, I turned to my men. "OrDERRRRP HARMS!"

The rifles made an agreeable slapping noise as they went to the tarmac. My guys were still rookie enough to remember this stuff from basic training.

"Open ranks...HARCH! Dress right... DRESS! ReadYYP FRONT! Present HARMS!" All followed in short order. I did an about turn facing the Prime Minister, bringing my arm up in salute.

"Detail ready for inspection, sir!"

He returned the salute, expressionless in his sunglasses. Then, accompanied by Gentry and Hayes, looking very impressive in his khakis with the four stripes on his epaulets and all his Vietnam ribbons, badges and patches, the inspection took place and was concluded.

As I put my men at ease, Hayes came and stood beside me as the PM mounted a short platform whereon was placed a podium and microphone.

"Worshipful Lord Mayor of New Britain... Militiamen and people of St. Margaret's...."

"You're being ordered home," Hayes whispered to me as Colgate's speech droned in the background.

"Not surprised."

He managed a half smile. "You'll be in the right hand seat."

"Yessir."

"You're gonna do some flying."

"Yessir. Any word on my court-martial?"

"We'll talk later... Well done, Cassell. It floored these bastards you somehow came out of this. They think you're some kinda' miracle worker."

I managed a half smile.

"Not the fuck-up with incredible luck I know you to be."

I managed a full smile. "When do my men get pulled outta here?"

"They're *my* men Cassell."

"Yes, your fucking majesty."

"You and I turn right around and pick them up."

"That's good news."

"Thus inspired... we will continue to move forward into the sunny uplands of progress... progress for all our people! Our Destiny as one... independent and united... *together!*"

Enthusiastic applause broke out for Colgate as he acknowledged the crowd, then descended from the podium. As he went into a huddle with the Mayor and his Ministers, I ran to our shack and got Sybil packing. Then, after an emotional good-bye Syb and I both shared with the men, me repeating Gene's words of their imminent pullout to their bright smiles, we departed, leaving them under the command of Subaltern Burns. Back to the East Coast, and the fate that awaited me as the killer of a non-commissioned officer. *Yetu safari a hatari* was now over... mine about to begin.

Chapter Eight

THE *JUMBE* FLIGHT LIEUTENANT'S COURT-MARTIAL

Tuesday April 3, 1973... twelve days from Independence: the Headquarters of the Ministry of Defence, Government Plaza, Port Albert, Isle of St. Margaret's

My fourth day back from New Britain saw me in Defence Minister Gentry's outer office in the Transfer of Power building. My summons to appear had arrived yesterday, served personally by a Ministry of Defence staff member. Gene was ordered to appear as well. The summons said I should bring a lawyer, "solicitor" was what they were called here. I passed on the opportunity. I knew what I did and why. I didn't need to pay hundreds of pounds just to have someone say it for me.

"What's supposed to happen today, sir?" I asked him as the secretary returned to her typing after directing us to be seated. Gene had told me from now on I needed to be formal when we were in public.

"Dunno, Flight Lieutenant. You're causin' them a whole bunch a' problems, havin' to invent a court-martial system... and on the eve a' independence too."

"You mean they never had one before this?"

"Not for an offense punishable by firing squad."

I swallowed nervously at the reminder. Since coming back, aside of finding Joe sublimely happy with Tucan, who seemed sublimely happy with him, and aside of a smile or two cracked because of Sean, who was now seriously thinking of 'laying hold' of someone himself, life had yielded little but disturbing or at least curious happenings.

. . . .

My first full day back, a Saturday, found me once more at the RSMC building, huddling with Inspector Pereya. He invited me into his office then pulled a file folder from the ancient wooden cabinet. Lighting a cigarette, he sat down at his desk and opened it, scanning a few pages.

A few minutes later, he looked up. "Sorry, Flight Lieutenant. I just needed to refresh my memory."

I nodded.

"We appear to be at a dead end. About the only break we've had, if you want to call it that, comes from a signal I got from a friend of mine with the authorities in Bridgetown."

I leaned forward expectantly.

"A night clerk at Mrs. McElroy's hotel remembers two people loitering in the lobby. He distinctly remembers this was *before* Mrs. McElroy came back and reclaimed her key for the evening."

"On the nineteenth?"

"Yes." He shook his head. "Unfortunately, he doesn't remember if they were there or not after she returned."

"Any kind of a description?"

"Both black... the male very huge...very dark... mean-looking." The inspector chuckled. "This was why he didn't say anything to them."

"And the other one?"

"A woman... young, attractive. Mid-complexioned."

"That's all?"

"Yes."

"What about her grandparents in Puerto Rico? Has anybody contacted them... asking for money? Anything?"

"Well I don't know, but I can ask in San Juan." He looked at me sympathetically. "We've really very little to go on. Would there be anyone else who might be the recipient of a ransom note?"

I searched my memory with frustration. "Connie's folks lived in a Newark, New Jersey tenement slum. I'm not even sure if they're still alive, or if she even sees them. She was chief of staff for a powerful member of the New Jersey Assembly but has had no contact with him for at least a year."

We lapsed into a frustrated silence. The description of that male hadn't been lost on me, but he took me back in Florida, and there was no woman involved in that whole horrible episode. I'd seen lots of very large islanders since I'd been here so his incredible size was no longer as unique in my mind as it once had been.

"They *are* checking hospitals, the morgue, stuff like that, aren't they, Inspector?"

"Yes... I transmitted the photo you gave me the very first day."

For the moment, I was out of ideas. Feeling powerless... a gnawing sense that Connie was alive somewhere living in terror. It brought tears to my eyes to think I was being no help.

"We'll keep checking, Flight Lieutenant," Pereya spoke sympathetically. "Unfortunately, in this part of the world, Puerto Rican women, even young, pretty ones, aren't a rarity."

My head was down. "I know." Finally I hauled myself to my feet, shaking his hand. "Well thanks, Inspector, I appreciate all you're doing."

"I'll keep at it, Flight Lieutenant. I'll let you know. Feel free to check back if you think it's been too long."

I certainly couldn't ask for better help than that. Stumbling outside, I went into the General Post Office, a couple doors down. There was a letter in my box from 'Doby & Loller, Attorneys-at-Law' in Miami Beach. For a moment I blanked, but then remembered I'd sent my Miami Beach next-door neighbor Marty Loller a bank draft for £200 to make the best deal he could to end Sybil's lease at her apartment building, and also to collect any money due for her job at PCTC. I tore open the envelope, finding a check inside for most of it back, and a single sheet of memo paper.

FROM THE DESK OF MARTIN LOLLER, Esq.

☺

Hey Bro!

Man, you're still crazy as a bedbug for my dough! Your friend Sybil Jack never leased that apartment. It's held for

Business purposes by a shady group called Caribbean Horizons Ltd. And her old boss doesn't owe her anything. She left not long after you did! Think she was missing you or something?

So I'm returning all but $52.19, four hours, plus tax of my investigator's time finding this shit out!

Be well, man

Marty

That wasn't Sybil's apartment? Or she's connected with Caribbean Horizons? Whoever they are. Had it been PCTC it would've made sense. *But she left right after us? But didn't arrive here until the twentieth?* It was all too much to contemplate on an empty stomach... or maybe it was an empty head. I thought of confronting Sybil with what she was doing running around Florida those two weeks, but she wasn't mine then... I had no right to know. Besides, after the way she came through for me on the mission, I had no thought of cross-examining her about her past. She was young, she was beautiful... things happen. I stuffed Marty's memo in my pocket.

The break of dawn on the morning of my appointment at the Defence Ministry found me walking the beach. Sybil and I were spending nearly all our time here, rather than my big house with all the servants on Mantilla Heights. The turquoise waves were putting on their usual scenic show slamming against the shore. The sun was coming up a bright red ball this morning. *Red sky at morning... Sailor take warning! Good thing I'm not in the water militia, or whatever they'd call it... if they had one.*

I had to admit, with all hell about to break loose over me with this court-martial, that things hadn't been nearly as bad as I figured. Colonel Christian had been right not to send his troops along with me. The Communists barely put up a show of hassling us. I guessed that meant that Colgate's sending valuable equipment and skilled labor with the military equivalent of cub scouts hadn't been sinister either. The man simply knew his country, and its enemies. There still remained the question of Ferdinand though. *Who had assigned him to me? Why?* After all, the mission would have been just as much a fail- ure if I hadn't shot him. He had the men on the verge of desertion.

I know why I was tapped for this mission... but I can't figure you... His words at our camp that night came back to me. What was he trying to tell me? Maybe it was nothing more than an effort to get me de- moralized. Maybe it was, as I suspected at the time, that he was one of Colgate's secret police and was trying to get incriminating comments from me on tape.

Tape! Get comments on tape! A twinge of fear hit me right between the eyes. If he had a wire, it would still be on his dead body. Maybe it would also contain the evidence that would convincingly show wheth- er I was right in killing him or not. *Oh God! If he is secret police they'll know he had the wire and were likely retrieving it... likely had retrieved it from the moment my morning reports hit Gentry's desk.* I shook violently as I contemplated the tape recorder played to a packed courtroom, showing him the loyal agent of his prime minister.

"Hey *mume!*" Sybil was wearing a yellow bikini. She had decided to join me.

I went over to her and, ignoring her laughing protests, picked her up and carried her into the ocean. She had a comb stuck in her afro, but I fortunately pulled it out and heaved it up onto the beach, then got down to serious business forgetting all my cares and woes.

....

The intercom buzzed on the secretary's desk. She picked up the receiver. "Yes, Minister? . . . Yes, sir." She replaced the receiver on its cradle. "Go in gentlemen."

We did. Defence Minister Gentry was seated at his desk, wearing a gray suit and tie in this heat. He was squat, not much more than five nine or so as I remembered, dark complected with a fringe of gray black hair. He wore gold-metal framed glasses and his wide mouth and large eyes seemed perennially fixed in an expression that trans- mitted anger. I didn't like him, not from the first moment I met him... at the ceremonies commemorating Willett's Last Stand.

In contrast, the man seated at a chair in front of the desk was tall, lean, had a full head of gray hair worn in a short afro and black, heavy framed glasses. He looked like an intellectual, but he wasn't. He was the Attorney General, Granville Browne.

Gene and I approached the desk, our officers' caps stuck under our left arms. We brought our right arms up in salute almost in unison. Gentry looked impassively at Gene, then with hostility at me before returning the salute. "You two know our Attorney General?"

"Yessir," we both answered as the man inclined a pleasant smile at us.

"All right then... siddown." We did.

"Did you engage a solicitor, Flight Lieutenant?"

"No sir."

Gentry shot a hostile look at Browne, then an even more hostile look at me. "Why not?"

"I know what I did, sir... and why. I don't need..."

"There's a lot more to a criminal proceeding than that, Flight Lieutenant," Browne interjected. "You really should have a lawyer acting on your behalf."

"With all respect, sir... I'm gonna tell my story to the panel of officers. They will buy it or not."

Gentry let out an irritated sigh as he leaned back in his chair. Casting a quick look at Browne, he nodded, then faced me. "Well, in that case, I'm appointing Capacious Cargo as your solicitor..."

"*Who?*"

"Capacious Cargo, a Member of the Bar here. He will be there to advise you in case you get smart and seek professional help."

"Yessir." I wondered what a man named Capacious Cargo could possibly look like... be like.

"Solicitor General Solon Grimes has the brief for the Crown," Browne now spoke, looking at me. "Your prosecutor... I will be the Court's legal advisor."

"I see."

Gentry reached across the desk and handed me a list. "This is your Court." I looked at the list. Lieutenant Colonel David Moreland, commanding Fedderson Company of the Militia, was the President. Captain Harold Newgate, Captain Addis Moseley, Lieutenant Conner Dellums and Subaltern Felonious Burns, Jr. were the members.

Burns was the only member of the Air Militia on the panel, but then besides Gene and me, he was the only Air Militia officer.

"Any objections to this panel, tell me now." He inclined his head toward Gene. "Ask your commanding officer any questions you desire."

I showed Gene the list. He shrugged, then nodded.

"No sir, I have no objections."

Gentry looked at Browne in a way that signaled he'd put something over on me, but not knowing the man, I might have been wrong. "Now," he continued, "oh *Christ*! We need a goddam court reporter!" Angrily, he picked up his intercom and barked an order. A few minutes later an attractive black woman came in, carrying the familiar machine. She set it down in front of yet another chair in the Minister's office and sat down, hands poised over the keys.

After giving the date, time and place, and announcing that this was a preliminary proceeding in the court-martial of Flight Lieutenant John Cassell, Gentry now had me repeat my comments about hiring a solicitor, recited the appointment of Capacious Cargo to advise me, and again solicited the fact that, after consulting with my commanding officer, I had no objections to the Court after he once more read their names.

"You ever been in the military Flight Lieutenant?"

"No sir."

"You ever been a criminal defendant before?"

"No sir."

"All right." Gentry furtively looked down at a piece of paper on his desk. "Maybe it's just as well because we have our own procedure here. Your trial will be on the ninth of April. Sentencing will be on April 20th."

"Why wait so long?" I asked, skipping over the obvious first question.

"Because until the fifteenth, only the British can sentence to death. Your crime carries the death penalty, so," he spread his arms with a shy smile on his face, "we're just going to wait them out... see?"

"Yes, sir. That's pretty clever."

"Thank you, young man." He didn't seem to get it, but no matter how many zingers I threw at him, it was my life on the line here, so I could hardly say I bested him in any duel of wits.

He then read the charge. "Capital murder of a non-commissioned officer whilst on a mission under arms. Penalty... death by firing squad. Specification... that on the ninth day of March, Year of Our Lord 1973, the aforesaid Flight Lieutenant Cassell, whilst on a mission under arms and having neither justification nor excuse, willfully, feloniously, and with malice aforethought didst shoot Colour Sergeant Lionel T. M. Ferdinand three times pointblank into the chest, thereupon causing his death." Gentry looked up, feeling very satisfied with the tenor of his words. "Do you agree or disagree, Flight Lieutenant?"

"Twice, sir."

"What?"

"Twice... the first shot went wild."

Browne's head was down, shaking back and forth. Gentry looked like he'd just picked up three aces after drawing four to an ace in five card draw. "That's your only problem with the charges?"

"Wait a minute, Mort," Browne interjected with some heat in his voice. "The man has no solicitor. Enter a plea of not guilty."

Gentry looked like a spanked juvenile delinquent. "Oh... all right. You plead not guilty."

"You really should make it a point to work closely with your solicitor, young man," Browne now cautioned me. "You obviously are unschooled in what is happening here."

"Yessir. The people who tried to kill me before never used all these fancy words."

Gene looked down, suppressing laughter. Browne looked shocked. Gentry looked insulted. The court reporter *did* laugh.

Gentry shortly regained his cool. "All right. I declare the Court-Martial convened. So we go right into the giving of evidence on Monday. No preliminary fooling around. Independence Day is less than a week later and we all have things to do."

Browne winced, probably at the thought the young lady was working her fingers all through this. "Yes," I replied, "I have some things to do too."

Gentry shot me a *you've gotta be kidding* glance. The proceeding, if that's what it was, shortly ended. Gene walked me over to my Land Rover where Joe and Graham were waiting.

"How'd I do, your fucking majesty?"

Gene spit out a short laugh. "I was just a grunt, John. But I think that was about the lousiest performance I ever heard of."

"Oh." I turned to him, now deadly serious. "I was right, Gene... I *know* it."

He put an arm on my shoulder. "Maybe so, buddy." He stuck out his hand. "Luck, huh?"

I shook. "You gonna be there?"

"Wouldn't miss it." A final good-bye and he walked back to his Land Rover.

I felt as if I were in a dream... that this nonsense had nothing to do with eighteen terrified young men, ready to desert because of the treason of a Judas amongst them... desertions that would mean no airstrip... and the loss of valuable human and materiel resources at a time the island was going to need them most. *Nope... it had nothing to do with what counted out there that horrible, frightening morning.* If I'd have given it much thought, I'd probably have been enraged these game-playing bureaucrats were now actually thinking they were going to kill me.

Monday April 9, 1973... six days from Independence: the Court-Martial Chambers, Colonial Military Reservation, Fort Cornwallis, Port Albert, Isle of St. Margaret's

Fort Cornwallis was divided into two very unequal parts. The larger was termed the British Military Reservation. The smaller was the Colonial Military Reservation. Here was situate the headquarters of the Militia and Air Militia. Within the Militia Headquarters Building was a special room used for court-martials. That's where the vultures gathered on the Monday just six days before Independence, before the *real* shooting started. It really made me laugh. Six days before they'd be fighting for their lives and they were playing some silly games trying to take mine! Gene told me I had the wrong attitude. But it was my life, God damn it. I felt I was entitled.

I awoke the morning of the Big Day feeling listless and *angry*. Dully watching out our ratwired, louvered windows as the turquoise waves slammed into the shore, I recalled that an impossible mission had been handed me, along with twenty men in no condition by virtue of either training or experience to accomplish it. Yet we *had* accomplished it. In the face of terror and uncertainty we had come through, delivered the goods, got the airstrip built. My reward: court-martialed, facing the death penalty.

Sybil stirred beside me. She tried wrestling, smooching, and all her other magic tricks but nothing was working today. Finally dragging me out for a morning swim, she at least got my blood flowing. We headed for the fort with Graham, Joe, Tucan and Sean at 0730. She wore a hot pink minidress, 'to improve my morale', as she put it. I wore my khakis.

Entering the courtroom, it was like none I'd ever seen. The ground floor area was no wider than three shuffleboard courts placed side by side. It led to a table with several chairs. One level above it was a long table with five throne-like chairs. A heavy curtain was behind that.

To the left of these tables, which were obviously for the Court and its legal advisor, five long rows of benches rose upward like a stadium or a theater. At the top was a wooden pen with a small counter at the front and a chair. This, I was told, was the prisoner's dock. My place. On the other side of these tables were another five rows of long benches. Above it all was a balcony, running around the entire room like a horseshoe, the open end being where the Court's tables were located. We were drawing well. The balcony was already crowded, a good hour before this circus began.

Giving Sybil a quick nervous kiss, and shaking hands with Joe, Tucan, Sean and Graham, I glumly went to the dock and took my place inside. A few moments later, Capacious Cargo, all four hundred pounds of him waddled in. He had met with me the previous night. Six foot four inches tall, almost as wide, though again like so many here it was all solid muscle, he had a shaved head, a coal black complexion and wore pince-nez glasses when reading. "We're gonna put these dipsy-doodles through their paces," he thundered, nearly blowing the walls of our beach house apart with his booming voice. "Reverse discrimination! We'll not stand for this! Unabashed rev..."

"NO!" I finally bellowed, getting him to pay attention to me for the very first time. "I'm gonna do the talking. I'm gonna tell my story."

"You just leave it to me. Reverse discrimination! These dipsy doo..."

"NO!"

Now I found I was sitting way to the back, while Capacious Cargo, in his short white wig and black gown which no doubt was once an undertaker's tent it was so huge, was sitting in the very first row. He was shortly joined by one similarly bewigged and begowned man in the front bench, and some three more carrying piles of books in the bench behind.

Solon Grimes came in next. Dressed the same way, accompanied by the same number of people, also dressed the same way, taking their seats in the same approximate places on the opposite side of the three shuffleboard courts. Then came the Attorney General, the legal advisor, as he put it. He sat at the table below the judges' table, flanked by two similarly dressed people carrying books on either side of him.

I had to laugh. Unlike American courtrooms, the judges here, dressed as they would be in their uniforms, were the only people *not* wearing robes. Other robed people took up positions around the legal advisor and both attorneys. These, I were told, were ushers. They handed around exhibits and whatever else needed handing around. They didn't have wigs... that was how you knew who they were. Directly across from me, also on the top shelf of this bottom level, was another wooden pen, only this one had no chair. This was the witness box. Witnesses had to stand here I was told.

Except for Joe and Sean in the gallery, and later Gene, everyone was black. It was an interesting turn-about to some scenes I'd heard of in American courtrooms. Yet I didn't feel on edge. I'd been here long enough to tell the good guys from the bad guys. And when all eighteen surviving members of my detail came in and took seats in the balcony together shortly before the proceedings started, I felt actually *loved*. They gave me thumbs-up signs, a couple even saluted, despite the military impropriety. Sybil went over to them. They smothered her with kisses. We'd all grown very close. I suddenly didn't feel so *frightened*.

The clock above the curtains said 9:23. The court reporter was down below as well, in front of the legal advisor.

"SILENCE! Be upstanding in Court!" Everyone rose as from behind the curtain, five officers appeared all at once and took seats at the table on the stage.

"All persons privy to the matter of the Court-Martial of Flight Lieutenant John Cassell and the issues to be tried therein between Our Sovereign Lady Elizabeth II and Flight Lieutenant Cassell draw nigh and give attendance. God Save the Queen!"

Whew! That was a mouthful. I had nothing against the Queen and I'd bet she had nothing against me, but that's what the man made it sound like the battle was over. Our unresolved issues. My attitude was turning bitter again.

"Be seated!" One of the ushers called as the last of the members of the Court sat on their thrones. The gallery was totally packed now. I didn't take long to realize that every member of the Air Militia was there to give me support. Now I felt very grateful and loved once more.

The legal advisor next read the charge, then turned and addressed me. "What sayeth you to the charge, Flight Lieutenant? Be ye guilty or not guilty?"

"I sayeth I'm NOT guilty," I replied to snickers from my men and elsewhere in the gallery.

The legal advisor next read the specification, then turned and addressed me. "What sayeth you to the specification, Flight Lieutenant? Be ye guilty or not guilty?"

"I sayeth it was twice... and I'm NOT guilty," I replied to loud laughter.

The legal advisor shot me a dirty look, then turned toward the Court. "The prisoner sayeth he be not guilty of both charge and specification. You are convened as a court-martial by the Right Honourable Morton Gentry, Her Majesty's Minister of Defence of the Isle of St. Margaret's... and it be your charge, having heard the evidence, to find whether he be guilty... or not." The legal advisor turned to me, shook his head with exasperation, then sat down.

Lieutenant Colonel Moreland cleared his throat. "Very well. Mister Solicitor General, you appear for the Crown?"

"I do, Lord President."

"Mister Cargo, you appear for the prisoner?"

"I do, Lord President."

"He do *not*, Mister... uh... Lord President!" I retorted. "I doeth... uh... does... uh... *do*!" All the funny English was making me confused. I hadn't meant to say it that way, but that's how it came out, to fulsome laughter.

"Just a moment, Flight Lieutenant!" the Lieutenant Colonel snapped. "You..."

He stopped dead as the Attorney General stood up and whispered something to him as the other four officers leaned in to hear.

"Oh..." he faced me once more. "I see. Very well, Flight Lieutenant. But Mister Cargo is here to advise you and I urge you to take advantage of that advice."

"How, sir?"

He looked at me, puzzled. "How *what*?"

"How can I get his advice, sir? He's way down there... and I'm way up here."

More laughter convulsed the spectators.

The Colonel was puzzled by that problem, as were the other four officers. "Oh, I don't know... just raise your hand or something."

More laughter washed over the room.

"Thank you, sir."

The President nodded. "Right. Care to begin Mister Solicitor General?"

"Call Aircraftsman Crewe!"

His name was repeated about five times as the young man stood up and moved to the steps, then came down and walked over to the witness box.

"Take the Testament in your right hand, and read from the card," an usher boomed.

"Uh… I swear by Almighty God that the evidence I shall give shall be the truth… the whole truth… and nothing but the truth." He put the card down, then looked up as Grimes rose in his seat and turned around to face him. This was about the dumbest layout for a court-room I had ever seen. Browne was facing away from the Court he was supposed to advise, Grimes was facing away from the witnesses he was to examine and Capacious Cargo was facing away from me, and located miles away besides.

Grimes shortly elicited that we were on a mission of danger, under orders, carrying weapons. He got him to say that on the morning of March 9 while talking to the men I had suddenly called out the colour sergeant's name, then drew my revolver and fired three times, killing him. He established that Ferdinand had made no threats, was not pointing a weapon… had done nothing more than answer my question when I called out to him. A hushed silence was over the room as Grimes sat down.

"Hello Aircraftsman Crewe."

"Hi, Sir." Crewe had a big smile on his face as did I. At least two officers on the Court noticed it.

"Do you recall what had happened just before I called out the colour sergeant's name?"

Crewe's face screwed up into a pose of concentration. "Oh… yessir! You were answering questions from the men, sir."

"Do you recall what the question was I just answered? Who asked it?"

"Uh… let's see…," Crewe was concentrating hard. "Oh yes, sir! It was Micah."

I nodded.

"Micah *who?*" Grimes snapped irritably, getting to his feet.

"Address your remarks to the Court, Mister Grimes," the President snapped.

"Oh yes… objection, Lord President! Let's get the declarant's last name."

"It was Dooley… wasn't it *jumbe* Flight Lieutenant?" Crewe asked.

The whole courtroom again dissolved into laughter.

"Yes it was," I recalled.

"Objection! Objection! Objection!" Grimes bellowed. "The prisoner is testifying."

"I was just answering his question," I replied innocently.

"SILENCE!" bellowed the President. He shook his head. "Now let's get organized here. Prisoner, you ask questions. Witness, you answer them."

"Yessir!" we both replied.

"It was Aircraftsman Dooley, *jumbe* Flight Lieutenant."

The Court was mightily amused by the obvious affection between us. Grimes was fuming.

"Do you remember the question, Crewe?"

"Yessir! It was something about how would the traitor know where to find the Communists in the dead of night."

"Now why was that question asked?"

"Objection! Calls for speculation."

"Sustained!"

"Why?"

"Prisoner! When I sustain an objection you can't ask the question."

"Oh... sorry, sir. I thought I was sustained in my asking of it."

More laughter washed over the room.

I didn't know why I couldn't ask the question, so I raised my hand. After a short consult with Cargo, who had to waddle up to the dock to talk to me, I tried again. "What had happened right before this question and answer exchange?"

"A voice spoke to us from out of the jungle. Threatening us with death for fighting with you, sir, against the Communists."

"What were the men thinking of doing?"

"Objection! Calls for speculation."

"Sustained!"

"Uh... what were *you* thinking of doing, Crewe?"

Crewe looked down, an expression of shame on his face. Then he looked at me gratefully. "Until you talked us out of it, sir, we were going to desert."

Several members of the Court shot me furtive approving looks.

"What did I tell you after I shot the colour sergeant?"

"Objection! Hearsay!"

"Res gestae," I heard the Attorney General whisper up to the bench.

"Overruled."

Crewe looked at me, puzzled. "Go ahead, Aircraftsman."

He smiled. "You told us to take a vote on whether to remove you from command. You said that you knew you'd have to face a court-martial, but if you hadn't acted, the mission would be destroyed, because the colour sergeant was working with the Communists. You said that's how Aircraftsman Locke died. He thought he was addressing his superior NCO, but he was really a Communist operating among us. You said you had to act quickly, sir."

"What happened to the mission after the colour sergeant was killed?"

"We made it safely, sir."

"Thank you."

"Thank *you jumbe* Flight Lieutenant. You got us through, sir."

The courtroom erupted with loud objections from Grimes and wild cheering from my men. I was nearly in tears. The President dutifully ordered my men to shut up and struck the last remark from the record, but it was obvious the Members of the Court had anything but stricken it from their minds.

On that note, the Court rose for lunch, as they put it. An hour and a half later when we resumed, Grimes was looking like the cat that ate the canary.

"Call your next witness, Mister Solicitor General."

Grimes hauled himself triumphantly to his feet. "Call Constable Inspector Gayle."

As the name was bellowed five more times, we all looked anxiously around the courtroom. A lean, fit light-complected man in a gray business suit walked in, carrying a reel to reel tape recorder and a small case. He took the oath and Grimes introduced him, established that he was personally aware Ferdinand was working 'in a law enforcement capacity at the time of this mission' and that, as part of those duties wore a wire... a voice-activated tape machine on his person. He testified that, based upon my morning reports, he was dispatched with a party of lawmen with a Militia escort along Highway

Two to the place where Ferdinand was buried. He said the body was exhumed and a device recovered.

Grimes now had the device identified and marked as evidence. He then introduced a tape, which the witness identified as being in the machine at the time of Ferdinand's death. He said that other than determining the machine still worked, he in no way tampered with the machine or the tape loaded into it. Grimes then stated on the record that he had removed the tape and placed it on a more sound-enhanced machine, that the tape still worked and that it would clearly reflect the actual murder.

He paused to revel in the unbearable tension that gripped the courtroom. "Lord President," he now began in stentorian tones, "I now ask that the tape be played."

Lieutenant Colonel Moreland looked at me. I'd been giving this a lot of thought ever since I recalled my suspicion Ferdinand might be wearing a wire. The stakes were as high as they could be... my life. Granted I wasn't obligated to show Ferdinand *was* a Communist, only that the circumstances within my grasp at the time reasonably entitled me to conclude he was. But clearly if the tape showed otherwise, my chances of acquittal would drop irretrievably below the horizon. "Sir..."

At this point Capacious Cargo could stand it no longer. He rose to his feet. "Lord President, begging your indulgence, I *must* intervene to prevent a tragic miscarriage of justice."

Granville Browne was vigorously nodding his head.

"My young client here does not realize what is involved. But on his behalf I strenuously object to the passing of this exhibit off as truth on the foundation we have. The Crown's witness doesn't know if this is the same tape Ferdinand wore or not in his machine... if in fact he wore one at all. He *wasn't there.* Furthermore, the Crown didn't even know where to look for his body until my client's morning reports made the long trip back from New Britain, *at least eight days* after the event. Recall also, this was an area where the Communists engaged this force, so we know they had the opportunity to exhume the body themselves and plant whatever evidence they cared to. For all we know this tape was made in a sound studio in Havana, the foundation is so poor. I ask the request be denied."

Capacious floored me with that speech. He'd hit on some things I'd have never thought of. The President was obviously impressed. Browne was more than impressed, he was signaling that the evidence be excluded.

The President now looked at me as the courtroom grew deathly silent. "Your solicitor's point is well taken, Flight Lieutenant. Have you anything to add?"

I looked up into the gallery. My men were all riveted on me. "May I listen to the beginning of the tape, sir? I think I'd likely know if it were genuine."

Browne, Cargo and the five officers of the Court were all looking at me as if I were one gigantic fool. Grimes was licking his chops with glee.

The President looked first right, then left among his fellow members. They knew Cargo was right, but they were military men and even the most skeptical among them was, to some degree, fascinated by the mystery of what had occurred in that mountain fastness on the mission they all no doubt thought at the time was utterly doomed. They nodded at the President.

"Come forward, young man."

As gasps issued from the gallery, I moved down to the floor, past my distraught counsel, to where Grimes stood with the tape machine. He pressed the button.

"This is volume three... the evening of March 8... I'm going to check on the Girl Guide now... see what he's up to."

"That's the Colour Sergeant's voice," I told the President.

"Good," interrupted Grimes. "Let's fast forward to the murder."

"No Mister... uh... Lord President," I protested. "If this is the true tape, we're about to have a conversation. He finds me working on citations for the two men who went with me to destroy the mortar emplacement..."

"That's irrelevant," Grimes snapped.

I looked up at the Court. "Is it, sir? Didn't the Crown's counsel mention something about this man being in a law enforcement capacity? I think this conversation might give the Court a somewhat different view."

"Yes," Lieutenant Colonel Moreland replied immediately, not even *looking* at his legal advisor. He did, however, cast a very disapproving look at Grimes. "And shame on you, counsel. This lad was home free on this evidence. I was going to exclude it. Don't you think in fairness you *owe* him a stipulation that parts of the tape important to him be played?"

I guess Grimes was too much of a slick lawyer to overlook the fact he was losing points with his hardball attitude when I had just handed him, in the Court's view, the bullets for my execution. "Naturally, Lord President."

"All right... let's hear it."

You could hear a pin drop as the entire courtroom leaned to the edge of their seats. I could *feel* my men praying for me, and once again it moved me to tears. Grimes hit the switch.

"I admire that, sir... You know it won't get 'em squat though."

"There's damned little else we can try to do for 'em, Colour Sergeant."

"Wait a minute... stop the tape," the President ordered. "Flight Lieutenant, I want you to go up there and take the oath, right now." He pointed to the witness box.

"I object! This is my..."

"Overruled."

I took the Bible in one hand, the card in the other, reading the oath.

"All right, Flight Lieutenant, what is being referred to?"

"I was roughing out citations for the men who silenced the mortar emplacement, sir. The Colour Sergeant came up behind me and made that comment."

"I see. All right, continue the tape."

"Our goal for tomorrow."

"Begging the Flight Lieutenant's pardon, sir..."

"What do they have against you, sir?"

"Go in the tent, Syb. I'll join you shortly."

"Ndiyo mwenyeji."

"I don't want you talking this stuff in front of her, Colour Sergeant."

"Sorry, sir."

"You were saying?"

[sound of lighting cigarettes]

"You know we're both being sacrificed, don't you?"

[silence] The officers of the Court had very disapproving looks on their faces as Ferdinand's remark registered. Grimes clearly lost whatever he tried to gain by showing his 'victim' as engaged on some secret secondary mission for Maggierock.

"I know why I was tapped for this assignment... But I can't figure you."

"I think it's just that I don't know what I'm doing.... I think they're saving their best officers for the death struggle on the east coast."

"Maybe... but then this project is supposedly so important, I just wonder..."

"The PM is playing a difficult and deadly game, Colour Sergeant... Factors within factors within factors.... He's a very capable man."

"Pardon the liberty, sir."

"It's okay, Colour Sergeant. I'm very grateful you're here."

"Will that be all, sir? I'd best turn out the night guards."

"Yes... that's all."

There then followed Ferdinand's loudly barked orders to the sentries. For a while nothing happened to activate the machine. My heart was wildly pounding.

"Halt! Who goes there!"

"That's Aircraftsman Locke's voice, Lord President," I gasped. "Our sentry that was murdered that night." I found myself wiping away a tear despite my unbearable anticipation. This was the big moment. It would either be there or it wouldn't.

"Sergeant Ferdinand."

"Oh... good morning, Colour Sergeant."

"Have you noticed the movement in those trees behind you, Aircraftsman?"

[strangling noises] We sat, horrified, listening to our fellow soldier being killed by Ferdinand. I burst into tears, sobbing for several minutes. A Merciful God had vindicated me, I had been *right*. I could feel the warmth coming from my men beamed in my direction... from Sybil too. I doubt I had ever been more overcome in my life.

A short while later, the machine was activated by crunching underbrush.

"Comrade Ferdinand."

"Here's the list. Now Prentice and Howard have wives, so threaten them with deaths of their loved ones. Crewe and that bunch I'm not sure.... it's all on the list. Oh, and don't forget to call out to the Girl Guide not to look for you. I guarantee he'll have his glasses dug into his fool head."

"Are you on a SIB job?"

"Sure... talked Colgate into puttin' me on this mission because of it."

"Wearing a wire?"

"Always."

"Make sure you erase this part of the tape."

"Don't treat me like a fool, Comrade. I've worked for the Party since before you..."

"Comrade Ferdinand we..."

"I'm on a walk-by and have to get back. I'll have the Girl Guide stop us at the Twelve Gorge Falls headwaters tomorrow... if anyone's left that is. It was a real break gettin' such a snot nose in command. It's another place like this... plenty of cover.

"We'll be there."

"Bye."

"Bye."

I felt arms go around me. Prentice, Howard, Crewe, Newleigh and Drayton were up at the witness box, their arms around me and each other as we sobbed uncontrollably.

Grimes suddenly looked over. "I object!"

"SILENCE!" bellowed the President. "Leave those men alone... they... they're... entitled." I don't think there was a dry eye on the Court, though ours were so wet I couldn't tell. The reels of the machine continued to turn, the sounds of Ferdinand coolly completing the walk-by playing to the stunned Court and gallery.

There then followed the loudspeaker attack, the efforts I made to get a reading on the direction-finder, my anger with Ferdinand for seemingly being overcome with fear of the supernatural. Then Ferdinand's half-hearted bellowing in response to my orders.

"All right, men... now listen. You are not soldiers of the *mgeni jumbe* Cassell. You are soldiers of the Prime Minister... the nation.... the *Watu* or 'people' that Communist who was talking over a loudspeaker kept trying to claim for himself.

"Back there, I have the Prime Minister's written orders... I'll be glad to show you if you want.

"On April fifteen, the British are leaving. This is something you've fought for now since Ghana's independence in 1959... Do you know Ghana has been ruling itself that long now? They didn't have to *sell out* their freedom to Communists! To exchange one kind of slavery for another. And neither do you.

"Don't you *realize* that fighting people like that voice trying to scare you was what Willett's Last Stand was all about?

"Don't you understand that..."

"How did that voice *know* which of us did what yesterday, jumbe Flight Lieutenant?"

"What's your name, Airman?"

"Crewe, sir."

"Oh yes. Well, there's only one way that could have happened. It's why Aircraftsman Locke was killed...."

"Someone in this camp went out... through that jungle... and contacted the rebels. Someone who, masquerading as a brother, knew all of it. Hell, anybody here knew all of it."

"But... everyone is here, *jumbe* Flight Lieutenant."

"I know. He's back with us."

"But how could that be, sir? How would the traitor know to find the rebels in the dead of night?"

"Colour Sergeant?"

"Sir!"

[three loud gunshots, horrible gasping sound, dead silence]

"Wait a minute!" the President held up his hand. "Stop the tape!" He turned to me. "Why did you call out the Colour Sergeant's name before shooting him, Flight Lieutenant?"

For several seconds, I stood there, gripping the railing of the witness box, hyperventilating. The last couple minutes had been very powerful for both me and my men. I felt I was reliving all the fearful agony... the overpowering sense of drowning in deep waters on dry land, that I felt on that awful morning.

"Take your time, son... Several of us have been there."

"Thank you, sir." I struggled to get control, not really sure I'd ever decoded the reasons among the blinding white flash of *reaction* that guided my physical responses in those minutes. Yet I knew I must have had a reason. "Well, sir... I remember *knowing* the men were panicked beyond reason... frightened by this voice that was naming them and threatening death to their loved ones... At that point I felt anything could happen at any moment..."

The President and two of the senior officers were nodding.

"They were talking... wanting answers I so *desperately* wanted to give them." I felt a couple sets of arms go across my back.

"Sergeant Ferdinand's responses throughout the... the attack were ....*strange... alien.* The white civilian supervisors were ready to trigger a bloodbath... they of course were panicked too." I shook my head, wiping at the tears that just *wouldn't stop.* Slowly, I felt a calm descending on me as I struggled for breath and the courtroom hung on my every word.

"I remember already figuring it just *had* to be a traitor among us... but it wasn't until Dooley asked his question that it all suddenly came together."

I looked into the empathetic eyes of the President. "I was *nauseated*, sir.... when it suddenly clicked. I don't know what was keeping me upright. Somehow I knew I had to kill Ferdinand... that I could never best him in a verbal exchange... that he had weeks to plan what I was coping with in seconds..."

The President was nodding, riveted to my words and expressions.

"He was somewhere behind me, sir. He was an experienced soldier. I knew in any fair fight he'd win." I shrugged, looking down. "I guess... I think.... I think I called his name to get a location fix... so I'd have some idea where he was... if I needed to shift position... if anyone were in the way... I was so *tangled up.*" For a while I was hyperventilating once more. Then the calm returned. "His answer told me he was just over my left shoulder... a yard or so behind. Then... things just happened..."

The President waited for several seconds, then nodded. "I see... thank you, son." He turned to Grimes. "Continue with the tape."

"It's like this, men... Last evening, Colour Sergeant Ferdinand insisted we stop here. As you may remember, we had plenty of daylight left to find a spot not so hemmed in by the jungle.

"He was just too experienced to make such a move... But I was too inexperienced to see it. But of course this had been arranged in advance. He *had* to stop here. The heavy underbrush so close to our bivouac gave him a chance to make quick contact with the Communists... to give them the information that made it look as if a supernatural force were peering with evil eyes into our very midst. Quick contact... say... in the course of a walk-by."

"I think that's why Aircraftsman Locke didn't sing out when he was attacked. He thought it was his superior noncommissioned officer... and it was. But it was also a Communist in our midst."

"Flight Corporal Preston!"

"Sir!"

"Flight Corporal Preston, you are now the ranking military member here. I am surrendering my sidearm to you."

"All right, men, here's what I want you to do. I want you to assemble together and take a vote. Whether to remove me from command. I realize I face a court-martial for what I just did, but I happen to believe that this was orchestrated so that we would never come out of this alive.... any of us. Therefore I had to act immediately. Now... if you vote to remove me, Flight Corporal Preston will assume command and I will travel as your prisoner. If you vote to keep me on, however, I will re-assume command and there will be no more said about this until I contact my superiors when we arrive at New Britain. I now ask you to retire and make your decision."

"Sir?"

"Yes."

"What do you think is going to happen, now that Colour Sergeant Ferdinand is dead... to us I mean... on this trip?"

"I'll tell you. I think the Communists are very short-handed at the moment. What have we faced so far? Some desultory rifle fire from the heights that barely reached us and a deadly assault, but by only two mortars. I think they're massing for some independence showdown somewhere else. I think that's why they needed a plant among us. So that their meager resources would have maximum effect. This little thing today was supposed to make you desert... and would have ended the mission. It was all very cleverly done."

"From here on out, whatever limited resources they have will have to stalk us from the jungle. If they try to shadow us from the road we will see them. They are going to have a very difficult time mounting a serious military challenge to us from here on out.

"Of course, whoever will be command, myself or Flight Corporal Preston, will make sure we stay alert.

"For as you know, a bullet fired from a small, weak force kills you just as dead. But I think the death of the traitor will throw our pursuers into darkness. They will wait for inside information that will never come.

"Any more questions?" [silence]

"Very well then, retire and make your decision." [inaudible talking, Preston's bellowed orders, the grisly sounds of the body being buried as truck engines loudly started and idled brought the tape to its end]

The President was positively moved, as were all the officers. Browne, Cargo, everyone I could see except Grimes, who appeared in shock, were also moved. My men and I just kept sobbing up at the witness box.

"You have anything else?" the President asked after a paralyzed silence.

The Solicitor General looked up, shrugged, then shook his head.

"We're going to take a short recess," the President barked as the five officers suddenly stood up.

They were halfway to the curtains before the usher recovered from his own thralldom to bellow "be upstanding."

As everyone rose, Sybil joined us, sobbing, and we rapidly thatched her into the knot we had made with our arms around one another. Up in the gallery, the rest of the Air Militia was now and then wiping their eyes. Here and there a sniffle could be heard.

. . . .

"Be upstanding and come to order," the usher bellowed some twenty minutes later.

We pulled apart.

"You can stay with him, you men," the President called before the tribunal had even reached their seats. By now, all eighteen were up with Sybil and me. "I want you to pay close attention to this, though."

"Yessir!" several of us answered as we went into a loose 'at-ease'.

Once more you could hear a pin drop as the Court finished seating itself, the President leaning forward, peering at some notes he had hastily made during the recess. Then he looked up.

"A unanimous Court has some remarks we are going to put on the record here...

"It is impossible to divorce these proceedings from their larger historical context. In a very few days our nation will be fighting for its life. We worked long and hard for that independence, but some among us are determined to, as the young Flight Lieutenant told his men on that fateful day, trade one form of slavery for another."

He cleared his throat, then took a sip from the water glass in front of him. "Now... we will all have to make sacrifices in the coming struggle, but those of us under arms... every member of this Court... the young men up there by the witness box... and the many in uniform in the gallery... will likely have to make them most frequently and under the most life-threatening circumstances...

"The Members of this Court want to make it absolutely clear, that before we ever heard the tape, we were *profoundly* impressed with the bond in blood that we observed formed by the young men of that detail and their young commander... we saw it in the young witness as he first greeted his commander... we saw it in the body language between them during the examination... and in the young airman's repeated slip of the tongue, addressing the young officer in the manner they no doubt adopted out in the bush." The President was grinning in spite of himself, as were several of the Court Members and all of the most experienced. They seemed to be reliving, almost wistfully, their own days out in the middle of nowhere... in Harm's Way... with only each other to rely on.

"It only adds to our admiration... and our hope for the future... that the eighteen enlisted were the native sons of Maggierock.... the young *jumbe flight lieutenant*," he couldn't help grinning as he said it, even mimicking Crewe's inflection almost exactly, "a white *mgeni* from far away who joined us just in time to try to help make a difference."

The President now paused, allowing everyone in that courtroom to calibrate their own dread of the coming days, their fond hopes for the future, with the tenor of his remarks. I was stupefied. I had seen somewhat analogous communities formed out of nowhere when our island was hit with a deadly storm in 1962, but that came up suddenly. The people of this island, by contrast, had months to turn the com- ing 'deadly storm' over and over in their minds. And there they were sitting... professional and unemployed, soldier and civilian, poor and rich, white and black... citizens of Maggierock all... one giant close- knit *community*.

"Now you young soldiers..." He was looking straight at the men of my detail grouped around me at the witness box. "You did some highly questionable things there, and might well have found yourselves faced with a firing squad had things turned out differently. But... when it really counted... when you stood poised at this deadly crossroads... far from your base and far from your mission's objective... you pulled yourselves together with a courage and presence of mind that inspires us, and, we are sure, will inspire our people in years to come when they hear your story. We salute you."

At that moment all five officers rose, came to attention, and saluted my men. I joined them. All were in tears. After an amazing silence, they ordered arms and sat back down.

"Flight Lieutenant Cassell... You had no training and certainly were blindsided by the situation suddenly confronting you. During the course of our recess, the more senior members among us shook our heads a time or two at some of your actions."

I reddened.

"Nonetheless... again when it really counted, your instinctive re- sponses, which so well demonstrated your respect for your men and your devotion to the accomplishment of your mission... you acquitted yourself in a manner we are proud to recount among the other tales of courage and leadership which constitute the rapidly growing tradi- tion of the St. Margaret's officer corps... And we salute *you* sir."

Once more they rose and saluted, my men joining them.

Sitting down once more, the President shot me an almost boyish grin. "It ain't much, Flight Lieutenant... but as you yourself told the traitor in your camp that night, there's simply little else we *can* do. We're a poor nation... and our resources are stretched to the breaking point."

I wiped at my already puffy, red eyes.

"The Court hereby enters a judgment of acquittal as to both charge and specification. We can rathole the papers and the trappings of these accusations... unfortunately, we cannot rathole the fear, anxiety, self-doubt, and all the many other negatives you were forced to endure because of them." He let out a long, regretful sigh. "We only wish we could... all of us."

I barely heard the concluding remarks as they rose and departed one final time, nor the tumultuous cheers that erupted from my men and the gallery as they did so. All I could think of as I was lifted onto the shoulders of my men and carried out of that funny-looking courtroom where everyone was in robes except the judges, was that they had done a mighty damned good job of *trying*.

Chapter Nine

WE'LL REMEMBER ALWAYS...
INDEPENDENCE DAY

Thursday April 12, 1973... three days before Independence: the beach house, Settlement of New Gatwick, Isle of St. Margaret's

"Hey LOOK, *mume!*"

Sybil and I had been enjoying an afternoon swim at our beach house. I was scheduled to report to the 'airbase', as the old Hayes Airstrip was now somewhat hopefully called, at 1600. First the mission, then the court-martial had caused me to be out of touch with the frenzy of pre-Independence Day activities that had gripped the island in the past month.

A lot had changed, and many changes had taken place in the Air Militia. For one thing, my mission and the attention it had attracted had been a real boon to recruitment. Some fifty new recruits were now in our ranks, and the recruit school was about to graduate another thirty. My loyal Flight Corporal Preston was now a second subaltern and in command of the New Britain Airstrip. The two biggest surprises were, first, that we had gotten two Cessna aircraft, all decked out in the green around black target insignia and second, that I was now the pilot of one of them.

Since our flight home on March 30, Gene had been driving me like a madman, and had finally pronounced me 'qualified'. As with sailing several years before, the learning process had been difficult, but I thoroughly enjoyed the doing of it. I could never fly in an area of traffic, or even with a traffic control tower that expected you to calculate distances and fly 'on instruments', and my landings still had everyone diving for the slit trenches, but we were in desperate need of a second pilot, so that's what I was called. My uniform wings now had a crown on top, indicating I was a flyer, much to Sybil's delight, and my new title was 'deputy commander of operations' or 'DCO'.

What I lacked in skill I was certainly making up for in volume of flying hours. My mission at the airbase this evening was to fly the Commander of Sedona Company of the Militia over to New Britain to meet with Captain DeFreeze. Time was *really* running out now, and the Militia was taking a hard look at its deployment in anticipation of heavy fighting. Except for those 'Stone Age' settlements Gene had mentioned, and which remained unmapped and in many cases undiscovered (or at least the discoverers never lived to tell it), long stretches of our coastline south of the Doran plantation and north of the Autrey plantation were *believed* to be uninhabited... and *known* to be completely undefended.

In fact, Captain DeFreeze's platoon was the only armed force on the west side of the Central Highlands besides the fifteen men we had at the airstrip and about thirty constables in New Britain. Philip Doran was rumored to have at least two hundred thugs under arms at his plantation, under the command of Sybil's brother Anselmo. Darius Jack, another brother, supposedly led about the same number at the Autrey plantation to the north. A third mercenary force, called the Westside Planters' Security Consortium, numbering about fifty, were located in New Britain and guarded the taro warehouses. This consortium was one of the few cooperative efforts mounted by the two planters. Their convoys remained separate, and tales abounded to the effect that many of the convoy ambushes were the work, not of the guerillas, but the rival planter's thugs.

Wiping the water from her latest efforts to dunk me from my eyes, I looked out to sea where she was pointing. There, to my unbelieving eyes was an aircraft carrier, a much smaller but impressively luxurious-looking vessel, a large troop carrier and about five destroyers.

"*Damn!* Wonder what *that's* all about?"

"Maybe the rumors are true *mume!* Wouldn't that be *something!*"

"What rumors?"

"That the Princess Royal... or maybe Princess Margaret... is coming for the Independence ceremonies and State Opening of Parliament. Oh wouldn't that be *something!*" Sybil was definitely something of a rebel when it came to being a dutiful daughter of Maggierock. Since turning sixteen, she had angered her mighty and dictatorial father, Fortunus Jack, many times... wearing miniskirts and high heels, finally running off to get a job and live the life of a swingin' sophisticate in Miami. Yet cocoanut milk ran in her veins, as the local expression went, and in many ways as a somewhat more settled young female hydrogen bomb of twenty, she was a fiercely proud islander. The thought that a member of the Royal Family would come to this floating looney bin to see it off on its journey as an independent nation obviously pleased her. For several minutes she just stared, entranced, out at the awesome sight.

I found myself doing the same thing. Whatever else was in that impressive Royal Navy battle group now slowly making its way up the coast to Port Albert, that troop carrier told me that the 18th Berkshire Rifles were going to be departing immediately... and the thought made me cringe.

"Isn't that the *Britannia?*" she asked excitedly, pointing to the luxurious-looking vessel.

"I don't know," I replied, squinting across the millions of sparkles the shimmering afternoon tropical sun had placed in the turquoise waters. "Wish I had my field glasses."

"Just a sec, *mume!*" Before I could stop her, Sybil splashed her way toward shore then sprinted toward our back door and disappeared.

I flipped over on my back, closed my eyes and floated for a while. The outcome of the court-martial had been more gratifying than I would have ever thought possible. I really felt I *belonged* here. There was no televison (which I was actually finding to be a blessing. I didn't know how nice it could be foregoing the nightly yammering about Watergate on the American news until I'd tried it for a while)... our diet consisted almost exclusively of canned meat and boxed frozen chicken. The power was constantly going out. The cheese at Kwan Lu's store was always expired, the odd-looking meat, devoid of the

'USDA' purple stamp I'd taken for granted all my life, in the freezer case was always freezer-burnt. But my relationship with Sybil, my growing job skills, the feeling I was really *needed* and the many nice people I'd met here combined with the healthy life of swimming in warm tropical seas bathed in the brilliant sunshine and naked with Sybil at midnight had managed to make me happier than I could remember being.

There were still those other things... and when they hit they hit hard. But there was nothing I could do about them and so managed for the most part to keep the anxieties they caused confined to the moments I had to deal with them. I could tell from the feeling of heat on my face that I was going to be sporting a sunburn on the mission tonight. *Yuk! One... possibly two... nights in New Britain!* Our old rotten wood house at the edge of the airstrip was now its BOQ, so I imagined that's where I'd be staying. I really wanted to take Sybil along but my craft was a two-seater. We'd heard that one of the periodic outbreaks of dengue fever over there was currently in progress. I hoped they had managed to replace the torn mosquito netting over the bed that I remembered from last time.

I heard splashing behind me. My brain sent me the signal to get on my feet but in my drowsy tropical reverie it processed too late. I barely managed to take a deep breath before Sybil sent me to the bottom, clamping my head between her legs, giggling all the while. I dimly recalled she had my field glasses in her hands, so I couldn't do my usual number of standing up, holding on to her ankles as she continued to grip my head, then dunking her upside down in the water until she let go. Instead I compromised with a maneuver that wound her up riding on my shoulders, still giggling all the while.

"Here, *mume*." She handed the glasses down to me.

Locating the luxurious vessel in the glasses, I looked to its stern. "Wow, *mke*! That's the Royal Standard!"

"Oh *yeah*! Let me see!" I handed them up. Excitedly, she clamped them to her face, then let out a joyful squeal. "Yeah! I wonder who it is!"

We happily preoccupied ourselves with that mystery until it was time to shower under the outside showerhead and go inside. I was busily pulling on my khakis when Sean burst through the door. He had been up at our main house on Mantilla Heights. "This just came for ya Boss up at the big house."

There was neither stamp nor address on the envelope, indicating it had been delivered. I opened the envelope and pulled out what was obviously an invitation.

Your neighbours Norbert and Clara Perkins
Cordially invite you to a backyard barbeque
In honour of our Nation's coming Independence

Friday April 13 beginning at 6:00P.M.
Semi-formal, Undress uniforms

RSVP

"Oh, *mume*! Can we go?"

Norbert Perkins lived two houses down from us on the Heights. He was the Leader of the Marxist-Trotskyite Opposition NLP in the new Parliament. That aside, he'd been a pleasant neighbor and, along with his wife Clara had been very helpful when we first moved in. His former housekeeper Tucan, of course, was now making Joe feel twenty years younger in their little cottage behind our main house.

"Sure, baby. If I get back from New Britain in time."

"Ohhhh!" Sybil joyfully threw her arms around me, smothering me with kisses.

"Think that's a good idea, Boss?" Among his other talents, Sean's nimble Hell's Kitchen wits had made him well versed in the political realities of our new home... realities that my more spacey concentration either gripped me with terror or were blissfully ignored. I seemed to alternate between the two. I knew exactly what he was trying to tell me.

Before I could react, though, Sybil put her hands on her hips and faced him with a petulant expression on her face. "Oh Sean! You're such a kill-joy. Now don't you be gettin' the *mume* all scared or I'll tell Sunflower to paste you between the eyes when you lay hold of her!"

Sean turned a beet red as my glance darted between the two of them. "What's this?" I asked, amused at Sean's unusual blushing. I had seen it recently on Joe, of course, and so knew exactly what it was about. I just hadn't been up to speed on the goings-on around me recently enough to know who was involved or how close the big event was.

"Uh... well, Boss..." Sean was *stuttering*! I burst out laughing.

"My older sister Sunflower," Sybil piped up. "This lummox thinks he's gonna lay hold of her..." She turned angrily to Sean. "Not if you louse up this party, you filthy mick! I'll tell her to take the cocoanut and tattoo it on your thick head!"

We were all laughing now. "Okay! Okay!" Sean stammered, grinning. "Forget it!"

"When's the big event, Sean?"

He shrugged. "I dunno, Boss. Soon as I can work up da noive, I guess."

As I gave him a look that no doubt reminded him of how unconcerned he'd been over *my* attack of nerves that day at the Customs House, Sybil now jumped in, her tone more conciliatory. "Tell you what, Sean... you play ball on this party and you can just go buy the salt fish, tinned beef and taro right now!"

"You mean..."

"Don't forget the cocoanut and machete," I grinned, very proud of myself I had already traversed this rite of passage.

"Yeah," Sybil continued. "I'll fix it with Sunflower."

"You think she likes me, Miss Sybil?"

"You just play ball."

"Okay! Okay!" Sean reddened once more. "When?"

"How about tomorrow?"

"GEE! You're a peach, Miss Sybil!" He grabbed her, planting a kiss on her cheek. "Ferget what I said about da party Boss! Me n' Sunflower'll be joinin' you guys there." He looked hopefully once more at Sybil. "Right?"

"Just leave it to Sybil," she said smugly.

We all laughed hysterically as Sean happily charged outside to the jeep for the trip back to the big house, no doubt with a stop at Kwan Lu's now programmed in.

． ． ． ． ． ． ． ． ． ． ． ． ． ． ． ．

"Militia Three calling Cornwallis Tower... over." I spoke into my headset as I glanced at the clipboard Aircraftsman Drayton handed in to me. He was one of my men on what was now being called almost with reverence 'Mission Impossible' and had been trained by the Convair people.

"Cornwallis Tower, Militia Three... go ahead."

The walk-around checked out. The clipboard said all was well with my aircraft. I initialed it and handed it back. "Happy landings *jumbe* Flight Lieutenant!" Drayton smiled as he saluted.

I returned it, smiling, my verbal salutation interrupted by the tower transmission. "How's the sky tonight?"

Drayton shut my door and headed back to his fire extinguisher to monitor my start.

"Busy... the 4th Ark Royals are in the air over Port Albert... Royal Family security sweep... over."

"Roger Tower... I'll be west of there... Militia Three out."

The engine turned over and began warming. I ran through my final pre-flight. All appeared well. I nodded to Drayton who pulled the chocks and we began our taxi to the end of the tarmac. To the east, the foothills, the city and the harbor stretched out before me under the bright late afternoon sun. As we taxied, the Militiamen manning the sandbagged emplacements at the runway's perimeter saluted my passenger, Lieutenant Colonel Romulus Augustulus Jones. His parents hadn't given him a name that passed muster in a schoolyard, but they sure knew their history. Romulus Augustulus was the last Roman emperor in the west... fourteen years of age when deposed by the barbarians.

"The men look sharp, Flight Lieutenant," the colonel sighed with satisfaction.

"Yessir. I think the Last Stand really had an impact."

"You were there that night, I understand."

"Yessir. Next morning too." We reached the end and turned.

My heart leaped to my throat as it always did just before takeoff, though it was nothing compared to the terror just before landing. *Oh well... little by little...* I throttled forward until we were shaking hard and the RPM's were just right, then released the brakes and we were on the way. Pulling back on the stick just shy of the hangar, we lifted off the runway.

The radio station appeared on my right, the beautiful panorama off to my left. The British battle group was at the harbor now, adding to the magnificence of the sight. Our jeep ride to the airport had been magnificent too. All along the waterfront, Government Plaza and the diplomatic quarter, palm fronds had been tied to every available column, garlands of ginger blossoms and frangipani were everywhere as well. Knots of British soldiers were at regular intervals along the road. There were no loiterers these days by the side of the highway in shanty town.

It was hard to believe, but the flight to New Britain was less than an hour. I had wanted to do a long slow turn to the east and enjoy the sights of the city, but those helicopters were around somewhere and I wasn't looking to tax my meager flying abilities. So I banked to the right, then picked up Highway Two and my compass heading, and we were on the way.

"Expect to be long in New Britain, sir?" I was very anxious to find out how long I was going to be stuck there, especially with the party tomorrow night.

"Hard to say, Flight Lieutenant," Colonel Jones responded. "Depends on how DeFreeze has things organized."

"My CO is convinced that's where the opening attack is gonna come from."

Jones smiled. "Yes... we're familiar with the Hayes Theory."

"I understand *your* CO doesn't buy it."

"No."

"Why not?"

"No anchorages. All that equipment pouring in from Cuba he's so worried about could never be brought ashore."

"Oh."

"Besides, I think the rebels are afraid of the planters. I think they have more men under arms than we do."

I guess it made sense, but then I had no experience taking over countries from bases in the mountains. My passenger's eyes swept the green carpeted highlands now stretching out on all sides below. "They're out there *somewhere*, all right," he spoke ominously.

They were indeed. I found myself casting frequent downward glances at Highway Two, looking like a huge coiled snake... turning and turning and *turning*.

"That was quite an accomplishment, Flight Lieutenant," he spoke after a silence of several minutes.

"What was, sir?"

"Your mission... down there."

"Oh... yeah... I had a lot of good men."

"Dave Moreland told me he was very impressed with you and your men at the court-martial."

"Dave Moreland, sir?"

"The President."

"OH! Oh yes! I was very impressed with him."

Down below, a military convoy of some ten vehicles was winding along up a run of interminable switchback. "Reenforcements for DeFreeze," Jones spoke, reading my mind. I'm sending him New Gatwick's Second Platoon."

"I see."

"They may not make it by Independence day... it'll be close."

"Think the shooting will start right then?"

He shook his head. "I doubt it. Especially with the Princess here. There's rumors the Royal Governor has been trying to set up a meeting between Webster and Colgate... to get a truce. You heard of that, haven't you?"

"No... sounds good though."

Jones looked *very* surprised. "You *haven't*? Word is Colgate's gonna take you along as his military aide."

"*Really*? Why me?"

"Everybody knows you have some sort of magic touch with Webster."

That remark floored me. "*Me*? What on earth for? I've never met the man... wouldn't know him if I fell over him."

Now it was Jones' turn to be shocked. I knew I had something else to keep me awake as I sweated and swatted mosquitoes tonight in the New Britain Air Militia BOQ. Jones was unable to tell me any more, besides adding that the rumor was common knowledge in the Militia.

"Nobody tells me anything," I sighed to his laughter.

We were at New Britain. I banked our aircraft to the right, making my gradual turn to the north to set up my final approach.

"See that coastline down there?" Jones spoke.

I managed a look between the more important looks at compass, altimeter, and mountains. The strategy for this landing was to drop to four hundred feet, keeping myself to the west of the mountains looming above me, then come right down the slot to the airstrip. I did manage a quick look though. This part of the coast at least looked rocky and inhospitable, with nothing useable for a harbor anywhere I could see.

"Yessir. I see the Colonel's point."

"If we've got time, you can take a quick look to the south."

"Maybe on the return trip, sir. The sun'll be in my eyes soon."

"Forget it!" Jones said with a very familiar twinge of fear that made me laugh. "You just get us down."

"I'm for that, sir. Maybe on the trip back if we leave early enough."

Jones nodded.

The airstrip loomed ahead. Now down to two hundred feet, I extended the flaps. I didn't need to worry about the landing gear because the wheels were fixed. Now I was carefully watching the artificial horizon and the rapidly approaching airstrip. Keeping the nose up, but not too much. *I hated landings!* We touched down with what was called in the Air Militia a 'Cassell jolt', bouncing right back up again... then down... a bit more softly this time. Then brakes, working the engine, throttling forward in reverse, then down. All the rush of things to do burned into my mind by the terror of burning to death if I forgot them.

We were on the ground. I could see my men coming out to take care of the plane. I taxied to a spot on the tarmac near the small hangar and came to a stop. I could see Second Subaltern Preston coming toward me in his blue coveralls, each epaulet mounted with a single stripe. He'd been in my corner when I needed it most. Captain DeFreeze was with him. Letting out a sigh of relief that another trip was complete, I cut the engine.

"Preston!"

"*Jumbe* Flight Lieutenant!" we greeted one another after the brief welcome for the Lieutenant Colonel was complete and DeFreeze had extended an invitation to dine at the Officers' Club at the Militia post and, after a glance at the rotten wood BOQ, was accepted. The four of us walked to the Militia jeep parked nearby and began the drive into New Britain.

"Congratulations on your commission."

"Any chance of going back to being a Flight Corporal?"

I patted him on the back sympathetically. "Kind of a hole, eh?"

"*Kind* of... you have no idea, *jumbe* Flight Lieutenant."

Our journey took us through muddy streets past shanties and rotten wood buildings. As Jones and DeFreeze talked across the passenger front seat, I got the update on life as commander of a small Air Militia post in New Britain. There were few surprises. The *other* Militia post, where we were to eat, was located just to the east of the warehouse district, which was located practically on the water. By the time we had entered to the salutes of the sentries and our jeep had ploughed through a sea of mud to our destination, I was feeling profoundly sorry for Second Subaltern Preston.

Barbed wire and sandbags, a rusted out quonset hut and several of the usual assemble-it-yourself barracks that America was giving away by the hundreds at the end of World War II was pretty much all the place had. The 'officers' club' was one of three rotten wood houses standing in a row not far from the flagpole which still streamed the Union Jack.

We went inside and took our seats at one of five long tables the place had. Three Casablanca fans tried to muster the motivation to turn on the ceiling, while two miniskirted waitresses and a bartender whose feet were obviously moving to the calypso beat at the moment leaned against the bar.

Catching sight of Jones, one of the waitresses came over. She wasn't too bad-looking, considering the rest of the place, but I figured her for a fugitive from the brothels and so paid little mind. We ordered a round of warm beer, then heard that a shipment of North Atlantic flounder had just arrived, so we all ordered that. Being so recently from America, it never occurred to me to ask 'from where?' or what 'just arrived' meant.

"How long are you gonna be here Cassell?" DeFreeze asked at one point.

"Just until Colonel Jones here is ready to return." Preston shot me a look of extreme envy.

"Did you meet Heather Cressey last time you were here?"

"No."

"Well you may see her later tonight. She wanted to meet you."

"Who's Heather Cressey?"

"The mayor's daughter." The prospect hit me kind of sideways. On the one hand, the thought of spending tonight in my rotten wood paradise sweating and swatting mosquitoes was bumming me out, but besides that it was too hot to think of doing anything except think about leaving.

We had barely begun eating our flounder, which actually tasted pretty good, when a heavy downpour began outside, drumming on the sheetmetal roof with a ferocity that caused us to bellow at the top of our lungs anytime we wanted to be heard. It was some time during the worst of the downpour that the bartender ambled over to DeFreeze and whispered in his ear.

"Oh yes! Bring it on!" he grinned, leaning over and whispering into Jones' ear.

"What's up?" I roared.

"Kifo! They got a bottle in today!" All three islanders were now smiling broadly, looking at me.

"What's that?"

"Cocoanut liquor, *jumbe* Flight Lieutenant," Preston answered. "A local specialty."

That sounded much better than Heather Cressey in terms of speeding up the arrival of tomorrow and hopefully getting out of here. "Let's have some!"

We did. I found myself utterly astounded that the innocent little white stuff that tasted so good in a wedge of Horn & Hardart's cocoanut custard pie when turned to liquid could, in short order, render you unable to do anything but laugh hysterically as you fell out of your chair, too weak to get up, and see bright purple tracers anytime something moved.

The next thing I remember, Preston and I were stumbling around in ankle deep mud, often pitching face-first into it... sometimes together, sometimes separately... in total darkness, the sight of our revolvers strapped around our waists our only protection against the hordes of bandits that stalked this mud paradise at any hour of the day or night but particularly now, our arms across each other's shoulder, making for the dim lights that marked the airstrip, bellowing at the top of our lungs the little song the four of us composed, lying on the filthy, rotten wood floor of the Officer's Club, to mark Independence Day, to the tune of *Graduation Day*.

It's a time for DAMES
A time for BEER
A time to wonder
How the hell we got HEEERRRREEEE!
We'll remember always... Independence DAY!

When hostile trails
Are far behind...
No matter if...
Our way we'll FIIIIND!
We'll remember always... Independence DAY!

"Letsh do the verse about the whores, *jumbe* Flute Lightenant."
"Oh yesssh! Shubeckon Shubaltern."
"Okay... and a one... a two... a three...."

When it's horny that...
Ourselves we...

"Halt! Who goes there!"

"Ah dry up, buddy!"

"Yeah go fuck yourself... uh... where were we?""

"Stand and be recognized!"

"Aw go stick yer head in a toilet or somethin'. And a one... and a... OWWWW!"

It was only after the muzzle of Aircraftsman Dooley's rifle had struck Preston, knocking him over into the mud, and jabbed me in the stomach, causing regurgitation of things best left in the stomach, that the astonished sentry recognized both his CO and the *jumbe* Flight Lieutenant.

Profusely apologizing, not that he had any reason to, other than the fact he liked us and had served with us on Mission Impossible, he managed to turn out several sleeping airmen who somehow got their two officers where they were supposed to end up for the night. The guys who dumped me in my bed even managed to remember to pull the mosquito netting shut, as I later found out when I ripped it to shreds trying to get out of there over to the commode in time before I heaved Kifo and everything else inside yet one more time.

So ended just another day in swingin' New Britain, the Malaria Capital of the Caribbean.

Friday April 13, 1973... two days until Independence: the Air Militia Base, Settlement of New Britain, Isle of St. Margaret's

It was close on 1300 when Leading Aircraftsman Marsh, who was assigned as my aide by his very hung over base commander the next morning, stuck his head in my miserable quarters.

"De Lieutenant Colonel is ready to go, *jumbe* Flight .... Uh... what happened to de mosquito netting, sir?"

"Oh... it sort of fell down."

The young enlisted man looked puzzled for a moment. "De *jumbe* Flight Lieutenant's khakis are covered with de mud, sir."

"Wazz yer name again?"

"Marsh, sir."

"I think it rained in my bed last night, Mud. Turned everything to Marsh... uh... the other way around...ohhhh, my *head*!"

"You have de bad head, sir?"

"Ndiyo."

"Anything I can do, sir?"

"No thanks, Mud... uh Marsh... just help me to the plane."

A wave of nausea hit me as the light from the dark leaden skies stabbed mercilessly at my eyes. My plane had been rolled out and was ready to go. The young airman took me almost to the door. "Thanks, Marsh... I hope next time we can have a longer conversation."

Poor Marsh looked as if he hoped there wouldn't be a next time as he brushed some mud from my khakis off his blue coveralls.

"Sorry about de leaky roof, sir."

"De leaky roof?"

"That turned everything to mud and ..."

"Oh... oh yeah." I gave a wave of my hand, nearly falling over from the weight shift. "Well, things happen, Marsh."

"Yessir... happy landings, sir."

"You too, Marsh."

"I'm not going anywhere, sir."

"No? Too bad."

"Amen to that, sir."

I patted him on the back, then opened my door to see Lieutenant Colonel Jones sitting in the right hand seat, an ice bag on his head, his khakis covered with mud. "Something happen, sir?"

"Ummm. Some Communist moved the steps leading from my quarters."

"Ummmm. The Communists were very busy last night. They put a hole in my roof."

He nodded sympathetically, the motion nearly making him throw up. "Isn't there anything but *mud* around here?"

"Dengue fever, I hear... ohhh!"

"Ohhhh!"

I picked up my preflight, but saw everything was written there three times, in the same sentence. "Oh fuck the checklist." I stumbled through the sequence of knobs and switches, eventually getting the prop turning. "Damn, sir... how do you stand that shit?"

"Kifo?"

"Uh huh."

"We don't."

I tried to laugh, but the echoes nearly blew my head off as we taxied to the end of the tarmac. Turning the plane, I revved the engine, watching all three RPM meters.

"Oh God! It's so *noisy*! My fucking *head*!"

"Yessir! Sorry sir!"

"Oh God, it's like being inside one of those *washing machines*!"

"Yessir! Ohhhh, my *head*!"

"Just fucking *move* us, Flight Lieutenant!"

"Yessir! Sorry, sir!" I released the brakes and we started our takeoff roll.

"Oh God! Can't you shut this thing up a little?"

"Sorry, sir." I pulled back on the stick. We lurched upward... the engine coughed, then died.

My life flashed before me but again a merciful God decreed it wasn't my time yet. Surely it was His hands that suddenly did a lightening fast re-start, throttled forward, yanked back the flaps and managed to bring us down with an even more dramatic than usual 'Cassell jolt'.

Few things would sober me up faster than the sensation of plummeting to earth in something that would catch *fire* as it splintered all over the runway. Without another word I taxied back to the hangar.

"What the hell are you doing Flight Lieutenant? Let's move out!"

"Negative, sir."

"That's an order, Flight Lieutenant."

"With all due respect to your rank, Colonel Jones, I'm the captain of this ship. I'm gettin' some coffee. You want some?"

"Ohhhhh... my head."

The prop still turning, I opened my door and looked around. I saw Aircraftsman Newleigh, another veteran of Mission Impossible, running toward me with a huge fire extinguisher on wheels. "You all right, sir? Looked like you nearly bought it!" He was looking very scared... very concerned.

"I'm okay, Newleigh... just getting my quota of behaving like a goddam idiot out of the way for the next year or so. Can you get us some coffee?" I reached into the pocket of my muddy, sweat-soaked khakis and tossed him a half-crown.

"Will do, *jumbe* Flight Lieutenant." Leaving the extinguisher there, he sprinted inside the small hangar, shortly reappearing with two large styrofoam cups.

"Thanks, brother." I handed one into the Colonel.

I waited until I'd gulped it down, then got back in the aircraft and taxied once more. This time I didn't give a rat's ass *how* much my, or Lieutenant Colonel Jones' head hurt from the noise or the vibrations. I'd learned a bitter lesson today. My head was pounding, but I was still alive... and that was a start.

Still overcome with the close call, I banked us to the right, heading out over the malaria capital of the Caribbean... then out to sea, I then did a wide turn to the left, coming in somewhere over the uninhabited southern part of our coastline.

"What are you *doing* Flight Lieutenant?"

"Just celebrating being alive, sir. Checking out the coast like you... hey! Take a look at *that*, will you sir? One thirty low."

There, to our unbelieving eyes, was a medium sized boat, about the size of a tugboat, sitting inside a very small cove. Just opposite it, on-shore, was a clearing with *structures*. "Any idea what that is, sir?"

"No! Other than that it *shouldn't be there*... according to our maps." Romulus Augustulus Jones now appeared as traumatically sobered up as I was.

"Yeah... and it's fed from the outside... not the jungle. Holy fuck." I *hated* to ask this question... I was *scared*. "Wanna go in for a closer look?"

"Yes... do it."

"Yessir." Heart hammering all the while, I climbed for the heavens, then banked to the right, beginning a one hundred eighty degree turn. Well out over the water, I now descended quickly, increasing our airspeed as we approached the cove. We hit the coast and looked down. It was *gone*! Completely disappeared. Only the boat was still there to remind us we hadn't hallucinated.

"What the hell!" I gasped.

"Camouflage net," Jones answered. "Let's get a location fix on this, Flight Lieutenant."

Watching the airspeed closely, we 'paced off' the distance, flying in a straight line, to the beginning of the New Britain sprawl. I wrote down the figures and handed them to Jones.

"Let's head for the barn."

He didn't have to tell me twice. We had stumbled onto something here. Some people had come ashore and had constructed some sort of base. All the way back, Jones was thinking hard... no doubt about what to do about it. We had no watercraft except for a police launch at Port Albert. The nearest Militia force would take days to reach this mysterious base moving through the miserable jungle.

Once at New Britain, I had picked up my compass heading and began the trip home. "I wonder if you could persuade the British to use those PT boats one last time."

"Maybe... but not likely. They're gonna be on Royal Family security from now until they leave. I was thinking Clendenon... you know him?"

"I've heard of him... we've never met."

Nothing more was said during the entire trip. At the airbase, he gave me a lift in his Land Rover. Dropping me at the beach house, he told me "you're on standby tonight, Cassell. We may at least want to try to photograph it."

"We'll never see it from the air again. That camouflage net..."

"You're on standby."

"Yessir, I'll be at the Norbert Perkins party in Mantilla."

At first he was looking at me like I was being insubordinate. Then he just nodded. "Thanks for the ride, Flight Lieutenant."

"Yessir." I closed the door of his Land Rover as he sped off.

Saturday April 14, 1973... the very eve of Independence: the home of Norbert Perkins, MP, on Mantilla Heights, Settlement of Mantilla, Isle of St. Margaret's

A silence settled over the eight to ten separate mealtime conversations as Norbert Perkins' pendulum clock chimed the hour of midnight. Sybil gripped my hand. The body language displayed around the long banquet table showed strong emotion... hope and fear... much as I had observed at the court-martial.

Perkins slowly rose to his feet, picking up his glass. "We are now but twenty-four hours from Independence, brothers and sisters... To Maggierock! May her future be bright and free!"

"Hear! Hear!" Dollie Fishbine, the Notary-General and deputy prime minister echoed. She was a leathery old dame. The only member of Colgate's cabinet to attend the party, though all had been invited. I gathered she thought for herself, and always had. Her thick cataract glasses and heavy-set body gave an almost buffoonish impression, but it was wrong. She made Enid Worthington look like a shrinking violet.

We all drank the toast. Much of the neighborhood had been there for the barbeque part. Only the seven NLP Members of Parliament and their spouses remained, along with Joe and Tucan, Sean and Sunflower, Sybil and me, plus of course, Dollie Fishbine, for the midnight supper. One reason we were still there was because we hadn't arrived until eight. That was due to the fact that I just *had* to do something about my pounding head, and my housekeeper Melissa Torreon, a three hundred pound Hispanocaribe, one of the world's rarest ethnic groups, who 'came with the house', had to do something about my khakis.

She had... and now I sat at the table looking pretty spiffy, the only guy in uniform, occasionally wondering what had happened to Lieutenant Colonel Jones and Colgate's meeting with Webster. Both supposedly were going to involve me, yet here I sat. Of course we'd gone to the big house on Mantilla Heights almost as soon as I got in the door... but then everyone would have known to look for me there.

I was being treated with respect by all the NLP Members of Parliament. It was obviously because they thought it took a lot of moxie for me to come to one of their parties, when Colgate was now hours away from declaring martial law and throwing them all into concentration camps. They never tried to draw me out on any of that... they just kept coming up and thanking me for coming. Of course I knew exactly the side of Colgate to which they were referring, and as the evening wore on I was getting more and more nervous. I kept coming back to the point that if the deputy prime minister was there, it couldn't be *illegal* for me to come. But as the hours passed and I saw how much of character she was, I realized she just always did what she pleased.

"Flight Lieutenant?" I had been outside now about twenty minutes just gazing at the vista of the coastline from the Heights, enjoying the languid serenity of the magnificent tropical night, the gentle ocean breeze caressing my face. Sybil was inside debating some obscure point of Maggierock reality with one of the Opposition MP's, and enjoying herself immensely. She'd no doubt been arguing with Fortunus now for many years, and was very confident in her beliefs.

I turned around. It was Perkins. I couldn't help but like him. He was tall, thin, and walked stiffly with the aid of a cane. His white Van Dyck beard and afro made a striking contrast with his face, which betrayed a rapid-fire wit and keen intelligence. He had gone out of his way to make me feel very welcome tonight. "Sir?"

"Would you join me in the library?"

"Yessir." I followed dumbly behind as he hobbled stiffly ahead of me. The library was paneled with finished pine, and looked out of place in this war zone of building materials with the elements, where the former always seemed to be losing. It was even *air conditioned*. I hadn't enjoyed *that* feeling in ages. I rapidly concluded I could *live* in this library.

He took a seat at a polished desk, and beckoned me into a chair opposite. "I appreciate you coming, young man."

"I'm sorry more didn't," I replied. "It was a nice party."

"I don't really blame Desi," Perkins sighed. "He has lots to do right now. Bertie too. He's been learning how to be a governor-general for the last month now." Perkins smiled. "I don't envy him."

"I was afraid I'd be called away, sir. There was talk of a truce while everyone celebrated. I was told the Governor was trying to arrange a meeting of Colgate and Webster."

Perkins nodded. "I don't think there'll be a problem with that. For a few days, anyway."

The thought made me happy, and more than a little relieved. Perkins had a pendulum clock in here too and for a while its rhythmic ticking was the only sound besides the low, steady hum of the air conditioner.

"You're not the least bit uncomfortable... are you, Flight Lieutenant?"

"No, sir... not in the least." I didn't see what he was getting at though his look told me it was something.

He smiled broadly. "The young Militiaman and the old Communist... just as comfortable as can be."

"The air conditioning sure helps."

He burst into laughter. "Oh come now, Flight Lieutenant... don't sell yourself short."

"What do you mean, sir?"

"It's a rare gift you have... Accepting people as they are... able to enjoy the qualities you admire... able to overlook the qualities you detest."

I shifted in my seat.

"You *do* detest Communism... don't you, Flight Lieutenant?"

"Yes, sir."

"And yet I actually see respect in your eyes when you look at me."

"Yessir... I *do* respect you."

"I was at your court-martial."

"Really? I didn't see you."

"Yes. I agreed with the President. The way you came across on the tape showed you respected your men a lot."

I nodded, reddening. "They were easy to respect."

"And I am easy to respect... or at least you appear to do it so effortlessly."

"Yessir. You're easy to respect."

"How come? When I've devoted my life to something you detest. Am *still* devoted to it?"

"Oh... your human kindness... to me when I first moved in... so distraught over the loss of Connie."

"She means a lot to you, doesn't she?"

"Yessir. We've been through a lot together. She's already suffered so much in her life. She just wanted to get back to me... and..." I tried to stop it but I burst into tears. "I'm sorry, sir," I sniffled, reaching for my handkerchief and wiping my eyes.

"It's all right." He waited for me to pull myself together, then returned to his earlier question. "Anything else... about me, I mean? I'd really like to know. Young people like you are somewhat rare in my life."

"Well... your hospitality in organizing this party. Your almost... well, kind of childlike optimism in inviting the Prime Minister and your other political enemies... I dunno... lots of things. You're just a neat guy."

"And yet soon we may be shooting at one another."

"Well... we have this moment. I say we ought to cherish it."

"You like our country, don't you?"

"Yes... I really do. I don't know why it's true Mister Perkins, but it's been my experience that the people who seem to have to deal with the most tragedy are often the people who make those around them the happiest."

"An interesting observation, young man. I agree with it." He let out a sigh, eyes on me all the while. "You may shortly be asked to do some very disagreeable things."

I know my eyes were widening, but I couldn't mask my shock. It was as if he had been in Colgate's office that day... knew I was a lieutenant-inspector in the secret police... knew how much the very thought of it made me retch.

His 'omniscient' look was shortly replaced by one I'd call 'understanding'. "Think you'll be up to them? Able to do them?"

I shook my head. "I just don't *know*, sir. I just wish politics would *leave me alone*."

"And therein lies the role of History in our lives, young man."

"You mean God?"

"I don't... but you do... yes. God, History, Fate... we're talking about the same thing. Those forces... that Force... which demands we be tested."

My head was down.

"Will you? I guarantee you that you will *not* be left alone."

"I suppose the answer is down the road.... I just don't know." Tears were forming in my eyes again, my head still down, struggling with the agony of it all.

"I'll tell you a secret Flight Lieutenant."

I looked up at him.

He smiled. "You seem to have the same reaction to 'secrets' or 'surprises' that Desi always had."

"He must have hated them"

"He did. In most ways you remind me of Bertie... he was always our arbiter.. The *fair* one."

I managed a rueful smile.

"I think the look on your face about reflects what Bertie must be feeling right now. His post is largely a ceremonial one... but constitutionally there is a mailed fist beneath the velvet glove of the governor-generalship."

"You mean his emergency decree power?"

"Exactly. You've been reading up on us."

"Yessir. It was in the factsheet... his constitutional powers."

"Uh huh. I'd be bound Bertie is staring into his looking glass this very moment, wondering if he'll be up to it. He's too smart not to know it's coming. It's just a question of when."

"But Colgate has a two-to-one majority... elections are... what... up to four years away?"

"You watch, Flight Lieutenant. He's going to be asked for the Royal Assent on some very disagreeable legislation very soon."

I nodded... Colgate's cryptic comments ringing in my ears from that horrible office visit.

"But anyway... my leader in the House of Councilors told me your appointment to the Upper Chamber by the Chamber of Commerce arrived today."

"Oh my *God*."

"Yes... it's going to... shall we say... accelerate your trip to the Crossroads."

"So *that's* why the planters wanted to talk to me."

He looked amused, despite the obvious sympathy. He'd no doubt seen hundreds of young men broken on the wheel of political fortune, but I gathered he'd never learned to enjoy it. "How did they strike you?"

"Hard men... like the ones who tamed the American West."

"And made it wild."

"Yes. Interesting men. Very inner directed."

"To be sure. Apparently you made a most favorable impression."

I must have looked gutshot. "I don't know why people always translate 'respect' to mean 'doormat'."

"A most common linguistic error."

I nodded sadly. "Colgate thinks I'm a born pushover... my old buddy Gene did... apparently the planters did." I looked at him. "For all I know *you* do, sir... with all due respect."

He waved off my concern he'd be angry with a gesture of his hand. "It's a fair comment, son. I'm not angry."

I shook my head. "Well *I am*... It's a goddam shame things are going to get so violent around here."

He smiled, then got a far off, wistful look in his eye. "You'll never know just *how* shameful, young man."

I looked at him with confusion, thinking that was more or less what we'd been talking about. He caught the expression, smiled, then leaned back and pulled a framed picture off the wall. Then he leaned forward and handed it across the desk to me.

A soot-covered building with a brass plate that said 'King's College' was in the background. A gorgeous young black woman with ironed hair and five smiling young black men with very short hair were in the foreground, all bundled up against the penetrating London cold.

"Recognize any of those people?" He asked, smiling.

A tall thin young man with one pant leg fasted up around the knee, leaning on crutches, caught my eye. "*You*, sir?"

He laughed, nodding. "King's Caribbean Rifles... just mustered out. They hadn't gotten my new one yet." He slapped the cane with a loud crack against one of his legs... obviously artificial. "El Alamein."

"My God."

"See anyone else?"

I looked hard, then let out a gasp. One of the young men with his arm around another had very distinctive eyes. They weren't so full of hate then, but their peculiar slant was very familiar. I pointed to him. "I don't know this man's name, sir, but I saw him in a poster once, and later met him in person."

"You did indeed," Perkins nodded. "That's Nat Webster."

Now I really gasped. I had saved the life of the man out to turn this island Communist.

Perkins laughed. "He told me a week or so ago about meeting you. He was on the way to meet one of his agents when he was jumped by three Our Destiny Party goons. He was very impressed with your kindness."

There was a part of what he just said I'd have to get back to. I just nodded for now.

"Any others?"

"The man Webster has his arm around looks familiar... but..."

"He should... that's Desi Colgate."

"They were very close once upon a time. We all were. Desi, Nat and I along with the lady, that's Dollie Fishbine by the way..."

It never ceased to amaze me how old age could destroy even the best of looks. In the picture she was *gorgeous*.

"...all went to King's College. We lived on tea, steak and kidney pudding, when we could afford it, and burning ideals." I thought I saw a tear in his eye as he looked at the picture one more time, then again handed it back. "The young man in the British Army overcoat and cap is Bertie Tibbets, who was stationed at Aldershot... the other young man is Thompson Ritter... he went to a nearby redbrick." He looked at me with misty eyes.

"Damn... you all go back a long way."

"We certainly do. We'd get together, the only people from Maggierock in all of England. We were all quite close. We'd talk about independence... pursuing our own destiny." He frowned, then smiled as if recognizing that time made tragedy a funny war story. "Desi stole that phrase from Nat... named his party after it."

He settled back in his chair, looking up at the ceiling. "Now... all these years later... we've *got* it... and it just breaks my heart we all couldn't get together one last time." He turned away as I did the same. Obviously that had been his fond hope for this party.

"I'm sorry, young man. I'm rather tired now. Would you mind?"

"Not at all, sir." I hauled myself to my feet. "Thank you for this conversation, sir."

He nodded.

"You'll be at the Mahali tomm... uh tonight... won't you?"

"Yes... I'll be there."

I reached out my hand. "Good night, sir."

He took it in a firm grip, looking me dead in the eye. "Good night, son. I hope one of us is not in the unhappy position in the coming days of pulling the trigger on the other... directly in your case... indirectly in mine. I mean that with all my heart."

I returned his look, nauseated as his obviously knowing comment left me. "Devoutly to be wished, sir... truly."

He managed a final nod, then I left the library in search of my party for the trip home.

I made the return trip to the beach house lost in all kinds of thoughts. My own sense of a coming collision with Destiny had me once more boiling with anxiety, yet flattened by depression. On top of that, however, Mister Perkins left me profoundly wishing I could witness the reunion that had so unjustly eluded him this night. Of course they'd all be there... in about twenty-two hours, when the new flag was hoisted. The Mahali had been built in my absence into a kind of stadium, with the Wall of Heroes in the position of the centerfield wall, if this were a ball park. Yes... they'd be there, but separated from one another both by seating and years of bitterness I knew nothing about. In my boyish, everything-in-its-rightful-place mind, I thought it was rather tragic.

Chapter Ten

COACHES INTO PUMPKINS...
OR VICE VERSA

Sunday April 15, 1973... Independence Day: The Mahali, Port Albert, Isle of St. Margaret's

April 14, 1973 was a day like no other in the history of Maggierock. From the time the sun rose, people were on the streets, throwing firecrackers and cherry bombs, loudly wishing one another 'Happy Independence Day', throwing garlands of flowers upon the necks of friends and enemies alike. Beginning about noon, everyone with a musical instrument was outside playing it. From every electrical outlet came the sounds of blaring records, as long lines of people snake-danced their way through the streets.

The Air Militia jeep had called for me at the beach house promptly at 0800. My orders from Gene were to proceed to the fort and take custody of the Air Militia part of the British Command Post as well as three of the barracks buildings that were allocated for our men. I was then to supervise the installation of the large headquarters ham radio that was our only link to the two airstrips as well as any of our three aircraft that happened to be in the air at the time. There weren't any today. Our outfit had been ordered grounded from now until the Princess left. Jet fighters from the aircraft carrier were flying constantly over the island, as were helicopters.

That task completed, and installing Flight Sergeant Prentice in command of what would be a constantly manned position from now on, I was next to take possession of the air traffic control tower. The British had removed all their electronic equipment from the command post, leaving us only the detail map of the island hanging on one wall. They were, however, leaving us all the equipment in the tower.

Once those tasks were completed, I went over to the parade ground to check on the preparations for tonight. First Subaltern Felonious Burns was busy drilling the honor guard that would march with the other Militia, who were also drilling, in the ceremonies at the Mahali. Like me, they were all in their blue coveralls because, like me, they had to save their khakis for the big occasion. Another set for all of us was supposedly on the way, and I had ordered another set of ribbons from a specialty company after my only set came home somewhat damaged from my New Britain escapade. They weren't here yet. Our harbor was also sealed by the British until after the departure of the Princess. Only the seaplane was coming in on Tuesday, and that was because it originated in a Commonwealth country and the British would be carefully screening the passengers before they boarded.

It was nearly 1600 when I finally hauled myself back to the jeep for the return trip to the beach house where I was to link up with Sybil and pass the time until we joined the rest of the island at the Mahali for the gala independence ceremonies. We had seats with the other military officers in the section behind what would be the 'home plate' part of the stadium. Joe and Tucan, Sean and Sunflower had seats somewhere in the reserved civilian section.

By now the atmosphere along the roadway was electric. Islanders swarmed up and down... singing, drinking from bottles, waving Union Jacks and the island's new flag in their hands. Many of the British soldiers stationed in small groups along the roadway had garlands of ginger blossoms around their necks. In the course of our journey, I saw several put there by young, weeping island women. I gathered these had been the girlfriends of the particular soldiers during their time here. There was much nostalgia in the air, much joy... and one hell of a lot of electricity. I was finding it fascinating... witnessing the birth of a nation.

Sybil greeted me at the door of the beach house, dressed in a flaming coral bikini and holding an impressive parchment-looking paper adorned with a gold seal streaming black and green ribbons in her hands. "Oh *mume!*" she chirped excitedly as she handed me the paper. "Look what came for you!"

It was a document styled 'Writ of Summons', from Emory Jack, Lord President of the House of Councilors, to me, 'commanding' my presence on the floor of the House as an 'August Councilor of State' for the State Opening of Parliament on Monday April 16. The document recited that I was to occupy the bench of the Chamber of Commerce. The gold seal had been affixed at the Office of the Notary-General, and carried Dollie Fishbine's signature attesting to the authenticity of the document.

Sybil searched my eyes, a look of puzzlement suddenly in hers. "What's the matter, *mume?* Aren't you *thrilled?* This means I get to watch the State Opening of our very first Parliament in the 'family section' of the balcony!"

Seeing her look brightened my own... at least a little. I threw my arms around her and we kissed. "Well," I finally managed, "this was the last thing I wanted. But if it makes *you* happy..."

"Oh it does! And you'll be serving with my eldest brother and eldest sister! It'll be like a family gathering!"

She'd already told me about Emory. "Who's your sister?"

"Apple... a very strong willed woman let me tell you."

She didn't have to. I had never met a Jack that wasn't. The name floored me though. "*Apple Jack?*"

She shrugged, giggling. "Uncle Amadeus had quite a sense of humor."

"So he did." Amid laughter that was doing a fair job of papering over my anxieties, Sybil helped me out of my flight suit and into my swimming trunks for a late afternoon swim. Then we showered, me getting into my khakis and her into a flaming coral minidress for our trip to the Mahali.

A cool breeze perfectly complimented the clear night as we sat in the 'military section', looking out on the large flagpole, flying the Union Jack, with the VIP section beyond that had been constructed especially for the occasion up against the Wall of Heroes. At the entrance, we had been given two very nicely done souvenir programs with a formal portrait of Princess Margaret on the front page, with full page formal portraits of Bertie Tibbets and Desmond Colgate on pages two and three. The other cabinet ministers appeared on succeeding pages.

Between the flagpole and the regular stadium seating, a speaker's platform had been constructed under an awning, and JoJo Child, the popular disc jockey on Radio Maggie was hard at work, leading the crowd in boisterous singing. Outside the stadium, knots of British soldiers, accompanied by business-suited men whose pasty white faces told me they weren't from around here, were at each entrance screening the members of the crowd as they entered. Occasionally containers were opened, but mostly the searches were confined to checking passes with identification. The strange men, I was told, were agents of Scotland Yard's Special Branch, in charge of security for the Princess.

The crowd sent up a cheer at shortly after nine p.m. when Desmond Colgate and his cabinet filed into the VIP section. Several of the others in the section were already there. Looking in my program, I found out these were the diplomatic corps. St. Margaret's had two High Commissions, including the British. The new High Commissioner was none other than David Phillips, the outgoing Royal Governor. The other was Jamaican. Already an independent country, Jamaica's Governor General had played host to Bertie Tibbets most of the last two months, educating him in the responsibilities and ceremonies that went with the job.

Below the High Commissions in protocol was one embassy. I cringed when I learned it was Cuban. The ambassador was dressed in the dark green of the Cuban People's Militia. The program said his name was Colonel Heriberto Córdova. Below the ambassador were four Ministers of Legations, from the United States, Soviet Union, Argentina and Israel. The Argentine minister was also in uniform. He was General Antonio Imbert y Colona. The Israeli and American ministers were both women.

Seeing the American minister named as Donna Goldstien, my heart skipped a beat. Very glad I'd bought my field glasses, I put them

to my eyes for a look. She was a little older, and much more digni-
fied looking, than I remembered her that afternoon in Paris when we
were smoking my hash at a party on the Left Bank. She'd been in
blue jeans at the time, and was introduced to me by Gail Alexander,
another diplomat posted as a vice-consul to the American Embassy
in Paris. Yes, the years had left a mark of sorts, but Donna still looked
utterly gorgeous. She had been only the second diplomat I had ever
kissed. Now, all these years later, the number still stood at two.

Below the ministers were three consuls, the Dutch, French and
Swiss. All the diplomats were present, all the ministers of state were
present when, at eleven o'clock, a huge clock with only one hand was
hoisted, to the oohs and aahs of the crowd, up from behind the Wall
of Heroes.

"Only one hour to go before independence!" JoJo Child crowed
to tumultuous cheers. They had barely died down when two Honor
Guards, the British 18th Berkshire Rifles and our Militia and Air Militia marched out to a song played by the British military band from
the fort. The soldiers lined up on either side of the VIP section in
front of the flagpole. Looking again at the section, only four throne-
like chairs at the very front were empty. The Reverend Damian
Wallace, vicar of St. Martin's Church of England Mission mounted
the platform and pronounced the invocation. The main part of the
ceremonies were about to begin.

Suddenly the air was split with the sounds of an approaching helicopter. The crowd waited expectantly as it flew over the Mahali, then
came in for a landing between the two honor guards. It was a large
ship, with ROYAL NAVY painted across the fuselage. As it touched
down a tremendous roar went up. The soldiers went to 'present arms'
as Sir Bertram Tibbets, resplendent in his Commonwealth Service
white uniform, his many military decorations and the red sash of the
Order of Knights Companion of the Thistle making for a glorious
sight, stepped out, holding out a gloved hand to Princess Margaret,
who then stepped out. They were shortly joined by Lord Snowdon
and Lady Helen Tibbetts.

The band broke into an emotional rendition of *God Save the Queen*
as Tibbetts saluted and we all stood. After an inspection of both

honor guards as the helicopter departed, they mounted the speaker's platform where Princess Margaret administered the oath of the Governor General to more cheering. I was full of goose bumps by now. The ceremony was extremely well done, with both the raw emotion and the historical gravity of the ceremony coming through with full force. Following the administration of the oath to Tibbetts, he then summoned Prime Minister Colgate and his Cabinet to the platform. After each of them did a neck bow and kissed the Princess' white gloved hand, Tibbetts administered their oaths, to more tumultuous cheering. Then they resumed their seats in the VIP section, with the Princess and other arrivals from the helicopter occupying the four thrones.

There wasn't a dry eye in the house as, at one minute until midnight, to a drum roll and the solemn strains of *God Save The Queen*, the Union Jack was hauled down from the flagpole, dazzlingly lit by several floodlights. The big hand of the clock moved to midnight...

Then with another drum roll as the crowd held its breath, the green-black-green horizontally striped flag of the new nation slowly moved up the pole, ablaze in the floodlights, as the band struck up the new National Anthem, *O Fair St. Margaret's Island Home* to the tune of *A Mighty Fortress Is Our God*. Thousands of voices, already hoarse from cheering, took up the song.

O Fair St. Margaret's Island Home...
Thy bounty richly blessing...
'Neath golden sun and shady tree...
Our People labour praising thee...

Our triumph ever sure...
The tempests we endure...
Though Satan's host assail...
Our People will prevail...

Until Thy final victory....!

Wild cheering resounded throughout the Mahali as I recalled, grinning, staggering through the New Britain mud with Preston saying 'let's do the verse about the whores'. I wondered what he and his men were doing and thinking this minute, besides feeling profoundly gypped they were unable to share in this amazing spectacle.

From beyond the Wall of Heroes an incredible display of fireworks lit up the Port Albert sky. It was official... a new nation was born. Tears streaming down our cheeks, Sybil and I tightly embraced one another, much as all the people in the stadium were doing. There were many things to criticize here, many more to laugh about, but I don't think anyone could have possibly witnessed what we did without feeling deeply emotional toward the new nation and her fears, hopes and dreams for the time ahead.

It would be close to three a.m. before Sybil and I were finally able to inch our way through the traffic of deliriously happy snake-dancers and arrive back at the beach house. Graham was at the wheel, Joe gripping the shotgun. His beloved Tucan was riding in the Land Rover behind, with Sean and Sunflower, Melissa our housekeeper and Colby Hanlon, our groundskeeper and brother of the deserter-turned-hero Marvel Hanlon. It had finally happened, peacefully and with a universal sense of community. I had witnessed history this night, and it left me profoundly moved. I dreaded the inevitable return to reality tomorrow would bring... I think everyone did.

Monday April 16, 1973: the State Opening of Parliament, Chamber of the House of Councilors, Government Plaza, Port Albert, Isle of St. Margaret's

Arriving at Government Plaza shortly after eight a.m., I saw for the first time the green-black-green flag flying from the pole amid the gardens. Gone were the British Army sandbagged emplacements that had marked the final month of the colonial administration. In their place was a cordon of constables around the Houses of Parliament and many more of those pasty-faced guys. A large helicopter flew overhead, every now and then joined by a flight of jet fighters streaking in from the carrier, headed to the mountains, then back again.

Showing my Writ of Summons, Sybil and I were directed to the entrance for the Upper House, and thence to the 'robing room', where each Councilor had his own wardrobe cabinet. Gene had ordered us all to be in uniform until further notice, expecting, as I believe most people did, an all-out offensive as the last strains of *O Fair St. Margaret's Island Home* died away at the Mahali. Thus far, that hadn't happened, though it was plainly apparent the display of British air and sea power and all those Scotland Yard agents probably had something to do with it. Therefore I had to leave the officer's cap, Sam Browne with revolver and blouse inside the wardrobe, putting on the black cotton robe and white yoke over teeshirt and trousers.

"Gidday mate!" a dark tan, leathery faced guy built like he made a living wrestling kangaroos and wearing the same color yoke as me called out as I entered the Members' Lounge after escorting Sybil to the family gallery.

"Hi."

"Cassell, right?"

"That's me."

"Perry Herbert." He stuck out a calloused hand and nearly crushed mine with a brief shake.

"Oh yes... the naturalist! I've been hearing about you since I arrived."

"So that's what they call me behind my back... a naturalist." He spoke with a thick Aussie accent I found almost impossible to follow.

"Yeah... they say you live up on Point Loma Hermose... getting your brains scrambled with the wind."

He chuckled. "That's right, mate. You gotta go far and wide to escape people nowadays... but it's worth it. If it's got less than six legs, I ain't interested."

I had to admit I could sometimes see his point, though not the part about the legs. "How do you get here? There's no roads."

He gave me a look that translated 'citified sissy'. "Believe it or not, mate, people traveled before roads... got me a ten wheel drive Land Rover... Just me n' the bumps and the jungle on one side, sea on the other, all the way to Port Albert. Don't come 'ere often. Hate the bloody place."

"Hmmm."

"Only 'ere today for the State Opening... then I'll give my proxy to Szabo n' that's the last they'll see me 'till something important crops up."

"Proxy? Szabo?"

"Right. They got a system 'ere where you give a proxy to your favorite leader. He can't vote with it, but 'e can use it to enable a quorum... or lack of it. You gonna do that?"

I looked around the lounge. Paneled walls, stuffed chairs and sofas, darkwood writing tables and chairs... politicians in black robes with red, blue and white yokes. "I can't see spending much time here."

"That's the ticket."

"Who's Szabo?"

"NLP leader in the House."

"Ohhh."

He eyed me with disapproval. "Don't tell me your ODP."

"Okay... I won't."

He laughed.

"Tell me... how'd you get drafted for this?"

"Don't rightly know. I've been here for years. I guess when the Chamber of Commerce was tryin' to fill the seats they just thought of me. How 'bout you?"

"I really don't know... but I don't like it."

"You n' me'll get on fine, lad." He put a solid arm across my shoulder. "C'mon, let's go in."

The Chamber of the House of Councilors was two horseshoes stacked on top of each other. The top was the balcony... already crowded. The bottom were three groups of those benches, rising upward toward the back. There were about ten seats in each row, done in red plush, with armrests in between. To the front of each bench was a small, inclined row-like table on which Members could place books and papers.

The wood was dark, the floor was white mosaic tile, about like an old Atlantic City hotel bathroom. At the open end of the horseshoe was a large black marble bench, on a platform or dais accessible by climbing four steps. Behind the bench were two thrones. To the front of the bench was a big long table at which several people already sat, some were writing, some reading... some staring. A red carpet ran from the front of the opposite benches all the way to the long table, then beyond it up the stairs. The same carpet came down the stairs to the side of the platform as well, leading to a door. The dark wood paneling on the walls of the lower level gave it an appearance something like a church.

"We sit at the apex of the horseshoe, all five in the first row. The benches to our left, and the President's right, are the Government. They wear the blue yokes. The benches opposite are the Opposition. They wear the red."

I snickered. "That figures."

A small Oriental man, similarly gowned and yoked as us, was the only person sitting in the far benches at the moment. "'ere, mate... I'll introduce you. Tran?"

The man looked up. "Hello Perry."

"Tran this is John Cassell... also of our bench." The man nodded, giving a slight smile. I nodded back.

Herbert and I took two seats on the left hand side of the Chamber of Commerce row. I looked up and saw Sybil. I gave her a wave which she returned with a big smile. Within minutes a bustle of activity occurred as all the rest of the Members seemed to appear at once. I recognized Felonious Burns, the Government Leader, almost immediately. That was because he looked so much like his son. He took a seat in the first Government row, nearest the platform.

"I better go say hello to Burns," I told Perry, getting up.

"Fascist, are ye, son?"

I turned to look at him. "I don't know what I am, but I'm not a Communist. It just so happens I work with the man's son."

Herbert nodded, then looked away.

As I made my way across the House floor, several young people came in handing out programs. I got mine, then completed the journey to the front of the first row of Government benches. "Mister Burns?"

He had been talking to the man beside him. Hearing me, he looked up. "Yes?" Seeing my white yoke, and white face, I don't think he knew what to expect.

"I work with your son.. In the Air Milita... I..."

Now a big smile stole across his face. "The *jumbe* Flight Lieutenant?"

"Well... yes... but..."

"Oh I know all about you. Welcome to the House, son."

"Thank you, sir. Your son is a fine officer and acquitted himself very bravely... that night."

The Government Leader nodded, smiling. "Let me introduce you to the other Members here. He did, in rapid-fire order that caused me to forget every name except Olive Fishbine. I remembered her because she was introduced as the old Notary-General's daughter... and because she had her mother's stunning looks I remembered from the photo, though with an afro instead of the old fashioned ironed hair.

"Olive is a solicitor," Burns told me. "Just admitted to the Bar out of King's College London."

"Ashes to ashes," I found myself mumbling. Then to Olive "so you're just back?"

"Yes."

I couldn't help but be entranced. I also dimly remembered that the main job of this House was to be the Supreme Court of the nation. "When we do our judicial work can I come to you with questions?"

She gave me a bright smile. "Of course."

There was suddenly a banging noise. "Better get to your bench," Burns whispered. "We'll talk later."

"Oh... okay." One last look at Olive and I picked my way around two thrones that sat between the platform and the beginning of the Government and Opposition benches, then headed down the carpet to our benches.

"John!" The loudly stage-whispered voice caused me to whiplash up to the gallery. There, looking down on me, dressed in a modest white dress was Donna Goldstien."

"Well HI!"

"John I don't believe it! I saw you down there and of course recognized you, but until I saw your name in the program..."

"Yeah! I saw you at the Mahali. Can I come over to the Legation some morning?"

"Of course!"

"Great seeing you, Donna. I gotta get to my seat."

She sort of wiggled the fingers of her white gloved hand. I gave a final nod and smile and headed for our benches, now full, taking my seat next to Perry Herbert once more as the door near the platform burst open. A distinguished looking dark-complected man in morning dress came out first carrying some sort of gold baton, with a crown and cross on top.

"Be upstanding!" a voice bellowed from the side of the platform. Everyone rose as The Reverend Mister Wallace came in next, wearing the white stole for feast days over his cassock and surplice. After him, a huge, coal black man with snow white afro, wearing a magenta robe with ermine stole.

"That's Emory Jack," Herbert whispered.

I nodded.

"Who was the babe?"

"Olive Fish..."

"No... no... NO!" He indicated the gallery. "The olive-*skinned* dish?"

"Oh. Donna Goldstien, the American Minister."

"Hmmm," Herbert whispered. "Things are looking up round here."

"She's only got two legs, bud."

"Very nice ones I'd be bound."

"You said it... but that rule of yours?"

He gave me a smirk. "There's exceptions to everything, mate." Indeed there was, and Perry Herbert had chosen his exception well.

"The House will come to order." Jack now intoned. "August Councilors Cassell and Torgeson approach and take the oath."

"Hi Ollie." I hadn't seen the airstrip's project manager since before it was completed.

"Cassell." Torgeson was something of a stick in the mud, so I didn't expect a fulsome reunion.

We both made our ways to the President's throne and were sworn in. Something about Jack looked familiar, but I guessed it was a family resemblance I was picking up. Not that he looked anything like Sybil in my book, and judging from the white hair had been born at least thirty years before her, though you sure wouldn't know it by his smooth skin.

"We're all but in-laws, Cassell," he whispered, smiling, as he nearly crushed my hand with his grip after I took the oath then signed it.

"Yessir," I responded shaking my mangled hand to try to get the circulation going again.

"Did I hurt you?" He looked amused.

"Well… it's just that this is the second time today."

He gave me a wink. "Third time's the charm, Cassell." I retreated back to my bench not really sure what he meant by that. I was getting very strange vibes from this place, and the people in it.

"We will shortly be joined by the other place," Jack now intoned. "Then we'll proceed with the State Opening." He nodded to a page, several of which sat on the steps leading up to the platform. The young man nodded, then took off out the door Jack had come in.

He'd barely done that when another page came in, looked over to the Chamber of Commerce benches, then headed in my direction. "Councilor Cassell?"

"Yes?"

He handed me a note. I opened it, turning it away from Herbert's prying eyes.

THE GOVERNOR GENERAL

16 Apr 1973

TO: Flight Lieutenant John Cassell, MHC

Come see me, Flight Lieutenant, at the conclusion of the State Opening. Over at Government House.

Tibbetts

Oh brother, I thought to myself. *What NOW.* I barely had time to add to the thought when the doors burst open and some twenty or more people in suits and dresses came in.

"The other place," Perry whispered.

"Why do they call it that? Why not House of Assembly?"

Perry shrugged.

Prime Minister Colgate and his Cabinet, all in what must have been stifling morning dress, took the row of seats behind Burns and his Members. Another four took their places in the third row. On the other side, Norbert Perkins and his six other MP's sat behind the Opposition Members.

I had to admit I'd been wrong about Colgate. The tape played at the court-martial had answered the last of my nagging questions about the mission. Ferdinand had talked him into the assignment. It had been nothing sinister.

I saw Perkins looking in our direction. His eyes met mine, then he held up the program, made a show of turning to the second page and pointing to something somewhere in the middle. Then he gave a wink, turning back to the front.

"You are friends with Norbert?" Herbert whispered.

"We're neighbors." I opened the program to the page, then looked about halfway down.

The Address from the Throne is the traditional mechanism by which the Government of the day sets out its Programme to the Members of Parliament. The address is delivered personally by the Sovereign or her representative. In Commonwealth countries such as ours this is done by the Governor General, though H.R.H. Princess Margaret, sister of the Sovereign, will be presenting the speech on this occasion, our very first Parliament.

"Hmmm."

I looked over at Perkins, showing my puzzlement.

He just winked back, then turned away once more. I suddenly knew what he was telling me. *Listen closely to this speech, young man, the axe of dictatorship is about to land on the neck of a free people.* It angered me people around here were always getting me suspicious of other people around here. Weren't leaving me in *peace.* Perkins looked over once more, caught the frustration on my face, then burst into laughter.

A tall, thin man of great age, like the Lord President coal black in complexion, like the rest of us in this chamber except the Lord President wearing a black robe, unlike any of us wearing a long white wig, took the throne next to Jack.

Jack saw him and his eyes immediately bulged. He hurriedly summoned a page, then whispered something in the young man's ear. He ran out of the chamber.

"Who's the other man on the dais?" I whispered to Herbert.

"The Speaker... Jocko Cummings." Herbert jabbed an elbow in my side. "The man's older than sin, but at least *he* remembered."

"Remembered what?"

By way of answer, Herbert nudged me once more, indicating the dais with his head. As a trickle of laughter washed over the room, the page returned carrying another of those long white wigs which Jack jammed on his head.

"Oh." I had just begun to laugh when Jack cast me a glare that turned my blood to ice. Just me... no one else. Again I found myself wondering what it was about him I was picking up on.

Another banging noise... repeated three times, caused everyone to go silent. I now knew it was a staff striking the tile floor. "Lord President!" a voice boomed from the doorway leading to the carpeted path between our benches and the Opposition's. "Her Royal Highness the Princess Margaret! His Excellency the Most Honourable Sir Bertram Tibbetts!"

As one we rose to our feet, rendering a very enthusiastic standing ovation. Out of my right hand peripheral vision there shortly appeared a black robed man carrying a staff of some sort. Then came the Princess in a white gown, a tiara on her head, clutching a thin red book in one gloved hand, the other resting lightly on the gloved hand of Bertie Tibbetts. She wore a blue sash and a jeweled brooch I'd seen the Queen wear in formal portraits. The Governor General was again resplendent in his Commonwealth Service uniform, the red sash of his order and his many military decorations again making an awesome sight.

Once more I was full of those goose bumps. I couldn't believe I was witnessing this scene as a Member of the Upper Chamber of a Commonwealth nation's Parliament. The fact it all traced directly back to money that had been left to me made no difference at this magic moment. This wasn't about my earning the right to be here... it was about being here period. That was the pure joy of it.

My eyes drifted to Sybil, tearfully applauding, overcome with emotion as I was. Then to Donna, whose eyes drifted to mine with a brief, lovely smile and an expression that shrieked *who woulda' thunk it, Cassell? That Sunday morning back in 1969!* Who woulda' thunk it indeed.

The Princess and the Governor General reached the thrones below the dais, turned, bowed to the assemblage, then stood until the applause died down. "Be seated!" Jack intoned.

"Let us pray," the vicar countered. I'd almost forgotten he was here. He'd taken a seat beyond the Government benches beside the dais and was out of my view. Everyone's head was bowed.

"Heavenly Father, we humbly and heartily thank thee for that thou hath vouchsafed us to the day of our independence... and hath blessed us with this assemblage and our participation as free people in it..."

My eyes involuntarily looked at Perkins. The sly old dog gave me another wink, enjoying my frustration. I think I now knew what the phrase 'Communist agitation' really meant. The man was intruding on my peace of mind... and loving it.

"And for the gracious kindness of a Sovereign who hath caused to be with us her beloved Royal sister, to join with us in this celebration of our freedom. God Bless the Princess Margaret! God bless the Government and People of St. Margaret's! God Save the Queen!"

"AMEN!" we all gushed with a vigor that would have made old Enid Worthington proud.

A breathless silence, punctuated with a cough here and there and the brush of fabric against wood, now ensued. The Princess opened the thin little red book.

"Lord President... Mister Speaker... August Councilors of State... Honourable Members of the Assembly... the People of St. Margaret's..."

The Princess cleared her throat. I'd have been *dying* of nerves by now if that were me.

"From my beloved sister... Our Noble Queen... and Her husband I bring you heartfelt good wishes and prayers for our nation as it begins its journey on the road of independence... Lord Snowden and I add our own... for we are one family, united in purpose... devoted to freedom... and dedicated to the pursuit of our destiny as one united People..."

There was no doubt who'd written *this* speech. *And yes, the old bastard was grinning at me, reminding me that the line was stolen from Nat Webster all those years ago.*

"Time... for a People no stranger to want and poverty... is a precious commodity... and Her Majesty's Government pledge to you that we shan't allow the opportunity of this first Parliament to be wasted in our quest for a better, more fulfilling life here on this sainted Isle...

"Our Ministers will therefore shortly lay before you legislation which will provide an expeditious registration procedure for those in our midst who have joined us from other lands... enabling them to enjoy the full benefits of citizenship and full participation in the civil life of our nation..."

The dual citizenship bill, I remembered.

"So as to provide for a safe and tranquil environment in which to accomplish our rapid maturity as a self-governing nation, legislation will shortly be brought forth which will increase the Militias and the Constabulary... and enable them otherwise to be better able to counter aggression which bitter experience has taught us lurks never far from our shores...

"But defence by force of arms alone cannot effectively nurture the growth of democratic responsibility, and it shall therefore come to pass within the week that a series of discrete proposals, collectively labeled the Civic Responsibility Growth Act, shall be laid before you by Our Ministers..."

Perkins was looking hard at me now. I tensed.

"Among the separate components of this cornerstone of our freedom will be proposals to encourage..." The Princess actually did a double take. Very subtly, but in my suddenly heightened state of nerves I clearly caught it. Bertie Tibbetts did too. He turned in her direction, glancing down at the text held on her lap.

"Uh... to encourage the growth of... patriotic thinking and civic responsibility... to provide for a continual, wholesome public education in democratic virtues, that those in our midst lacking the proper tools to effectively participate in the realization of universal democracy shall be enlightened... that each citizen be empowered to do his or her part in the overall function of the body politic..."

My how politicians could fuck with words! This called to mind the slogan that the Nazis, who were among the first brilliant mass 'democracy' politicians, put over their hateful concentration camps... Arbeit Macht Frei... something like that anyway...'work makes us free'! The Princess was blushing, albeit ever so slightly. Tibbetts, who had practically been dozing, was wide awake. Perkins was still looking straight at me.

"To provide for a sufficient allocation of resources, both fiscal and human, to carry the programme of public education to all our people... to ensure the realisation of a society happy and free..."

Yeah...Arbeit Macht Frei... stop looking at me Perkins! I turned to look at Colgate and Ritter. Their expressions were utterly impassive.

"Our Ministers will lay before you in due course proposals for youth groups and local civic responsibility organisations... open to all... the freedom to say 'yes' and the wisdom to exercise that willing assent an asset of the body politic withheld from no one...." The Princess coughed.

Tibbetts was staring straight ahead. I kept recalling Perkins' description of the harassed Governor General, standing at his looking glass, with all those Royal Assents to think about. There was no doubt all this stuff would pass... 14 to 7 in the all-powerful Lower House. With a chill down my back, I then remembered our Chamber. If every Chamber of Commerce Member voted against it, the thing could be tied. Of course then Jack would cast the deciding vote. I glanced in his direction. He was staring at a spot on the wall beyond and above the Chamber of Commerce benches opposite... utterly impassive.

Of course we could only veto it for a year... But then a lot could happen in a year, particularly in a place like this, where people were just beginning the feel their oats as members of a supposedly free society...

I stole a look at Donna. Her nimble brain was obviously working overtime, decoding this amazing Queen's Speech as well. By now Princess Margaret was positively nonplused, though was doing an expert job of concealment. I doubt a Windsor had ever been asked to read such a speech. I wanted to be a fly on the wall in Tibbett's office when the two of them got back there.

Then I remembered my summons. I didn't have to be a fly on the wall! I resolved to head there first thing.

"... And thus convey to you my dear sister's affectionate wish for your happiness and well-being. God bless you all... God Save the Queen."

I'd apparently spaced out the concluding proposals contained in the Speech, though I'd certainly heard enough. The entire Chamber erupted into applause as we all got once more on our feet. Princess Margaret closed the book and exchanged a split second look with Tibbetts. Then, with the applause for her still resounding off the walls, the two of them rose and walked out the same way they had entered.

Monday April 16, 1973: the Office of the Governor General, Government House, Government Plaza, Port Albert, Isle of St. Margaret's

"What in God's name is the *rush, mume!*" Sybil gasped as I practically dragged her along the pathway from the Houses of Parliament to Government House.

I had charged out of the Chamber as soon as dismissed, getting to my wardrobe cabinet and climbing into my uniform once more, then began the frenetic journey, Sybil in tow, to Tibbetts' office.

"In due time, baby! I gotta appointment with Tibbetts!"

"Oh!" a smile lit up her face. "You're sure going places, *mume!*"

"Glad you're happy about it, luv."

The grounds of Government Plaza were mobbed. I was hailed twice by constables and once by a Special Branch agent outside Government House, but Tibbetts' signed note was the skeleton key that opened all doors.

Depositing Sybil in an overstuffed chair outside his office, I showed the note to his secretary. She obviously knew of it. "Go right in," she replied, handing it back, without even picking up her intercom.

Opening the door to the inner office, I beheld the Governor General, now in tan slacks and a short sleeved light blue dress shirt, standing with his back to me, looking out the four wide louvered windows behind his desk. Princess Margaret, now in a plain light blue dress, was to the side, facing more in his direction than mine.

"But of course if ODP stood together, you'd find it virtually impossible to form a majority government." The Princess was talking in a low voice.

Tibbetts glumly nodded.

I coughed, causing both to turn around suddenly. "Beg pardon, Your Excellency," I gasped, bringing my arm up in salute. "I was told to come in."

"You're Cassell?" Tibbetts asked as he returned the salute.

"Yessir."

He nodded, then eased himself into the large swivel chair, gesturing to his left. "Her Royal Highness Princess Margaret."

I managed something approximating a neck bow as the Princess smiled, also taking a seat.

"Sit down, son."

I took a nearby chair, very nervous in such august company. Here I'd planned to get all the inside dope on the Head of State's reaction to the Speech, yet when actually in his presence and that of the Princess was too nervous to think of doing anything except getting out of there.

In person, Tibbetts was of medium complexion standing just under six feet, with a solid, stocky build. He wore his salt and pepper hair very short. His silver-framed glasses gave him an almost professorial air. He seemed *worried*, but quickly flashed a smile.

"Thank you for coming, Flight Lieutenant."

The Princess once more stood up. "Well, Bertie, it's a puzzle... I'd best get back to the High Commission and get ready for the trip home."

"It's a pity you couldn't manage a visit to Mustique whilst here."

The Princess gave him a look of frustration. "Yes... all this lovely tropical water and no place to swim... the shadows won't allow it."

She looked at me, giving a warm smile. "Good to have met you, Flight Lieutenant."

I had gotten to my feet when she did. "An honor, ma'am. Did you want a place to swim?" I don't know what possessed me to blurt that.

I guess I just felt sorry for her, as I did for all the Royals, ever since I learned that they had less privileges than the man on the street, their lives constantly directed by other people.

The Princess had started to turn away, then whiplashed back toward me as my question registered.

"Sybil and I have a very nice beach house. You'd be most welcome."

Tibbetts was looking at me as if I'd gone mad, yet not without sympathy for my efforts to reach out to his royal visitor. I swallowed nervously, then looked back to the Princess.

At first she shook her head with frustration, but then a mischievous look began to steal across her face. "You know, Bertie, every now and then I just *dream* of giving the shadows the slip. I've less privacy than a goldfish in a bowl."

She turned back to me. "I was told today I needed to be back in London. I'd been hoping to go to my place on Mustique for a fortnight or so... you sound American. Are you?"

"Yes, ma'am."

"You wouldn't mind?"

I couldn't believe my ears. "No ma'am, not in the least."

Wearing the same mischievous grin, she thought a few seconds more, then picked up the phone on Tibbetts' desk, dialing three numbers.

"How are you going to give your protection the slip?" Tibbetts asked, now amused at the turn things were taking.

The Princess flashed a big smile. "Oh... just a thought I've had recently. An idea I got from a cinema."

"Maude?" She turned back to the phone. "Put Mattie on." ...

"Mattie? Remember the light blue dress you laid out? Bring yours... the white hat... oh, and the swimwear, will you?" ...

"Yes, Government House... Yes... Goodb... oh! Put Tony on, will you?" ...

"Tony? I'm going for a swim. Care to come?" . . . A dark cloud seemed to pass over her face. "Oh all right. Just don't panic when I turn up missing for a bit. I'll be at..."

She turned to me. "Where will I be at?"

"Uh... the Cassell beach house, between Mantilla and New Gat-wick... next to the Serena Blackstone house."

She repeated it. "Yes Tony, just for a bit. Goodbye." Now she looked positively excited. "Oh I hope this works," she sighed as she put down the phone.

She looked at me. "Young man, I'm afraid you're in for a bit of cloak and dagger."

"It's quite all right, ma'am," I replied, wondering just what I was getting into with my flapping mouth. "But I really should bring Sybil in on this... we may need her help with your getaway."

The Princess laughed. "That's the spirit."

I went back into the outer office, motioning Sybil to join me. She let out a delighted gasp as she saw who was in the room, doing a very good curtsy. She became even more excited when I explained the plan.

Some ten minutes later, a sandy-haired lady came in carrying a small suitcase. She was introduced to us as 'Mattie', the Viscountess Matilda Romley-Dunlop. Up until this minute, the closest I'd come to British aristocracy was shaking hands with the Lord Bishop of Warwick and Leamington after a service I'd attended in 1969. Anglican bishops, I'd long since been told, ranked as barons and sat in the House of Lords.

"You brought the sun cream, I hope, Mattie."

"Yes, ma'am."

"Wouldn't want Teddy to have a fit I burned a holding of the National Trust."

Within minutes the 'switch' was complete. Mattie did sort of resemble the Princess from behind, and with the white wide-brimmed hat managed to conceal her different colored hair. The Princess pointed to the spot where we needed to bring the Land Rover, and Sybil joyfully ran off to get it done.

"Now Bertie," the Princess finally said as we were ready to put the plan into action, "you'll give me an hour at least, right?"

Tibbetts by now was immensely enjoying himself. "Your Special Branch chaps are very persuasive," he replied, picking up the phone. He placed a call to Lady Helen, telling her he was going to lose himself for a couple hours and not to worry. Then he gave a similar message to his secretary and left with Mattie out the back way.

We watched tensely as the two began a walk side by side in the direction of the High Commission. "It's working!" the Princess exclaimed excitedly, pointing out the group of pasty-faced men who were following the two of them. She was now in a print beach dress with a floppy straw hat which partially concealed her face. She apparently had more changes of clothes than James Bond, but I guess that was as it should be.

Sybil was outside waving. "Ready, ma'am," I gasped.

"Right. Let's go!"

We now ducked out the back way too. Joe, looking utterly astonished, pulled open the door of the Land Rover for the Princess. She, Sybil and I got in the back. Then with an equally astonished Graham at the wheel, we began picking our way through crowds of people making their way from the Houses of Parliament. Several constables were directing traffic, but the brim of the floppy hat successfully concealed the Princess' identity, and we were shortly on Highway One headed for the beach house.

Since coming to the Isle of St. Margaret's, many unique experiences had come my way. This, so far, topped them all. I never did learn what the Governor General wanted with me, but he had left first and so was apparently willing to put it off.

"How many people live here, Sybil," the Princess now asked as we passed through the warehouse district.

"About thirty-five thousand or so, ma'am."

The Princess was horrified by the poverty of shanty town. "Yes, ma'am," Sybil had answered her comment. "Some eight out of ten of our people live that way. Something needs to be done."

I happened to glance at her as she made the comment. Her eyes burned with an energy that made me suddenly uneasy. Sybil and I had never talked politics. In fact, she always seemed around me to be blissfully unconcerned with the world around her. I don't know what triggered it, maybe the unease started by the Queen's Speech, but I found myself recalling Colgate's comments about her. Colgate was not a man given to hysterics, but his take on Sybil was downright vituperative. I recalled her entry into the room while the man I later found out was Webster was lying on the couch. I thought nothing of it at the time, but now I recalled Sybil had looked at him, almost expressionless, then spoke to me. She *never said a word* to him, and that was totally unlike Sybil. She always spoke to people, especially in her house.

He was visiting one of his agents, Perkins had told me off-handedly. Other clips of this disturbing cinema began to play in my head. Connie had disappeared the night before trying to get back to me. Sybil had shown up instead on the very plane. A big 'mean-looking' man and an attractive, medium complected woman had been hanging around Connie's hotel in Bridgetown just before she returned for the evening, then was never seen again. That described thousands of women, but Sybil was included... *and if she came on the twentieth on the seaplane, that's exactly where she'd have been the night of the nineteenth. I have to return to Florida in a week,* she said the day I 'lay hold of her', yet Marty told me she had quit her job sometime around the first week in February... when we came here. Her apartment was held 'for business purposes' by the 'shady' group Caribbean Horizons Ltd. I was kidnaped outside her apartment. *That look on her face when she first saw me outside the Customs House.* I still couldn't make sense of that one, but it was very different from the bright smile that shortly followed.

I was always one of those people who let worry intrude at times I should have been enjoying myself. I usually resented it, and I was resenting it now. The problem was, I didn't know where to go to get answers. I faced front, trying desperately to enjoy the once in a lifetime event of having Princess Margaret over for a swim. Yet my mind was racing. I thought of Donna Goldstien. I don't know exactly what I expected she could do for me, but I decided the American Legation would be the first place I'd visit when the opportunity presented itself.

Meanwhile, we were now an independent nation. Midnight had arrived and the coach was a pumpkin again... or maybe it was vice-versa. Whatever the Communists had up their sleeve, and it *had* to be *something*, we'd likely know very soon. My job for now, I finally decided as we reached the turnoff for the beach house, was to make sure I wasn't eliminated at the outset, or maybe held and used to fulfill their agenda, by a very clever agent who'd managed to get very close to me... if that's what she was.

My final thoughts along this dark highway of the mind, before I forced them into the background for the next couple hours, were realizing now why those people wanted me to come on to St. Margaret's, passing up over half a million dollars in the process. I'd gotten close to every important enemy the Communists had here. I at least could see them virtually any time I wanted to. Always in uniform, I was always armed... and no one thought anything about it. Maybe they had my girl captive somewhere, ready to use her to make me do something really awful. Up until now, my fears were related to what Colgate might make me do. Now I was wondering if maybe I'd been looking in the wrong direction all along.

Tuesday April 17, 1973: the Headquarters of the Ministry of Defence, Government Plaza, Port Albert, Isle of St. Margaret's

"You're a goddam idiot!" Defence Minister Morton Gentry shrieked as I stood helplessly at attention, Gene red and furious, standing helplessly at attention beside me, in the Minister's office.

"Here you are, an officer in the Air Militia, one of the men we rely on to keep this country safe, and you *conspire* with a visiting dignitary to spirit her off, away from her protection, to a place where Communist guerillas and God knows *who* else could have killed her or kidnapped her."

I swallowed, utterly scarlet-faced.

"Pretty goddam piss poor judgment, Cassell."

"Yessir... I'm sorry, sir."

"You *certainly are*."

"Group Captain?" Gentry now looked angrily at Gene, causing me to really cringe.

"Sir."

"Is this the kind of man you advance in the ranks in your service?"

"Well, sir, I..."

Gentry chopped the air with his hand. "Never mind. I don't want to hear it."

Now Gene swallowed.

"I trust you have some sort of punishment in mind for this fool."

Gene's jaw tensed. "I certainly do."

Gentry flashed an evil smile, looking once more at me. "I'd court-martial you right now Cassell... *this very minute...*," he exhaled sharply. "Except for two reasons."

"Yes, sir?"

"First... there's no offense that quite covers this... and second, I wouldn't want the British Royal Family to carry you out of the court-room on their shoulders after you were acquitted... because then you'd *really* be impossible."

I cracked a grin.

"But you better believe you're gonna *suffer* for this. It took the Royal Navy and Scotland Yard two hours to locate her... and you just better *believe* we were all dying a thousand deaths throughout that time."

It had been a happy two hours. Princess Margaret had enjoyed herself immensely. She was even talking of making us some secret recipe tropical salad of her's when the sound of a helicopter's rotors split the air. It landed right on our beach, some ten Royal Marines in full battle dress quickly alighting, pointing some very ugly-looking rifles at Sybil and me. The Scotland Yard people then came roaring down the packed sand and pebbles pathway some twenty minutes later as the Princess finished changing back into the beach dress. They were busily working me over until the Princess angrily told them it was her doing. I'm sure they knew that all along, otherwise I'd have probably been shot.

"Yessir... the security men tried to make me die a thousand..."

"You're at attention, Flight Lieutenant."

"Yessir."

"All right, Hayes, get this incompetent fool *out of my sight!*"

"Yessir. It won't happen again."

"Probably because no country will allow its VIP's to ever come here again once this story gets around. All right, the two of you, *out!*"

Gene and I walked outside, then down the path to his Land Rover. I could tell he was steaming. Gene was always red-faced, but when anger had him by the throat, he got so red his short, curly blond hair practically appeared lime-colored. He was that way now.

"That jerkoff's just pissed because he didn't get to kill me, Ge…"

"*Sir or Group Captain.*"

"Yes, your fucking majesty."

Gene turned on me, grabbing my Sam Browne. "Look you moron, don't you think I've got enough trouble right now? You know Gentry's always resented a white man holding such a job." Gene's voice was laced with bitterness. "Even though I bought the whole fucking air force out of my pocket."

"Oh relax… sir. We're doin' all right. We got over a hundred men now. Mission Impossible really made us popular with a lotta young men. I just wish…"

"And I just *wish*…" He stopped me cold. "That you'd stop doing whatever came into your goddam head."

"All right!" I pulled his hand off my strap. "Just what did I do… besides the thing with the Princess?"

Gene stood there a moment, then hung his head. "Oh… I don't know. I'm just frustrated Cassell." He looked up at the mountains. "The Commies are up there…. *somewhere*. But we can't find them. They're up to *something*! But *what*?"

"Was anything ever done about that report I turned in?"

"You mean about the secret base?"

"Exactly."

"Jones says it never happened."

"*What?*"

"You heard me."

Another mystery was now on my radar screen, already too full of mysteries. I wanted desperately to confide in him my plan to go see Donna, but I didn't dare, not in his present mood. The Communists had everyone in both Militias on edge lately, simply by doing nothing, or at least appearing to be doing nothing. Yet I was exploding inside from the doubts I was suddenly having about Sybil. Granted it had only been a split second look, but I never forgot that they brought down one of the biggest spy networks in the United States because the leader had stupidly given a fake coin with concealed microfilm to a newspaper boy, and he had stupidly dropped it, causing it to break in half. When you found yourself immersed in those circles, you didn't get many clues. Connie was still missing. There just *had* to be an explanation. My nerves were rubbed raw.

As for the latest revelation, I wondered what had changed Jones' mind. I thought often of that secret base... wondering what was going on there. It *was* an anchorage... the thing they said didn't exist on the west coast. And things *had been* landed there. What's more, for them to have a huge camouflage net ready to go like that meant they damned well had something to hide.

"Do *you* think it never happened, Gene? I'm telling you it did."

His harassed eyes studied my very confused ones. He exhaled, shaking his head. "You ever had Kifo before this, John?"

"No, thank God."

"Well... things happen on that stuff. And with all the acid you musta' done in your hippie..."

"Freak"

"Yeah... yeah. Look, John, I want to believe you."

"It would certainly account for the Communist silence."

"It's only been two days since independence. The Princess only left this morning. Maybe..."

"Oh cut it out, Gene! You don't believe that yourself."

We resumed walking. A few minutes later he let out a long, frustrated sigh. "Okay, Flight Lieutenant... what's your idea?"

"Send an armed force to take a look."

"But that's Jones' area... he says it didn't happen."

"Then go to Christian."

"You know goddam well what he'd say."

I remembered what he told me when I'd tried to get him to maneuver with my convoy. He immediately linked it to Gene's theory... essentially saying I was trying to prove it. Stalemate. "Okay, send our own men."

"Are you kiddin'? Move half the Air Militia across Highway Two, all the way to New Britain? Then down through the Doran..."

"Okay then, head west from Ormsby."

"There's no roads, Cassell."

"Perry Herbert says..."

"Perry Herbert's a goddam lunatic."

"Yeah, but he makes the trip down from Loma Hermose. We can blaze a trail ourselves."

"And how long would *that* take?"

"Fuck if I know, Gene, but I'm tellin' you something's out there, and if we wait until they suddenly finish whatever they're doin' and spring their big surprise... we're gonna get slaughtered."

"Oh Cassell..."

We made it to the Air Militia Land Rover and got in the back. The driver gunned the engine and we headed back to the fort. Gene was obviously lost in thought the entire time. It *was* asking a lot, diverting the bulk of the Air Militia from their primary mission, which without fighters or bombers wasn't much more than a reconnaissance operation, but still, that was our job.

"Well," I finally said, "how about letting me fly some missions in the area... take someone else along with a camera... at least try to get some proof."

Gene finally nodded. "Okay, Cassell, but you've got some healthy punishment to do first."

I guess I knew now how awful Chicken Little must have felt. All sorts of things were just not right... very close to me... on the other side of the island. Yet Cassell would have to do his punishment first.. So the politicians would feel better. Yeah... midnight had come and gone, we were on our own now, but nobody seemed to be wearing a watch.

Chapter Eleven

INTRIGUE AT THREE THOUSAND FEET

Wednesday May 9, 1973: the Legation of the United States of America, the Diplomatic Quarter, Port Albert, Isle of St. Margaret's

The American Legation was a three-storied stucco house with large louvered windows shaded by tall banyans and surrounded by a wrought iron fence. Until coming here this dark, cloudy morning I'd never explored the 'diplomatic quarter', though had passed it many times on my way out Highway Two. The quarter was an L-shaped complex of what, on Maggierock anyway, would pass for stately residences. It bordered Government Plaza and its own L-shaped group of official residences to the west and south. The American Legation was reached by driving past the Plaza on Highway Two, then taking the first left past the turnoff labeled 'Residence of the Governor-General'. The 'L' was formed by one continuous graveled road running parallel to Highway One, then turning east and running parallel to Highway Two. The entire area was full of banyans, palm and tropical pine.

As Donna told me when I called her for my appointment, the Legation was the third house I would encounter, the first two being the Jamaican High Commission and the Cuban Embassy. Immediately after it was the British High Commission, followed by the Argentine Legation.

. . . .

I'd wanted to come much sooner. My conversation with Gene outside Gentry's office, particularly the part about Jones obviously changing his mind and denying the existence of the secret base we had both clearly seen with our bleary but otherwise perfectly functional eyes, had really sent me over the edge. But there was that punishment to do first. Gene had sprung it on me the very afternoon of that conversation, when we'd arrived at the fort.

"You're on OD duty at the command post, Cassell. Beginning at 1600."

"Yessir. Until when? 2000?"

He let out a caustic snicker. "Until I say so. This is your punishment Cassell. It's the nearest thing I can figure to imprisonment..."

"But..."

"*Don't interrupt!*"

I swallowed.

"...After your misadventure with the Princess. Believe me, if I don't lower the boom on you, Gentry's never gonna get off my ass."

"He won't anyway....*sir*." I was enraged. The surprise of it all, when I was full of thoughts about how to figure out whether my suspicions of Sybil had any merit, made it even worse than it otherwise was.

"We'll see. You're to go home, get in your flight suit, tell 'em all not to wait up for you the next few weeks, and report back here like yesterday... you understand?"

"But Gene, I've got some problems with Sybil that..."

"Absence makes the heart grow fonder, bud. Now get with it."

I stood there in a towering rage, but Gene was unmoved.

Thus it came to pass that from April 17 to May 8 Flight Lieutenant Cassell lived at the Command Post at Fort Cornwallis, watching as my NCOIC's and ANCOIC's, who were low-ranking enlisted men, changed every four hours. There was a cot in a small room where I slept between crises. My meals came in cans or boxes from the post mess hall. My contact with the outside world was limited to occasional surreptitious phone calls and a discussion over the radio with Subaltern Preston talking from New Britain. For consolation I could at least tell myself he was imprisoned like this until further notice just by virtue of being stationed in New Britain. But then he didn't have a mistress who might be a Communist and working with others to force me into doing something awful on the eve of the Communists pulling whatever they were going to pull.

The Air Militia shared the command post with the other Militia, so there were several people besides my own assistants to meet and talk to. As a result, I got to know just about every other officer in the Militia considerably better, including some who had been members of my Court. The same was true of the NCOs and airmen of the Air Militia. Even so, my simmering fears just worsened as the weeks passed with me unable to do anything about them.

Of the two sets of suspicions, Sybil bothered me the most. In all respects we had a fabulous relationship. I often wished I'd never seen that hateful glow in her eyes for the split-second when she made her comment to the Princess. As the days passed and I missed her more and more, I felt even worse, thinking those things about her. But then I'd recall the very suspicious coincidences connecting Connie's disappearance with Sybil's arrival, and back I would fall into the quicksand of doubt.

For a while I contemplated putting Inspector Pereya onto Caribbean Horizons Ltd. to see what possibilities might be revealed, but then I hesitated over speaking its name over the phone... letting whoever might be listening know that I had heard of them. Our command post phone lines ran through the Ministry of Posts and Telegraphs central switchboard and thus were capable of monitoring. I'd been told the lines were secure, but I'd been here long enough to know that Maggierock was one big sieve, and that the 'cocoanut telegraph', as it was called, was more efficient and far-reaching than Ritter's more commonly recognized electronic variety. Then too... how did I know I could trust Pereya were the investigation to suddenly leave the realms of street crime and enter the arena of the larger Communist-Government fight over the future of the island?

Such were my wretched preoccupations as I stared at the large detail map on the wall and listened to our silent radio and phones and the other Militia's silent phones and radio, waiting for all hell to break loose. An event we all *knew* was soon to be coming, but which day after day as my watch dragged on through the weeks never did.

My other paranoid preoccupation, the secret base, had at least some development when, on April 25th, Lieutenant Colonel Jones strode into the command post to check on his OD.

"Colonel!" I called to him from across the room, waking up my two helpers with a start.

He saw me and his eyes widened, then immediately resumed their previous expression. "Flight Lieutenant! Good to see you. Hear you're practically part of the furniture around here these days."

I didn't appreciate the humor, but managed a small laugh. "Colonel... I need to speak with you... privately."

"Maybe some other time, Cassell, I..."

"It won't keep, sir." My look must have convinced him I was ready to tell my story on the floor of Parliament and some mollification was called for.

He pointed inside the Militia OD's room with the cot, and I followed. We took seats at a small camp table. He somewhat nervously cracked his knuckles, then looked me in the eye. "Okay Flight Lieutenant... what is it that's so important?"

"Exactly what you're no doubt thinking, Colonel." I continued eyeing him, my look bordering on disgust.

"Our little hallucination?"

"It was no hallucination."

"Really... then how come it was gone when we came back?"

"You said it yourself, sir. The camouflage net."

He made an effort at a chuckle. "I was drunk, Cassell... That's pretty far-fetched, especially since the boat was still there. How could they have such a thing ready *before* it was even unloaded?"

"Interesting point, Colonel. How do *you* account for *that*... the boat being there, I mean?"

"Curiosity perhaps."

I laughed. "Come now, sir. *Nobody* visits the west coast of Maggierock for *any* reason. That's your whole argument discounting the Hayes Theory."

He shifted in his seat, then looked at me with something approaching contempt. "You've been here a matter of months, Flight Lieutenant. What do you know of Maggierock?"

"I'm merely reciting *your* arguments, sir."

"And I'm telling you there's nothing there." His tone was testy, defensive. I found myself getting *worried*. There seemed to be more here than simply a half-humorous debate on how hung over we were. I'd obviously struck a raw nerve.

"What we saw was a boat at an anchorage on the uninhabited part of our coast...*period*."

"Sir... I can't let this pass. We've got to take a look. This could be the reason the Communists have been so quiet. Our survival could depend on locating and knocking this thing out before they finish whatever they're doing."

Lieutenant Colonel Jones now fixed me with a bug-eyed glare. "*Drop it*, Flight Lieutenant. That's an *order*."

For a good minute we sat there eyeing one another. For whatever reason, Jones seemed almost hysterical at the prospect I might manage to convince someone to pay this place a visit. I had been confused and a little upset since I first heard of his change of story. Now... I was positively *alarmed*.

Jones rose from his seat and went to the door, pulling it open. Then he paused, hand on the knob, facing back in my direction. "You're a good officer, Cassell, with a bright future. Don't throw it away on some stupid experience two drunken officers thought they had after tangling with a quart of Kifo."

"Sir, if we do nothing about this base, *none* of us who are anti-Communist may have any future."

His eyes drilled into me some more. They were almost pleading now. "Don't." One last look and he was through the door.

For the next twenty hours or so I was more troubled than ever about *what just had to be* a secret base. My first reaction was that Romulus Augustulus Jones was a Communist. *But no! That's crazy! His split-second reactions when he first sighted the base took care of that suspicion.* So what else? I finally concluded someone had ordered him to back off... for some reason, including perhaps closet Communism, known but to them. Not knowing who that might be, however, ruled out my safest course of action, which was to take the problem over Gene's head to Gentry, thence to Colgate. Unless it was Christian, however, the person ordering Jones to back off *had* to be one of them. *No... lump in my throat or not... I've got to get outside help on this.* The realization I was likely destroying my standing in the Defence Ministry, such as it was, had me very depressed, but that would be an excuse of no consequence when I heard the last gunshots executing the last non-Communists on the island because I'd done nothing about what I *knew* I saw.

. . . .

So here I was, fresh out of my long imprisonment in the bowels of the command post, doing something likely to get me sent to real prison when it was found out.

"Hey John!" Donna gaily called as she came bounding into the otherwise empty reception area. She told me to come before 0800 and she got busy. It was now 0724. She threw her arms around me.

"Great seeing you again, Donna," I whispered as I squeezed her.

She pushed back, eyeing my flight suit, wings and name tag. "Well! You look impressive, John. This is about the last getup I thought I'd see you in some day!"

I smiled. "I thought I'd take you flying, Donna. Show you the island."

"Wow! *Really?*"

"Sure!"

"Do I need to bring anything?"

She was dressed in tan cotton slacks and a white short-sleeved blouse. Perfect for flying or doing anything else here, almost. "Nope... you're fine."

"Okay! Let me just leave a note here for Christy and we're off!"

"Christy your receptionist?"

"Yes... The Prime Minister's niece no less."

"I thought after Dominique you'd end the practice of hiring foreigners when it was your turn."

Donna gave a slight grin, then gestured upwards at the photographic portraits of Richard Nixon and William Rogers hanging above the receptionist's unoccupied desk. "*They* decide that... me, I just work here."

I laughed. "I'm surprised the President gets to decide anything these days... what with all the bullshit over Watergate."

Donna's face flushed with anger. "You don't know the half of it, John... what's coming up." She shook her head. "You know, there are many unkind things can be said about Nixon... things I'd agree with..."

"Yeah... he's no charm school honor graduate."

"But the man's a real visionary, John... especially in the area of foreign affairs. SALT I, the Red China initiatives, put him head and shoulders above any president we've had recently... *certainly* above those the men out to bring him down worshiped."

"That wouldn't take much. You'll have to catch me up on the things going on back home, Donna."

"You picked a good time to be away. The Democrats just can't understand why the electorate didn't fall in love with McGovern... They're gonna win in Congress what they lost in the election."

"You really think he'll be impeached?"

"I can't say...not yet. But they have the votes and are out for blood. I'm just afraid Nixon's paranoia plays right into their hands."

For a while we stood there lost in all sorts of thoughts. I had lots of reactions to recent American politics... how everybody seemed to be beguiled by smoke and mirrors since the election of 1960 was allowed to stand without any challenge to the obvious Democrat vote fraud. Just talking about it soon got me angry, though. "Aw hell... let's go slip the surly bonds... for a while anyway."

Donna laughed, then finished the note.

I watched as she wrote it, then turned again in my direction. "Two stripes on the shoulder... what's that mean?"

"Flight Lieutenant... equivalent to an American captain."

"You *are* an American, John. Don't forget that." Her face didn't betray if that comment was made in a negative or merely off-handed way.

"Yeah... but you heard the Queen's Speech, Donna. The dual citizenship bill passed and got the Royal Assent the same week."

Donna took the thumb and forefinger of her right hand, reached out and pinched my cheek. "Yes, dear, I know, but we don't recognize that sort of thing." She pinched harder. "So be careful."

"Of course... wasn't I just talking like an American? I just meant in the American air force. I promise I'll talk to you before accepting a title of nobility."

Donna beamed me a warm smile. "You do that." She picked up her purse. "Okay Group Captain..." She gave me her arm. "Fly me to the moon!"

"Flight Lieutenant."

She laughed. "Sorry."

Two hours later I had stopped at the General Post Office for a bag of mail needing to go to New Britain, then driven with Donna to the airport in an Air Militia jeep. While the ground crew, under the newly promoted Flight Corporal Drayton, trotted out my aircraft and got it ready, I took her into the small locker room off the main hangar area and found an extra flight suit for her to climb into. Then we walked back outside toward the plane. The skies seemed darker than an hour ago, and a stiff wind was blowing from the northeast. She seemed excited, particularly when she caught sight of our little plane with the RSMAM insignia on fuselage and wings. "Oh John, this is so *exotic!*"

"So was meeting you at a party on the Left Bank, Donna. We seem to get together doing interesting things." I pulled open the door to the right hand seat. "Hop aboard... uh... how do I address the American Minister?"

She gave my shoulder a squeeze, blushing slightly. "Donna... of course." We both laughed as she climbed inside.

"Jumbe Flight Lieutenant!" Drayton greeted me as he handed me the clipboard.

"Congratulations on your promotion, Drayton."

"Thank you, sir." He gestured to the clipboard. "Everything checks out... but..."

His tone was decidedly *worried*. "What's the matter?"

He indicated the sky with his head. "I dunno, sir. I don't like the wind. This is where all our hurricanes come from."

I shrugged. "It's nice and cool for a change." It was too... almost. As for hurricanes, the season was a couple months away. "It'll be okay, Drayton." I initialed the form on the clipboard, then handed it back.

"Yessir. Happy landings, sir." I nodded and we exchanged salutes. Then as he watched, I climbed inside, completed the preflight, then started the engine.

"How long have you been flying, John?" Donna asked.

"About a month... sort of. Excuse me just a second, Donna." I reached up and put the headset on. "Oh! If you wanna listen in, put it on." I gestured to the hook where the set for the right hand seat hung.

"Great!" Donna eagerly put on the headset.

"Militia Three calling tower... over." I spoke into the set. Getting no response, I tried once more. Then, after another minute, again."

"Oh... uh... tower here, jumbe Flight Lieutenant!"

"Who's this?"

"Aircraftsman Briggs, sir."

"Why the delay in answering, Briggs?"

"I jes find de switch, sir. This is de first time on de tower duty." Gene had told me the very first time I went flying with him that there was no air traffic control here. The British, at least, maintained the tower as an aid to navigation and, as we knew only too well, to spearhead rescue efforts for aircraft in trouble. When we took over April 15, a total of two men on the island were familiar with the equipment and how to use it. These two occasionally staffed the tower during un-usual occurrences, such as a flight involving high government officials. Mostly, however, they were conducting crash training for some fifteen others who would be qualified in about three months. Meanwhile, the tower was manned by people about as qualified for that job as I was to fly.

Donna's face betrayed worry as she looked at me.

"How's the sky, Briggs?"

"Fine, sir."

"No...I mean is there any traffic?"

"I don't know, sir." My own ignorance of the tasks involved with flying had made me more tolerant of others in the same position.

"Well, just look at the radar screen, Briggs. That big green thing... should be in front of you."

"De big green thing is black, jumbe Flight Lieutenant. Nobody turned it on yet."

I let out a sigh. "Okay, Briggs. When it gets turned on, let me know, huh?"

"Yessir, jumbe Flight Lieutenant."

I revved the engine and taxied the short distance to the runway. Because of the wind, we would be starting our takeoff roll from the hangar today. "You sure this is safe, John?"

"What?"

"Flying.... with no tower?"

"There's only three aircraft here on the island, Donna, counting ours. And both the others are right over there." I gestured. "The seaplane took off at seven-thirty, so it's gone." I revved the engine harder, watching the RPM's.

Releasing the brakes, we sped toward the end of the runway. I pulled back on the stick and we lifted off into the sky. "Oh John, it's so beautiful here!" Donna's attention was riveted on the panorama to the east.

"Yeah... I'll show you." I banked to the right, then we did a long slow pass over Port Albert, headed south and east out to sea, then came back over the coastline at Ormsby.

Donna was a fabulous passenger. She thoroughly enjoyed the view as I flew north along the coast, all the way to Loma Hermose, then turned left and headed for the west coast. I then turned south, heading for New Britain.

"Hear anything from Gail?" I asked her after we'd been cruising about half an hour.

"No. She's still in the diplomatic service, but we've lost touch."

"Too bad. She was a neat chick."

"Yes," Donna sighed wistfully. "Our first posting... and it was Paris."

"Those were the days." For a few minutes we lapsed into silence. "You're doin' pretty good, heading the American mission... at our age."

"Yeah. That's because I'm willing to go to an out of the way place. Small... uneventful. Gail liked the bright lights. I think she's still a vice-consul, but in Western Europe. Me, I wanted to *explore*."

"That's neat, Donna, but it must play hell on the social life."

She nodded. "But then I'm married, so I shouldn't have *too* much of a social life." A mischievous grin stole across her face as she said that, and it soon put a smile on mine.

"What does Mister Goldstien do?"

"Mister Goldstien is my father, John. He was a milkman for many years. Mister *Strachman* is my husband."

"Oh." I blushed. "I didn't *think* you were married when we met in Paris."

She laughed. "I wasn't."

"Where's your husband?"

"In Warsaw... first secretary at our embassy there."

"I'm married too."

"Yeah? Where's she?"

"Illinois. I got married the year after I met you. It didn't work out though."

"Often happens." A few moments later our eyes met and we burst out laughing.

The bulk of our ride to New Britain passed in such small talk. She got to witness the usual 'Cassell jolt' when we landed. Then, after I took the mail bag into the ops shack and introduced her to Subaltern Preston, we went into the small commissary for coffee and cans of c-rations. Outside the window, the sky was growing very dark, even though it was only ten in the morning. The wind was picking up as well.

"It may be kind of a rough trip home, Donna."

"Oh, I don't mind a little turbulence."

"I was more concerned with visibility. I can't fly on instruments. But there's something I wanted to show you... talk to you about."

Donna seemed unconcerned with whether we could make it back or not, though she readily picked up on the fact that New Britain was not a Caribbean hot spot. "Sure seems to be a lot of mud here," she observed as her eyes swept the field of weeds beyond the flightline. She'd already noticed the rotten wood walls and sheetmetal roofs of the city's buildings when I made my approach.

Preston had joined us with a cup of coffee. "I don't know if you want to try the flight back, jumbe Flight Lieutenant. There's a line of thunderstorms moving in from the northeast. They should be over our east coast in about an hour."

"Oh crap."

Donna shrugged. "What's to do around here, Victorious?"

"If you stay too long," Preston responded with a knowing glance at me, "you wind up drinking lots of Kifo."

"Oh gawd!" I gasped.

"Kifo?" Donna was obviously one of those chicks who were always game for something different.

"Liquid death," I hurriedly spoke up.

"A local delicacy," Preston added. "Cocoanut liquor."

"I always *loved* cocoanuts," Donna gushed.

"So did I.... until I had that stuff."

"Well, if we can't get out of here tonight, I say we have some."

"There goes our relations with the United States," I moaned to her laughter.

Preston seemed pleased by the prospect. "We can fix you two right up. You can party with Heather and me."

"Heather Cressey?"

Preston grinned. "Yup. Missed your chance, Flight Lieutenant."

Now I laughed. Even so, the prospect of the New Britain Air Militia BOQ, even with Donna Goldstien in the next room, was not my idea of a good night. So we decided to go up, so I could show Donna what I wanted to talk to her about, then see what the weather was like when we came back down.

"You sure are mysterious about... whatever it is, John." Donna spoke about five minutes after we'd taken off once more.

"I *have* to be, Donna. This thing has me all tied in knots."

"Good Lord... what *is* it?"

I then related everything I could remember about the secret base, from the moment Jones and I first sighted it, through all the shifting stories and orders to forget about it. She listened quietly, an expression on her face indicating agreement with my feeling she had not wound up in some diplomatic backwater as she first thought.

"No, Donna, it's just that the British kept everything really quiet for some reason. There's all kinds of rumors about World War III almost happening New Year's, but..."

"World War III? John, there was absolutely nothing on our threat board over that holiday."

"Well, its just that one of our Militia NCOs, who I met on my extended OD tour, told me he was working New Year's Eve attached as a guide to Third Platoon, B-Company, 18th Berkshire Rifles. He told me they were dispatched a ways up our east coast to a place called Blankenship Cove. He said he *saw* a submarine a short ways out to sea brimming with guided missiles..."

"They use those for defense nowadays, John, that's not..."

"He said it was the other kind, Donna. He said he knows the difference... he was a corporal in the British Army and had an MOS that required that kind of knowledge. *And,* he said, every member of that platoon was hauled before their CO and ordered to shut up about anything they might have seen, after getting some sort of pep talk about going home to England safely. They *did* release the fact that fifteen men were killed trying to land with a bunch of explosives. The men weren't black either, Donna."

"Meaning what?"

"Well... if the sub was Russian, which it would have to be to have nuclear missiles, then..."

"Oh John... I think you're assuming too much."

I managed a pleading look at her. "Please, Donna... all I'm getting is a run-around. Don't *you* give me one too."

For a while she looked at me, then exhaled. "You know, I just realized I know very little about you, except that you brought some mighty fine hash out of North Africa once upon a time." She continued eying me, as if trying to penetrate to my very soul.

"So you know very little about me. What does that.... why are you looking at me like that?"

"Why are you here, John?" Her look remained penetrating. I wanted to make a joke, but suddenly realized this would probably be the most important conversation of this journey. Donna had gone just so far with me on friendship. I hadn't asked her for anything yet, but I guess she must have realized that when I did, it was something that was going to require sticking her neck out.

"The answer is important to you... isn't it, Donna?"

"Yes." The penetrating look continued.

"Will you keep it strictly between us if I tell you the unvarnished truth?"

She continued staring. "Does it involve an ongoing or future crime?"

"No."

A final look into my eyes, then she faced front. "All right," she exhaled. "Strictly between you and me."

Now I exhaled. One false move and all I tried to accomplish by coming here would be thrown away. Now I was risking my personal safety on a matter of island security that no islander seemed to even care about. I wondered if I wasn't being a gigantic fool. *Go on... eat the mushrooms... join us... tell yourself it was a hallucination... Then you won't have to tell this chick with a direct line to the FBI everything she needs to send you to federal prison for a few years. Aw fuck it!* In the end I couldn't let it go. I took a deep breath.

"I'm fleeing from Don Clemente DiStefano... and the FBI."

Her face whiplashed in my direction. "Why the FBI, John?"

"They wanna talk to me about the murder of Jerry Fischer."

"Oh yes... the philanthropist."

I made a retching sound, causing her to look at me with surprise. "Did you kill him?"

"No... but I know who did... witnessed it with my own eyes."

"And you don't want to tell them?"

"That's right."

She nodded. "Okay... and Don somebody?"

"That's not a name, Donna... that's a title. He's a Mafia chieftain. I wound up in possession of some ledgers last year that could have sent him to prison. I finally got them to him last November, but have no idea if he's forgiven me."

For several minutes there was no sound but the loud hum of our engine filling the cockpit. Donna's eyes were focused on some point in the ocean. Once more I was regretting carrying Maggierock's burdens all by myself, especially since if anyone ever found out I went to the American Minister they would hang me from the nearest yardarm.

"Okay, John... what do you want of us?"

"We're coming up on it in a minute, Donna." I looked down until I saw the now familiar cove I had stared at on the detail map those weeks of my punishment. "Okay... see that cove?"

"Uh huh."

"It's right there."

"What is?"

"The *secret base*, Donna."

Donna looked and looked. When her eyes finally met mine, they had a look almost of pity in them. "Kind of well hidden... isn't it?"

We had just overflown the coast and were heading towards Orms-by. Suddenly I lost it. Banking to the right, I began a wide three-sixty, losing altitude all the while. Several miles out to sea and down to fifty feet, I aimed right for our coastline and 'floored it'.

"What are you *doing*, John?" Worry was in every note of her question.

"That was the nicest way I've ever been called crazy, Donna. But I'm getting tired of it." My eyes were riveted on the coast. "Keep your eyes peeled. I'm trying to give you peek under the net."

Thirty feet... twenty feet... fifteen feet. The coastline loomed ahead... above us. Three miles distant, two miles distant... "Okay, John... okay... get us up... I'll do it."

I didn't know how much longer I could stay at that altitude. I simply wasn't that good of a pilot. I hadn't seen anything incriminating when, at about a mile or so from the coast, I pulled back on the stick. Donna visibly relaxed.

"You *are* crazy," she gasped.

I continued on to Ormsby. Reaching the coast, I turned north, into buffeting winds. It was a race with a gigantic bank of black clouds, but

I got us down before they got there. We taxied back to the hangar of the familiar Hayes Airstrip as the heavens opened.

As the men took care of the aircraft, Donna and I sprinted into the small commissary at the back of the hangar. Taking seats across from one another with cups of coffee, she took a small tablet and a pen from her purse.

"You like *Gilligan's Island? The Beverly Hillbillies*, John?" She asked as she scratched away with her pen.

"No."

She laughed. "Well pretend you do. Come to the Legation after tomorrow and ask to see this man." She handed me the small slip of paper.

"Ted Spurlock," I said, reading.

"Uh huh. Officially, he's our cultural attaché..."

For a while I stared blankly at her. She gave me no help at all.

"Ohhhhhhh!"

"God you're *dense*!" Donna laughed.

Thursday May 17, 1973: Hearing Room Number Two, the House of Councilors, Houses of Parliament, Government Plaza, Port Albert, Isle of St. Margaret's

I would never have suspected that my position as a Member of the House of Councilors would allow me to be in position to observe the first real break in the mystery of Connie's disappearance, but it did. Thursdays were often given over to our judicial duties. I checked the bulletin board in the Members Lounge on Tuesday May 15 and learned Jack had put me on the panel to hear the appeal in the case of *Autrey Plantation v. Peavey Warehouse, Ltd.* We were assigned in panels of five to hear such things, with one member being designated the vice-president *pro tem*. The vice-president in this case was Apple Jack, the members besides myself were Tran Van Choy, Mitre Fisc and Harlan Debke. Jack was following his usual custom of putting three Chamber of Commerce Members on panels in cases involving commercial law issues, with one Government and one Opposition Member rounding out the cast.

I checked out my copies of the briefs from the House clerk and
took them to the beach house that evening. In reading them, I learned
that the Court of Queen's Bench had ruled in favor of Autrey, the
issue being whether a one-on-one negotiated contract provision covering risk of loss on a load of taro controlled over a written 'terms
of bailment' document Autrey drivers were required to sign when
dropping their loads at Peavey's Port Albert warehouse. The bailment
document had a different provision for risk of loss, one naturally more
favorable to Peavey. The Court of Queen's Bench had ruled that the
bailment document was a contract of adhesion and therefore not en-
forceable, adding as an alternative ground that the agency powers of
the Autrey drivers did not extend to revising the terms of the agreement negotiated with Peavey by their boss.

The ruling below sounded reasonable to me, though I planned to
listen to whatever the more knowledgeable panel members had to say
before casting my vote. Two thirty in the afternoon found me in my
seat at the high bench, second from the left of the vice-president.

The Peavey lawyer was a Port Albert solicitor named Peter Huggins.
He led off the appeal, arguing 'a contract is a contract is a contract',
adding that if making arrangements binding on their boss to store the
cargoes they had driven for days over the dangerous Highway Two
wasn't within the scope of their agency, nothing was. He added that a
contrary result would wreak holy havoc on the taro industry, with taro
trucks rusting in the tropical sun while their cargoes rotted waiting
for word from the plantation owners responding to the terms offered
by the warehouse operators for storing their crops pending shipment
on the next freighter. The thought was *frightening* to me, but then
this law stuff had never much captured my interest, outside of *Perry
Mason*, of course.

"Ah, but they already have arrangements in place, Mister Huggins,"
Vice-president Jack interrupted.

"Yes, Your Ladyship," Huggins countered, "but my client was pro-
posing amendment of those terms."

"But doesn't the contract provide a means for amending the provisions?" the vice-president replied.

"Yes ma'am, but the constantly changing circumstances of the warehouse and shipping business *must* of necessity allow for amendment where and when the amendment is most needed...," Huggins started to respond.

"But if the parties provided for a means of amending.... and agreed to this procedure as part and parcel of the contract, wouldn't the circumstances of the business be presumed to be taken into account?" Mitre Fisc, the Government Member, asked.

"Under normal circumstances, perhaps, Your Lordship," Huggins shot back, "but what business could long survive if..."

I was starting to tune all this out, watching Huggins' wildly gesturing arms instead. As I did so a flicker of gold against his coal black wrist caught my eye. It was in the shape of New Jersey and reminded me very much of a charm on a charm bracelet Connie used to wear. Her boss, Big Ed Foley had gotten that particular charm for her. Entranced, I watched more closely. In the next round of question and answer, a 'C' charm, then a 'Q' charm came into view. *The bracelet was Connie's!*

I completely spaced the rest of the argument. Then, as my colleagues filed in to the conference room to talk, I came around the bench, still in robe and white yoke and buttonholed Huggins as he was shoveling papers into his briefcase.

"Where'd you get that bracelet?" I gasped.

"What? This?" He held up his wrist.

"Yes!"

"Why the interest, Your Lordship?"

"Because it belonged to my girlfriend... she came to the island with me."

Huggins became defensive. "It's mine, fair and square. Paid fifty quid for it in New Britain."

"*New Britain*? How could you buy something like that in New Britain?" I was practically hyperventilating.

"Don't you think this is improper conduct when you're on a case involving both of us?" It was the Autrey solicitor, Percival Dudleigh, who now spoke.

"Huh? Uh... what? Oh! The case! Uh, I'll take myself off the bloody case." I turned back to Huggins. "Would you answer my question?"

"Well," Huggins grinned, "actually I took it in exchange for a part of my fee from a New Britain client."

"And who would that be?"

Huggins was now getting spooked. "I'm not sure I should tell."

"Listen, buddy," I gasped. "I'll give you three hundred quid for it. But I need to know that information. My girl's been missing for two months."

Huggins swallowed, eyeing me suspiciously. Then he composed himself. "Actually I was giving my client a discount..."

"A volume discount," Dudleigh sneered. "He represents all of Posey's girls in Alderman's Court... makes a tidy bundle every year."

Huggins now turned on Dudleigh. "You shut your bloody trap, ambulance chaser! You represent..."

"Wait! Wait! Hold it!" I gasped. "This Posey... is this the one who gave it to you?"

Huggins was still eyeing me very suspiciously, but Dudleigh's presence apparently helped loosen his tongue, since apparently Dudleigh would tell me anything he didn't. "Why yes... Piusetta Posey."

"*Piusetta?*"

"Uh... yes."

Dudleigh smirked. "She owns Posey's Palace... one of the leading brothels in New Britain."

"THEE leading," Huggins blurted with pride in his client's healthy income. Then he looked at me. "Okay, Cassell, three hundred and it's yours."

"Okay, follow me to the robing room." We were just about to leave when Apple stuck her head out. "Are you coming in, Cassell?"

"Oh... sorry, ma'am," I gestured at both lawyers. "I suddenly realized I have a conflict."

Apple spat something under her breath, shaking her head, then retreated. I took Huggins to the robing room, got my bank drafts from my uniform pocket, wrote one for £300, then hurriedly changed into my uniform and ran over to the RSMC Building.

Inspector Pereya seemed impressed. "You're *sure* that's hers?"

"Positive! When can you go with me to New Britain. I'll fly us."

We went the next day, with two sacks of Royal Mail. Pereya arranged for us to be met by Inspector Thomassen, a buddy of his, who took us directly through the muddy, steamy streets to Posey's Palace, located right among the rusty, corrugated metal warehouses, about a block from the water.

Posey's was a dump. The heavy, stained, scarlet curtains with pink tassels you walked through upon entering the rotten wood building smelled of whiskey and sweat. The middle aged woman on duty at the counter cringed as she recognized Thomassen, then got positively frightened when she saw Pereya and me in my Air Militia uniform.

"We don't gyp the boys, here..." She squinted at my epaulets. "Uh... Flight Lieutenant."

"No ma'am...I just need to speak to Piusetta."

She looked relieved, then disappeared behind a door. Piusetta was three hundred pounds of solid suspicion. When she heard it was about the bracelet, however, she relaxed.

"Oh *that*! Pearly Gates be givin' it to me."

"How long ago?"

"Oh... maybe a month."

"Right around Independence Day?" Thomassen asked.

"Yeah! I give de volume discount to de boys on de Independence Day!"

"Which boys?" Pereya chimed in."

"De boys on de Doran return trip."

"Know where we can find this Gates now?" I asked.

Pereya cut me off. "We'll find him Flight Lieutenant." On the return trip, Pereya told me he was well acquainted with Gates. He was a merchant seaman who would occasionally double as convoy security for a return trip if the ship was in and he had the time. The freighter was his main livelihood, however, as it plied the seas between the major and minor Caribbean islands. He went with me to the shipping office, and learned Gates had shipped out last Tuesday, and wasn't due back for a month. Pereya promised he'd be there when next the ship docked.

"How would a seaman wind up with Connie's bracelet?" I thought aloud as we walked away from the shipping agent's office.

Pereya eyed me with sympathy. "I think you should assume the worst, Flight Lieutenant."

I think I already had.

"Probably the people who kidnaped her, and that's certainly what this looks like more and more, took it and either traded it for drugs or lost it in a poker or dice game. Don't worry, we'll lean on Gates pretty hard once we have him back. I'll let you know, Flight Lieutenant."

"Thanks, Inspector," I mumbled weakly as we parted company at my Land Rover, where a grim-faced Sean Kelly waited with Graham Jack to take me back to the beach house.

Tuesday May 22, 1973: the Legation of the United States of America, the Diplomatic Quarter, Port Albert, Isle of St. Margaret's

I was becoming an all too frequent visitor to the American Legation. My friendship with Donna was the cover, though the cover was doing nothing to help my relationship with Sybil. I finally promised her I'd stop going, but there was one more visit that *had* to be made. That was because Spurlock had gotten something back on 'that little matter we were discussing' as he always referred to it.

Spurlock was in his early thirties, with black hair and brown eyes, a stocky build and a Tennessee drawl. We'd gotten to be fairly friendly although it wasn't the sort of friendship that I expected would override orders from Washington... or more accurately, Falls Church, Virginia. Still, I was very useful to him, it turned out, being his first 'source' in Maggierock. In his line of work, and it wasn't *really* convincing Colgate and his Minister of Education and Welfare, Daphne St. George, that reruns of *The Beverly Hillbillies* were just what St. Margaret's needed to bring its children into the Twentieth Century, sources were as important to him as I was convinced getting the truth about the secret base was to me. So for the moment, at least, we were a perfectly symbiotic relationship.

I would come to the Legation, then talk to him after taking Donna for walks in the Diplomatic Quarter, occasionally on my mail runs, holding hands as we'd leave the reception area. These latter activities were blatantly designed to trick Christy into secretly telling her uncle I was secretly doing a thing with Donna. So much for cloak and dagger on a small Caribbean island. I didn't mind giving Spurlock information about our defense capabilities since I knew damned well the United States had no intention of invading us, and could probably get the same information from its British ally any time it really wanted.

Today, however, was the payoff. Christy gave me her usual smile when I entered and took my usual seat after lamely asking 'if the boss was in', like I always did. Like she always did, Christy said to take a seat and she'd be right with me.

"Come in, John," Donna spoke with unmistakable *excitement* in her eyes when she stuck her head into the reception area a few minutes later.

Nervously, I jumped to my feet and followed her to her office where Spurlock was waiting.

"You were *right*, John!" Donna whispered as we walked down the short, carpeted corridor to her office.

My heart was pounding. I was already trying to think of how best to reveal the information to my superiors when she opened the door, revealing Spurlock looking at two papers spread in front of him on Donna's conference table.

What appeared to be an aerial photograph immediately grabbed my attention.

"Hiya, buddy!" he called cheerfully as Donna shut and locked the door. "Come over and pull up a chair."

"You just ain't gonna *believe* what we got here!" he exclaimed as I took my seat.

My look must have told him my discomfort at seeing a top secret CIA memo lying next to it.

Spurlock's manner became more subdued, though no less relaxed. "Sure, John. You go ahead and read it. We want you to…"

"Under the circumstances," Donna quickly added.

"Yeah," Spurlock echoed, "under the circumstances."

I did.

CENTRAL INTELLIGENCE AGENCY
CONFIDENTIAL MEMORANDUM

TOP SECRET

TO: RICHARD HELMS, DIRECTOR

FROM: TED SPURLOCK
                 CULTURAL ATTACHÉ
                 UNITED STATES LEGATION
                 PORT ALBERT, ISLE OF ST. MARGARET'S

ROUTING: CENTRAL AMERICA DESK, STATE DE-
                 PARTMENT
DATE: 18 MAY 1973

SIR: ATTACHED AERIAL PHOTOGRAPH TAKEN AT
FLIGHT LEVEL 500 BY U-2 RECONNAISSANCE AIRCRAFT
EX-MARCH AFB CALIFORNIA 16 MAY 1973 PER COUR-
TESY OVERFLIGHT REQUESTED BY MINISTER DONNA
GOLDSTIEN (STRACHMAN)

REQUEST PROCESSED FROM LOCAL AIR FORCE
CAPTAIN (SOURCE) ALLEGEDLY SPOTTING TUGBOAT-
SIZED CRAFT IN ANCHORAGE DURING OVERFLIGHT
13 APRIL 1973. SOURCE ALLEGED CONCERN OVER
COMMUNIST MILITARY BUILDUP, REQUESTED AGEN-
CY ASSISTANCE AT LEGATION IN PORT ALBERT 09 MAY
1973

PHOTOGRAPH SHOWS PORTION OF COASTLINE IN
SOUTHWESTERN QUADRANT OF STM. DARK AREAS
TO RIGHT IDENTIFIED BY SOURCE AS DORAN TARO
PLANTATION. RECTANGULAR OBJECTS SHOWING IN
RED BELIEVED TO BE PROCESSING PLANTS OF UN-
KNOWN KIND. DARK MASSES BELOW BELIEVED TO BE
UNIDENTIFIED CULTIVATION [SUSPECT OPIUM]. EL-
LIPTICAL SMALLER STRUCTURES SHOWING IN RED
BELIEVED TO BE INTERNAL COMBUSTION ENGINE VE-
HICLES [SUSPECT MILITARY ARMORED CRAFT]

NOTE: SOURCE IS AMERICAN EXPATRIATE OF UNCER-
TAIN RELIABILITY. LEFT COUNTRY IN FEBRUARY 1973
UNDER SUSPICIOUS CIRCUMSTANCES [SUSPECT IN-
COME TAX EVASION]. FULL ULTRA-CONFIDENTIAL
DATABASE CHECK REVEALS INTELLIGENCE FILES

MAINTAINED ON SOURCE BY ALBUQUERQUE (NM) POLICE DEPARTMENT NARCOTICS UNIT (FEB 1970), NEW YORK CITY POLICE DEPARTMENT MANHATTAN SOUTH BOROUGH COMMAND INTELLIGENCE UNIT (MARCH 1972), FEDERAL BUREAU OF INVESTIGATION, MANHATTAN FIELD OFFICE (OCTOBER 1972).

NCIC RECORDS CHECK 17 MAY 1973 RESULT: NO AR-RESTS NO CONVICTIONS WANTED FOR QUESTIONING BY FBI MANHATTAN FIELD OFFICE RE: MURDER OF JERROD FISCHER 31 DEC 1972XXXEND OF MEMORAN-DUM

Ted Spurlock

From the moment I saw myself used in vain on a memo that had gone to Richard Helms, one of the pariahs of my generation, the photo was blown out of my mind. Sitting down once more after taking it from Spurlock's outstretched hand, I read it thoroughly, shaking all the while. When I next looked into the faces of the two grim American diplomats, my mood was bitter. "Looks like I really put my head in a noose coming to you guys," I remarked angrily as I tossed the paper back toward Spurlock.

"That's SOP anytime we develop a source, John," Spurlock drawled.

"But showing it to him definitely isn't," Donna added.

"No... it isn't." Spurlock added, looking at me utterly without remorse.

I shrugged, no less mollified. "Okay... I'll bite... why *did* you show it to me?"

"Because you already told the most damaging part of it to Ms. Strachman..."

"Goldstien."

"Oh... sorry, ma'am... Goldstien."

"So we thought you might want to explain the rest, John." Donna added.

For a few moments I stared into the faces of my erstwhile allies. I really didn't know what explaining anything would do. It was just possible Richard Helms had other fish to fry besides dredging up one and three year old intelligence files on some obscure expatriate. If so, then a follow-up memo might just attract attention that otherwise simply wouldn't be there. But what they did behind my back, especially when I was trying to lay low enraged me. Made me *want* to cram the truth up their smug, by-the-book asses. It would only be later I would ask myself if that wasn't their game all along... exactly what they *wanted* me to feel. The problem with being an unqualified second in command of a small country's pathetic Air Militia was that I necessarily was encountering issues and playing with people way over my head. Maybe I was growing up fast from all this, but it was definitely at high cost.

"I'll do better than *tell* you, *esteemed countrymen*," I sneered. "I'll show you." Getting up, I left Donna's office and returned to where Joe Fallon and Graham Jack were waiting, giving Joe directions to retrieve a photograph I kept at the Mantilla Heights house.

. . . .

"I had no idea a man like Fischer was into all that," Donna remarked quietly some three hours later, staring at the photograph I brought for them to see as my tale came to an end.

"And some of *your* boys made it all possible," I told Spurlock.

He nodded, not untouched to some degree, at least, by my story.

The photograph was the obvious reason for his reaction. It showed a young man and young woman, intense, searing pain etched into their soot-blackened faces, being led away from a burning farmhouse and barn by two grim-faced New York state troopers. In the background was Sergeant Rick Gariglia, his face contorted with horror.

"So *that's* what the FBI was up to."

"Yes, Donna. And my role as a main witness against Fischer made me both someone they wanted to harass into silence *and* pin the goods on for Fischer's murder."

Donna shook her head.

"And your undercover investigation against Fischer prompted the NYPD intelligence entry?" Spurlock added, his eyes riveted to the photograph.

"Mike Devlin wanted to make sure I stayed dead and buried if he ever had to come after me for stealing his daughter's affection."

"Hmmmm." Spurlock looked up. "That investigation won you both medals, right?"

"The Medal of Valor came from the business at the farm."

"I see. And the New Mexico entry?"

I shot a furtive look at Donna, who immediately reddened. It was fairly obvious to me that she was grateful I'd protected her by limiting the dope issue to myself. I figured many people who found themselves cornered by such investigations might be tempted to swing away at any of their oppressors they could hit. It would have been a cheap shot, but then for my dough so was this. I was taking the high road today. "That was legitimate. I *was* dealing dope... for a brief period. If you follow that one up, though, you'll find it was made by Robert Dugan and his partner Ed Gallagher. One was killed trying to murder me later that year, the other is serving time for kidnapping and beating me a year later." A tear came to my eye as I thought of Toni. Had Gallagher not intervened, we'd be married by now and I'd be some schnook bureaucrat, using my college degree as I should. They didn't need to hear about that one, though. I'd dredged up enough emotion for one day.

"Well, Flight Lieutenant," Spurlock drawled, "I guess I should..."

"And as for this income tax suspicion of yours," I interrupted, "go check with Abe Horowitz, a New York lawyer. He'll show you my tax returns."

The atmosphere of tension released in Donna's office was broken only occasionally by heavy sighs over the next couple of minutes. I stared at the photograph. Donna stared at me, Spurlock stared at his memo. "Want me to send a supplement?" Spurlock finally spoke. "I'll be happy to do it."

"I just don't want a goddam target on my back from this. I don't want the FBI learning my whereabouts. Now you tell me what's the best way to accomplish that... supplement or no supplement?"

Spurlock thought a moment, then sort of grinned. "Helms won't tell Patrick Gray any more than he'd tell Hoover. You're safe either way, John."

"Would the supplement wind up filed with this?" I pointed to the memo.

"Most likely."

"Okay... then send it."

Spurlock nodded.

I wasn't completely satisfied, but was at least sufficiently relieved to turn my attention back to Maggierock's problem. I picked up the aerial photograph. "You were quick enough to suspect opium cultivation, and my tax evasion," I told Spurlock. "Why don't you hazard an educated guess on these processing plants?"

"The redness on the image indicates a fair amount of heat," Spurlock began. "I'd say they're for processing heroin."

"I'll be damned. *Here*? On *Maggierock*?"

Spurlock shrugged. "It's a puzzle all right. That's why I hesitated to put it in writing. The BNDD boys would laugh their asses off."

"So you're saying this is new talent."

"If that's what they are, that's what I'm saying."

"*Could* this be a military build-up?"

"Unless they're making ammo and firearms in those rectangles, I doubt it. Mind you there's a fair concentration of military equipment there, but it's deployed defensively."

"Son of a *bitch*."

"So you were right all along, John," Donna spoke up. "It *is* a base of some kind."

"But *whose*? For *what* purpose?" I was more confused than ever.

Spurlock and Donna exchanged a quick glance that told me they'd given some thought to this question.

I had obviously grown in the esteem of both Donna Goldstien and Ted Spurlock, so I decided to cash in on it. "I caught that look, you two. What is it?"

Donna shifted in her seat. Spurlock kept his gaze on her, taking refuge in her position as his nominal superior. "Well, John," Donna finally spoke after clearing her throat, "based on the other things you told us... about that lieutenant colonel... Group Captain Hayes..., we think it's your own government."

"That's *absurd*!"

"*Is* it?" Spurlock shot back. "It's obviously not the planters, because... see those long black lines there... near the suspected military vehicles?"

"Yes... very clearly."

"Those are some sort of very dense barricades... obviously anticipating an attack from the planter... who was it?"

"Doran."

"Yes... him. So who does that leave? It could be the Mafia of course, but they already have their own facilities and they're producing all they need."

"What about the Commies?"

Both American diplomats shook their heads. "They wouldn't put such a thing on hostile territory. At least it's highly unlikely."

I guess I was relieved the secret base wasn't part of the Communist scheme of things, at least if these two knew what they were talking about. But their explanation bothered me almost as much. "How about local criminals?"

"I doubt it," Spurlock answered. "Those military vehicles are more sophisticated than anything you guys have here."

"But we're really only guessing," Donna added to Spurlock's immediate nod.

"But why would Colgate want to do something like that?"

Spurlock shot me a *glad this ain't my problem* grin. "That's fer you to find out, buddy."

"Yeah... lucky me."

I spent the remainder of my visit telling them about the young lady in that horrible photograph I'd showed them earlier. Told them of her disappearance... of my finding her bracelet on someone's wrist and what I'd learned about that since. I told them about the coincidences surrounding Sybil... her job at PCTC, the apartment, Caribbean Horizons Ltd., the information out of Bridgetown. They told me they'd find out what they could and tell me.

I guess in the end my going to the Legation had been a good idea. My intrigue at three thousand feet had paid off. Only problem was... learning what I had about the secret base seemed to create more questions than it answered... and on Maggierock, there just was no place where those kinds of answers could be found... at least that augured well for continuing life as a free man... or continuing life period.

Chapter Twelve

PREPARING FOR THE WRATH OF GOD

Tuesday June 5, 1973: the office of the Deputy Commander for Operations, Royal St. Margaret's Air Militia, Fort Uhuru [formerly Fort Cornwallis], Port Albert, Isle of St. Margaret's

I leaned back in my swivel chair, propping a boot up on my desk as I stared listlessly out the ratwired windows that took up almost the whole wall of my office in the Air Militia Headquarters Building. Even with the louvers fully open on all of them and even with both Casablanca fans turning on the ceiling above me, I was uncomfortably hot in my flight suit. I probably wasn't helping the situation drinking my fifth cup of coffee of the morning, but I needed the caffeine boost.

My windows looked out upon the circular stretch of lawn, gardens and concrete that held Fort Uhuru's main flagpole. Colgate had ordered Fort Cornwallis renamed a month ago. I was told *uhuru* meant freedom. The skies were leaden at shortly after 1000 hours, but it was still infernally hot... and incredibly still. I found myself hoping we'd have a rainstorm or something to stir the air a little.

I guess in the grand scheme of things Maggierock would never be considered a 'happening place'. This was especially true now that we had reached the month of June. According to the islanders, this was the beginning of the six month long season of *Mori Mungu*, which I was told translated as the 'Wrath of God'. Colorful, I thought, yet it got the point across. This was the time of year nobody envied Minister

314

of Education and Welfare Daphne St. George. Almost any morning my duties took me from the fort to the airstrip I could see her, haunting the complex of old warehouses behind the fuel docks located to the south of the Interisland Airbus Terminal.

The last freighter had brought the first shipment of cots, blankets, cleanliness items, C-rations and medical supplies for the mass shelters she and her Ministry people were feverishly setting up in the old warehouses. I was told that once the hurricanes started, hundreds of people from both north and south shanty towns would be living there. The toll of destruction among these pathetic cardboard and sheetmetal structures where some eighty percent of the island's people lived was close to one hundred percent in every hurricane.

While their unhappy and desperate owners took shelter and were fed in Daphne's warehouses by night, the days were spent by them frantically collecting enough cardboard, lumber and sheetmetal to put them up again. I was told I had to be there to see it, but that I would wish I hadn't. Many people were killed each year fighting over scraps of building material. The frustration caused by their homelessness led to many other incidents of violence and looting. *Mori Mungu* just wasn't an ideal time to be here.

When I first heard the Minister's name, I figured her for some kind of 'Cindy Smooch'. That was far from true. Daphne St. George was two hundred pounds of 'can-do'. She was elected from a district most of which was located in south shanty town. She had to be one tough old dame to even show up there to campaign... but to win? Both the other Port Albert shanty town electoral seats were held by the Communist NLP.

The freighter docking on June 19 was rumored to be bringing much more in the way of hurricane supplies. I was fully intending to be present for that event, but not because of the cargo. This was the ship that would be bringing Able Seaman Pearly Gates back. Inspector Pereya had promised me he would be taken into custody the moment he shipped off, and grilled thereafter until we had all the information he could give us on Connie's charm bracelet and how it had wound up in his possession.

While Mrs. St. George and her Ministry were busier than ever, the rest of the public sector seemed in the opposite mode now that we had reached *Mori Mungu*. Prime Minister Colgate had the Governor General prorogue Parliament, then along with Defence Minister Gentry and Group Captain Hayes had departed for London to attend a Commonwealth Air Ministers Conference.

As Gene left me in command of the Air Militia, he excitedly told me he was expecting to return with all sorts of goodies for our outfit, or at least the promise of same, and even more ideas for us to put into practice. We were now an outfit quite different from the one officer and eight ground crewmen I first observed the evening of February 6. We were now up to 115 personnel and airstrips on both sides of the island. Another recruit school was in progress at this very moment. Air Militiamen, like the other Militia, drew almost nothing in the way of pay, but they were fed, clothed and housed, which with Maggierock's poverty made a slot in our outfit or the other Militia something most families here found very attractive for their grown sons. Willett's Last Stand, Mission Impossible and the exasperating silence of the Communists since Independence had all proven boons to recruitment.

With Parliament prorogued, many of the other cabinet ministers were away on vacation as well, as was Colonel Christian. His Militia was being run by Lieutenant Colonel Moreland, while the country was being run by Deputy Prime Minister Dollie Fishbine. Just yesterday she had summoned Moreland and myself, as well as the heads of just about every other government agency into the Executive Building, formerly the Transfer of Power Building, conference room. The old dame kept it short and to the point. After waiting almost an hour for some of the less motivated agency heads to arrive, she strode into the room.

"You all know your jobs... Just keep doing them. That's all... you're dismissed." Then she strode out the way she came. I *loved* meetings like that!

The Governor General's prorogue order had the effect of shutting down the House of Councilors' Supreme Judicial Court duties as well. The Lord President had gone off to Miami for a visit. It all reminded me of the B.J. Thomas song *Everybody's Out Of Town*. Jack's absence, however, had an additional significance for me. It meant that he would not be there, as the clan's eldest surviving son, for the wedding of Sybil and me on the fifteenth. Sybil had talked me into it close to a month ago. When I pointed out I was already married, she explained that we were to be wed 'island style', which ignored any previous off-island ceremonies. It wasn't recognized in law, but it was recognized in custom. Even the Court of Queen's Bench applied it in cases of intestate succession, to send property not claimed by any formal marriage to the 'island-style' spouse. When I began seriously looking into this phenomenon, I discovered many people were married that way here. The old Patriarch Fortunus had given his blessing and would be performing the ceremony. I still had all my old concerns, ranging from Connie to my worries about Sybil, but after Mission Impossible, I owed her, and besides, she had been and still was a fabulous mistress. As I had already told myself several times, I was in a different world now. I simply vowed to play life by Maggierock rules for the time being.

The wedding was to be on the sprawling Jack estate, beginning at the southwestern edge of New Gatwick and continuing quite a ways into the heartlands. As I spent many hours gazing at the large map of the island that hung on the far wall of my office, I couldn't help but notice how close the southwestern border of my future father-in-law's estate was to the place called Atrisco Bay... the anchorage where the secret base was located. I couldn't help but think that somehow my status as family member might well be a big advantage some day were military movements in that area to become a necessity.

The buzzing of my intercom nearly caused me to jump off my chair. I picked up the receiver. "Yes, Flight Corporal?"

"De man from de Legation be here, jumbe Flight Lieutenant," Curly Howard responded.

I hadn't expected to see Spurlock, much less here and now. I had figured our last meeting at the Legation was intended to be just that. I was suddenly feeling ill at ease. "Send him in."

"Yessir, jumbe Flight Lieutenant!"

I barely had time to get my boot off my desk and turn my chair so as to look busy when Spurlock entered, dressed in a loud island shirt with a camera hanging around his neck. He had a pretty good poker face, but it was obvious he wanted something.

"Hiya, Ted. I wasn't expecting to see *you here.*"

"You about to go flying or something, Cassell?" He was eyeing my flight suit.

"No. We use 'em like fatigues." I indicated a chair to the front of my desk and he sat down. For a few moments we eyed one another tensely. Suddenly I knew this was not a routine visit. I stiffened in my chair. "Uh... what can I do for you?"

Spurlock wasted not a second. He leaned toward me, speaking in a low voice. "You can exterminate the secret base."

I studied him, wide-eyed, as he pressed on.

"I just got a top secret cable from Helms. Those are his orders."

"*WHAT?*" I gasped. "What does Helms care about some opium field grown by my government..."

"It's not your government, Cassell."

"But that's what you told me."

"I know... but that was just a guess and I also told you that."

I nodded at the memory. "But then..."

"It turns out the photographs taken by the U-2 were studied using...uh... other technology. Stuff I can't share with you."

"But..."

"I'm serious. Helms wants the base destroyed... and he wants you to do it." Spurlock's eyes were drilling into mine.

"But *how?* You identified some sophisticated military vehicles, with barricades..."

Spurlock held up his hand as he exhaled sharply, cutting me off. Then with a glance in the direction of the closed office door he leaned as far as he could across the desk, dropping his voice even lower than before. "Listen, Cassell, we'll take care of that. Do you think you could round up... say fifty men... for a four week training period? We'll supply the trainers and the equipment... all of which we'll let you keep. We'll also provide you some limited support and intelligence for the operation itself."

This was hitting me like a ton of bricks, though I had to admit the idea of destroying that cancerous growth appealed to me. "You mean… you'll train and equip a special unit of my Air Militia?"

He nodded. "Sure will. You and the other fifty men."

"Starting when?"

"Round 'em up today… we'll start tomorrow. I noticed a large marshy area on the south side of your base here."

"Yeah… the British used it for jungle training."

"Ideal! Give the word, Cassell, and my guys'll be here in the morning."

With Colgate, Gentry and most importantly Gene gone for several weeks, I actually could pull off the first part of it anyway. The idea began to excite me. Nodding at him, I picked up the phone, telling Howard I wanted to speak to the Air Militia's head NCO, Air Sergeant Major Rufus Killebrew. As Spurlock waited, I instructed him to round up all the enlisted from Mission Impossible, plus some thirty men of excellent ability of his own choosing, and have them mustered at the south drill pad at 0730 tomorrow morning for a special mission.

Killebrew had often told me he wished he'd been given a chance to go on Mission Impossible. He had seen combat with the British Army, had joined the Air Militia to mix it up with the Communists, and often chafed under the burden of his primary duties of running the recruit school. "Is this another of your special projects, Flight Lieutenant?"

"Yes… it is."

Killebrew sounded *excited*. "Can I be your NCOIC on this one, sir?"

"Certainly."

"Yes SIR! They'll be there. And *thank you*, sir!"

I replaced the phone on the receiver, turning to Spurlock. "We got the men."

"Outstanding!"

"Yeah… there's just one more I want to get… my NCOIC from last time. He's now the CO over at our west side airstrip. I'll fly over there this afternoon."

"Okay Cassell." He started to stand up.

"Just a moment, Spurlock." He sat back down.

"You're not gonna leave us on the beach... like with the Bay of Pigs?"

A wave of anger washed over Spurlock's face, then he regained control. "This is Nixon... not Kennedy. By the time you step off, you're gonna know just what support we'll give you, and you can count on it."

"Also... I need this kept top secret. The only orders I've gotten from my government have been to forget about this place... so my neck's out about twenty feet."

"Yeah... I know, Cassell. You told Strachman all about it." He eyed me curiously. "Just how do you plan to fade *that* heat?"

It was a good question. I had been so wrapped up in the blessed relief of being able to finally scratch that itch I hadn't even *thought* of the possible fall-out for insubordination. "Just a second." I got up, opened the door, then got myself and Spurlock a cup of coffee at the pot Flight Corporal Howard kept going throughout our duty hours. Just at the threshold of my office I paused and looked at him.

"Flight Corporal, contact the Hayes Airstrip. Have them ready Militia Three and pick up whatever sacks of mail need running to New Britain."

"Yessir." He stood up.

"Then go over to the command post and have the NCOD send a message to Subaltern Preston I'm coming to see him this afternoon."

"Yessir."

"Then, after you get me to the airstrip, go to my beach house and tell Syb I may be at New Britain tonight, but will try to make it back... then you can take the rest of the day."

Howard loved days that got him out of the office. As a taxi driver he was used to working out of doors. A big smile crossed his face. "Yessir!"

"And tomorrow, we'll go from here to the south drill pad at 0730. You and I have another mission to handle."

Now his grin was as wide as it could be. "Yessir, jumbe Flight Lieutenant!" He happily picked up the phone as I again closed the door, handing Spurlock his coffee.

Easing myself into my chair, I took a sip of the coffee. "I guess I'll just present 'em with a *fait accompli* ... you know I always thought I could never live with the responsibility of keeping silent about that base... no matter *who* told me to do it."

"Who has told you?"

"Jones... the guy I first saw it with. Only it's very obvious his orders come from higher up."

"Know who?"

"No... that's the bitch of it, Ted. I swear someone above me is a Communist, but I don't know who. It's driving me nuts." A smile stole across my face. "But now they're all out of town... and my men are just itching for another slugfest with the bad guys. Sooo...," I stuck out my hand to the CIA operative, "we're happy to help you, Ted."

He jumped once more to his feet, pumping it heartily. "Okay, Cassell... we'll see you tomorrow."

. . . .

The south drill pad was located next to the large, marshy area of the fort that Spurlock had mentioned. A barbed wire fence ran along side of it, restricting access to the marsh, which had been used to train British troops for some of the adverse jungle conditions they would be facing on Maggierock. A huge sign located next to a guard shack announced that entry was forbidden without authority. The drill pad itself was used only for drilling active duty units for special parades and occasions. As per instructions, it was here the men of Mission Impossible and those selected by Air Sergeant Major Killebrew gathered at 0730 on Wednesday June 6 to await the arrival of our American friends.

It was 0735 as Subaltern Preston and I got into a jeep at the Air Militia Headquarters Building with Curly Howard to make the trip. I had gone over to New Britain to pick him up yesterday afternoon. He was *thrilled* I'd chosen him to be my vice-commander for the mission, but less enthusiastic than I thought about leaving New Britain. It turned out he had 'lay hold' of Heather Cressey a while back, and they were both getting along very well, to the great benefit of his morale. As we pulled away from the building, it suddenly occurred to me that the Americans hadn't told me how they were going to join us. I wondered if I needed to leave orders at the Main Gate, but finally figured I'd better get used to telling as few people as possible about anything connected with this mission, so I simply took a radio with me, telling the gate sentries where I'd be.

Once again, the skies were dark lead. Once again it was very still. Sybil told me last night with a worried look on her face that this kind of weather portended a hurricane. Hurricanes so early in *Mori Mungu* were rare, but they were certainly possible. She was worried it would somehow interfere with our wedding the fifteenth. I was worried it would somehow interfere with this mission. I didn't know exactly how long Gene and the others would be gone, but with four weeks of training staring us in the face first, then several days moving through the jungle before we could attack, we could hardly afford to lose even a day.

"Tennnch HUT!" Killebrew's voice resounded throughout the upper Caribbean Basin as we drove up. He turned on his heel and gave me a flawless salute as we piled out of the jeep. "Fifty personnel present and ready as directed by the Flight Lieutenant SIR!" he boomed.

I had never met him before, but we had spoken on the phone. He was the scourge of every enlisted member of the Air Militia. No one had gotten through basic training without jumping through his rather demanding hoops. His appearance was very imposing. Six feet, two hundred thirty pounds or so of solid muscle, his coal black shaved head mounted firmly in a huge neck. His uniform utterly flawless, his boots like looking glasses. His starched, creased flight suit boasted Royal Air Force Vulcan bomber aircrew wings and British Army paratroop badge.

The men snapped to attention standing in seven ranks of seven. I returned the salute as Howard, nervous at seeing the Pariah again, hurriedly sprinted to the rear of the formation. Even Preston cringed, but as an officer remained at my side.

"Have the men stand easy, Sergeant Major."

Killebrew now bellowed the command as I looked around, saw we were quite alone, then faced the men once more. Killebrew even had me intimidated. I began to get the sinking feeling I would open my mouth, revealing a high, squeaky voice that would set the men laughing. I worked hard reminding myself I was a disc jockey and knew how to speak from the diaphragm. Looking into their faces, I began to calm. Many were smiling back at me, happy to be going on another mission together. All were obviously glad to be here though no one knew exactly what this was about. The months of Communist-orchestrated silence had grated on everyone's nerves.

"You have all been specially selected for this mission.," I began. "It is a mission of the highest importance to the security of our new nation. From this point onward you are all under orders to maintain absolute secrecy about what you will be doing here, what and who you will be seeing here, and maybe most important, why you have been assembled here."

I began to hear helicopter rotors off in the distance. The men, including Killebrew, were all paying rapt attention to my words. "A Communist base has been detected in the uninhabited part of our south coast. It is apparently well armed and defended, and located in a spot very difficult to reach."

The rotors were getting louder, but the men remained riveted. Several had gasped when I mentioned the base. "You are to commence a four week intensive special training program. You will learn some things we've never learned here before. You will be taught to handle equipment you've never handled before... It will be difficult, but once it is complete, we will be moving out together to destroy once and for all this dire threat to our security. So give me all you've got, men, so that when we take on these invaders, you will be in the best possible position not only to eliminate them, but to come safely home. That's all... rest... smoke if you got 'em."

Several men lit up, as did I. We all were shortly watching the sky in the direction of the now quite loud helicopter sounds. Before our cigarettes were finished, two large helicopter gunships descended through the clouds into view to the collective gasps of us all. As they got lower, our bug-eyed fascination was replaced with confusion. The ships were painted a bright blue, and all across the fuselage, which bore the picture of a smiling gray-haired old lady, were the words 'Mrs. Blodgett's Caribbean Tours... Experience the Magic!'

Now the men were looking at me and one another, very puzzled. I could do no more than share in the puzzlement. The two ships shortly touched down and the hatchways swung open to reveal about thirty young white men, all dressed in loud island shirts with cameras around their necks, many wearing funny-looking straw hats. They immediately piled out, loudly exclaiming how *exotic* everything was here, and asking 'what kind of bird is that', 'what kind of tree is that' and several other inane touristy questions. Each one of them carried a suitcase or travel bag, many with stickers and other ridiculous paraphernalia stuck on them.

As we all watched with amazement while thirty bug-eyed fools wandered around the dismal drill pad with its stinking marsh beyond, making inane comments about how beautiful it was here, Killebrew came over to me. "CIA?" he whispered in my ear.

I nodded, he grinned, and we both lit up another cigarette. The reason for this charade was shortly made obvious, though Killebrew had seen it before it happened. The helicopters had attracted crowds of soldiers from elsewhere on the fort. They were standing close to us, gawking, until the funny tourist activity had them making swatting motions with their hands and laughing, then returning to whatever they were doing.

It was at this time that a six foot four giant, who looked like a world-class body builder, stepped out of the ship, bursting through a teeshirt that said 'Mrs. Blodgett's Caribbean Tours' on it, then came over to me, accompanied by a man dressed in short sleeved dress shirt and slacks and carrying a clipboard.

"Flight Lieutenant Cassell?" he asked, eyeing my epaulets.

"Yessir."

He gave out with a soft chuckle. "I'm just Harry Ives, your tour guide." He stuck out his hand, crushing mine until I yelped.

"Sorry," he grinned, blushing slightly. "Dunno my own strength at times."

"Heh heh." I shook my hand to try to get it working again.

"These your men?"

"Yess... uh... yup." The guy was obviously military, probably Special Forces, but I figured I'd better play it his way for now.

He nodded. "Mind if I say a few words to 'em?"

"Be my guest."

"Hi men!"

"HELLO, SIR!"

"Heh heh. I'm just plain ole Harry Ives. You all and my tour group's gonna have some fun the next four weeks so get ready to relax and enjoy."

The men were looking at one another, very puzzled, then looking at me.

"A course y'all will enjoy it lots better if ya like marshes, cause that's where you'll be the whole time." He pointed to the dismal fields beyond the barbed wire. "What I want you to do now is come up to Mister Taylor here," he indicated the man with the clipboard. "Give him your uniform sizes and answer his questions, then report to the second ship there and haul whatever you're asked to out there about two hundred yards into that field. Y'all got that?"

The men were too confused to verbally answer. There were some nods. Ives chuckled, then turned to me. "Let's start with you, Flight Lieutenant."

"Sure."

He turned to Taylor. "How we gonna show his rank?"

"You're the equivalent of a captain, right, sir?"

"Yes."

"I can give him three diamonds on each collar."

"Yeah," said Ives, "that oughtta do it. What are we gonna do for that crown on his wings?"

"Aw... no problem. I can fool with a command pilot set from SAC."

"You're a genius, Taylor," Ives chuckled. Then he turned to me. "Flight Lieutenant, of course you won't carry anything, but what I'd like you to do is talk to your..." his voice trailed off as he looked at Killebrew's insignia, which was the St. Margaret's coat of arms. "Say, what *are* you, fella?"

"Air Sergeant Major, sir."

"Heh heh! I'm just Harry Ives, the tour guide. Well anyway, Flight Lieutenant, I'd like you to pick me out fifteen mortarmen and fifteen infiltrators while we complete the sign-in process here, then meet with me out there. Okay?"

"All right."

Ives finished with Preston and Killebrew, then we headed out into the muddy marsh and began the selection process. I wanted Flight Sergeants Prentice, Crewe, Newleigh and Drayton in the mortar teams. Killebrew readily identified the best qualified infiltrators over the next three hours as the process was completed back at the drill pad and the skies turned even darker. I had a very strange feeling about Ives and his come-on. He clearly was keeping us at a distance, had no intention of getting chummy with us. I began to wonder just what sort of experience this training was going to be.

I started to get some idea as the men began lugging tents, cots, and some lightweight (unless you had to carry them for several miles) tent flooring out to where we were standing. Flight Sergeant Prentice was the first to arrive. "Where do you want these, sir? Mister Ives said we were to set up a tent city."

I turned to Killebrew. "Get it done, Sergeant Major."

"Yes sir. Where do you want yours?"

"Oh, that's all right" I laughed. "I'll just be in and out, monitoring the progress here."

"I don't think so, sir," Prentice broke in nervously.

"*What?*"

"Yessir. Mister Ives said you were to get the tent of your choice, sir."

My head was suddenly swimming. *Four weeks of this shit! Spent HERE! My God! I'll miss the wedding! I haven't told Sybil ANYTHING! Oh my God!* I could feel myself reddening. "Wait here, men."

"Yessir," Preston, Killebrew and Prentice answered as I stalked back toward the drill pad, determined to set this 'tour guide' straight about a few things.

As I closed the last of the distance, I noticed the 'tour group' members lugging the walls, flooring and furniture of what appeared to be a small building, as well as metal boxes of ammo and what looked like disassembled mortars. They weren't even puffing with the effort though I was nearly out of breath just watching them. I realized that I had been completely fooled by the funny get-ups. I began looking closer into their faces. They were *all* body-builders, many with hollow eyes that bespoke long experience inflicting death under *very* hostile circumstances. I was starting to feel very intimidated. Several of my men passed me, their faces wreathed with broad smiles as they hefted several American M-1 rifles each and boxes of ammunition.

I was plenty nervous by the time I reached Ives, standing by the second helicopter, talking in a low voice to Taylor. He noticed me and immediately looked up. "Well, Flight Lieutenant! What brings y'all back in this direction?"

"Uh... well..." My courage was failing as I looked into Ives' eyes. *God damn! They're hollow too... really hollow!* "Uh... there's been a mistake, Mister Ives."

"Aw shit... *really?* What mistake, Flight Lieutenant?"

"Well, ya see, I'm just sort of dropping in and out. Uh... I got the whole Air Militia to..."

"Well shit I reckon, Flight Lieutenant. I'm sorry. Y'all take off."

A wave of relief washed over me. "Gee thanks, Mister Ives, I'm sorry about the mixup. Killebrew has the list you wanted. I'll drop by tomorrow."

He smiled, then gave a wave. "Bye Flight Lieutenant."

I nodded, then turned and headed for the jeep. "Oh by the way," Ives called over my shoulder.

I turned around. "Yes?"

"Would you ask the one they call the 'jumbe Flight Lieutenant' to join us?" Ives smiled shyly. "He was the guy we was expectin'."

I reddened. "Uh... that's me."

"That's *you?* But I thought we made a mistake."

"Well, no... uh... I mean yes. You see..."

To my surprise, Ives pulled this ridiculous hand puppet of a smiling, gray haired old lady out of his back pocket and put it on his right hand. "Uh Ms. Blodgett, ma'am... do you think we might make an exception in this man's case. I mean, after all, he's got the whole Air Militia to..."

"Absolutely *not*, Mister Ives!" Ives spoke in this high pitched voice, shaking the puppet in his face. "We're gonna teach him some things... things *nobody's* gonna walk around knowing until they've used them the way we want. Now get with the program Harry!"

"Shucks, ma'am. I'm sorry." He looked regretfully over at me shrugging. "Guess we can't help ya Flight Lieutenant. The old lady's on the warpath today."

I looked at the puppet, then at him. In spite of myself, I gasped. *His face had turned into Doobie's!* The eyes showed incredible cruelty... incredible *emptiness*. I stumbled backward, swallowing hard.

"Right back that way, Flight Lieutenant," Ives grinned. "Say I know what... let's you n' me take a jog. You'll feel much better. How far do you run daily, anyway?"

My head still swimming with the bizarre hallucination of a moment ago, it took a while to register the question. "Uh... well... three miles."

Ives looked at the old lady puppet. "Sounds good to me, ma'am."

"Land sakes, Harry! The secret base isn't right down at the corner... it's five days into the trackless jungle. Now just what kind of fool are you turnin' into. *Six* miles, Harry!"

Ives actually blushed. "Sorry ma'am." He looked regretfully at me once more. "Sorry, Flight Lieutenant... the old lady's *really* on the warpath today!" He grinned. "I guess we do six. Let's go."

Too many things were slamming into me at once. I hadn't even felt the rage inside me when 'the old lady' told me I was a prisoner here for four weeks and would miss my wedding to the daughter of one of the island's most powerful clans. I hadn't felt it... yet. But it damn sure was there. "Uh... well, my running shoes are back at my office. I'll just be a few minutes."

"Why sure, Flight Lieutenant." He was rolling up the hand puppet, sticking it back in his pocket.

I nodded again and headed for the jeep.

"Oh Flight Lieutenant," he called out behind me, almost as an afterthought.

I turned around to see him unrolling this map of the island. "Uh... 'afore you do that... would y'all step over here and mark the running trails leadin' to the secret base. We didn't know there was any a' that... thought it was all trackless jungle." He held out his pen, spreading the map just inside the hatchway of the first helicopter.

Once more I reddened, heart pounding. "There aren't any... it's all jungle."

"Heh heh... well then we wouldn't be doin' y'all a favor gettin' ya up to six miles in runnin' shoes, now would we?"

I stood there, positively crimson. Ives winked. "Go pick yerself a nice tent, Flight Lieutenant. I'll be along for our run shortly."

I nodded, then turned, enraged, heading back to the marsh.

"Oh Flight Lieutenant?"

I turned back again.

"Just so's ya know. Each tent has two buckets a' sand come with it. When ya ain't fightin,' runnin,' or shootin' yer hand's in that bucket... jabbin' yer fingers in... over and over."

"Uh..."

"Startin' *right now.*"

I swallowed, nodded, then turned away from Doobie's evil face.

"I'll be along for our run in about twenty, Flight Lieutenant. Plenty a' time fer some good finger exercise."

I nodded without turning around, continuing on my way to the marsh... *very* depressed.

. . . .

It *couldn't* have been much more than twelve noon as I stumbled back to the tent I shared with Subaltern Preston gasping for breath, a piercing pain in my side, my legs so numb I could barely put one in front of the other. But it seemed like it *had* to be 1800, three days later. Somehow I got my feet up on the plastic planking that was the floor of our tent then literally fell onto my cot, my left leg hanging over the side. I couldn't even muster the motivation to pull it in.

A short while later, as Preston monotonously kept plunging his fingers into his sand bucket, I managed to take off my boots and soaked socks, my soaked flight suit, then my soaked teeshirt. Wet or not, I used it to sponge the rivers of sweat off my face as I lay half dead on my back.

"Well shit I reckon, Flight Lieutenant, I'm sorry!" It was that bastard Ives. He'd been, literally, running circles around me throughout our 'little jog', bellowing *The Ballad of the Green Berets* at the top of his lungs. Once or twice he'd even lapped me... 'just for fun' as he put it.

"You ain't fightin' are ya, Flight Lieutenant?"

"No," I gasped.

"And ya sure ain't shootin'," he chuckled. "So's I musta interrupted yer runnin'." He grinned a sheepish grin. "I'm real sorry..." He swept an arm toward the outside of my tent. "Please... don't let me stop ya... continue."

"But... I..."

"Here, Flight Lieutenant, let me get that nasty ole sand bucket outta yer way. We don't want ya trippin' over that while ya run." He grinned some more as he moved the bucket.

"Oh *fuck*," I mumbled under my breath as I painfully reached for my left boot.

"Naw, Flight Lieutenant, don't get dressed on my account. Y'all jes keep running like you obviously must a'been doin'… seein' as how yer hand weren't in the bucket."

The world was a hideous study in red and blue as I stumbled around six more miles of marsh, barefoot, in just my undershorts. I don't remember what else happened that day, but when we were rudely awakened at 0430 the next morning, my fingers were still stuck in that sand bucket.

On the second day of training, we were each issued a brand new M-1 rifle. My men had never had the luxury of repeating rifles before. We learned to disassemble it and clean it. We were then divided into four tracks. Fifteen 'infiltrators' went with ten of the 'tour group', fifteen mortarmen went with ten others, and twenty 'assault troops' went with the final ten. Killebrew, Preston, the three NCO's we'd designated as section leaders and I were left with Ives and Taylor. We ran six miles twice daily, fired our M-1's twice daily, and spent several hours fighting hand to hand with each other and practicing lethal moves on specially designed dummies. Every moment in between, our fingers pounded the sand. Every muscle screamed with pain, every joint ached to holy hell. We had bruises everywhere.

On the third day's fighting block, we were each issued a small triangle. When you pressed the clasp though, it turned out to be a piece of piano wire connected to two triangular handles. We fought each other for the right to strangle the dummies, then strangled them. We didn't get a 'kill' until we snapped the neck off. Three tries without a kill netted you a 'bonus' six mile run.

On the fourth day, we learned something else. "It's the reason y'all been workin' yer fingers," Ives drawled as he stood in front of three life-like heads with bright blue eyes. "Now ya can use just about any fingers ya want, but ya got the most killin' power with the first two." He then showed us how the eye socket of a human being permitted entry to the brain. And if you struck the brain, your opponent was dead.

"Now yer not aimin' fer the brain," Ives stressed. "Yer aimin' fer that palm tree fifty yards in back a' the guy's head. And ya better hit it too."

With that, we lined up at each of the dummies. A buzzer sounded when we had penetrated deep enough for the kill. This charming little exercise became a part of our daily routine as well.

By day six, my attitude was evaporating. I chose Killebrew as my fight partner. He was a monster, and sent me crashing to the ground over and over. But I kept getting up and throwing myself back at him. He began going to the ground a time or two. That afternoon I felt someone patting me on the back. I looked around. The back of Ives head was all I saw as he walked away. By that evening, the buzzer was sounding regularly, the necks were snapping off. I was hitting the target with the M-1 *and* could bellow '*Funky Nassau*' at the top of my lungs for part of the six miles.

Meanwhile off in the distance, the dummy mortar rounds set off the 'on-target' buzzer more and more frequently. We were looking at each other, and ourselves, with a pride and respect we'd never before experienced.

On the late afternoon of June 14, just as I was despairing over the wedding, yet taking it in my stride, we all were assembled together.

As we sat in the marsh, Ives paced a raised platform, dressed in his black flight suit and combat boots, the uniform the entire tour group had been wearing for quite awhile now. As at the beginning of this adventure, the skies had been leaden for the past couple days, but now a breeze had started to pick up. Rumors of a tropical depression had been running through our camp like wildfire.

"Y'all are doin' mighty fine," he drawled. "Mrs. Blodgett has decided to give ya an 'on yer own' tour from 1600 this evenin' to 2000 tomorrow night." He looked at me as he said the times, registering my stunned gratitude.

"A word about yer conduct on the 'on yer own'... You've learned some deadly things here. Y'all can kill almost any human being you'd come up against on this island about ten different ways." He looked menacingly at each of us. "What you learn here, you leave here. Once yer mission is complete, you can keep all you've learned with all yer equipment. Until then, it all belongs to the United States Government... I'm serious as a heart attack, gentlemen. Anybody does any maimin' out there, yer makin' it more likely the enemy's gonna know what yer up to... and if the enemy knows what yer up to, there's a damned good likelihood you won't be seeing about half the men now sittin' around you when your mission's over. Y'all catch my drift?"

"YES TOUR GUIDE!"

"All right. You'll report to me individually at the building for your passes."

Naturally as the commanding officer, I went in first. This was the gray prefab building I saw the tour group hauling in pieces the very first day. Ives lived in it. A cot was against the far wall, a small camp table and two chairs were in the center of the room. Ives smiled when he saw me. "You've come a long way, Flight Lieutenant."

"Yessir... thank you."

"Don't thank me, John. You always had balls. All you had to do was overcome yer tendency to be a crybaby when things don't go yer way."

"Yessir."

"When I saw who you picked for your fight partner, I knew you had it knocked. You don't just wanna *win*, John. You wanna *learn*. You wanna bring your boys home safe after a successful mission, and yer willin' to spare yerself no amount a' trouble to make it happen."

My head was down, even as I felt myself warmed by his words.

"We pretty much figgered it was a matter of time. We know they don't award the New Jersey Law Enforcement Medal of Valor to creampuffs."

My eyes whiplashed to his. He smiled, then got back to business. "Now you will speak to your father-in-law, right?"

"Yessir... first thing." I hesitated. "There is one thing though..." I was *very* reluctant try Ives' patience, but knew if I succeeded we'd have a major advantage when we attacked the secret base. If old Fortunus gave us a pass across his land, that would mean his hundred or so field hands would do the hacking of the underbrush through several miles of the trackless jungle for us. We'd arrive quicker, and less drained.

Ives narrowed his eyes. "What is it, Flight Lieutenant?"

"Well, sir, I don't know how much you know about this culture, but I was supposed to bring gifts to the old man to wed his daughter."

Ives looked at Taylor and they both laughed. "Pretty good racket."

"Yessir. Now I didn't have time to get anything, but you happen to have something he'd take in a heartbeat... *and* I think would open doors for us."

"Yeah? What's that?"

"Give me about five additional M-1's."

"Hmmmm." Ives face darkened as he scratched his chin. "I dunno, John..."

"Actually, sir, I think it might help with the disinformation campaign."

Ives now looked up with interest. "Oh? How?"

"Well... if our outfit is the only one that winds up with American rifles after you're gone, it's gonna shriek 'military aid'. But if a powerful heartlands land baron has some as well, it's gonna look like a gunrunner came to town and anybody lucky enough to get to him first cashed in."

Ives and Taylor exchanged a look. Then Ives laughed. "Well shit I reckon, Flight Lieutenant... you ever thought a' bein' a con man?"

I laughed, and was still smiling when a case of ten M-1's was loaded from the helicopter to my jeep as Flight Corporal Howard prepared to drive me home. I took a last look for a bit over twenty-four hours at that dismal marsh with its twenty-some tents and small gray building. Its running track and target ranges... all the other training locations where my men and I had exchanged a lot of skin and sweat for some amazing knowledge... knowledge that just might enable us to drive the Communists into the sea, and return to our base to tell about it... It was almost like leaving home.

Sunday June 15, 1973: the estate of Fortunus Jack, J.P., the heartlands west of the settlement of Ormsby, Isle of St. Margaret's

The wind-driven rain was coming down in buckets as we entered the Jack estate. I had never been this far south on Highway One. The settlement of New Gatwick boasted many what would be called 'lower middle class' houses elsewhere. Graham told me as we left the highway to make our westward turn that many government workers lived here. Of course there were the ever-present shanty towns, but on the whole the place seemed to be saddled with far fewer extremes than Port Albert.

A low stone wall at the end of a dirt road marked the beginning of the Jack holdings. A guard shack was on the right hand side. Beyond it, just inside, was one of those awnings under which was placed outdoor accommodations for some ten security men. All were grouped underneath it on the rainy day, but two immediately came out when the first of our two Land Rovers stuck its nose into the entrance. Seeing Graham, they immediately waved us in.

It turned out our journey at this point was less than half over. The old man granted the sub-estates in this area to his elder children. Emory Jack's house was the first we saw. Going down a palm-lined path we next encountered Apple's, then homes belonging to Darius and Anselmo, whose lucrative duties on the west side pretty much guaranteed they were seldom here. Now some ten miles into the property, we encountered a fork in what could only be called by now a 'beaten trail'. We were already using our four-wheel drives before being called upon to choose whether to take the path rising steeply into the foothills, or the one skirting the tail end of the central highlands headed south. This latter one was the path Graham took. He told me it went on for ten miles or so, then turned west through low rolling jungle-carpeted hills to the Old Man's place. In the area we were traversing now were houses belonging to several of the older Jack grandchildren.

"De Old Man prefer de heartlands," Graham explained. In fact, the older Fortunus got, the more he was reverting to the Stone Age life-style into which he had been born. Fortunus and his brother Amadeus were the third generation of the clan, believed to have been started when a young girl recently escaped from the slaver *Annabelle Treen* mated with one of the surviving sailors of the Royal Navy corvette HMS *New Gatwick* that was chasing it. Legend had it that the sailor's first name was Jack, but after finding refuge with his mate in the dense unpopulated heartlands he simply stopped using his last, perhaps to assist in breaking the ties with further Royal Navy service, perhaps because of outstanding warrants back home, it depended on which of Sybil's millions of relatives you spoke to which story you got. Anyway, that beginning accounted for some of the lighter skinned members of the clan as well as its odd surname.

When the escaped slaves made it to shore, the vast majority settled in what is now Port Albert, simply because it was convenient. Some of the more traumatized members of that inhumane cargo, however, just kept running. It is their descendants that today comprised the so-called Stone Age settlements of the heartlands. They took with them their native language and erected replicas of their villages back home, and for perfectly understandable reasons would butcher any white who blundered into their area. That remained true today, the terror of their abduction being passed down in an oral tradition from generation to generation.

For that very reason, it was all the more remarkable that Fortunus and Amadeus emerged from that direction and began picking up land toward the coast, instead of the other way around. No one really knew how old Fortunus was, as the British maintained a strict policy since they claimed the island in 1846 of leaving the heartlands entirely alone. Thus no births were registered which occurred there.

The best guess, however, was that he had to be in his eighties, possibly late eighties.

When I first caught sight of him, as our vehicle drove into his compound at shortly before ten a.m., I'd have put him closer to sixty. He was sitting on a pile of cocoanut mats, under two large banyan trees, carving up a papaya with a bush knife and popping the pieces into his mouth. Beside him was a large stoneware jug, which Sybil told me was full of Kifo, if he hadn't killed it off yet. A few feet from him, was a small little cottage where he now lived. A few feet beyond that, into the jungle, was a crude still. The hundreds of cocoanut shells piled all around it testified eloquently to what he was making. Directly opposite the cottage, forming a compound clear of foliage and covered with palm fronds, was a crude wooden outhouse with palm frond thatched roof.

"I always pictured your dad in a huge mansion," I remarked to Sybil as I eyed him with fascination as we came to a stop in front of the cottage. He had a ramrod back, and despite the wind and rain was dressed only in a loincloth. His broad shoulders, arms and chest seemed to bulge with muscles, his skin was almost what you would call smooth, and his eyes seemed sharp and clear.

"He was," she answered. "For many years. Now, however, he's 'reverting', as he calls it. Each year since mama died, he's been doing it more and more. He says he's waiting for the spirits to guide him home to be with her."

Sybil had tears in her eyes as she beheld him. Mine were full of admiration and wonder. "Damn."

"Papa!" Graham bellowed as he cut the engine and stepped outside. Sunflower and Sybil pretty much did the same thing. Graham and the old man embraced, then he pulled both his daughters down on either side of him. Sybil was in the traditional white, clinging island wedding dress with sandals. Sunflower wore a traditional island festival dress, navy blue with colorful designs at the collar and sleeves.

I was dressed in my khakis, Joe and Sean in loud island shirts, and Tucan also in a traditional festival dress. Hers was red. Almost at the moment we arrived, the three token Jack families who were to attend our wedding drove up in pickup trucks, and began unloading and setting up a long low table around which we would all sit crosslegged for the wedding feast. If it rained, I was told, we would simply get wet. The entire ceremony and celebration had to be outside, according to the old man.

I went over to the old man and was introduced as *mume* by a blushing Sybil. We'd had one hell of a reunion last night, and we wanted to get home in time for more of same before I disappeared back behind the barbed wire for another three weeks at eight this evening. "Good day, sir," I saluted.

Fortunus returned it. He supposedly served with Lord Allenby in Palestine during the Great War. His salute was as good as many I saw with the 18th Berkshire Rifles during their last days here. "Call me 'papa', boy." His voice ricocheted off the jungle trees, his lungs as powerful as the rest of him.

"Yessir." He bade me sit next to Syb on the pile of cocoanut mats. I secretly reached around and rested my hand. *God she felt good*. We had both been ravenous for one another.

For the past half hour or so, the rain had let up, the wind had stopped, but the skies remained dark. "This would be the eye of the hurricane," the old man said, looking up into the sky.

"You have brought gifts?" He asked a minute or two later.

"Have I ever, papa. You're gonna love 'em too."

The old man appeared very curious. He gestured toward the Land Rovers. "Show me... eh?"

I motioned to Sean and Joe. Within five minutes the old man's lecherous eyes were feasting with glee on seven M-1 rifles and two metal boxes of ammo. I had kept three of the rifles and one of the boxes back for Sean, Joe and my personal use. I had one at the airbase, of course, but thought I'd better keep one at home as well.

The old man grabbed Sybil by the arm and shook her as she giggled. "This one my Mori Mungu... I have to atone with her." I gathered he was calling her his problem child.

"You keep her in her place, boy. She's a spot of bother, let me tell you."

As her eyes locked onto mine, making promises about this evening, that was about the last thing I'd call her. There were now present the twenty or so people who were going to attend the wedding. No more were expected. I excused myself to use the outhouse.

"Use the cottage," the old man said. "The outhouse is for suckers." Then he broke into a hearty, almost demonic laugh that came close to reminding me of the one I heard in Florida that awful day.

I nodded and went inside just as another pickup was driving into the compound. Hunting the commode took me through the back door, where the old man had placed a construction project chemical toilet, his wedding gift, I later found out, from the husband of Hy Jack, short for Hyacinth, another daughter, and obviously from Amadeus' side of the house.

I had barely finished when Sybil unleashed an ear-splitting scream. "*Mume! Help me!*" she shrieked.

Running quickly around the side of the house, I watched astonished as Sybil was being tied to a cocoanut tree by her wrists by a four hundred pound monster. The old man was watching impassively, as was everyone else.

I drew my revolver, causing the Jacks present to send up a loud groan and Graham to come racing over, grabbing my arm. "No, jumbe Flight Lieutenant," he gasped. "He is laying hold of her."

My eyes darted to the bed of the shabby red pickup. In it were the three cases of tinned beef, salt fish and taro.

"But we're getting married!" I bellowed as the evil hulk turned on me and began taking off his clothes.

"He challenges you to a fight to the death," Graham whispered.

I must have been crimson. My heart was pounding. I looked to the old man.

"You want an island wedding, Lieutenant... you free my daughter from his grasp island style."

I wasn't tuned to this hassle at all, but obviously I was one of its two stars. As the family members excitedly chattered in patois, no doubt getting bets down on the hulk, I dressed down to shorts, just as he was in a loincloth. We didn't even have shoes.

"Free her," I ordered Joe.

Fallon stood up, but was immediately halted by a command from the old man. "Only the Flight Lieutenant can interfere with his laying hold."

"De man bug her since she sixteen," Graham whispered. "He a no-account now and then farm worker. You lose... she his slave the rest of her life."

We faced each other murderously across the compound. Sybil was trying to saw her bonds against the trunk of the tree, tears of terror and desperation rolling down her face. Obviously the rules surrounding this custom were different in the heartlands.

What you learn here... leave here, the words of Harry Ives short-circuited my enraged plan to send this bastard to the Promised Land by the most direct route. As I attempted to rationalize this commandment, the man grabbed me by the arm, spun me around, and began tearing at my face as I struggled.

I finally reached behind his neck then doubled over as fast as I could, lowering my center of gravity enough with my newly developed strength to dump him on his back. I jammed my foot against the bridge of his nose. If I'd had my boots on it might have ended the fight. Instead, as he bled profusely, he grabbed my ankle and gave a vicious twist, sending me crashing to the mud face down.

Holding onto my ankle as I tried to kick at him, he got up, bleeding all over me, and began turning in circles, faster and faster, swinging me around like a rag doll. To the excited chattering of the younger Jack spectators, I went flying into the jungle, fortunately landing in a stand of elephant grass instead of slamming into a tree trunk.

For what seemed like an eternity, I lay there, too dizzy to get up. I was shortly hearing the sounds of this monster crashing through the underbrush, getting closer. I tried to raise myself but just couldn't. Sybil let out a frightened scream as the man dragged me by both feet this time back into the compound. Then he picked me up and, to the laughter of the Jack spectators, heaved me into the thatched roof of the outhouse, sending me crashing down inside.

A popular expression back in America these days was 'you don't know jack shit.' Despite my misery, the thought that no one, at no time and in no place could ever say that to me again actually made me laugh. It also focused me. I could see the old lady puppet taking a large bite out of my ass, maybe worse, but this guy was going to louse me up so bad I would be unable to pull the mission. I was just going to have to disobey Ives, with the devil taking the hindmost.

I stayed there among the Jack shit, laughing hysterically. The laughter enraged my opponent. He practically ripped open the door. I was waiting for him. There was no palm tree directly across the compound, so I aimed for the cottage door. Damn near hit it too. Looking quickly around, I saw a small *ufagio* (island broom) standing against the wall of the outhouse. To cover what I'd done as much as possible, I jammed the stick into his empty eye socket, turned him to look like he fell on it, then walked out, utterly amazed at the effect Mrs. Blodgett's Caribbean Tours was having on me. I truly was 'experiencing the magic'.

Slamming the door of the outhouse, I walked across the suddenly deathly silent compound to the outdoor shower and pulled the cord. Still shivering from the cold water, I walked over to Sybil and freed her from the tree. Then I turned to the old man. "I guess I better get married like this, papa. I need to dry before I get back in my uniform."

The old man nodded as Sybil clung to me and Joe and Sean gave me looks approaching vaporlock. "You need to call the cops or something?"

"I'm the law here. Justifiable homicide." I then remembered he was a heartlands justice of the peace.

I nodded, and we went onto the ceremony.

Monday June 16, 1973: the marshlands at the south end of Fort Uhuru, Port Albert, Isle of St. Margaret's

Subaltern Preston, Air Sergeant Major Killebrew and I stood outside the officer tent in the predawn darkness, studying our daily training schedule with a flashlight. Our eyes had popped open automatically at 0429, and we'd been surprised to find no one yelling at us to fall in. Today, though, we didn't need any encouragement. We wanted to put on our new uniforms.

"Free time until 0800," Preston read. "No wonder they didn't wake us up."

"*Free* time!" Killebrew exclaimed. "I can't believe it." He looked at me. "I say we start buildin' some Ranger tradition here, Flight Lieutenant."

"Said and done, Air Sergeant Major. Turn out the men."

"Yessir!" he saluted, smiling, then began bellowing the appropriate orders.

We were about as pumped up at this point as it was possible to be. We'd each come back from our 'on yer own' to find two sets of jungle camouflage fatigues and one field jacket, an American helmet wrapped in jungle camouflage material, a sixty pound American infantry field pack, two pair of American jungle combat boots, socks, underwear, boonie hat, flack jacket, and, for mortarmen, infiltrators, and everyone flight corporal and above, a black nylon gunbelt with .45 caliber automatic and loaded magazines laid out on our bunks. They'd done a beautiful job of recreating our special badges and our British-style rank. Over the left shirt pocket was **ROYAL AIR MILITIA** in black letters against green. Over the right were our names.

The *piece d' resistance*, however, was high on our left sleeve of both fatigues and field jacket. A patch of the green-black-green St. Margaret's flag with the word **RANGERS** underneath. Nobody did much sleeping. Within a minute of Killebrew's first command to fall in, all fifty-three of us were there with packs, weapons and helmets.

"Rangers! Tennnnch HUT!" you could feel the men bursting with pride as they stiffened. Killebrew did an about turn, bringing his arm up in salute. "Detail all present, sir!"

"Very well, Air Sergeant Major." I returned his salute, then faced my fifty smiling Air Militiamen. "A new Maggierock legend has been born, men. We need to nurture this legend and make it grow. Now it says we have free time until 0800, then we have our usual track schedules. The St. Margaret's Rangers are going to spend that time on a six mile run, during which we are going to select a marching song and practice it. It should be something that reflects our pride in our new nation... and our new unit."

There were many nods among the smiling faces.

"Any suggestions?"

"How about *Ballad of the Green Berets?*" a Militiaman toward the rear spoke up.

I thought a moment as the suggestion registered mixed reactions in the ranks. "My problem with that is the song has people dying for those oppressed. We're gonna make the oppressors do the dying. I want you men to come home safe." Actually I had *many* problems with the song, but Ives loved it so I kept them to myself.

Murmurs of approval filled the air.

"How about *Funky Nassau?*" Flight Corporal Drayton spoke up. There were several enthusiastic nods. JoJo Child played the song constantly on Radio Maggie, so we all knew the melody and lyrics written to commemorate the independence of the Bahamas, which was taking place next month.

"What do we put in place of Nassau?"

"How about 'Maggie', sir?"

"What do you say, men?"

"Yes SIR!" the Rangers bellowed in unison.

I turned to Killebrew. "What do you think, Air Sergeant Major?"

"As long as I get to do the base part solo, sir."

We all laughed. "Very well. Let's try it men. Air Sergeant Major, get us underway."

"Yes SIR!" Killebrew and I exchanged salutes. "Right FACE! Weapons at high port...column left by columns... forWARRRD... doubletime....HARCH!"

Off we went. The amber lights of the rest of the base glowed dimly in the distance on either side of and between the dense black silhouettes of the helicopter gunships still sitting on the south drill pad. The predawn air was damp and humid, with heavy clouds blocking out the stars, but our hearts were as light as could be. We'd stretched ourselves out in single file except for Killebrew, Preston and myself when Preston started it off.

You could *feel* the pride in their marching song start to take hold of the men.

Killebrew bellowed his first base part like a seventy-five millimeter cannon. I was seeing a different side of him this day. The song was bringing out the men's personal emotions… I liked it.

Crewe chimed in next. Several men did a fair drum part, to laughter.

Killebrew reduced us to hysterics with yet another fabulous rendition of the base. He must have done it every day for weeks driving to and from work.

A team effort produced a pretty fair guitar imitation….followed by the horn part. It was as if *everyone* had been practicing favorite parts. "Dah dah DAH DAH!"

On and on my soldiers sang. I guess as a marching song it was a bit unorthodox, but the beat was right if you helped it along, it was island and it was proud, and I could *feel* them pulling even closer together as the song and our hike went on.

Ives had pretty much forgiven me, or at least understood my thinking on the killing of the hulk, especially when I related the steps I took to cover up the cause. But, like me, they were also extremely happy to hear that not only was the old man going to send his groundskeepers to hack our way through the jungle for us in advance, he also gave us permission to occupy a five square mile tract of highlands for the final part of our training. He had marked it on a map for me before I left and I gave the map to Ives. The M-1 rifles, and probably my victory over the hulk, and made a very favorable impression on him.

The remote training site was especially good news, because despite a ridiculous sign hanging on the barbed wire which read:

SITE OF MRS. BLODGETT'S CARIBBEAN TOURS
CAMPFEST 1973!

DID YOU MISS THE MAGIC THIS YEAR? DON'T WORRY!
SEE YOUR TRAVEL AGENT TODAY FOR THE BETTER
THAN EVER CAMPFEST '74!

we were definitely attracting attention and, once the others got a look at our uniforms, it would be all over. Additionally, the helicopters would not be seen taking off on the day of our step-off, something that had often worried me, funny fuselages or not.

We were coming around the tent city for our second pass. I could see Ives and two or three of his tour group standing on the steps of his gray, prefab building, looking in our direction.

"Mrs. Blodgett's listening Rangers! Bring it on home!" Preston bellowed. They did too.... All the way.

The men sang more spirited than ever as we charged past our trainers, making them shake their heads with approving wonder. Ives even shot me a 'thumbs-up'. The St. Margaret's Rangers were off to a good start. Ives would later tell me the 'free time' was put there to see what we'd do with it. Apparently, we got the highest possible score for our response.

. . . .

Our final two and a half weeks of training seemed to pass twice as quickly as the first one and a half. Now, other than intensified courses in fighting and marksmanship, everything else was accomplished by means of practical exercises. The infiltrators were working with mockups of vehicles believed at the secret base, learning how to plant explosives. The mortar team worked on blowing up a simulated mockup of the base's buildings, the assault troops on accomplishing what the other two might be unable to.

Preston, Killebrew and I now rotated daily among the three tracks, learning how each team was to do its job. On our fifth day back from the 'on yer own', after I delegated command of the Air Militia to a very puzzled Subaltern Burns, the Rangers were airlifted out of the marsh for the final time, to the desolate meadow and jungle of Fortunus' highlands. Harry Ives now ran the program entirely through myself and my staff, which consisted of Subaltern Preston, the vice-commander, Air Sergeant Major Killebrew as NCOIC, Flight Sergeant Tino Prentice as team leader of mortar section, Flight Sergeant Aaron Sampson as team leader of the infiltrators, Flight Sergeant Lucien Reeves as team leader of the assault troops and Flight Corporal Curly Howard as my unit clerk.

From that point until the end, we had a series of wargames, where one section would stand the other two as aggressor versus defender.

On July 3, the second to the last day, a very unexpected event happened, giving us a powerful indication of just how frightening our elite unit looked to the rest of the island. I was leading the assault troops in a rank-order sweep of a large meadow, headed for the mock 'base' of the other two, when from out of the jungle, ten terrified, half starved men in black, eight islanders, two Cubans, appeared with their hands up.

"Don't shoot Americans! Don't shoot!" the man in the front pleaded as they approached.

Reeves and I looked at one another stunned, then we quickly surrounded these men, searched them, then had them sit on the ground well out in the open meadow while I radioed for 'Mrs. Blodgett' to 'come for some new customers'. Following the advice of Subaltern Preston, we took their clothes, put them in a pile and burned them. Preston explained that, in island culture, the burning of the possessions of a captive blocked his path back to 'face' or self respect forever. One of the helicopters appeared in fifteen minutes. As soon as I handed the field radio phone back to Howard, one of my men, Aircraftsman Merlin, came to me, wide-eyed.

"Thought you want to see this, jumbe Flight Lieutenant." He handed me a very worn, wrinkled piece of paper. Propping my M-1 against my hip, I opened it one-handed.

> **La oficina de Caribbean Horizons en Miami dice que hay una fuerza imperialista nueva en 'La Isla'. Todo han salido de la fortaleza Uhuru el 20 de Junio a las 5 en la mañana. Dónde están?**
>
> **CBE**
> **22 Junio 73**

"Christ Almighty!"

"What is it, jumbe Flight Lieutenant?" Flight Sergeant Reeves asked.

"It's a note... probably written by someone who speaks Spanish as lousy as I do... saying that we left Fort Uhuru at 0500 on the twentieth."

His eyes bulged. "Yeah... we did."

"And this was apparently known to an outfit *in Miami*... named Caribbean Horizons... two days later."

We looked at one another... stunned. "CBE," Reeves read over my shoulder as I started to turn away. "Wonder who that is?"

"Obviously somebody highly placed in their outfit." I turned to Merlin. "Who'd you take this off of?"

He pointed to a Cuban sitting at the far end of the line of prisoners. The man immediately looked down when I faced in his direction.

"Oh! This was what it was inside of, sir." It was an envelope, postmarked Miami, June 22.

Reeves and I walked over to the Cuban, standing above him. "Como se llama, soldado cubano?" I asked.

The man just stared back at me.

"Dígame! Pronto!"

The note meant many things. The most important for us, was that the Communists on the island knew about us, and that we had departed the fort for points unknown. Obviously, every Communist installation would go to heightened readiness, including our target.

The man just stared back at me, flashing a look of contempt.

Reeves, also holding his M-1 against his hip, landed a powerful kick into the man's chest, sending him toppling backward... screaming. "Por favór, señor capitán! Por favór!"

He was obviously reading the rank on my collar. "Dígame! Pronto!"

"Por favór, señor capitán! Miguel Cienfuentes!"

"De las fuerzas armadas de Cuba... no?"

He stared up at me with terror in his eyes until Reeves kicked him again. "Sí, señor capitán! Por favór, señor capitán! Por favór!"

I turned to Reeves. "He's a fuckin' Cuban soldier." I looked into the faces of some of the islander prisoners, finding one pissing all over himself with fright.

"Jack that one up, Flight Sergeant," I pointed to the man with my M-1. "See what he tells you."

Reeves went over and grabbed the man by his fulsome afro, as he whimpered, dragging him over to a point some twenty feet away from the others. Two more Rangers went and stood over him, blocking his view of his comrades. I heard gruff questions, then the heavy thud of Reeves' fist, then a shriek. Then things got quiet. A short while later Reeves returned, leaving the other man sobbing.

"He's from the secret base, jumbe Flight Lieutenant. They all are. They were looking for us. That bastard you were talking to is the leader... a major in the People's Militia."

"Well... we're gonna get some updated intelligence." At that point helicopter rotors split the air. I wanted to ask Major Cienfuentes many questions.. Like who 'CBE' was? how many men at the base? who was behind Caribbean Horizons? and who were their spies on Maggierock? but I didn't know enough Spanish.

The helicopter gunship touched down, its rotors continuing to turn as Ives stuck his head out of the hatchway. "What the well dressed terrorist will wear," he chuckled. Then he looked in my direction. "You St. Margaret's folks is aw right!" We wound up turning them all over to him. He told us he'd 'take care a' all them questions.' Then they took off.

Graduation Day loomed with the prospect of the St. Margaret's Rangers shortly going into action against Cuban regulars. In our youthful exuberance we were willing enough, but that didn't change the height of the hurdle suddenly confronting us in what the History of St. Margaret's Isle would forever record as The Battle of Atrisco Bay.

THE END OF PART ONE

ACKNOWLEDGEMENTS

LORETTA TOWNSEND and FREDERICK J. O'BRIEN who read and commented upon the chapters of this book as they were completed

EDDIE SOLIAI, MD, IOTAMO SALEAPAGA, MD, and WILL W. ANDERSON, MD whose compassion, devotion to the welfare of their patients and professional skill at different times and places over the three year period encompassing the birth and growth of this book helped me overcome illness and its constant pain sufficiently to complete the writing and publication process

TRICIA SGRIGNOLI for her truly magnificent cover and professional talent and skill in the interior layout and design of this book

MASHA SHUBIN for her sharp eye and professional knowledge in reviewing the manuscript and providing several helpful suggestions

MASHA SHUBIN, LINDSAY BURT, TRICIA SGRIGNOLI and the others at INKWATER PRESS who, as always, have made the publication process unbelievably pleasant

HIGH TALKING CHIEF TAESALIALI'I who made possible my continued functioning throughout the period of the birth and growth of this book that took place in American Samoa

To my son-in-law DEWEY SHIELDS, to LORETTA TOWNSEND, SUZANNA TIAPULA, my son PHILLIP CASSELL, DAVID VARGAS, my brother BARRY CASSELL, TRICIA SGRIGNOLI, ALAN SABER and WINNIE MAGGIORE who have been exceptionally supportive of my writing efforts

WORKS BY JOHN W. CASSELL

∞ BOOKS ∞

CROSSROADS: 1969

ODYSSEY: 1970

HELL'S QUEST: 1971

DE VILLIERS COUNTY BLUES: 1972

UNCERTAIN PARADISE: 1973 (part 1)

∞ UPCOMING BOOKS ∞

UNCERTAIN PARADISE: 1973 (part 2)

∞ SHORT STORIES ∞

ALL IN A DAY'S WORK

LEST WE FORGET

THE FLOWER OF ST. MARGARET'S

HE IS RISEN

"PUT ME IN, COACH"

Breinigsville, PA USA
05 January 2010
230245BV00001B/57/A